THE LAST
BLACK HIPPIE
IN
CONNECTICUT

THE LAST
BLACK HIPPIE
IN
CONNECTICUT

A Novel by

Charles Fort

Quale Press

On the front cover: *Strapping Into the Electric Chair*, photo by James S. Metcalfe, appeared in *The Royal Magazine*, 1899
On the back cover: photograph of the author, by Jerry Blow

Sources:
Pages 40–41: HandWiki: *Encyclopedia of Knowledge*, "Chemistry: Sulfur Mustard," https://handwiki.org/wiki/Chemistry:Sulfur_mustard; the sections "The Antidote for Death," "The Woman in the Petrified Forest," "A Poem for Wendy (Love's Labor Found)," "Letter to Wendy Frm Sister" and "Ben Cocoa, Professor of Blacksmithing" appeared in *Reynolds Review* (2002); the sections "New Year's Eve," "After the Rehearsal" and "In Memoriam" appeared in *We Did Not Fear the Father* (Red Hen Press, 2012); letters on pages 110–115 reprinted courtesy of Elizabeth Wassel, John Montague, Maxine Kumin, Dana Gioia, Donald Hall, Kate & Fred O'Brien and Julie Buffaloe; pages 139–140, material on Elizabeth Cotten adapted from Wikipedia; page 149, material on the Large Hadron Collider from "Physicists Calculate Mass of Top Quark, Heaviest Elementary Particle," Huffington Post, March 22, 2014 by Tonya Lewis; pages 161–162, based on "Eye-for-an-Eye Incivility," by Charles M. Blow, *New York Times*, May 4, 2014; text on the Popigai Crater in "CNN Breaking News" (pages 185–186) adapted from Wikipedia and other source material; text in the section "Get Plenty to Eat" (page 235) adapted from the Fort family history *Witness to Injustice* by David Frost; five methods of execution in the section "Laughter in the Iron Lung" (pages 241–243) edited from texts by Dr. Deborah Denno, Fordham Law School, "Lethal Injection Chaos Post-*Baze*" (*Georgetown Law Journal*, 2014), "The Firing Squad as a 'Known and Available Method of Execution' Post-*Glossip*" (*Univ. of Michigan Journal of Law Reform*, 2016), "The Lethal Injection Quandary: How Medicine Has Dismantled the Death Penalty (*Fordham Law Review*, 2007) and "When Legislatures Delegate Death: The Troubling Paradox Behind State Uses of Electrocution and Lethal Injection and What It Says About Us (*Ohio State Law Journal*, 2002); and in Appendix 2, text on iron lungs adapted from Wikipedia (pages 305–308), text on pages 309–317 adapted from Ray Jasper's "My 'Final Statement on Earth'," a letter to Hamilton Nolan (Gawker, February 2014) and pages 317–322 adapted from Steven Alejandro's reply to Ray Jasper published on the web in 2014 and since deleted.

ISBN: 978–1–935835–34–9 trade paperback edition

LCCN: 2025932457

Quale Press
www.quale.com

Contents

Here at the quiet limit of the world.
—Alfred, Lord Tennyson

Prologue #1

They walked Ben Cocoa from the foxhole to his death row cell under the remnants of praise and affliction found in everyone's blood that was dark and borrowed. We were the citizens that walked the atlas of woe and enchantment and met at the grand fountain before our journey to heaven or hell. Ben stopped under the holy shadow with a fear of angels, empty tombs, and falling stars.

Ben was a very hard worker and excellent student, busy, and at times reckless. When asked what message he had for the sudden wave of young black hippies, Ben responded "Be a brave witness to the terror and absurdity in the world."

Prologue #2

WHAT HAPPENED HERE once happened to the world. The warden walked into the death chamber followed by the executioner he watched tighten the leather strap borrowed from Bob's Barber Shop given by the inmate's father who received the shop rather than a blind blue mule. Ben Cocoa was scheduled for the firing squad on New Year's Eve. Leap years had prevented his execution for a decade. Ben was given several choices for his death. Electric Chair. Gas Chamber. Lethal Injection. Whipping Post. Horse Drawn and Quartered. Boiled in Three-in-One Oil, Robotic Firing Squad, and one revealed by the C.I.A. and Pentagon: A.I. A.I. was Ben's final choice. He was lifted and placed inside a discarded iron lung found at a junkyard scrapheap, a pyramid of poison pointing to auroral activity, filled high with Ovaltine and Fluffernutter jars, car tires, clothes pins, yellowed pages, and a Slinky. A.I. was Ben's final choice. It designed the iron lung equipped with a black rotary phone used by Wallace Stevens, a rear-view mirror, two portholes, hourglass, sun roof, space heater, license plate, embossed with BEN COCOA, JR., WAR HERO, made by his fellow inmates on his last birthday. They had tried the gas chamber and lethal injection on Ben when he turned 18. Those methods left Ben paralyzed from his neck to his toes. One of his eyes popped out of its socket into a glass of water the warden held in case Ben experienced dry mouth before the lever was pulled. The gas chamber shriveled his veins and decreased his height by four and a half inches. The lethal injection was attempted seven times and stopped after the M.D. deemed the eye in the glass that stared at him too cruel too unusual at lunch time. Suggested by A.I., the iron lung was shot into outer space on the latest X rocket with no return address. Ben was set to float forever. The warden did not tell Ben that the iron lung was electrified by NASA scientists in case he tried to escape.

Black Flugelhorn

The mouth of the soldier filled with aphids.

They found a green canteen full of holes roped to his waist.

He played taps on the fugelhorn to announce the end of the war.

Ben Cocoa was the last man killed in the war three weeks after the treaty was signed.

They looked at their scalded faces, fiction in front of mirrors caught between the living and the dead.

The flared notes of the fugelhorn floated into the tops of trees.

It was the lilac wild in a garden at the turn of the century.

The riderless horse stormed the Ides of March. The tourniquet of the century saved a few men.

The nurses and doctors under the tent worked blue magic under the futile stars.

The hands and feet of child blown off by a land mine. Was that a skipping stone across the blue pond?

They unearthed bags of gold coins.

The coins spinning to earth fell over a birch tree. The man wearing a stovepipe hat pointed the fugelhorn to the sun.

They wished the world well in the wishing well. There was a choir swaying in white robes.

Children danced in the baptismal waters. The animals floated in their stalls.

Ben placed his clicking teeth into a jar of Fiji water birthed out of volcanic baptismal waters into a whirlpool of baking soda and H_2O.

It was the town clock burning.

The bullet catchers wore stovepipe hats.

They tried to save the witness to peace using a robotic tourniquet invented at the turn of the century.

They buried the workers along the cast iron fence. He tossed the spoils of war into a pot of chitlins beans and rice, goat ribs, alligator mambo, wooly andouille sausage.

The prisoners of war were sent to the Mojave Desert for spring break.

They carried the Mojave green snake in baskets. Who were the deranged and prosperous men of war? I will dance for food.

I will speak in underworld patois. Who filmed Kafka's fugue?

The fugitives released from prison were never found.

Ben Cocoa fell asleep inside a time machine and awakened inside the iron lung.

The birds were screaming for their lives. The birds were screaming for their lives.

Coltrane blew notes of "These Are a Few of My Favorite Things" into the iron lung.

Children wish for angels and dream of war.

June 27,

PM
27 JUN
1987

RALEIGH, NC

U.S. OLYMPIC
FESTIVAL
JULY

Julia Ward Howe

Hello Claire -

See the dancers?
When you want to dance,
daddy would like to
dance with you. Daddy
dancing & Mommy & Claire
dancing. Let daddy brush
your teeth for you today
See you soon.

Love,

Mommy

Claire A. Fort
706 Timber Lane
Wilmington, N.C.

28405

7

The End of the War Gave Us

Children wish for angels and dream of war. They sentenced the last black hippie in Connecticut to death by electric chair. He was caught blindfolded in a crawlspace foraging love letters and falling into peony and exile. The prison doctor for the criminally insane held a stiletto above the man's broken eye socket and poured holy water over the embers under his bare feet. He was looking for a pulse and not looking for a pulse. The retrievers of the dead met at the chained door of the cathedral, lowered the flag, and bowed their heads. Some of them slept and all of them grieved.

After being shot in the back of his neck trying to escape near the barbed-wire guard tower, he was left paralyzed in the dirt cellar breathing like a bluebird inside an iron lung. They waited for his resuscitation and practiced on a ventriloquist dummy seated in a barber chair used on Mondays as a time machine until he was able to walk on his own two feet to die.

His father, Ben Cocoa, Sr., recalls that after his son was wrongly placed on death row, doctors insisted that he not touch him for fear that he or someone else would contract the disease. He said they predicted he would soon die.

The guards installed a generator in the prison yard as a backup power system, and many times Ben Cocoa sat with his son overnight, fearful the machine would shut down.

Ben knew his time praying for his son was limited and they worried about his execution inside the iron lung instead of the electric chair.

He was rolled onto an ambulance for his ride to a New Year's Eve Party Fundraiser sponsored by the Salvation Army.

"He wasn't unplugged more than a couple of minutes," Ben said. "He said, 'I'm going if it kills me.'"

Ben wore a tuxedo designed for him by a local seamstress and a top hat. When he was wheeled into the room with an American flag draped over the machine, he received a standing ovation.

"The Salvation Army will take care of Odell when his parents can no longer afford to do so and the money will be set aside for that care."
"I've had a good life," he said.

Two pennies were set into his eyes as he sat in the electric chair. They dropped rose petals into a circle. It was midnight. The crowd gathered below the rope bridge. The guard read a proclamation on the day of the execution.

"The brownfield does not know who's under it, does not know my name carved into a bar of soap, does not know the thunder above hollow ground, does not know the cadence of the ghost steps chained at the ankles and dragged to the electric chair, does not know how the delicate rain seeps like fire into soil and over rock into the roots of wild oaks above the monument of the war dead and bereaved, does not know how the fire spread and cut the tops of trees, does not know the names of birds screaming for their lives. Today was the tom-tom tambourine parade. The crowd arrived with blankets and wicker picnic baskets and lemonade. One basket would hold his tongue. One carried his wild brown eyes to the river. The woman held his splayed yellowed penis like a serpent against her neck. His charred testicles were wrapped into a plaid shirt. Teeth were removed with Stanley Tool pliers. His skinned fingers were placed in shirt pockets with pens and protractors. Nigger toes were a delicacy on white linen, prized possessions sent by pony express to senators and congressmen, citizen's councils, and the chamber of commerce set up to send out mass mailings on mass killings. We proclaim this a day of reflection, a memorial for those less fortunate, less behaved in the mutilated days ahead."

Ben Cocoa won a trophy for the longest softball throw at Smith Elementary School and first prize for photography at the YMCA in New Britain, Connecticut, when he was ten years old. He held a silver clarinet and wore a blue blazer and white pants for the Memorial Day Parade. There was news about strange lights over New Britain above Batterson Park

One year before he was drafted into the Vietnam War, Ben Cocoa was the last black hippie they found sleeping in the Litchfield vineyards. The most well-known vagrants in New Britain were Red Tarbox and Piccolo. Mr. Tarbox always carried a *New Britain Herald* paper bag and delivered to the factory bars that circled the downtown far into Park Street, a bowling alley into the working-class nest between the Blue Mirror Bar, Wedge Restaurant, and the Diamond Bar. Long before they uprooted the trees in New Britain's Central Park, perhaps to reveal what never appeared under the canopy, street level, eye to eye, they say as the trees were torn down the gold angel lifted her wings.

Piccolo walked Hartford Avenue like the city shepherd, his burning staff directing the night shift workers into the smoke and woe of a furnace. Piccolo was the mayor's illegitimate son, born on a prom night Shuttle Meadow excursion under a half-moon convertible, they say he hid money inside a mattress at his last unknown address.

The mechanic at the auto repair shop took his pistol and shot his homemade bullet into the rabid dog's ear.

The man on the third floor of the tenement walked out naked during father's barbecues, they say he was a WWII German veteran, disguised as a clown who survived the Hartford Circus Fire, and had his genitals cut out in one final act of war.

The woman on the second floor carried a large frying pan and knocked the pigeons, homeless city chickens, out of the sky, and the children wondered if she de-feathered and boiled them into what she called her Happy Stew inside her kitchen.

The woman on the first floor collected neighborhood kittens, their whispers like the holy bells and wind chimes, she wrapped them inside a wool blanket, rolled them into the backyard inside a shopping cart, picked the kittens out of the blanket and one by one with her one good hand, dropped them into the barrel of fire. Ben, trained as a sniper and turned into a bullet catcher, was thrown head first out of the tree by a tank that tore its roots and shook the earth, he was taken under the tent and they examined that his senses had been temporarily altered, he saw a rainbow above a tall ship, the manikin in the display window remarked that it was a lovely day for a regatta and grandmother's ricotta, who made wedding cakes for the dispossessed.

Ben Cocoa gave his sore thumb a golden snap and he remembered his daughter coming home crying after her classmates made Mother's Day cards and her mother was gone, and the phone call from the school to pick up his daughter who had started her period. Ben found that *we are ultimately alone.* It was the pewter canteen he used as a flask for his black whiskey he loved.

LUCKY SEVEN

THE NEW BRITAIN police caught the gentleman behind a white birch tree. The only one seen off I-84 West by a half-sleepy child in the back seat counting light poles on the highway. They found the sticks and bones and broken yellow teeth beneath the autumn torch set down by the charred hand of God. There was sushi, barbecued ribs, Subway sandwiches, gasoline station, brake repair, Bed, Bath & Beyond, Kinko's, D & W Shoes, China Pan, Michael's, TGIF, Border's, L.A. Fitness, and Filene's Basement. The trial killer had taken one past the American Mausoleum of American Art to go bowling at Laurel Lanes in Plainville. They boarded the bus at Stanley and Park, and they watched the children climb the tree at Walnut Hill Park. They heard the South Congregational Church bells at the bottom of the hour, the fog made it seem like the town clock burning. The bus drove past Angelo's and Stop & Shop and two rummage sales next to each other, CVS, McDonald's, and a liquor store where the night before he had bought a long bottle of tequila with a large worm at its bottom, a shallow pool of wet soil, his footprints left in the snow disappeared. Had the killer's muse led to him kidnapping six women and one man, was it the lyric of *Helter Skelter, you may be a lover, you ain't no dancer,* that altered his memory and in a temporary gift of rage, set his hands upon the innocent, left them in a fetal position, unspooled their hands and arms and legs and buried them spread eagle into the earth, and left them face up as if the light over their bodies called a velvet wolf to the ridge as its New England Claw pawed at her forehead. The husk of a rainbow fell next to him as he turned away from her body. He was told as a child not to be heard or seen, go to trade school, become a car mechanic, a shoe repair violinist like his grandfather, homemade Chianti, ouzo, fresh red tomato, basil, arugula, his backyard garden, honeysuckle, blue grapevines, beehive, pigeon cage, barbed wire, electric chair, gas chamber, firing squad, drowning, cross bow, quartered, burning oil, tar and feathered, gangplank, morning glory. He lifted the woman he had strangled into his arms like a bird, her doll's head lopped to one side. He rolled her body into the incline, he followed her with his stuttered walk, and he buried her among the lucky seven, a short drop down a slight hill into the meadow of the dead.

Ben Cocoa's father stood in front of the Polaroid Land Camera. He always looked away from its electric eye and pointed one finger toward nobody in particular, perhaps toward the crippled ghost he saw walking across the pasture under the moon's apparel, a half mile from the churchyard, perhaps it was what he knew of old school charm, his way of knowing how the universe worked inside the factory, a pensive glance into the camera a way of smiling, his face slightly turned for a brief moment, away from the world, the only tattoo he saw as a child was I Love Mom on the Marine's forearm, and a bullet hole through his elbow, a rare Sunday afternoon and Ferris wheel on the beach, the pond full of silver dollars, the low ceiling of the third-floor apartment, the fire escape nailed into ceramic siding, a nest of birds falling to the sidewalk, the trimmed hedges nearly kept out the smoke from the warehouse fire, brass knuckles in a shoebox under the table at the motorcycle club house, full of deranged teen provocateurs, automobile gangs, tinsel hung on the window sills and the Frigidaire handle, and the third-grade classroom where the red-haired kid had a seizure, epileptic, or was he *Joey the mechanical boy*, half-human, half-spirit, breathing in the vapors of the civilized world, a furnace of molten steel, the underground fountain of youth, the toy soldiers on the throw rug in his room, a shipment of gas masks were swept into a whirlpool, lost treasure map at the Mausoleum of American Art, they jumped into the trenches, tombs of noise, wearing death's apparel, cannisters of mustard gas fell at their feet, toy cars, they fell on top of each other's bodies, their arms attending arms, warm flask of black whiskey, canteen of beauty, army tank under the bunk bed, silver hub caps, the doors of

Amato's Toy Store closed after a firefight broke out the large pane glass windows into a chandelier swept into the grate, into the river of rivers beneath the hardware city of the world, and they brought in ten thousand dump trucks filled with hot tar, poured over the rooftops of tenements and cathedrals and abandoned buildings, they say three angels with charred wings appeared in the sky above the city, they hovered above smokestacks, one was caught in barbed wire at the entrance of the elementary school, the second was found half-alive crawling on the stage of the Darius Miller Music Shell, the third angel was heard laughing in the vestibule as the arsonist paid by contractors and sub-contractors and told to set fire to the living and the dead and burn the city to the ground, the hot tar covered the rose garden, city hall, school children, homeless, baker's dozen, diners, bondsman, sheriff, city jail, parks and procreation, the Mausoleum of American Art, the public library had opened its doors to the critically wounded and the ministers stood in line to feed the poor with jelly donuts, yet it was to no avail as the northern wind and hot tar aided the efforts of the minotaur with its tail throwing fire as the flames swept over the brownfields, the robes of the church choir caught fire in Central Park, holy water would not douse the flare of desire.

They drove their chariots into the underground tunnel. There would be no recourse, the smell of burning flesh would linger ten thousand years inside the rings of the white birch. The waters of the sea would rise above human shelters, over mountains, and receding into the corridors of the earth. They sent armies to scour the filth. They would find the remains of a civilization, signs of discourse, tablets of alphabets, discarded bodies, skeletal bluebirds in mud, gold coins and music boxes, signs of life and no signs of life, a cathedral for the poor, a cathedral for mourning, stepping stones to sacrifice found in the rivers of glory and pestilence, the one-eyed pirate who lost a gangrene leg on a gangplank battle for the right to land on the shore of another country on the border of a holy war for those who believe and those who do not believe, they found the diary of a madman in the isolated cell who grew his own wings and the evolution of his wings and heart into a human face.

One hundred planes dropped flares into the tops of trees and seeds of light fell from phosphorescent clouds. The sky pilot found the husk of a rainbow in the orchard. He left the scaremonger effigy leaning against a wall in the dirt cellar. It had embraced him as he fell thousands of feet. Was father in a shark skin suit, wingtips, money clip, in cuffed and pleated pants at the Elk's Club Christmas Ball? There were flames in the eye sockets, and its cow tongue was painted blue. It had the ears of a sleeping child and the pink mouth of a dancing clown. One part, the human half, uttered a psalm. The other half, the inhuman part of its body, webbed feet and fingers as long as a water moccasin or a splintered copperhead. His arms became a wing of the noble angel. There was a thin shadow tumbling and cursing above their heads. Was it Satan riding shotgun inside a rumble seat on death's carriage in heavenly freefall trying to bless the burning globe in his ragged hands? It had blown a tire taking a hairpin turn at the northern stop sign and eastern ghost star. Satan held the aluminum tree between his red hooves and a reindeer's foot in his bad teeth. The hunger of gravity pulled them together at a long dining table with well-seated patrons of vice and damnation feasting on serpents, domesticated alligator, and goat ribs. There was a pale and hungry crowd knocking at the door. They started singing the blues for hours. A shuttle bus moved them back to the malls of salvation. There was one way down in the glory of the deranged and prosperous lovers. The soldier turned prisoner had lost his way. The carrier pigeon was lost in the mustard gas. His compass had fallen off the roped bridge. He tried to touch hands with the carnal sinners who passed by him in fertile despair wide-eyed and floating in a wintergreen snowfall. There were no signs of love on this rumble seat of desire. It was the whistle of the meteor that nearly startled him into weeping until the screen door slammed on his back porch and he fell out of his rocking chair amused yet wary as the yellow-topped grasshoppers snapped into flames in the brooding waters. It was the only way down, to separate the music from the laughter of cattle, the happy dog gruel of terror and beauty on a three-day pass of redemption where the men and women are blown about forever in the barbed wire hereafter and falling backwards into and land feet first unafraid of the next step.

The Mojave green rattlesnake was found warm and curled under his U.S. Army helmet. They found a diary in his shirt pocket. It was dated 1969. High school. There was a bullet hole in the pewter canteen. The drops of pond water fell down his forehead to his tongue. There was no antidote recorded in the small village, no elixir bottled at the apothecary of desire for the homesick and heart breaking into splinters. He slept inside a rail car rolled in a blanket with a shipment of Africanized bees in the season of drought and dereliction of duty. There was no antidote known to the descendant of the Mojave green serpent. They had one vial from the last living specimen that was genetically altered to bring aboard the defunct space shuttle. The astronauts were to mix it with Tang, shake three times, rattle off the names of Apollo, Zeus, and Hercules, and roll it into a buttermilk pancake mix. There were minor concerns what would occur at zero gravity. How had the serpent uncurled and disappeared into thin air? Was the venom the antidote for seclusion and fear? Who would place a small vial into the hands of the populated world, children served first, followed by the men and women in the underground lavatories? Was one drop in one eye needed or three drops in both eyes? Had they properly discarded the small bottles into fire? The mixture of venom and mustard gas worked best. There was concern about the late arrival of trains from the West Coast. The dust storm had taken the breath out of the falling stars, and snow drifts of dust in the eyes of children and their dolls, covered the men who played bocce and women who walked in summer dresses. One radio signal was captured and lost in seconds. Whose curdled voice sought good fortune in such ruin? The men were lined arm's length apart as they walked the Connecticut retrieving the miniature globes of venom. They took boats to the geodesic nuclear repository. They lifted men and women and children out of the scalding water. They placed one drop of venom into each eye. The water continued to rise. This was no miracle of science or accident of birth. It took mere centuries for light to reach the back of the eyes. A bluebird vanished though a bank teller's window. Schoolyards were abandoned at noon. Lunch boxes were emptied and thrown into large trucks. They had altered the colors of the rainbow and the hunger of gravity. There were no pennies falling in a cracked jar.

Water filled the dirt cellar. They heard a small animal in the crawl-space and found a WWII folding shovel and school desk. The drilled holes in the wall were full of light. The young girl screamed and ran into a corridor illuminated by what death had taken apart inside the architecture of her heart.

The military holiday was signed along with the peace treaty. It was called *The Blessing of the Hogs.* "You write such big stories, and what does one do with the little haiku," he said. They boarded a night train for the coast. A sniper was found inside the town clock, his lifeless body covered with blue bees. The award-winning equestrian team from a small college in Ohio was flown in for the Memorial Day parade.

She sat at the card table in a fur collar. His brother who smoked Lucky Strikes and drank six bottles of booze each day was dragged into the asylum shouting: *Protect the rich!* They say he was found half-buried in wet snow believing his winter hat was a crown. As a child he had nightmares of motorcars, wild horses, a pig's bloated eye, and burning chariots. He was a bar owner, high school teacher, father, musician, high school football player, hated the genius of jazz and rock 'n' roll, modern dancer, smoked dope and cigarettes, loved the ocean, for the war, never joined the war, single, married, divorced from the Boy Scouts, only-the-strong-survive kind of man, knocked out on his front lawn, duck pins, summer projects, anti-intellectual, a corn pipe, apple eating, god-fearing and godless, drag racing Saturday night dirt track, midnight homosexual golfer, seaworthy and worthless, lover of racist men and women, brothers and sisters, mothers against everything, films with brief nudity, taxi-cabs in New York City, apple pie and black eye, fool's gold in a fool's hand, AA, you get the "creature off your back" then move on to a better day and night, there was nothing wrong with her, he just forgot her birthday kind of day, your sister and brother who smoked, neighbors who drank and smoked long cigarettes on the beach, scarecrow with a whiskey bottle for a heart, ski-jumping over the fucking moon, wearing wedding wingtips, had he played the third act of his life in a tuxedo, a small red rose pinned to his lapel, a slapped child hiding under the bed, the hour and last dance and electric slide downhill racer found outside in a museum of flowers and photographs of the life of a drunk clown face down?

She closed the book of photographs. One heard the blues of a mumbling train on the tracks near the shore of the Connecticut River. There were soft knocks on the screen door. She turned the music box key.

"They found no sign of life on a distant star," she said.

They unwrapped the figurine found in the red clay under the sea wreckage. It had a face carved in dark sapphire. There were stockpiles of grenades and mustard gas under the blue coral. The blue light on the star chart was first believed to be a radio frequency left tumbling at the end of a meteor.

"New life forms in complete darkness," he said.

The small light traveled for ten thousand years and passed over them in their own time. It felt like a brief sun shower on the eyelash.

They moved the weapons to Plum Island. Former war prisoners taken out of the asylum who were given holiday tours for their courage prepared the uniforms and death masks of the citizens. The sought-after corsage was sold at every Walmart for every senior prom in the world. They were taken out of the arms of wives and children by a riderless coach into the wildflowers and rolled into lime dust by soldiers who buried their dead brethren in unmarked graves outside small towns and large cities. The rainbow husk fell out of the sky. It was retrieved out of the flash flood after the firestorm left the tops of trees smoldering. It spread through farmland, cathedral, factory, and sealed tombs. Nothing moved. The coffers of silver and gold and paper money were gone.

The gentleman read the funny papers. The president spoke of the angel found in the high mountain. He addressed his countrymen and the laws without punishment in the field. He said those laws were written by men who in their sleight-of-hand disguised their open wounds with the salve found under the wheel of death's carriage. He spoke of abandonment, children some born without eyes, some awakened without arms, and those lifted from the ground without legs. There was no warning, no flare in its futile arc across the sky.

There were half-stepping helmsmen. The Ministers of the Heart in white suits who gathered the living and the dead out of the field and threw them into the rising sea, half-alive.

The wind in the low hills burned the skin. The moon's ladle held a floating candle. There was a pulse. The fingers on his charred right hand were lifted off his chest.

"They called out his name and his eyes turned colors," she said.

He rode a bicycle on a dirt road to the next town. The war debris was taken to a high cliff by a hundred trucks. Bulldozers dumped flowers into the sea. They pulled ten thousand white crosses out of the earth to prepare for winter. Animals were carried to the railyard cut open and bladders torn out with branding tongs.

These were the vagrant hours under the moon's wreckage, a choir of the bereaved, and a riddled apparatus of the soul. They fell to their knees in the warm and mortal air. Planes landed on farmland. They were taken into the tunnels built by the first humans who gathered rock, found fire, invented sport. They caught wild hogs with long knives that cut the earth. The men tied thick rope to their ankles and climbed tall trees. They jumped head first to the ground. Heads bounced inches from the fertile earth and they were taken to the wedding room. Some of the heads hit the ground and they were carried away to a waterfall.

The crowd gathered at the first movie theater for a newsreel of the end of the Earth. Its demise was filmed at night under circumstances to be announced during intermission. It would not happen. The reel snapped into goat feathers. The magic man arrived and rubbed a blue crystal ball. A large crow under his top hat disappeared in a wink. He poured a water jug into his red suspendered pants and they collapsed into laughter. They stopped after he asked a woman to come to his aid and she disappeared. A monkey with a pink ass was lowered from the ceiling. The manikin he inflated with a hose from a rubber tube walked off stage. A noble angel in a black dress and pearls snored like a world champion.

"What the hell's so funny?" somebody shouted.

The crowd threw Molotov cocktails onto the stage. The magic man behind the movie screen burst into flames. Those in the balcony ran to the exits. Next weekend they returned to hear a lecture based on *A Rap on Race* with James Baldwin and Margaret Mead on long hot summers in American cities and the widows on a small island who were sleep-walkers holding hands that suddenly caught fire.

The guard in the straw hat snapped his leather razor strap like a whip. The prisoner's shirt had large black pin stripes that wrapped around his body. The priest placed a penny into the front flaps of his loafers and a penny on the tip of his swollen tongue. His ankles and wrists were tied down with pieces of charred hanging noose. He was lowered into a barber's chair with a thick leather seat and trim, taking his last breath inside a porcelain bowl. The forged steel handles lifted his soiled legs like a puppet in a three-piece suit, a pocket watch and chain inside his vest pocket. They wired his neck below the headrest. He wore a light brown uniform, white t-shirt, and black work boots. His wrists and ankles were buckled to his throne. The swivel chair floated in the room filled with mothballs and jars of Vaseline. It turned toward the one-way mirror. The executioner's mask left two almond shapes on the glass. No one saw inside his own chamber nailed shut with slats of cedar.

This was a shrine to finality and mortal charm to a man who did no wrong, a play in three acts, one for the small town stage right on page 21 without dialogue, a violin left at his back door on New Year's Eve, two for the wildfire center stage inside her eyes, three for the captain's globe stage right at the equator of the heart. The guard read a letter to his wife:

I woke up in a pool hall, my head cracked open by the eight ball. The jukebox kept playing "Stop Talkin' and Start Chalkin'." It was the game of the century. Two of us circled the table like serpents in a duel for love. The ball flew straight into the air and slammed into the middle of the table. Heads turned. It was the last game of the night. The moon settled into my bottle of bad whiskey. I do remember the kitchen staff pulling out knives from under their aprons. There was smoke coming out of the back wall. They wrapped damp towels around their mouths and eyes. Somebody threw a chair through the window. I was found nude under the pool table. They had cut out my tongue.

Had they seen lightning sketched across the Great Plains on a freight train? Who brushed against the chimes under the peasant's grapevines? What hour would the town clock stop? Was it a holy bell in the undertow of the underworld? There was salvation in what he knew of the world as he fell asleep under the stars in the window, and a certain comfort, too, in the music that played above his nodding head.

They removed night-blooming flowers from the prison yard. Bleach was poured over workout benches until the blood ran clean. The electric chair was sent overseas to repair the conductor wires. Jars of spearmint and wintergreen were placed on shelf. They built the viewing stand a foot from the barber's chair. They lifted barbed wire like tinsel from man's face with scalpels. The hanging noose on the holy bell in the guardhouse snapped and they turned a hand-cranked siren. Their children carried goat horns and grim rice on their hunched backs. If they looked up, copper freckles of mortality fell from the ceiling pipes into their eyes. If they looked sideways, they would see the image of a human face carved by their shadow and illuminated by their shadow, they would not look sideways for long as if a hand pressed against their straightened faces. If they looked away from death's robe and weary arms, they would not look away for long as the sunken light inside the prisoner's eyes brightened their own eyes. If they looked down as the needle punctured the veins in his neck and arms, they would not look down for long as the candlelight flared. If they would not lift their heads, they would not be lowered for long as the psalm they recited awakened what they would not speak. If they turned away from each other, they would not turn away for long as they heard the name of the man. If they turned away from the mortal light behind the window, they would not turn away for long as a halo floated above his head. If they sought comfort, it was not found in the vagrant hour. If they leaned against the window as if begging for mercy, they would not beg for his life for long. If some had covered their closed eyes, they would not be closed for long as they were surrounded by what they had not seen. If some stood to find a better view, there would not be a cleansing of the darkness. If those who fell on their knees sought refuge in the articulation of holy light and prayer, there was none. They lifted his head. Life was gone. They lifted his arms. Life was gone. They opened his eyes. Life was gone. They lifted his legs and removed his boots. Life was gone. They washed his body down. Life was gone. They pulled his mouth open. Life was gone. They removed his clothes and burned his body. Life was gone. On shore there were footprints in the sand dunes smooth as Darwin's thumbprint. If they remained silent, they would not remain silent for long.

He was found half-asleep on a park bench after a lunch of head-cheese and black flies. The yellow sparrow landed on his bad shoulder. *I will tell you my story. I will tell you my song.* It was his last will and first testament to the living. Although the guard spread newspaper under the barber chair and prisoner's feet, they were not prepared for the blue halo that formed above his head. What were his last cursed words, a wisp of a dragonfly, the calling bird's whistle, a brief minuet of the heart's desire, the peasant's amulet, a soldier's diary, green canteen, the small rivulets of nouns that echoed from his lips? They wheeled in a machine covered in cloth to resuscitate in case the prisoner would not let go of his soul dressed in rags. The Minister of the Heart read a blessing: *There was no life beyond his life for a man trained to take a life.* They found a music box and miniature skeleton key inside the machine. The prison doctor ordered sourdough bread and a glass of salt water. Those who stood in the viewing room had worn black hats and red capes, led into the tunnel with piccolo and drums, they lowered their heads in psalm. Outside the prison, behind the barbed wire, near a meadow and river with bluebird and wildflower, the choir emerged barefoot out of the baptismal waters, after boarding a night train in the high cliffs, after the last buffalo was shot through its eye, after the face with sapling eyes and thin lips formed inside a pink hourglass, and whose name he had called up from Hell proper before his last breath in three slow syllables, a family name, blood relative, first cousin, the human bloodletting, raised pitchfork, uncommon speech, the museum of sediment, choir of blind fortune, mouth of a blue mule, after the ships arrived on the gold coast, after he read a love letter to his high school charm, after he packed his belongings, after he watched the barrels of fire rolled into the sea, after the trees burned to ash, holy water, after he read a passage written in blood, after it was winter becoming winter again, autumn's torch, after banishment and song, after the iron gate collapsed, after the noble angel landed in quicksand, after they attached copper wire clips to his ears, penis, toes, eyelids, pursed lips, after the moon shed its ghost skin, he rode a wild horse out of the inferno of the living, out of the corridor of the deranged and prosperous men.

"The prisoners made a run for it into acres of quicksand," he said.

The guards threw paper airplanes out of the guardhouse across a full moon. They filled the wooden cart and waited for death's carriage. There were muffled sounds in the crawlspace, a blue mist on a third-floor tenement, the woman's arms flailing against curtains like a wounded bird rolling on the sidewalk, butterfly and honeysuckle, spearmint leaves between factory sidewalk and a chicken store with low-hanging birds, bare-chested men with their webbed feet on bumper cars at the Saturday night races, women outside the bowling alley in high oval skirts, science, for the division of cells and matrimony, art, for the gifted and cursed tongue, religion, for the healed and damned, evolution, for the larger brain and smaller heart, crime, redemption, punishment, for crime, warfare, for the peacemaker, nuclear winter, for evolution. It was a posse in search of the dispossessed twins separated at birth and placed on the orphan train through North Platte, Nebraska, overgrown weeds and thistle lean as the cattleman shot in the head off I-80, a cowboy thief who stole nothing in particular and attempted to rope the stars with a calf's umbilical cord, a drought of biblical proportion inside a small town wishing well, a child's first bicycle with streamers and baseball card in the spokes, stolen and left stripped at the next door gas station, flood waters in the hardware city, a highway and city to no goddamned place in heaven made *60 Minutes*, the hometown a ghost town of tar and pigeon feathers, ball brownfields and ghost factories, the wrecking ball above the town clock, patrons, thieves, governors, mayors, Central Park, underground lavatories, *urban renewal became Negro removal*. The gold angel dropped through the trees and landed feet first on the totem in the middle of downtown. It was struck by lightning on a Friday, rebuilt during the war, and replaced by a man who sold wingtips and toasters door to door.

The factory doctor placed a whistling African bee under his eyelids.

"After he crawled and opened the dirt cellar door, the sheriff's red-tailed lariat took the man's eyes straight out of his head," she said.

"If you break a horse, you can break a man," he said.

His execution by electric chair was set for midnight, May 23, 1920. The ceremony would begin with a foxhunt and boxed picnic lunches prepared by the prison staff with light Spam and Wonder Bread on the shore of the Dismal River. It would take place twenty-one days after the twenty-minute guilty verdict.

"There was no hung jury with this hanging judge," the preacher laughed.

The man's last wish was to read from his family Bible, penny loafers, and a long drink out of a pewter flask of Molotov riptide moonshine rum. They brought Japanese lanterns, fireworks, lawn chairs, blocks of ice, sailor's rope, riderless horse, telescope, penknives, two-dollar bills, pick-up truck, canoes, fishing poles, death certificate, cotton candy, English toffee, newborn calf, and bottles of Moxie. The wind stirred and sun hats flew into the river. They built a fire pit for the grand hog captured the night before in the church cemetery, roped and tied, and carried on the back of the all-star high school running back. They slit its throat and drained its blood into the outhouse latrine abandoned behind the schoolyard after the dustbowl. Homing pigeons were released from sailing vessels to honor the execution. They brought their wives and children and signed the guest book. Had they found the wedding of holiday and crime, blessing of the harvest moon, hunger of gravity, arc of human color, dance of the broken wheel, ribbon of carnality, parrot of the Tarot, long distance runners, unclaimed deed and massacre, unsigned love letter, gruel and torch of the common man?

"They gathered the animals during the blizzard," he said.

"They were taken into the dirt cellar," she said.

The sniper waited behind the Emerald Waterfall. He watched what slept in a crawlspace would reveal itself in shadow. Something moved under the ghost stars. He tracked a small man for three days and, with a golden snap of his thumb, the birds were screaming for their lives. This was the symphony of earth and sky composed by Ministers of the Heart, tall and thin hollow men, who carved their notes into trees. They had worshipped the pagan god of memory: school dance, slow dance, a turntable of 45s and *the rude mechanics of love.*

They met the explorers of the flesh at the Tavern of Fools who carried thimbles of blood into the prison, designed to clone those on death row. If they were declared innocent, they would live again and become new men and women with altered bodies and a throbbing ghost in the machine inside their heads. Those living were the innocent and the executed might live again. The bar floor was littered with paper chrysanthemums, needles, broken vials, false teeth, broken clock, a college degree was taped to the corner of a tainted mirror, a white rat inside the bird cage swinging on the chandelier, noisemakers, a penny candy machine with men who floated to the surface with baking soda, ribbon candy, *Grit* newspapers on bathroom stalls, Bazooka Joe fortunes, Radio Free Europe on a Zenith radio, Victrola with wooden slat speakers and green velvet top playing "Deacon Jones," "Blueberry Hill," and Negro spirituals. This was the way into the long corridor, footsteps and chains, wide oak doors and forged steel locks, slammed shut.

The guard walked into the field with a shovel. He dug a hole out of the red clay. The scarecrow leaned into the rain. The man played a violin in his cell. It was the last hour of a man's life and particular physics had its place on the drawing board at the tavern, the length of his last breath, heart rate, and the charred bottom of his shoes. *There was a tincture of blood dropped into the beer.*

Veins rose on the side of their necks, mouths wide open, clicking lips like a conductor's wand against a podium, Bibles opened, eyes closed, faces lowered, hands held hands, arms over shoulders, and some part of them shook and wept, and with their eyes opened their nostrils flared with the blood and burning flesh.

The bum luck men sang behind a drunken-ass mule, low roller confidence men coughed in their cuffed pants, a three-legged pigeon fell to its side, and night shift factory workers flopped belly up. They looked up half-amazed at the bloated angel as it fell, wings arched in full blossom until it caught the cupped hand of god and floated above their knotted heads into higher circles landing feet first at the border of heaven and highway to nowhere. The city planned a picnic the weekend of the execution and a video of the barber chair turned into the first electric chair attached to a iron lung by Stanley Works. One bronzed electric chair for every corner militia in every neighborhood by 2025 advertised on every TV and radio channel in the last small town owning the last chair. They first studied the blue meteor dust found on the wheels of the electric chair, followed by extensive probes of the spokes and Willie Mays's baseball card placed with sparklers as some kind of cruel joke by the executioner's tomboy after it had been stolen at the Peabody Museum and rehabilitated in the tunnels and launched on a Friday at sunset, and the whole world was watching a slow motion film of its trajectory over a millennium in the black-hole western movie, after it recorded its history in a three-minute breakneck capsule, after the six coats of chrome had disappeared down to the nub of its mahogany lever and raised three feet out the boiling waters of Saturn's red eye, after they removed the pink manikin from the driver's seat, after its human eyes recorded the constellations and movement of the planets, floating into the airless nights and flared days without sleep, after the weightlessness returned and its torn shoulder blade was removed by a satellite tethered to a helicopter, after the red leather padded seat was set fire by the sun spot between its forehead and the magnified glass of earth's globe, after the minister's goblet of holy water removed from the hourglass turned to blood in its bloodless veins, after the Teutonic plates on Earth caused the unstoppable and unforeseen brake failure on the electric chair wheels and tumbled out of heaven powered by heaven's distant light in a whirlpool of red clay and the clown kick loss of breath as the barbed wire tightened around the half-human manikin on death row and it smiled back at its scalp made wider seated in the barber's chair funny mirror and the hunger of gravity planted one evolutionary gesture of mouth into one immortal kiss.

They walked outside of the tenements and traced fingers across a brown dust on the third-floor banisters and windowsills. The church bus left Jimmy's Smoke Shop for Ocean Beach Park. The Ferris wheel was like a barber's chair, a slow circle game on top of the world and lower frequency of dolphins, ebb tide current of jellyfish, salt water taffy, slap of waves under the pier, articles of the seahorse, a runaway night roller coaster, *hold on sweet manikin, inside a chariot of time*, the landscape collapses into a square dark staircase, the pink hourglass placed in your plaster hand set you on course, lifts off in a field of wild flowers, under ghost stars, leaving the earth's orbit above the equator of despair, a mid-air collision of nano-verse in love letters inked in featherweight apparitions sketched by floating syringes tethered to the stars, patches of cotton wrapped around a cut wrist, sent first class, boiled in lard, the reused needles drawing blood out and drawing lethal horse injections into the pulsing neck and elbow veins, natural chemicals found in nature, natural living, natural dying, natural disasters, a bloodletting in the testament of the convicted and executed in every state of the union, a totem to the civilized warrior disguised as a peacemaker holding a telescope in the right hand on a houseboat observing the curvature of space and the alien war ships and the executioners in top hats and riding boots descending from sailor's rope to the floor of death row, in full regalia to the living, mustard gas as the second measure, standby for those they thought took their last breath only to open their wide eyes under the lilac light, sudden recovery, the gasp and curdled cry, life taken and life revived at the exact moment of birth, the re-set time clock, a deathwatch overtime, a last meal re-ordering of peanut sauce and chicken pot pie, a fine way to leave this earth, horse and buggy, barber's chair, chariot, a soap box derby, limousine of the heart, a rumble seat in the deepening waters of space, a taxi of stuffed animals, hula hoops, duck pins, calendar of the death row inmates, the astrological death dates, slow dancing in the widowed streets, the first step and last words in a last wish, gangplank science, parts of the time machine found in a rhubarb garden, portions of the viewing window found in red clay, and who miscalculated the temperature of the sun, the folding of angel wings, night landing, ten thousand miles off course and whiplash on the gangplank?

There was a back porch with metal poles and concrete steps, a varnished path children used for marble and golf holes around at the tenement. There was a petrified mud hole boot print of the butcher who stumbled each hour from Quality Market to Walt's Restaurant for a shot of hard whiskey. He dragged and mumbled on a pink cigar out of the side of his mouth, cursing to the world and homing pigeons, his bright blade sliced through cold cuts, and he offered us slices that filled our cheeks, a butcher with a heart. After school it was the Three Stooges, one episode of *The Woman Haters Club* and All-American jokes shaped a generation of backslappers and knuckleheads. The ventriloquist held his dummy like a lover. It had nigger lips. It was a creature the Creature of the Black Lagoon transformed into a two-legged boy genius. He spoke Chinese in Latin. His first job at sixteen was at Ace Cleaning Company. No ladders for children was the policy. The Stanley Works office had ladders that reached to the skylight, and we dusted lamps shaped like a 1950 UFO in a Flash Gordon movie. The third week of work found the door nailed shut, and the police looking for the owners who had stolen moneybags from the local bank. It brought images of tough men who fell out of those black and white TV tubes, *Paladin, Have Gun Will Travel*, and a sidekick, Steppin' Fetchit, who wore a large black hat, ran like a horse, laughed like a monkey with his ass on fire and slapped his side like a happy mule. *Amos 'n' Andy* sold nigger baby candy at the neighborhood stores in the city and to the schools in the suburbs, and the evening news became a what-the-fuck-had-gone-wrong in the country, riot of democracy, Tarzan beat the shit out of a thousand black Africans with a belt buckle, a kung-fu fucking Western movie, fair fight behind the diseased camera lens, *Birth of a Nation*, riot of democracy, protect the piggies in the dog-legged tub, a throat slit pledge of allegiance to the fucking flag and leave the despot in the extra large pot of boiling pygmies, the dummy had to find a TV that worked after the *Tonight Show*, national anthem at the Kentucky Derby, on your mark, get set, go back to sleep after a twenty mule team surveillance of your bedroom holding a Tarzan sex organ placed under your pillow on Christmas Eve, this was high noon at the soup kitchen, the school children unearthed charred bones of feet of workers next to the railroad tracks and the Lone Ranger waved on his white horse, Tonto in quicksand.

The World War II veteran stopped at the back porch and showed off the bullet hole through his left elbow to children. The barbed wire crackled and sundown left a swarm of honeybees floating above their heads. The sudden wind turned the clothesline into a lariat of despair. It was the hour of the crippled ghost who led the man, by his golden thumb covered by a pewter thimble, from death row to the balcony of viewers who wore masks that covered the eyes and nose. The mask would protect them from the indoor lightning caused by any frayed wire or syringe pushed into his veins. The lariat of light formed a halo around his neck. His eyelids swelled. His eyelashes burned. The mask held back the flames that curled out of his mouth. His arms were long and weary. His false and rotted teeth turned to dust. Several behind the plexiglass dropped their boxed lunches, buttermilk, and chocolate kisses. Several fell to their knees as if bullet proof and charmed into a kind of prayer, a remorse for one's unkind life torn out of alcohol and the puritanical gift of the plague house. This was the asylum of the brokenhearted, the wisdom-eaters, who dined with the crippled ghost on the covered bridge, along the river of mermaids and pirates taken out and down by a riptide into the glorious undertow of the underworld.

They were awakened one hour before the execution.

Were they signs of life or a glow of copper pennies inside his opal eyes, a ghost star, the meadow of the damned and reckless surveyors of the heart on a seaworthy expedition of the continents, the harpooned surveillance of loss and recovery, the locked door, a bare bulb, the serpent under the altar stone, a staff carried by the Minister of the Heart, broken wheel on death's carriage, a meteor across the sky, the man in a cloak with a white raven on his shoulder, the peasant holding his child in the floodwaters, the raft found down river, double moons under the unknown constellation, a sailor's telescope, sea of fire, burnt hair, ivory lobsters, the sunken ship on a map without coastal waters, his singed eyebrows, broken wrist, was this how his wooden leg tied to barbed and electric wire, dragged by a wild horse outside the prison walls, snapped into holy dust?

The child carried a basket of Concord grapes into Walt's Restaurant and heard a factory train backing up to the warehouse. The high school assembly included letter awards for the cross country and track teams, and a musical skit of "Rocky Raccoon."

"It was winter becoming winter again," he said.

"Brown water flowed out kitchen faucet for a week," she said.

"They shut down the reservoir," he said.

"Pigeons dropped from the city hall gargoyles," she said.

"The animals from city pound, who drank the brown water, crawled to the park on their hind legs," he said.

"They swept them into a wooden cart," she said.

"They canceled weddings for one year," he said.

"The flood started as children were let out of school," she said.

"The milk truck carried a few home," he said.

"Some were found a year later face down in the hollow ground of the meadow," she said.

The early snowfall covered the town square. They took their sleds to the Smith School hill. Aeroplanes lifted off a few miles away at the Army Air Corps base.

It was a summer of paper airplanes, hula hoops, whiffle ball, badminton, soft ball, ribbon candy, crabapples, cowboys and Indians, high school football, cross country meets at golf courses, medals and trophies, a pep rally for the hardware city of the world, paisley shirts and bell bottoms for a working-class mod squad, and the powder-faced children who ran into the street on Halloween chased by a policeman wearing a clown mask.

They delivered pizza to 341 Park Street in the blizzard on New Year's Eve. "What became of the young men who roamed Hartford Avenue. What happened to the Boy's Club and boxing a leather bag into feathers?"

It was summer becoming summer again and long nights of the newborn sparrow and dragonfly. The three-foot hedges in the city were trimmed with the precision of a factory saw. Nightfall. The Lithuanian Club on Park Street had dimmed the lights. Nothing like a last call on a slow night and thundercloud. The men with low shoulders stumbled into their factory apartments like duck pins struck by lightning. Two young boys hid behind the bushes in front of the tenement across the street from a warehouse.

"We got to get the money," he said.

"Take the brass cash register," he said.

"The door is thick as hell," he said.

"It has two small windows," he said.

"We can break the crystal doorknob," he said.

The boys ran across the street hit the knob clean off with a railroad spike. They ran past a rainbow of liquor bottles in front of a mirror of their lives. They hit the long brass keys of the cash register like their teacher who stood in front of the class on his Corona typewriter. They grabbed the nickels and pennies and dollars and dimes. They laughed in front of the funny mirror as their eyes disappeared into smoke and woe, their fingers holding a small bag of paper money and penny candy. The red siren floated above the street. The trees spread their leaves into shadows. They stood up in front of the oak bar and gave each other Boy Scout signals. Rain dripped through the tin roof. There was a broken honey jar under the gutter.

The policeman shot the young boy dead through the window on the front door of the Lithuanian Club.

What became of the dying city, brownfields, and ghost factories? Bricks were thrown through the stained glass of the church. There was Mrs. John on the Smith School playground, monkey bars, and a dairy farm over the schoolyard fence.

For executions, the prison guards wore black leather trench coats, camouflage, extreme winter, tropical, field blouse, peaked cap, crusher, fatigue, double braid, eagle, shoulder strap, collar tabs, field gray cloth, bottle green, shoddy, pleats, belt buckle, scalloped flags, internal belt, high-waisted, straight-legged, button-fly trousers with suspenders (braces), three internal pockets plus a watchpocket, tucked into jackboots, ankle boots, robust trousers, cockade, ear flaps, visored field cap, ski cap, soft headgear, stiff visor, black vulcanized fiber, patent leather, braided silver, aluminum, gold cords, tropical olive, jacquard-woven, tank headphones, guardhouse parachutes, coal scuttle, apple green, wartime factory, dark black-green, splinter-pattern, hand-painted, netting, chicken wire, black-white-red diagonal stripes on the right, eagle in silver-gray on the left, decals, calf-high pull-on jackboot, brown pebbled leather (blackened with polish), with hobnailed leather soles and heel-irons, breeches, kneeboots, deep turnback cuffed sleeves, ramp-buttons at the back of the waist to support the belt, wool gabardine, doeskin, whipcord, green collar and scalloped, pleated pockets, slate-gray trousers, French cuffs with officer collars, form-fitting thigh-length eight-button tunic, fine wool, without external pockets, dark-green Swedish cuffs, piping-edged collar, front closure, scalloped rear vent, silver braid belt, embroidered XXX, parade dress, steel helmet, jackboots, sword, white-cotton tunic, stand collar, black wool hip-length double-breasted jacket, six-button front, plain, barracks and guardhouse wear, rise-and-fall collar, removable buttons, shoulderboards, metal breast eagle, black wool hip-length double-breasted jacket and trousers with skulls, rose-pink armor branch, gold, for former cavalry units in the reconnaissance role, black and white twist, the black color made oil stains (blood stains?) less visible and a short jacket was less likely to get caught in the machinery. The trousers had tapered cuffs with drawstrings and tapes in order to fit into lace-up ankle boots, jacket buttoned to the neck in cold weather, worn open-collar with a field gray or mouse gray shirt and (in theory) a black necktie, self-propelled anti-tank artillery and assault-gun crews, first pattern jackets had deep lapels with square collars, second pattern added three buttons to close the collar, reduced the size of the lapels and had a more pointed collar, some second pattern jackets were produced without collar piping, a third pattern deleted the collar piping for all personnel but was otherwise similar to second pattern, a large black beret worn over a hardened-felt helmet which proved cumbersome and unnecessary, a field cap in black was worn, a crusher peaked cap for officers, crew tankers pinned their skull insignia to their lapels, reed green, zips running down the inside of dump leg used to zip both legs together to make a sleeping bag, heavy wool greatcoats, silver dimpled buttons that didn't reflect the light and sometimes painted green for camouflage, special winter clothing made by prisoners on death row, hooded waterproofed parkas, tropical medium-weight olive-drab cotton twill in service faded to khaki, the shirt and the seldom-worn necktie were green, embroidered in dull blue-gray on tan backing cloth, khaki or mustard-yellow cotton, Pith helmets, ankle boots with puttees, and lace-up canvas knee-boots, for prison riots standard steel helmets field-painted in a tan color were issued, vehicle interior sand-yellow or exterior brown-yellow, peaked caps made of olive-drab cotton twill lined with loosely woven red cotton fabric for protection from the sun and effective heat transfer from the head, a long visor, one-piece "false fold" rather than functional earflaps, and two metal ventilation eyelets on each side, a yellowish-khaki cotton twill or olive, the latter faded to a sage-tan color with use and sun exposure, its cut suited to the local climate than that of the early prison guard tropical uniform, with loosely cut trousers, a closed-collar tunic, and tan shirt, weapons cleaning and other duties likely to soil clothes, unlined, insignia-less uniform made of linen or cotton herringbone twill, two buttonless patch pockets on the skirt, undyed and off-white oatmeal color, a blue-gray, single-breasted, open-collared jacket with four pockets and flaps; white shirt and black necktie; blue-gray trousers; black leather boots; and a blue-gray peaked cap, side cap, for those who jumped out of the guardhouse, blue-gray, single-breasted, open-collared jacket with four pockets and flaps; white shirt and black necktie; blue-gray trousers, and black leather boots, a pair of trousers, a white and a blue shirt, a shirt-collar with three stripes, a silk neckerchief, gray gloves and a cap with two ribbons, a midnight-blue double-breasted reefer coat with ten gilt buttons and a matching peaked cap, jackets and over-trousers of brown or gray leather, a white peaked cap, full uniforms for full riot gear, light civilian clothing for picnics outside the prison, for vacations, seaman's jumpers and sleeveless shirts, lookouts in the guardhouse wore ponchos and sou'westers when on duty, bayonet, ribbons, wartime wedding photographs, piped dress trousers, collar, closure, cuffs, chocolate brown overcoat in cold desert nights.

It was winter becoming winter again. The prison guards sawed off the legs of prisoners and then heated them in ovens so they could thaw out and remove the boots in the long winter of desire.

God with us.   *God with us.*   *God with us.*

They found silver dollars inside a time capsule. If city pigeons are the rats of the sky, are prairie chickens the rats of the Great Plains? What happened to your charred hand?

"Do you have any last words?"

"I do," he replied.

"The alphabet," he said.

"Do not worry about my long sleep," he said.

"I wrote a letter in long hand for the prison archives," he said.

"They gave me a feather and inkwell," he said.

"It was the golden eagle," he said.

"I wish you well," he said.

They walked into the long corridor, on slanted floors, descending into death's chamber. There was a square window in one corner and the rabid eyes of animals in a crawl space. The electric chair was bolted into the center of the room like a king's throne. There was a garden of blue daffodils under the viewing mirror. The low ceiling had frayed wires from a crystal chandelier torn out of the ceiling. The Easter shoes, patent leather, horseshoe, wingtips, spurs, oxbloods, and high-top sneakers of the executed were thrown into a mud hole. Some of the men wished his audience well, how their time spent on Earth was a dirt road to nowhere, their birth determined by the ghost stars, a divining rod held by charred hands, a rolling pin thrown into the air, floating over the landscape, and landing in a meadow next to a waterfall, and thumb's up to the sight of rainwater, the demise of the silver clarinetist in white pants and blue blazer, the blessing of thorns, a beggar's chalice and holy bell, and some of them spoke well of the living before them, how they sang in Sunday school, prayed to the viper that moved across the floor under the altar stone, its head full of venom, moved like a pendulum, its pouched cheeks, from side to side, and crawled into the guard's cuffed pajamas, its flared and mortal kiss, the broken clock in one corner, family photographs, taped to the mirror in the prisoner's cell used to light the fireplace in the asylum, a commissary of bread and water, communion of fear and laughter, a music box found in a shed, a skeleton key in the family Bible, a harvest moon, easel, oils, brush, pastel, sketch book, birds, magnolia, and some of the men spoke of rose petals between pages of love poems and despair at the public library, a child lifted the book, and purple ash fell between his fingers, a poem written to the deserted towns and Ferris wheel in a faraway land, the manacled freed by the hand and burned by the hand, the calling of the human deed, a barn burning séance of flowers and disease, voodoo, black magic, hand-written sheet music blown off the window sill, notations of the constellations, weather vane, hidden planets, on a meteor a collision course with a wooden cart pulled out of the red clay, goblets, the blinded mule tied to a trough, how the circus tent burned into a theater of desire, a girl's lost shoe, how nobody foresaw the mishap of a bad penny inside a toy wallet, the alchemy of empty tombs and falling stars.

His hands were burned down to the knuckles inside the factory furnace. The door slammed shut on his weary arms.

"How old was the young boy?"

"14," he said.

"They dropped him off at New Britain General Hospital," he said.

"In a police car?"

"No."

"Yellow Cab."

The cab left Jimmy's Smoke Shop during a blizzard. His right hand looked like a large hawk had captured a small animal in the snow. They had to amputate his right hand. It was replaced by a pirate's clamp. They taught him how to lift a cup.

The factory doctor was a shy man. They gave the young boy a yellow-plated gold watch.

"For his left hand?"

The gold watch did not fit his missing wrist. It was night and the lilac wild. There was gunfire at the reservoir. He was married in rainfall.

There were no fingerprints left on the cash register. The young boy with rickets wore leather gloves the night he was shot in the head.

The story begins after the young boys played gin rummy before their rampage into low fog behind the hedges. The oldest boy stole burglar tools out of the backseat of the captain's Lincoln Continental, four doors for three boys on a joyride, speeding through locked gates, over railroad tracks and gravel parking lot at the opening day carnival. They bought root beer floats and rode the Ferris wheel, threw softballs at straw dummies, swung at the strong man totem bell, drank Avery soda, ate Capitol Lunch hot dogs, purple cotton candy, stared at the bearded lady and man with a lizard's tail, rode bumper cars, threw darts at balloons, rings over soda bottles, smoked fat cigars, a Laff in the Dark.

One boy who wore a derby to high school was killed in the Plainville Dirt Track Demolition Derby, one disappeared on a Greyhound bus, and the youngest boy was on death row for the six Donna Lee Bakery Murders. He was a member of the automobile gang turned motorcycle outlaws who rode their bikes through the senior prom parade, and ran out of town by the highway patrol to the Canadian border.

He misjudged the hairpin turn, held to the steering wheel a second too long, thrown face first through the windshield, landed face up in the mud, under a willow tree and moonlight, a straight man to a boy genius, sat next to a man on the bus who kept singing a lullaby, and sat up in the aisle.

"Help me, help me, help me," he repeated in a high-pitched voice.

The next bus stop for dinner was a hundred miles. The driver stopped on the side of the road next to a shallow ditch. The man sat in the back of the bus with a large carving knife. Everybody was told to get out of their seats and off the bus until police arrived. The young boy jumped over the electric barbed wire, caught his pants and tumbled into a stream, away from the sharp blade that nicked the side of his arm, under night's apparel of stars, and he ran toward a life, into the corridor of his past and those who might remember him unrecognized by his own deep-set eyes.

The boy was offered a glass of water, lethal injection, mustard gas, electric chair, crossbow, machine gun, stomped by buffalo, or boiled in oil. He opened his journal and read passages he had written years before behind a school desk in a dirt cellar. The glass of water contained a tincture of tainted elixir found in the subterranean caves on the Red Sea floor, lethal injection derived from a mule tranquilizer and placed into a pink hourglass, mustard gas sent into his veins with a hand pump used for flat tires on road trips, the electric chair option was ruled viable by the appeals court in a 5 to 4 decision, a crossbow used by King Arthur in a courtly love showdown gone awry, the arrowhead a replica of prehistoric hunters in drag, the machine gun with a built-in digital camera used for such events, death recorded in real time, stomped by a buffalo herd startled by a helicopter above the Wyoming River, boiled in fish oil made by Johnny Roach at the Berlin Ponds, yet it was determined that death would come too easily for the untrained eye, knowing water was alchemy and elixir rare, the guard might not be able to draw such water out of a wishing well, and the night before the execution the boy would be placed into a vat of lard up to his neck and it was determined by the Ministers of the Heart a pendulum would swing and be lowered one inch from his eyes and stopped.

"Punishment in the electric chair would be crime in the field," he said.

They sat manikins with their glowing opal eyes into chairs behind the one-way viewing mirror, backs straightened, white gloves, and hands in their lap. Each manikin had a recorded voice.

"Crime in the field would be punishment in the electric chair," he said.

"His small feet were placed into a bucket of eels," he said.

He would be sent into sleep.

They were released into the corridor. Their iridescent angel wings caught fire and left tiny drops of blue flame on his forehead. There were screams in the brownfield. Fire spread over the lilac wild. The ghost train derailed under a night rainbow and harvest moon. Mustard gas settled over the town. The smell of garlic and horseradish awakened the night crawlers.

Within 24 hours of exposure to mustard agent, victims experience intense itching and skin irritation, which gradually turns into large blisters filled with yellow fluid wherever the mustard agent contacted the skin. These are chemical burns and are very debilitating. Mustard gas vapor easily penetrates clothing fabrics such as wool or cotton, so it is not only the exposed skin of victims that gets burned. If the victim's eyes were exposed, then they become sore, starting with conjunctivitis, after which the eyelids swell, probably the result from the cholinomimetic activity of mustard. At very high concentrations, if inhaled, mustard agent causes bleeding and blistering within the respiratory system damaging mucous membranes and causing pulmonary edema. Depending on the level of contamination, mustard gas burns can vary between first and second degree burns, though they can also be every bit as severe, disfiguring and dangerous as third degree burns. Severe mustard gas burns (i.e., where more than 50% of the victim's skin has been burned) are often fatal, with death occurring after some days or even weeks have passed. They cannot be bandaged or touched. We cover them with a tent of propped-up sheets. Gas burns must be agonizing because usually the other cases do not complain, even with the worst wounds, but gas cases are invariably beyond endurance and they cannot help crying out.

The baby girl was lifted out of the crib, her flesh, burned thin as air, peeled off by touch, floated to the floor. She was placed into a wooden cart. He turned the miniature key to a music box. It was a melody of the lost flower. Yellow fire flared above the trees. The retrievers of the dead turned to grief and walked into the baptismal waters. There was candlelight in the Office of the Deputy and laughter in the bunker. Boxes of cigars and whiskey were small gifts to the men. Snow fell over the bodies piled into freight trains and thrown into the sea. It was winter becoming winter again.

The retrievers of the heart met outside the village.

The retrievers of the dead carried the children out of the asylum and placed them into wooden carts. The commander had not allowed for the pink hooves floating in their stalls, the quicksand, appearing as blue straw over the hollow, drawing the captain down up to his swollen neck and saved by a hanging noose, a sweet reminder of the lethality of the vagrant hours on the descent of a time machine's axis, nerve gas filling the lungs of the hopscotch young and bocce elders on the beach, how they forced out a pill into the flared mouths of the dying to resuscitate to give them enough air to kill them, how the rumble seat fit the electric chair, the electric chair made into time machine, sent the soul out of high heaven into the thin air of physics, into the veil of weightlessness, seated in a throne of time and death's leather strap buckle to the young boy's waist, bronzed with the archangel's sword, a low rider in a swivel chair thrown into a meteor shower of

gold coins, the small oval-shaped head first appeared in the sailor's telescope, too sharp ears, almond eyes, a mouth nearly too small for drinking buttermilk from the two-headed blue mule made out of a straw, the
faces multiplied across the constellations, transmissions were detected
on distant radio signals captured on Admiral and Zenith tubes and
turned into Valentine nano-verse into scriptures found inside a litter
bin of heaven and the footprints found in hell identified by scholars as the prehistoric, petrified, swift and three-hoof demons on their
annual binge of golden oxtail and red neck soup, executions had a way
of bringing out the beast with angel wings, fields of grim rice, opened
cages of wild dogs with long red tails and sunken eyes, a compass set to
the falling stars, sure-footed humans on the precipice of a town clock
throwing daffodils and sunflowers into the hands of the deranged
and prosperous kid goats on their hind legs baying to a disappearing
race, and somewhere in everyone's blood a witless seed planted in the
unyielding ear for proper balance walking on the gangplank of ghost
stars, one uneven step into the winter garden and nothing in the soil
can be saved on this earth and in heaven, the crackle, hiss, a curse set
upon the village on the sea of flames, animals found with human teeth,
and the ready, set, go-cart crowd chanting at the hour of the trap door
inside the asylum of trained killers, one tube and pulley connected to
all living things.

On earth as it was inside a time machine, they played "Scarborough Fair." Some went to war. Some went to college. Some worked in
the ghost factories. The cheerleaders threw flowers into the air at the
bonfire in front of the school. Autumn Torch. There were hula hoops.
Walking to the annual Thanksgiving football game. Willow Brook
Park. New Britain Senior High versus Pulaski. Who won most of the
games?

There were school dances near the park and records with James
Brown, Junior Walker and the All-Stars, black and white students,
jocks and hippies, smokers and dopers, Key Club Dollars for Scholars,
athletes with jocks straps around their necks, and homecoming queens
with false eyelashes and falsies who danced without music or boys.

What became of the whistler on the *Andy Griffin Show*, American Stock Exchange, basketball and football stars with dreams larger than the public library? Who rode in the Memorial Day parade the year after the Vietnam War ended?

"They never left the state or town where they grew up?"

"Nebraska?"

"No, Connecticut."

"How many died in the Vietnam War in your hometown?"

Flags were lowered to half-staff. Taps were played and their names were read until their blood ran clean.

"Made in China, Buy American."

"The flag pole was stolen from City Hall."

"They overturned gravestones."

"The golden angel wings were found floating in the reservoir of the dead."

He taught himself to sit still on death row behind prison bars on holidays. He had read the news. It was New Year's Eve. The prisoners filled a bathtub with jars of moonshine. They played Motown and Beatles on 45s on a record player found in the corridor that connected city hall to the asylum. The one-legged elderly prison cook found the factory doctor's medical bag in a trap door to the root cellar and used his one bottom tooth to pull a sewing needle straight out of the left foot of a guard working who had stepped on it and broke it clean in half on the deep rug inside the warden's office. He took the sewing needle out of his mouth and used it on the turntable.

They threw tinsel and colored lights over the barbed wire and bodies after the prison riot. The rooftop of the cafeteria was blown off first. There was no electricity except for a hand-wheel generator for the time machine. They dropped hundreds of ventriloquist dummies into their

cells with explosives stuffed inside their eye sockets. The clown dummies with red lipstick floated into their cells. Helicopters landed on the
playground and mines were placed under each of the baskets. Molotov
cocktails flew out of windows. One dummy landed on the lap of the
executioner and he ran for his life in the snow. Molotov cocktails flew
out of windows. One landed in the beef stew of the warden who cursed
in Spanish and called the governor for reinforcements. The National
Guard left their posts at the border. Submarines floated to the surface
with periscopes set to the stars. The local militia gathered at the YMCA
and Boy's Club to recruit able-bodied men and women, sitting in parks
and at social services, able to wear steel boots and carry long knives for
one hundred miles. The children were told to stay at school and not
return home. The children and animals at the zoo were given shots
against nerve gas. Army tanks were inoperable. Naval blockades were
planned on the Atlantic and Gulf coasts. Satellites broadcasted the fires
spreading across the earth in eruptions of red geysers. Computers were
down. Cell phones were down. What started out at the prison claimed
telephone poles, football stadiums, mountains, skyscrapers, and all
things illuminated by the guard-house spotlight, splintered like ghosts.

They built the Willow Street playground on top of a junkyard.
Burned automobiles, demolition derby bumpers, and scrap metal pierced the earth, pylons of debris and human waste stacked high
enough to be seen from Smalley School, weathervanes pointing due
north behind the sun, a ticket stub from the 1964 World's Fair between
the seat of a living room couch, aluminum siding, copper pipes, bricks
clawed by a crane, mounds of plaster board and stained glass turned
into a fine asbestos dust by a wrecking ball crew, the alchemy of desire,
a cruel and unusual punishment, eye for an eye, penis for a penis, one
black, one white, and both splayed by a razor under the altar stone at
the Museum of the American Gargoyle, occupied by those who sat in
their pews on Sunday morning, a small wafer of baked penis placed on
the tongue, the lower wages of sin and the parted ocean turned into
sewer water flooding basements for ten thousand years, night fires in
the brownfields, forged steel turned into ball bearings for jet fighters

and marbles for the neighborhood children, radioactive whiskey, magnifying glass, charred Victrola, toaster, pinball machine, hammer, nail, coffee maker, shoeshine box, hometown newspaper, bicycle tubes and spokes, sander, screwdriver, honeysuckle on barbed wire, grandfather clock, one thin dime inside a bedroom slipper, mounds of smoldering tires, high school yearbooks, medals and trophies, a declaration of human rights, mufflers, shoe horn, broken mop handle, step ladder, hub caps, street light, wheel barrow, stop sign, windshield, horseshoe, buoy, duck pin, 78s, parachute, VW Bug, flag pole, a seventh grade journal, paperback books, complete set of the *Encyclopedia Britannica*, *Sergeant Pepper's Lonely Hearts Club Band* album, a photograph of the town clock burning at the turn of the century, a train signal, a program from the memorial service for Martin Luther King at South Congregational Church, one disco shoe with platform heels, a masterpiece painted by Minnie Evans, discarded by the Salvation Army Band Christmas Fundraiser, a piggy bank filled with nickels from the Burritt Bank, a large glass urn filled with butterfly wings thrown out of the attic of a spinster secretly in love with her cousin Violet, years after the man on death row a dressed in a khaki uniform had requested a jar of chunky Negro Peanut Butter and blackberry jam for his last meal and testament to the dereliction of duty beyond his means.

They lost the homecoming football game.

"Team got drunk the night before," he said.

The ambulance arrived for the coach. He fell on his head under the bleachers at half-time as we stood like warriors in our high school sweaters. It was the gridiron pigskin revival of town and country, a cotton candy pom-pom homeroom, penny loafer, the mascot pony tied to a parking meter, paisley shirts, black and white striped bell bottoms, five seniors inside a VW Bug riding to lover's lane at the reservoir, high heels, skirt to the waist, last ride to White Sands Beach, Wild Irish Rose, bonfire inside the iris of the seagull, shaking hand on the leg of the cheerleader, and who threw his father's handkerchief out of the back window of the time machine, a young man's tassel, his first school dance, teachers taking arms and pairing tall girls with short boys, short girls with tall boys, the slow dance inside a pink hourglass, a soft shoe waltz of the beggar's daughter and factory worker's son, the get-down wing span of Johnny Walker and the All-Stars and James Brown knees down on the ground, sorrow a caped and ragged man brought to his feet by the angel noble in a shark skin suit, his black cape in flames, young men and women clicking their heels like matadors in full regalia, wild bull snapping at their ankles, the midsummer's bluebird house and sailboat, graduating class of scholars for dollars, cross country, indoor and outdoor track teams, band members, young alcoholics, burglars, smokers of Hartford tobacco and trash weed, battle between WPOP and WDRC, long after the wind lifted his father's handkerchief above the willow tree, before the wooden cart filled with three neighborhood children ran brakeless down a steep hill in the middle of the road, past tenements, through a stop sign, past Quality Market and Walt's Restaurant, into a garden over the lily pond, honeysuckle, rhubarb, nasturtium, sunflower, miniature trees, and floated above a century of proms captured on a turnstile inside a minuet of blown glass, a rotating time capsule, thimble, needle, and lace unwinding on the gymnasium floor above a blue crystal ball of light, and nobody on Earth believed how a slow dance turned into a last dance and a first kiss into a long embrace inside a corridor and burning of leaves.

Three weeks after he started breathing inside his iron lung, a wicker birdcage was placed above his bare feet. They brought in a fair maiden of the electric chair for her expertise in natural dying and her handling of the bellow to create a short and steady breath. *Inhale and Exhale. Inhale and Exhale. Inhale and Exhale.* It ran like clockwork until at night the bird started to peck at his toes and stare into his eyes. He heard a foghorn. Was he near a pier and railyard somewhere between the city of his birth and Saturn? Was he transported by a Yellow Cab, the hollowed out Greyhound Bus, the re-wired ambulance used in three assassinations, rolled to the front door on a stretcher to the front door of Jimmie's Smoke Shop to purchase Cuban cigars handed out to children and sold on the street, marinated in pot liquor and stuffed with poison sumac, placed in the back row of a reconstructed aeroplane that dropped napalm over rice fields by a famed pilot of his generation with purple and bronze stars on his chest, a man of war and distinction who retired into the prison system, executioner of the century, fitted in a double-breasted herringbone suit, wingtips, fitted with a black hood with eye holes that peered into the eyes of the damned and prosperous man on death row he lifted off his knees into the chair like a wounded bird, suspenders tightened over his shoulders for the rapid departure of the soul to earth's inferno, a veil used to deflect the ultraviolet rays and cover what the face of a man who whispered something into his ear, the glass tubes inside his nostrils, orange syringe pushed into the side of his neck, and who would know the exact time of death, a stethoscope placed over his heart, finding a pulse before the electricity and gravity pulled him down, tumbling into thunder, rain, meteor, volcanic ash and lava, dust storm, inside a laboratory designed for eternal sleep and few distractions, comforts of the hearth and home, baked goods, meat loaf, roasted goose, sweet peas, cranberry relish, wild turkey, a pantry of canned goods to prepare for good after a marathon of Bergman films and popcorn with brewer's yeast and Guinness, after the final prayer and absolution a resuscitation on the killing floor of heaven after they warned him before he was slid into the chamber of the high levels of mercury in his blood, blindness, and toxic air, trapped inside the iron lung and time machine, altered the bronzed rivets, outer space, and mortal time? They found options other than electricity unreliable and the consequences often ended in misery. The silver box of vipers from the New Holy Ghost Church was pushed under the chair and by a defrocked priest bitten on his golden thumb and left him crawling on the killing floor with his legs amputated below the knees. One silver bullet in a blue velvet case exploded in the executioner's hand. The prison doctor replaced the hand with a bronzed glove. The medieval crossbow broke apart after sending its arrow through stained glass of the town and into the left eye of the bell ringer. The knife thrower sliced his finger pulling out a switchblade from the abdomen of the prisoner found half-awake and stabbed in the laundry room. The red button used to release poison gas became stuck and traveled into the air conditioning vent of the warden left comatose and his curdled split tongue dancing inside his mouth. The parboiled organs inside a sweet charred oak cask, leftovers used to pour over a prisoner tied down and fancy free, caught fire in the prison chapel and left his conjugal visitor fleeing into a shallow pool of burning rainwater. The roped prisoner drawn across the dirt road was nearly saved when the palomino bucked the guard and sent him into the river rock where he drowned. The body of a prisoner with a sailor's knot around his neck, dropped through a trap door, was never found. The strewn bodies of the damned and quartered were picked up by orphaned children who were paid one penny apiece to fill straw bags, hung low in the warden's dirt cellar for years, and thrown over the sea cliff. Death by firing squad sent smoke rings into the trees, birds screaming for their lives, and for a brief moment the sad eyes of the world piercing through dark spaces and the splintered light in the wilderness, above the hooded prisoner tied to a totem pole, yet it was death by fire that claimed his heart on the riderless horse, something about being burned alive and the wing span of grief circling above a temple of fire, the choir of mortality, shadows of dust falling into piles, one would almost see his sunken eyes inside the fire, his tilted head, collapsed shoulders, floating waist, a final gasp of blessed air in the undisturbed air, a voice breaking into song, his last meal, last words, his last will and testament, conjugal apparition over his mattress, last phone call home and on the last dance of his life his legs wavering in a mirage.

He found a quote in the prison library, among boxes of law books and medical journals, that *a true friend is rarer than a white raven.* He wrote down his three last wishes. He wanted to learn how to fly the World War I Lafayette Escadrille. He stepped on the wing and climbed into the cockpit, a sky pilot and aviator of the heart, sent into the clouds to drop letters tied in black ribbons, a declaration of clean and prosperous living after the war and final execution, for photographs of the sacred mounds of those who fled in exile. The first sign was children born without eyes. He recorded work completed by the retrievers of the dead and living on a burning landscape, those taken to the road by wooden carts, horses drowned in the rising rivers, vultures that circled above homes for hours before dropping out of the sky, charred by the mortal air.

He planned a long weekend for travel inside a time machine as he played a didgeridoo, rain stick, thumb piano, and his poems would be translated into all known human languages and into Morse Code. The second sign was the light above the mountain that appeared every third day. They say it was a white halo thrown over the world by the wounded hand of God. It would hover for a few hours like a rainbow and disappear slowly by morning tide. He would send a high-pitched radio signal with the music and poems to distant planets, one day returned with readable notes on miracles. The time machine was retro-fitted with diamond cut headlights, bullet-proof airbags, twin goat horns, rumble seat, and upgraded with two large Mason jars and fusion nano-injected flux engines filled with pigsty rainwater, anti-missile and tank rocketry, oxygen-producing light bulbs, death masks, marbles, periscope, one-way mirror, Polaroid sunglasses, parachute, Beatles and Motown cassettes, for its final descent from the heavens into hell's ocular eclipse.

There were no other clear signs except for the birth of one animal with three tongues. His last wish for his unearned suffering and redemption and was to fly a dirigible once commandeered by elite officers who he learned had floated for hours inside their amniotic sleeping sickness, awakened by the turbulent air and siren of the dispossessed caught in the hunger of gravity that ignited their apparels of flesh inside the aquarium of stars.

They stabbed all the pigs and burnt down the family barn. The family left Kansas for Oklahoma at midnight inside a junkyard car with bare tires, without bumpers and a cracked windshield. Grandpa said it was like driving in a rainstorm on a bright cheerful day, whistling on a flatbed truck, hot wind, your scarecrow, ears flopped, weeping out loud in the middle of nowhere, a fast getaway or a cell in prison for doing nothing bad, one wrong move inside Lucy's Love Palace and life is gone, a pitchfork plunged between the soft ribs of the manic drunkard and a siren blares like a dog whipped senseless into the air, its eye knocked out by a pool stick buzzard, the last hand of straight poker and his world ended, packed a bag of sandwiches and bottles of Moxie, it was a two-dollar bill taped to the mirror that caused havoc, somebody said it was a counterfeit and Confederate bill, somebody shouted the names of generals, another man with his ivory cane top said it was stolen from the five and dime safe, somebody mentioned the set of false teeth at the bottom of the large jar of boiled eggs, another said those teeth were found after the warehouse fire during the race riot, somebody said don't call me a fool, fool, somebody said I knew it when I bought you, somebody raised their hand for blood, another showed his fist in a pool room brawl that ended up outside and upside down in the sewer grate, somebody called the sheriff and everybody ran for their lives in the snow, they roped three men like cattle and rolled them against the back wall, two others were found under the altar stone asleep with Mojave green snakes inside his cuffed burlap pants, one left in the car with bad brakes, he ran with his family out of a one bar town, they sent dogs and a search team with long knives and torches, they crossed under a covered bridge, they came to his house near the railyard, they used crowbars and nightsticks to break out the windows, his house was burned to the ground and they waited for somebody to jump out of the attic window, and Grandpa said there was no one way to tell good from evil yet there would be signs, what one claimed their own, another found the abnegation of self, how one claimed love, another found false testimony given to the Ministers of the Heart, a freight train took a slow turn into the tunnel on the other side, one of the prison guards swore he saw the son of the devil laughing upright in a straitjacket with angels inside a box car.

Grandpa said you get chills and fever from a bad watermelon. They hung a crystal ball filled with newborn vipers above the electric chair. It was tied to the executioner's foot pedal as he sat in a barber's chair behind the viewing room to drop them over the face of the prisoner.

He pulled out a straight razor with HOLLOW GROUND engraved on the blade, sharp as a river reed, canoe drifting across the lake, slingshot, medicine bag, falconer's glove, eye patch, stethoscope on the amputated arm, fishing pole, family Bible and photographs, brooch, pearl necklace, class ring, marbles, the chandelier fell into the dining table at the warden's dinner party.

They placed the test dummy in the chair, its pink mouth open for pennies, they tried 5,000, 10,000, 30,000, and held at 100,000 volts, to tempt the goddamned dummy into speech, at first there were a few vowels, nouns, and guttural verbs in English, French, Spanish, Urdu, Swahili, Italian, Swedish, Scottish, Mandarin, Arabic, Bengali, Hindi, Russian, Portuguese, Japanese, German, Wu, Javanese, Korean, Turkish, Vietnamese, Telugu, Cantonese, Marathi, Tamil, Min Nan, Jinyu, Gujarati, Ukrainian, Persian, Xiang, Malayalam, Hakka, Kannada, Oriya, Panjabi, Romanian, Bhojpuri, Azerbaijani, Maithili, Hausa, Burmese, Serbo-Croatian, Gan, Awadhi, Thai, Dutch, Yoruba, and Sindhi.

They found the dummy a finely tuned vessel for the death chamber, its sculpted nose and lips, broad forehead, brain size, wooden teeth, chatter box on the armchair, dressed in a plaid vest, knobbed knees, pocket watch, short red hair, large ears, boxer shorts, black eyes, puffed cheeks, patent leather shoes, bow tie, they found at 5,000 volts, its charred tongue twisted into a perfect straw and its wooden legs turned to dust, they found a money clip with a Powerball in the dummy's overalls in his back pocket, it had been blown out of its seat at 30,000 volts, flames shot out of its mouth, ears, and eyes, they filmed the dummy crawling on the floor asking to be lifted back into the rumble seat with a repaired exhaust system, axle, GPS, flight pattern set to the stars, its charred face made him almost half-alive, and they tied a chain and pulley to the back bumper of a pickup truck used on the newborn calf in the Great Plains and tried with prayer and singing but little success prying his small hands off the captain's jar of blue honey.

They said they saw a blue halo above his head outside the iron lung. He had recited one line before he slept and dreamed he was walking in a sweet clover field.

The twin towers fell and my wife sat up in her hospital bed.

He was turned to his side once every two hours and played "Moon-light Sonata" on his childhood music box. He always wore its small skeleton key around his neck. The box opened and he opened his eyes. The black rivets he counted inside his tomb of noise became a slide ruler. He counted off the rivets far into the night and invented a code for time travel, how to X-ray veins in real time and capture a pulse as one sat in the electric chair, and how to lift the barber chair by a foot pedal if he were set free from his roped straitjacket in his minuet of gravity. He found himself floating and free falling over a landscape of desire, above the English garden of thorns, swan, canoe, fishing poles thrown from a shore of mud, blue iris, and starlings, dragonfly, peat bogs and vespers fathered by two lovers behind a waterfall, gold coins released from heaven's carpentry, fence post, wild horse, the sacred cross, amulet, opal, blackbird with emerald wing, a live wire planted into his tongue, pinned down into a wax tray, wrist, behind the knee, ankles, neck, eyelid, fingers, toes, cheekbones, connected to the inner ear like a psalm. He floated above the prison grounds. He had wished to be wheeled to the Great Cave and Blue Hole as he slept inside his iron lung. There was snowfall on the day of his execution. Hailstones bounced off the thick metal drum, and the guards were unable to reach him for three days with a search party on horses. The ice storm had knocked out power at the prison and guardhouse. His body was kept warm by the down feathers floating in the iron lung. They had pre-pared for the mutilated days ahead. He was able to press buttons with his hands and toes that released sleeping potions in various strengths and time-released capsules. He had sought weightlessness and good sleep for years. The medicine worked well when he was first rolled into the iron lung and with slumber under the moonlight oratory and chimes of the retrievers of the dead he found a certain comfort in this.

Johnny Roach held her hand against his chest. She wore a black dress and pearls to the dance. It was a waltz inside the iron lung and their late arrival on the dance floor. Somebody in the crowd threw sand, another told the disc jockey to play their favorite song well suited for the ballroom at the New Year's Eve Palmer House Gala, they held the red draped curtain to one side as the men marched and bagpipes played, the accordion was saved for their last dance under a chandelier of ghost stars. He wore a king's tuxedo, bow tie, and union jack boots. They circled the dance floor, his finger tapped her shoulder, she lifted her dress and took a promenade curtsy, maple leaf, gang plank, silk net caught a firefly, down to his knees for a wedding vow, opened the folded paper like angel wings with his thin fingers, depleted by a lack of natural light and drips of water and vials of oxygen, his swollen hands, aviator lips, chained in one position until welts spread appeared and spread over his body like tiny vessels in the eyes, and what kind of man claimed he was able to sleep blindfolded inside the iron lung, blindfolded in a straitjacket in a barber's chair with a straight razor under the ball of your neck, blindfolded the final descent of the time machine, monitored only by a thread of light sent by a telescope and connected to some unknown radio signal sent inside a candlelit nook under a glass dome and blown out as he whimpered in his sleep, what kind of men carried portable ground-to-air missiles over their shoulders in search of a time machine sent from a distant planet landing near a volcano into rivulets of molten lava that stalled its throttle and broke the launching pin and snapped a cable on the armchair, the noble angel staring into the windshield, hands wrapped tight around a lamb's wool steering wheel set to speed away from meteors lifted by a glowing pitchfork and kicked into the hunger of gravity by Satan's pink split hooves, this was the ride of a lifetime in a convertible, top down glory, rumble seat, *diamond in the back*, rabbit ears, three-channel TV, transistor radio clips on the dashboard, AM radio, and a prayer by the retrievers of the dead, the prisoner on death row inside the iron lung hourglass in free fall until he was awakened by the grim rice thrown over his black, blue, and beaten body until he was awakened by the holy water poured over his charred eyes.

They threw flowers and first dirt over the iron lung as it was submerged into the sea. This was a test flight. A dummy doll dressed in a red sweater replaced Johnny Roach. It had long eyelashes and a brace tacked to its broken back and a priest's handkerchief wrapped tight around the wooden sockets of the knees. The head rotated like a spinning bottle with large red lips that would kiss a woman off her feet and into the ground, brown teacup eyes, a long black curl of schoolboy hair on its bald head, elephant ears, wooden teeth, mouth wired to its lower jaw, natural pearl buttons, cowboy shirt, Madras Bermuda shorts, green canteen on the alligator belt, railroad pocket watch, wing-tip, gold-toed, spurs behind his boots, silver cleats on the bottom of its shoes, a certificate of promise for his war wounds, two purple hearts and one bronze star.

He was paraded into the town square in a wooden cart pulled by a half-skinned mule used in the post–Civil War plan to recover stolen paintings and music sheet by the composer of the heart's apparel. He had scored a symphony dedicated to his late wife, and he attended the premiere at the Grand Museum. The theater filled with dignitaries and pardoned thieves. There was a greeting line in the ballroom. They shook his hand and offered their condolences. They, too, were half-alive seated in front of the urn and grand piano among the sculpture and paintings from another era of redemption. They placed a black cloth over the urn in homage to the last dance of her life on these marbled floors. There was a psalm and song performed as the crippled ghost appeared in the garden window and gave a wink, laugh, and scowl at the trampled human flowers in folding chairs. They spoke low of how her hands suddenly caught fire. The children fell asleep in the wishing well.

There was no rain.

The nurse pulled out its tongue with pliers and observed a heart-shaped wound on his left shoulder. She stuffed its pink mouth with cotton balls dipped in mustard gas, placed a copper penny on each socket, closed the eyelids with its tiny head rested on the velvet pillow inside the iron lung. Ten, nine, eight. Seven, six, five. Four, three, two. One.

It was late September. Johnny Roach was first approached by a bouncer outside Lucy's Love Palace.

After the iron lung failed during the blackout, Johnny was transported by Yellow Cab and seated into the barber chair in the basement of Grill and Bones Restaurant on Hartford Avenue. The visiting nurse clipped his toes and trimmed his fingernails after the scientist found that his hair and nails grew faster and longer inside the iron lung. During holidays they pumped laughing gas into the iron lung and recorded Johnny's high-pitched howls, the kind heard in deep caves, a miner's cough, the kind of spirit with amputated arms left with sensation on fingertips long gone in the arson started by a firefighter at the warehouse next to the Lithuanian Club, its arms reaching out of the underworld trying to touch the husk a rainbow. After the barber chair failed to raise to the proper height for a close shave, they placed Johnny in a wooden cart and raced him to the bottom of Walnut Hill Park and around the corner to the front of Jimmie's Smoke Shop to board the time machine found half-buried in the brownfield outside of Fafnir Bearing, Co., and few blocks past Frary, Landers, and Clark. They rolled the barber's chair out of the attic and polished its chrome frame, they took two wheelchair axles, a headrest, soft white napkins, a bottle of witch hazel, a lather heating box, hollow ground, straight razors, leather straps, mirror, calendar, washbowl, brass cash register, red leather seats, boxes of Avery white birch soda, Martin Rosol kielbasa, and frozen Capitol Lunch hot dog sauce, Stanley Tool hammer, wooden folding chairs, leather and aluminum arm chairs, and these items surrounded the time machine like a museum gift shop, they pressed a button and the siren blared, they turned on the bulb hanging above the time machine and it gave off only a few seconds of dim light Johnny Roach rested his chin on his voice box. They had to find a spark plug before his mortal flight. Using the *Jaws of Life*, they converted the Greyhound bus into a room with a hospital bed. The bus driver used a ship's wheel for the time machine. There was no time for delay. The exhaust from the bus made him cough and wheeze. Somebody sounded the holy bell and the bus drove toward the highway. The transistor radio, tied to his wrist by elastic bands, played a minuet of flowers and burning rope and drops of water he was not able to wipe off his forehead.

Professor Ben Cocoa Led the Creative Writing Program
$100,000 Budget

Ben assigned poems and essays to use for discussion during class-es with the visiting writers. He also distributed poems and essays to departments. Ben wrote personal letters (never spoke to a single literary agent for any of the visiting poets) inviting the writers for a three-day stay. It took nearly a day to arrive in Nebraska at the Omaha or Lincoln airport. It did not end there. It took another two or three hours to drive to Ben's campus in Kearney from those two cities. On the second day they would visit creative writing classes. On the third day they would present a reading. The next day they would fly homeward.

There are many stories: Tillie Olsen arrived and nearly exhausted Ben with her endurance and probity. He drove to the hotel to take her to din-ner with other faculty, student reading assistants, and community writers. Tillie was nowhere to be found. Ben ran outside and in the distance on a long dusty Great Plains road he saw her slowly emerge out of the horizon. She had walked several miles. After her reading and great applause, she raised her fist into a shape and force Ben had not seen since 1969 and shouted: Power to the People! There was a long line waiting to meet her. She talked and signed each book past midnight in the tiniest handwriting Ben had ever witnessed. The next day he drove her halfway to Omaha with his wife and two daughters. Writer Brent Spencer met them and drove her to another partnered event at the University of Nebraska at Omaha— Omaha, Nebraska, where Tillie lived as a child. On the drive back from Kearney Tillie told Ben she had a heart condition.

Ben could not find the Irish poet John Montague and his wife, fiction writer Elizabeth Wassell before their readings. He came upon them in the darkest corner of our Midwestern bar toasting to the world in their grace and grief.

Ben spoke with Maxine Kumin after her interest in presenting a reading in the middle of Nebraska — nowhere yet everywhere. She had just fallen off her horse a year or so before and had a broken neck and ribs. Ben believed she wrote a book about it. She would not be able to attend without her partner to assist her. Ben agreed and paid her partner's travel and expenses, too. She, of course, read her poems, but not before giving a powerful speech against the Nebraska pollution from corporate farmers and the perpetual chemicals and pig waste that seep into the Ogallala Aquifer — one of the largest aquifers in the world.

The poet Leslie Adrienne Miller arrived with her four-month son. Ben prepared a "baby army" with student assistants to guide Leslie's baby back and forth to the university daycare between classes, readings, and dinners. Indeed, one student held the baby outside the classroom. There were several moments of delay and glee as Leslie ran out of a classroom to breastfeed.

Ben picked up Donald Hall from the Lincoln Airport. They drove by a sign: Crete, Nebraska. Donald pointed to it and said that is the town where the woman donated her bone marrow to try and save the life of Donald's wife Jane Kenyon. Ben asked him how he found where they woman lived, and Donald said he had written letters.

Donald met Ben's wife and daughters during the reading, dinner, and reception. As fate allowed, a year later Ben's own wife would pass away in nine months from the same disease as Jane Kenyon.

What happened to the Oxblood shoes you wore the last time we brought you back from the veteran's hospital after you became ill after eating oxtail soup that you swore looked like the devil's tail?

The bronzed compass based on the divining rod was first manufactured in the *Hardware City of the World* and used to chart the ghost stars. The steering wheel was set to autopilot for lift-off and re-entry. The time machine was thrown off course by a meteor shower for three years until it landed safely on top of a leaking septic tank. Johnny Roach had been fitted in a disposable biohazard suit as he slept inside his iron lung. He told his doctors he had dreamed of sitting in the back of a convertible VW Bug with the air dancing through his afro. He was on his way to White Sands Beach to meet his graduating classmates who kissed around a large bonfire that was seen from the lighthouse where they anchored the time machine for refueling. They drank apple and strawberry Boone's Farm wine. They threw driftwood into the fire that turned their faces into clown masks behind the flames. It was high tide. They ran into the water in search of unclaimed treasure, small trophies, cross country, middle distance, and medley relay medals, they sought comfort in the articles of the sea-dog that floated under the moon's wreckage, homeroom romance, cheer-leading Thanksgiving flowers, and what they had found and placed into their hands on this evening were the miniature charms of the past, present, and future at the exact moment the flames reached the beach house, and what they carried they threw into the fire, what they could not hold onto disappeared into the coral mouth of a sea cave, a place illuminated by small iridescent blue birds that lived underwater and smaller amphibians born teeth under the belly and eyes in the tails that shifted the sand into the shape of a human face, mermaids chained to masthead, sea snakes that nested and laid black eggs in their knotted hair that floated to the surface with gold coins, far below where they stood like a choir swept into the undertow and underworld by the charred hands of God.

The chestnut trees disappeared one summer and never grew back. It was a long walk home as autumn turned the leaves and a woman's kiss into the burning of leaves. Finding a chestnut in the snow was not like finding a dollar bill pulled up with a stick and gum through a sewer grate. It became a liberty silver dollar in a boy's palm, a creaking clothesline pulled by his mother's arms, his father's car horn as he drove past the factory bar and drifted by on soft wheels as you sat on your shoeshine box waiting for the steel-toed coronation of the weary workers who sat at the bar seats in a toast of straight whiskey and cigars, men who wept under the night shift stars circling above the smoke stacks, vultures in the high desert who waited for the piercing siren to open the locked chamber, workers who emptied a drum barrel of ball bearings and rolled it to the front of the factory gate and built a fire out of scrap wood pallets, the strike lasted three months through Thanksgiving, Christmas, and New Year Eve, a duel over pension and prayer, the wages of sin and despair, nothing like a U.S. Savings Bond behind a weekly paycheck inside a black lunchbox, food for the children, clothes for the women, shelter for the men, a psalm of the deranged and prosperous thieves, who will enter heaven in a wooden cart followed by three Ministers of the Heart, each holding a lantern, walking for miles to the sea cliff, waiting for the return of the charred angel buckled in a straightjacket inside a time machine that flew too close to Saturn and too far from redemption, caught inside the nest of green flies, a sailor's wide net pulling up the unknown species without eyes and its heart outside its body, and it a mortal descent for some and a mortal climb for others, one way to heaven and a dictionary to hell opened half-way to the precipice of desire, the living who sang a lullaby for the newborn, the dead who shall be raised, the coin toss, sword into stone, blackbird with emerald wing, lilac wild, a barefoot man inside a breathing controlled by a foot pedal and lever attached to strings that made his hands open, arms rise, legs bend, mouth open, and he came to believe that floating inside a cage was better than living alone, and the echo of his own laughter a good companion to isolation, and after the brief comfort the first time the guards clamped the iron lung and tightened knobs, he remembered how two sparrows flew into barbed wire?

The hemp rope pulling the iron lung out of the prison gate snapped into blue feathers. It went on a three-mile slide down Sleeping Giant over the forehead, nose, lift-off, mouth, breastbone, waist, knees, and its crooked foot under the birch stars. They sent out a search party for the iron lung in ski shoes, backpacks with Coleman lanterns, a St. Bernard with black whiskey under its chin, sleigh dogs and lariats for jutting rocks. The prison camp did not want any responsibility for the sky pilot locating a freezing man taking his last breath inside a cylinder left knocking on the iron side with a toothbrush between his teeth. They released carrier pigeons bred by the Nazis with emergency cell numbers clipped to their legs. Johnny Roach was able to place long distance calls inside the ghost in the machine by slight movements of his large brown eyes. Town folk sat in the prison chapel lighting hundreds of white miniature candles that framed the stained glass into a kaleidoscope of the holy ghost in the light, wisdom, and forbearance of all they had learned about the unseen world. The press had lined up at the local soup kitchen, one of thousands set up along the coastal towns and cities after the end of the great war, and waited for the first 911 call made from a time machine. The crowd went wild. They heard the call had not gone through after the gold tooth placed into the mouth of Johnny Roach disintegrated soon after launch into gravity and caused him to dial the wrong number on the wrong phone with the wrong area code and on the Times Square billboard they showed a red timeline of his journey into the past, present, and future. He had escaped after sundown under the harvest moon and the wheels on the iron lung were traced by the great-great-grandson of a Confederate Civil War scout expert in the ways of meteors, shallow rivers, high water, covered bridges, wild hogs, hallowed ground, a way of seeing through the eye not with the eye, rainbow, snapped twig, burnt rubber, maple syrup, false teeth, scripture, darning needle, tracking wounded animals in mud and snow, quicksand, waterfall, her deep set eyes and the riderless horse and divining rods used by the retrievers of the dead. Pulling the iron lung out of the quicksand took a little time, a pickup truck and hemp rope tied to a great oak in front of the town clock. The small pond had grown larger after the flood. Despite the wrought fence iron fence, barbed wire, and a warning sign, they say everything that walked or fell into the pond disappeared.

He nicknamed his tubular residence the Good Humor Iron Lung, it was covered in a royal Indian carpet, captured and returned to Gunga Din by the British conquistadors. Stained glass windows were blowtorched into each side of the iron lung and above his bare feet. They placed a poet's jukebox inside his medicine cabinet, and each time he took a pill a thunderous voice recited any poem of his choice. This was the dry season in the dunes. Temperatures rose to 130 degrees and water was rare. The small fan, run by one AAA battery, pointed toward his swollen face and was no relief inside layers of iron and cardigans. It was the hot sand that seeped through small cracks that caused discomfort as he tried to sleep. They placed a leech, a scarf of blood, over his forehead and in his nightly fever he heard the cooling water rushing over the top of his iron lung and pulsating into the rubber hoses beneath his body. They had found a design to lower the temperature of the rumble seat using blocks of dry ice inside a suitcase placed under his Sting Ray bucket seat found under the children's playground built on top of the junkyard. His music box and alarm clock were solar-powered although he had to use candlelight after a meteor shower blocked out the sun for three weeks and a fine dust filled the capsule and his NFL helmet used a century before in a last-minute attempt to lessen injuries and save the ghost in the machine. He determined by his compass that he was tumbling like a strange bird inside a pink hourglass, sand filling his mouth, half-buried and falling into the hunger of gravity, drought and pestilence on a black-and-white TV. He was surprised to find his iron lung was coal-powered by fillets of the rock lifted into a furnace welded to the bottom of his tomb by extended arms used in a dentist office to excavate fool's gold. It worked well to fuel the rumble seat and lift the barber's chair, yet carbon monoxide exhaust became volatile mixed with stardust inside a gas chamber and sparklers built into the electric chair.

His last rites were read by a Minister of the Heart, the choir sang spirituals and stood under the tainted light. He saw a swinging lantern on the high cliff in the mirror attached to his bad shoulder. The prison water boy, son of the warden, kept the devil's eternal flame glowing below the iron lung, kept a small fire burning in a large pit, and there was a certain comfort in watching the hourglass on top of the music box, a certain comfort being rotated with his buckled spine, a stuck pig inside the sweet chariot on the highway to nowhere one light city and blown through the heavens into outer space into the future with a $1.10 haircut, 80 cent shave, and 60 for children. The sign posted on the time machine: No PROFANITY! No CREDIT! There was no ATM inside the time machine, a large plastic Coca-Cola bottle filled with change kept the back door closed, against a three-quarter length white coat, against the flames rising in the dirt cellar and curving down the attic staircase, against the mouth's bridle, railroad spike, bedroom window, the warm bare bulb inside the iron lung, downhill skier, weightlessness, sneakers, tin can walkie-talkie, tunnel vision, cumulus, bag of wedding rice, gyroscope, fetal position on the bottom bunk bed, vase of chimes and lilac on the front stoop, George Washington and his slave's teeth in a Mason jar, the peglegged and beautiful dreamer, a rainbow of green flies above the barrel of fire, Concord grapes, tool shed, hometown and out of town driver, believer in observable things, the broken-hearted monitor attached to his chest at the whimsy of the scientist of earthly desires checking his pointer at the blackboard witness after they tied his arms behind his back and chained his legs. It took a garbage truck roped to a fallen log to drag the iron lung out of the river mud. The retrievers of the dead sat in the balcony writing down their names and counting their names. It was winter becoming winter again. One saw the white birch rise against the hardscrabble terrain of war. The last man standing was the last man killed. They found his pewter canteen between two rocks at the top of the mountain, a dueling pistol in his right hand and the ghost lantern in his left hand. He had a letter in his vest pocket. There was rain and lightning. Nobody spoke a word. They wrote their last names first and middle names last in chalk on a blackboard inside the last one-room schoolhouse filled with mortal verbs and mastodon nouns.

At the confidential request of Masters & Johnson, conjugal visits inside the iron lung were considered for a ten-year study. Johnny Roach was the exemplary choice after losing the use of his right arm and left leg and the limited blood flow to his extremities. He was six feet tall, and the woman would have to at least reach his waist and be able to hold on to the leather straps bolted into the side of the air vents. They would set up a collapsible card table, provide ample candlelight, and a bottle of Mateus. Clean oxygen would flow through the tubes implanted into their bodies at the sign of a first kiss that automatically started the film projector and dropped the screen. *Playboy* had supplied a splayed pussy and formaldehyde cock. They were of no good use in a time machine as the speed of light was no match for a love at first sight. Heavy breathing inside a prison cell, pacing twelve steps from the live oak to middle ground holding a dueling pistol to his chest, two strangers in a dark corridor embracing, under a willow on the river between two mountains, her mouth full of witless seed, her legs rising on a promenade of air, the fingerling of hair between his teeth, under-water dance, the off-key music box slowed down to a half turn and one note each minute serenade until nothing in the chamber moved, a train whistle of air between the thighs, what in the dark moved so slowly, the torchlight in her violet eyes, starfish arms clinging to a round stone, a surface where no human ever stood surrounded by tentacles, rainbow teeth, eyeless creatures and venom to kill every creature on any planet, and they opened his pantry filled with spoiled cans of food, black mold spreading through copper pipes, insects with tiny mouths feeding on electrical wire, hesitant throb and flared nerve-endings, molted wings and bloated lips, the spreading and lifting, the smoke, woe, whim-per, moan, and tumbling of stars and falling money in a cracked jar, what Frankenstein was after was the last fair deal in the foundry of his transplanted heart for what he claimed as love and he craved its elixir and sour taste after the barbed wire and gunfire would not slow his evolutionary steps into the winter garden as he reached out for her and collapsed in shame as he muffled her first name and held the last vial buried in the churchyard under the town clock, Tom Thumb's Love Potion, a carousel of bloodhounds in pursuit of the human scent.

There was love hereafter inside his homemade echo chamber, a breathing tube pursed his lips and pinched his tongue, mouth, and throat. Words multiplied by three in such close quarters in the alumi-num sleeping bag. He was given a green canteen flask of black whiskey and a straw. He was able to sip from a Mason jar borrowed from a red clay farmer in lowland Mississippi inside the iron lung. The farmer had hung himself during a long drought on one apple tree that had survived the dry season. They say the apples fell as the noose snapped his neck and apples would never grow again. The offshore fog rolled into the coastline and into the vents. He was awakened by the smell of salt water, and he asked to be carried to the front of the pier. They lifted the iron lung on a pulley above the sea and it swung like pendulum, a hammock, a swing at the schoolyard, the arc of wind and stars above his knotted head, primate paws, unbound, taken into the sky to a branch to earth and back again, the rise and descent, the body horizontal, on four wheels, the vertical arms, hands reaching for light. They lowered the iron lung into the seawater for cooling. The ropes tied to its anchor and welded to the door above his sternum gave way to a shifting constellation. The iron lung sank to unknown depths with fluorescent sea snakes tumbling out of a nest illuminating three portholes, one eye level, one at his waist, one above his feet. Red sea vipers floating into the vents and across his eyes, and he felt them curl around his ankles, between his legs, and kiss the side of his neck. He heard a sonar bell and muffled voices coming out of his radio speakers. The iron lung descended like a submarine and came to rest among underworld creatures, mouths of pearls and wings of fire, flowered tentacles, blue night crawlers, glowing nets spread across a large field of half-buried serpent eggs, husks of fallen rainbows, he saw flowers and a small face on the wall of the sea caves as he was raised above a shipwreck and gold coins spilled into the turbulent uncharted waters, he tapped his cracked waterproof retirement watch as he rose to the surface almost whole, and he was driven by a Yellow Cab waiting at the end of the pier and taken to a rest home with guardian angels who were thrown into weightlessness and landed on his back porch on top of his iron lung singing songs of love hereafter that were translated into psalms on the radio inside his coral throne.

They placed his iron lung into a hammock created from the silk of the black widow and the hammock into a catamaran. It was towed to shore and taken by a double trailer truck to the Lake Compounce Amusement Park and welded to the wooden roller coaster at his request for the ride of his tainted life. There was a small crowd of citizens and politicians against the death penalty and a flaming midget was used to pull the lever. It was a slow ascent like a red velvet curtain at the world premiere of an Ingmar Bergman film. The iron lung stalled for nine hours at the top of climb. A special unit of firefighters trained in wildfires and mountain climbing were called in from New Britain. They carried spring water and vials of spinal fluid for injection into Johnny Roach's 4th and 5th lumbar. There was a sudden high wind that threw the capsule down and the rails and around sharp curves. He felt the wind through the vents to the side of his head, waist, and the bottom of his bare feet. He was given a wooden whistle and clothespin in honor of his ride. The clothespin was placed over his nostrils that made his breathing easier. He blew hard on the whistle as the roller coaster left the tracks and flew over the pond like a missile and was last seen rising over the mountain. There had been a construction crew nearby that had discovered a lost copper mine and dinosaur bones. The iron lung descended out of a dark cloud and flew into the opening of the mine and landed on a rail car that rolled into the deep earth past the emergency staircase, past the wild illuminated ore, past a waterfall far below the sound of animal and human footsteps, in cavernous and hollowed walls turned into rubble and dust by a lit fuse and mining collapse, on short rails and wide turns, his lungs nearly collapsed three miles underground until he was able to re-set the oxygen tank by pinching his breathing tube with his false teeth implanted by the prison doctor on his birthday, fainting spells were known to occur at such depths and he wondered if he had blacked out as he awakened floating in a fountain of beauty or was it a wishing well in the middle of a ballroom as he crawled to the stage half-alive and somehow stood up for his waltz in the underworld and found his partner, breathing underwater, surrounded by fire, and the crowd turned their heads and lowered their heads to the last dance of her life in laurel and pearls wearing a canary blue feather hat?

The sky pilot who tracked the iron lung by tracing the night flares from his helicopter on loan from the savings and dime and during a spell of turbulent air ejected himself after spotting the husk of a rainbow on the rooftop of the Ministers of the Heart and was one of the first to arrive as they raised the cylinder out of the tunnel of love and helped to dislodge a corner of the iron lung and peeled off its first layer of metal and washed off the Hawking radiation with a garden hose attached to the exhaust pipe. The iron lung landed in a region of hell reserved for the retrievers of the dead who carried pouches of black widow spiders on their canvas belts. Johnny Roach felt the first black widow on his left foot and it sped up his shin and knee and nestled in his crotch, and one black widow felt like a thousand and the retrievers of the dead released a thousand black widows out of Mason jars, each painted with a pink hourglass and sold to the bell ringers of the Salvation Army in their preparation for war and the coming holidays. There was a false start in the effort to save him. The black widows began to fill the breathing tubes leading directly into his lungs, he opened his railroad pocket watch and found three black widows dancing between high noon and midnight, they bit down on the straw inside his mouth to keep them out of his morning glass of Ovaltine, they filled his music box, vest pocket on his sharkskin Easter suit, coffee filter, music sheets, white collar, jasmine tea bags, athletic socks, turntable, toothbrush, hope chest, medicine cabinet, Oxfords. The black widows were opal jewels on the small chandelier above his head, above his crib locked by wooden slats made of pine and sealed with tar, belly button, anus, entered his penis, and filled his hollow eyes, and the star dust made him sneeze and the black widows flew out of his mouth and floated into weightlessness, and the sky pilot and retrievers of the dead thought there was a chance he would survive not because of his willpower but because of nature's frailty as the spiders floated above him and swarmed like bees and were blown out of the vents into blue heaven. The experiment on a death row prisoner under drought, rabies, straightjacket, brown water, nuclear rain, brownfields, ghost factory smoke, Mojave green snake, rickets, half-body, right side, paralysis, blindfold, and scalding gravity, had gone awry. One black widow spider had crawled and remained inside his inner ear like a psalm.

The retrievers of the dead had one hour to locate the iron lung after it submerged in quicksand and Johnny Roach had only thirty minutes left of clean air. They were able to squeeze a bluebird through his meal tray slot to monitor the levels of mustard gas that hissed out of the small crack in the time machine. The rivets snapped into feathers as he flew past the sun, the horizon outside his port-hole transformed into a single knotted star, and he believed he had caught a glimpse of heaven if not for the drops of gasoline on his forehead, one spark from his Coleman stove blew him above the rails into thinning air, they had wrapped his stiff body in aluminum foil and a layer of 9/11 flame resistant overalls made in Iowa and invent-ed by elder farmers who had survived Hiroshima and the dustbowl, old war, young war, the necessary, inviolate war, dueling humans, preying animals, a caged and howling beast without a name to grace the earth, the hands that clawed the barbed wire, how he walked into the territory of the heart, climbed the ice cliff, broke apart rocks that turned into bread, the chorus that turned into sirens, the letter he found inside the abandoned mine that brought him to his knees, the harvest moon blown across the sky, the riderless carriage half-buried in red clay, the town clock left burning for months, the prisoners chained to chairs in the dirt cellar, the escapee and his broken spine, a midnight dance on the river and floating candles, fingers numbed by frost, what happened to the townspeople after they crossed the roped bridge, had their children placed on boats, the drought turned land into water, there were no books, dance, music, art, paintings left behind, nothing recorded and nothing saved, and he awakened and at first thought he was swimming into the sea in search of the ship they had placed him on for his execution until he recalled that they had slid his iron lung off the gangplank into the white waves and he thanked them for his release until what he felt was searing heat and dialed his black telephone with a number two pencil between his false gold teeth, it rang three times before he was cut off with a recorded message in a high-pitched voice that screamed for Johnny to call back between the hours of mortality and salvation when the night birds fell out of the sky like flares into the sea and the retrievers of the liv-ing, in riding boots, held copper shovels to dig into the robes of light and violets of despair. The spring thaw revealed traces of webbed feet and evolutionary claws used to climb to the tops of trees. They found footprints on fieldstone under snow leading to Sorrow Road.

He was placed on the train from New York City to New Orleans to Oklahoma and back to the land of the Connecticut Yankee. It backed into the station and rested against the Gulf Coast waters darkened by the *smoke, lilacs, and jade* floating in the great oil spill. The iron lung was strapped to the top of the Yellow Cab. They fed him red beans and rice and alligator sausage strained through a feeding tube. The taxi driver explained the Oklahoma red tape:

> *They tell you to go to the third floor and then down to the second and up to the fourth flour and back down to the basement. I was busted once for alleged distribution, but it was a foggy day in the night court. The lights went out above the hanging judge and the sheriff was arrested for a DUI. Who's driving, goddamn!? Who's driving that goddamned truck? The man was drunk as a long-tailed armadillo crossing a highway for home.*

It would be a 1,798-mile drive over mountains, streams, small villages, large pines and oaks. His two relatives arrived dead drunk drinking 151 rum out of a rubber hose tied to a radiator on a Saturday stroll for no good reason. They were not able to lift a bluebird in a cage. The piano stood straight up on a dolly for three days. Nephews and brothers and cousins were lost sailors holding the unsteady wheel on the ship of the crying damsel. They were stooges left holding a bottle of rum and a can of beer. Life story. The long-winded road and skeletal scarecrow on a three-day drunk in the burning wilderness of the deranged and prosperous underworld greeted them with a kiss as their shirts caught fire and those destined for hell were greeted in hell by the charred hand of God. There was great surprise when the door snapped off its hinges and the bottles in their hands melted inside the furnace of their sleeping chamber. The nephews and brothers and cousins were drunks, vagrants, bums, shit-eaters and homeless angels at the schoolyard rumble. The handcuffs were locked on their ankles and wrists and their bodies placed inside a straitjacket iron lung with a hundred proof bullet-proof vest made for the SWAT team pausing on their back porch. It was a holiday for fools at the asylum. They were not released from jail and they were left believing the door they had opened was a refrigerator full of liquor and laughter. The alcohol on their breath and inside their pork bellies was nothing more than the breaking of their mortal hearts.

The shackles were too large for his small legs bent by rickets and the electrode did not fit his small head and prison hat. At the park near the river outside one wall with *chevaux-de-frise*, children holding wildflowers danced under a maypole. A small body inside the iron lung left slightly more room to raise elbows to the porthole and rest his eye on the periscope for a view of a meteor shower or a wildfire or typhoon far above the earth. They had attached the iron lung to a satellite once used by Radio Free Europe and the War Department to capture distant radio signals that bounced off the mouth of Mount Rushmore, Crazy Horse, Wounded Knee, the motorcycle spokes in Sturgis, and the Rio Grande. A few of the signals carried a lone voice singing the national anthem sung by a soldier amputee seated on one of two models of a push lawnmower converted into a wheelchair for the brave and delirious warriors, one recovered a signal made by carolers who walked behind the retrievers of the dead working overtime on holidays, one bounced off the bat of a designated hitter in the last inning of the last game of the World Series, another garbled signal off a ship that carried nuclear warheads showed a countdown by the captain and it was made all too clear that the warning shot seen floating in a great arc across the moon's surface was not to be taken as a random act of God's charred hand, it was a single moment caught in the belly pool of time, between the arrow and splitting seed, laughter and mortal wound, plague and kiss, whimper and hanging noose, flared wing and heaven-sent, deranged and light on the feet periwinkle blue, back porch and psalm, webbed-hoof and decent, ash and starlight, minuet and famine, holy bell and homing pigeon, throwing coal into the furnace of the iron lung in snowfall and broken wheel, Sunday meal and call-to-arms, div-

ing into high water and bare-knuckled mannequin, X and Y and Z
and false start, half-a-crown and tainted cloth, chalice and bag of rice,
viper's eye and halo, requiem and curse, blueblood and parasol of rags,
hands raised and hands lowered.

He was able to read how the yearling poets and artists who escaped
the asylum fled into the wilderness. They were knaves and hard drinkers who abided by the swollen tongue of their fathers who coughed
in the fog under the ghost stars. They were the cruel drinkers who
put their fists shaped like serpents into walls and made their women
crawl into dog-legged tubs full of lard and smoked hams. They took
the bodies of their women in vain and their art remained a blank canvas in their nightmares and third-class letters lost in a mailbox in front
of the five and dime. They had little sense of mothers and daughters,
wives and grandmothers, friends and lovers. The curdled middle finger of their half-life was scalded in a mop bucket. The demons in the
heart imitated blow jobs in a public space. Johnny Roach believed the
feet of a monkey made their art. They learned to paint a pink ass in
bloom. Their *harmatia* shifted the alignment of the inferno sale with
heaven's border collie who ran its teeth across the canvas in a Saturday
tag blue plate special divine. They lived in a place without a past, present, and future. The drunken boat arrived at their back porch. The
pirates under the midnight sail anchored the ship and released the gangplank. The young were banished to the underworld each time they fell
asleep and were taken to the gallery of folk art masters and redemption of their gnarled and tragic souls with Playboy coupons and Green
Stamps for their bottles at the Stop-and-Shop of desire. They would
find epiphany or despair, recklessness or *teach us to sit still*, meth mouth
or sobriety, Margaret grieving and noble angel, evolution or nano-neu-
ro-doom, a swarm of blue bees or the wingless bird on their window
sill, a gathering of the dispossessed or a reunion of the false prophets
of art who smoked weed out of fire hoses and drank out of their bum
shoe at the grand opening of their inner life as they fell to their knees
and screamed for a life and some man stumbling on the sidewalk was

their father walking on stilts built to reach the sun. There was quiet. Somebody played the vibes and baby grand. There was nothing in their juvenile hearts to offer the *better angels* above the world. They awakened in a drunken stupor and set their art on fire as art and sent it floating into the dismal swamp.

He saw her eyes in the rearview mirror welded to the outside of his window. They changed colors like a whip. Was it the dance of night under the full moon that changed her eyes from black and white to blue and yellow? They had once walked into the Asylum of Roses at Elizabeth Park in Hartford on her birthday. The grave diggers removed flowers from the main garden and filled the wooden cart with irises for the retrievers of the dead. They lifted bags of lime dust. After the dust settled over the dead and wounded, they placed petals over their pink mouths and kissed them as if they were half-alive and they gathered their last breath inside the hourglass of shame tied to a canteen.

What thief pulled the historic iron fence out of the earth at the Fairview Cemetery? Whose bones rattled inside the music box covered in velvet in the rumble seat of death's carriage? Whose fingers turned the key and played *Moonlight Sonata* as the night train pulled away from the station?

The compass under a sun flare had taken the iron lung off course, and it landed in a meadow next to the playground at Smith School and left its wooden sled tracks in the snow and knocked over tombstones. They had filled the chamber with headless dolls with torn patches of hair and one good arm or one bad leg. They had traced his flight by peering into a crystal ball once used in the bowling alley for duck pins. One saw a world war and countless half-world-wars in one half of the world. The men of war and fame kept a lucky penny in their boots. The women carried their children on their backs and walked out of the city in their robes of light. In the eternal weightlessness he saw a mirage. He looked into the horizon and there was a Civil War nurse holding a long blade. There was cannon fire and ten thousand men.

A blue halo cut the tops of trees. The men turned their heads to the sky. There was no sound. The battlefield floated over the city. Who had turned the key to the ivory box and placed it inside the marbled globe that rested in a chamber surrounded by brick and mortar until the earth shook it loose and it sank to the bottom of the swamp after their next of kin were called to duty in one final act of war and they were left without food and water unfit for consumption after they had incinerated half the world?

He almost looked out from the iron lung and called out to the stars that fell to the earth like gold coins. He remembered the woman who danced without music or men and the last dance of her life. He felt the wings of a hummingbird on his forehead head strapped by a leather belt to avoid whiplash as the voltage reached the muscles of his neck and behind his ears. They watched from the balcony as they lowered the iron lung to the center of the opera stage. The backdrop curtain fell and revealed a castle surrounded by a meadow of fireflies. It was the study of the human eye. The prison doctor observed that the imprint of his dizzy and mortal eye retained feigned memory loss and fleeting amnesia. He remembered riding in a VW Bug around Shuttle Meadow Reservoir and floating in weightlessness and falling half-in-love. She was the most beautiful woman he had known with large brown eyes, long hair, and coral lips. The leaves flew over the road and splashed against the windshield. They never reached lover's lane on some off-road illuminated half by the water and half by white birch three miles down a rocky path. It was not what the eyes claimed to see but what would never be seen, it was how the crippled stars shed their light over the world, the way the eyes opened and settled and opened half-alive back into his head like a doll's broken eye socket, how the eyes paused before the miracle of death, the way his eyes closed as the blossom opened in her hand, how her kiss was a low tide and the burning of leaves. He believed in everything he saw perched in a hammock made from a bird nest found in the high cliffs of Madagascar. Large portions of the heat shield on the iron lung turned to ash and the leather straps on his ankles and wrist snapped like a shoeshine rag over his body. The executioner was unable to push down the one-armed bandit of death.

There was a malfunction in the delivery system with loud bursts of air through the vents. Those behind the one-way mirror fell to their knees. The priest had a seizure and was carried to the ambulance on a card table. A crane was brought from Yankee Stadium to lift the iron lung into a dirigible. Angels dropped out of the sky with large brown eyes that trembled in the dark.

The angels lifted him off his soiled mattress on the city sidewalk and into the iron lung and tied it to a wooden cart and *hi-hi-hee they hit the dusty trail.* They knelt at the side of the iron lung and kissed its small stained glass that created a prism above his head, a chandelier of fire and grace, copper-brown boar bristles in his great grandmother's hairbrush, pearl necklace, long black dress, a canopy of desire and parasol of rags, lovers under the spell of Tarot, wicker rocking chair, the unclaimed self-dispensing laundry box, the sharp curve turn on white flames, the brakeless foundry on four wheels, window opened and window closed, depleted oxygen in a breathing tube and the rarified air pumped into the ruby doll's mouth, riderless bumper cars, the soft pout on the strongest man in the world, the half-man on stilts was a goat with false teeth, the magic man who held a blue crystal ball that had floated to the tops of trees and landed in a basket on top of the Ferris wheel and carried on the back of a bicycle on the back of a pickup truck to the traveling salvation circus and taken by a team of mules into a dust storm, the high winds lasted three days until the sun broke through and the crystal ball was rolled into the iron lung and came to rest on the bellow he used with his good right foot to inhale and expel the fresh air out of his chamber, a soldier's flesh wound became his amputated leg replaced by a pegleg made of pine and cedar for the holiday, one leg up on a down pillow and one leg down the chimney was his motto, and they marched half in step with death to the back porch of the unknown soldier who some said was a man who wore a mask into his last battle, his artificial leg was a perfect match with the synthetic air, it was the perfect season for snow thunder across the burning landscape torched by the crowds who left the city for the meadow and threw their long knives into the sea, and he once danced the last dance with a woman who danced without music or men who stood in formation after the six-gun salute and the playing of taps and found comfort in standing at attention to a twenty-one gun salute and stared into Arlington's eternal flame until it burned yellow and burned blue in the iris and the hagioscope of the soul. He left the dance hall and climbed the long winding stairs into the town clock on his one good wooden leg that splintered into a fine holy dust.

There was engine failure in its final descent over the Indian Ocean and the hunger of gravity sent the iron lung tumbling into blue rain. He pressed the screen and the exhaust pipe fell off and the time machine was drawn into the curtain of satellites that flew above the surface of the earth and landed somewhere in the Great Plains. It left remnants of fossilized life forms from distant planets that once thrived in the belly pool of time and recognition. One child lifted a silver ball bearing out of the mud, another pressed his lips against a round stone. Johnny Roach was fitted well into the gas mask that fell into his lap, yet somebody had left the valve open in the emergency room. There was the viper hiss under his electric throne, a small opening of light under the closed prison door slammed behind him, the vent of fresh air as they attached the wires to his left ankle and right wrist, one foot inside a bucket of water, a bowl of chicken soup and loaf of sourdough bread. They stitched a buttercup to his collarbone using a hot needle and thread and removed his fingernails and toenails, they pulled out his teeth and replaced them with false wooden teeth made out of the finest teak, they made a dummy stuffed with newspaper out of the man with a bow tie and tuxedo and spats, a top hat designed for a bright monkey on a short leash that danced to a music box, they lifted the iron lung into a helicopter for a short flight above city, he pressed the screen and released roses into the air that floated into backyards and barbecue pits, a yellow parachute ejected and tangled in live barbed wire, a team of junior league aerospace engineers were called to set up rotary phones in the courthouse across from the county jail, they sought comfort in the priest who was called to give last rites and found he was not needed after the blue wire disconnected from the AAA battery, a young priest knelt before the prisoner, he touched his face and lips and kissed his forehead, they undressed him in warm water and pasted feathers to his naked body, they placed a pillow under his neck and removed death's palette and apparel, they had two hours until he awakened from his iron lung slumber, he was caught between the curved earth of sleeplessness and the crescent rail of sleeping sickness, he believed he was sleeping when he was awake and awake when he was sleeping, there was nothing real and nothing dreamed only a thimble of his blood for his kin.

The boat arrived at shore. They knotted a clean white cloth at the back of his neck and slapped a straight razor hanging from the side of the barber's chair. They clipped his bow tie and dusted his top hat. His oxbloods were buffed until they shined like Easter Sunday. He requested a blue thin pinstriped double-breasted jacket, gold corduroy pants, and a starched white shirt with opal cufflinks. He wished to be lifted into the balcony so he could look down upon the choir and retrievers of the dead.

He read a story about a young boy with rickets who picked winter collards grown in the city backyard, Concord grapes that grew into small globes in the sunlight, and captured hummingbirds in angel cloth nets floating over a garden of lilac.

There was no sign of life, no signal from a distant landscape inside the iron lung. He wore a wool scarf and gloves, and as he coughed, his breath curled into pink rings that became fetal snakes and fangs of smoke. He would draw his lips away from the breathing tube when her face appearing in his shaving mirror, walking into a covered bridge under the winter lilac, reaching out to embrace him, and he would kiss her as if she were still alive.

The executioner punched his time clock. He was given a fifty-dollar U.S. Savings Bond, a bonus for the holiday on death row. He was given white silk gloves that would be deposed in the warden's fireplace on New Year's Eve. They boxed and donated Johnny Roach's model race cars and electric train set to the Salvation Army Band Gift Shop. The newspaper editorials in the *Hartford Courant* rebutted the ones read in the *Hartford Times*. They argued for a peaceful march and memorial for the war dead in these times of the mad and prosperous army tanks that ran over fire hydrants and rose bushes planted in front of city hall. There was a call for the National Guard to separate the hard hats from the hippies, the prisoner from the Thanksgiving foot-ball crowds who demanded reparation for their losing team at their homecoming games, and after the national anthem they remained standing as the loudspeakers were connected to his voice and the AM radio taped to his forehead with a bandanna made of hemp and they listened to a cello and piano concerto playing in the background of a rainstorm and wild horses and the breaking apart of his tin voice under a dim light and requiem for the twenty-first century.

There was a woman in Idaho who entered the iron lung as a small child at three years old, and after forty years, she found comfort there, her small neck under the silk pillow, patent leather shoes, a silver cross necklace, and she wore a red skirt with large black dots that appeared in the sky as the time machine appeared in a corner under the eclipse of the moon. She remembered her father on his knees at Christmas dinner. *Jesus Wept*, and Jesus must have wept for me said the little girl in the iron lung wearing tortoise shell glasses. They set her breathing tube to the pulse of her heart.

There was a meteor shower under her parasol of ghost stars as she felt her young ribs against the metal drum. The porthole was designed to open whenever the time machine lost power and the generator turned on the space heater that tilted with the gyroscope inside the pink hourglass and bare bulb with its cord above her head swung like a pendulum of desire.

It was at her first dance and the last song where she stumbled to the gymnasium floor and it shined like a silver mirror in the girl's lavatory where she had smiled and left a kiss she had lifted her off the expected at the end of the prom. Her lungs were depleted and they lifted her off the floor like a sparrow half-alive on Sorrow Road. They placed her on the school bus parked outside the football stadium and drove her to New Britain General Hospital on top of Walnut Hill Park where she had found a silver dollar at the Easter egg hunt, watched the athletes running cross country past the music shell under a rainbow above the smokestacks, under the wrecking ball that shook the earth and took down a movie theater and left its balcony rising out of the ash and wonder in the city of workers who toiled on the night shift making ball bearings that proved immutable inside the wheels of the iron lung, and they were used to fuel the eternal blue flame under the time machine.

They have covered me in grandmother's quilt with its patches of black-birds, birch trees, and her aquarium of dreams. I sleep well curled inside a wishing well.

The rainstorm fell over the city as if the metered sun had collapsed, recoiled, a psalm written by the light of her body and delivered to her father's hands.

They placed the young man with rickets into a dog-legged tub filled with lilac beads to soothe his suckling thumb cut and his soul tainted by the speed of light. He left his hand outside the porthole of the time machine, and his nimble fingers brushed against the debris of space, silly putty, bank safe, its captain's wheel set at day's end to the shifting Labrador stars, string attached to soup cans, cardboard hot-rods, a deck of Tarot floating to a the back of his eyes, yet it was the poison ivy that twisted around his wrist that flared under the plaster cast on his left leg, and he caught the measles despite being inoculated at the Connecticut State Fair at the NO SWIMMING hole with the swine and mud, he played the games of chance under the tents, O-rings over coke bottles, darts and balloons, strong-man hammer, water pistols, rifles with corks, pewter tea cups, Ouija reader wearing black silk gloves, miniature men in high heels dressed like toy soldiers, war heroes on a chessboard of fame and fortune, the gentleman sailor with a pegleg said to be the last living veteran who in a final act of war car-ried a glass eye hidden inside a music box and taken to the command post behind the twenty-mule team infantry, the human skulls scattered among the animal bones by infrared surveillance by a telescope welded to the bottom of the iron lung were commonplace on hollow ground, and the blind retrievers of the dead walked lightly on the undisturbed earth and as their red-tipped canes pierced the soil, and they recorded the exact moment the soul left the body in the belly pool of the time machine, and the after-school children were paraded in front of the monkey in a three-piece suit who was kept alive and somehow awakened speaking English inside the iron lung and seated on a hope chest and kept behind a red velvet curtain wearing a monocle, and they were told at the assembly how the monkey was able to read out loud and dance to Mozart and was well behaved behind a one-hundred-year-old haunted typewriter with a poem on the roller titled: "Hospital Gown," and was able to drink holy water out of a pewter spoon and wooden bucket taken from a shallow wishing well.

"He was a good soldier," they said.

From the top of his cap to the medals on his jacket down to the happy oxbloods he wore at the Rodeo Prom for Displaced Warriors.

"I was his first date. He carried me to the ice sculpture, sat me down in a wooden folding chair and placed a blindfold over my eyes," she said.

"He had a crease in his pants that could cut through steel," they said.

"He was a Johnny come marching home jolly good fellow comelately," she said.

"What happened to him in the war?"

"They tried to take a machine gun bunker on the sea cliff before dawn," they said.

"He was ambushed as he crawled under a net of ghost stars," she said.

The bullet traveled through his left eye, mouth, throat and rested between the 4th and 5th lumbar and made his spine convulse like a serpent under the altar stone. He suddenly spoke French for the first time in his life. They had set his broken back in Egyptian cloth and rolled his body cast into the iron lung. They attached a video camera to the ceiling and a colostomy bag under the iron lung. The ten-story rocket was painted in blue stripes and set to launch after a week's delay with a category 5 hurricane rising off the coast. They welded the rivets and tightened his oxygen mask with duct tape. They placed Stephen Hawking's *A Brief History of Time* next to *Gideon's Bible* on his elevated card table. Although there was a call to evacuate and sirens blared, thousands of peasants were unable to leave the city, and the line of Greyhound buses stood empty and screeched their exhaust like cicadas on the shore, and the rockets were prepared for a break in the opal sky, angelic light, the ill-defined halo, heaven-sent, falling over the pink scar across his forehead.

They placed a miniature aluminum Christmas tree at the end of the pinstriped mattress, a prison-issued recycled memory foam found at Railroad Salvage. The warden placed the cafeteria on a one-potato-a-day diet with a plate of butter beans grown on the side of the road leading to the prison gate. They sprayed jackal poison over the tomato vines after they grew over the fence and into the barbed wire. The plant made its way to the guardhouse and started breaking apart the concrete walls behind the underground urinals and outdoor latrines. They sent medical staff to the prison from the Center for Disease Control to investigate how the vines were traced back to a train wreck on the Pontchartrain Bridge leaving New Orleans for Mississippi after they were discovered on the wheels under the baby crib of the warden's newborn baby. The baby was placed in a cage until a serpent crawled into a pillowcase as the warden slept with his drug-free fiancée.

This was the dust recovered between the living and the dead by the retrievers of the dead who sailed aboard the time machine using a refurbished sundial and tampered gyroscope. There was eternity in weightlessness and fuel supplied by the dried and crushed wings of the monarch butterfly. What floated above his head floated closer to you than the stars to heaven, and you claimed they were the opal eyes of God looking down at him inside the kaleidoscope borrowed by the Office of Corrections from Hell Proper.

This was how one lived inside the iron lung, reeling and tumbling, shifting to one side of the body depending on how the unalterable light caught the departure of the soul, how the widower, captured in the blue net and hunger of gravity, rode shotgun on death's carriage, attempting to hold off the hourglass and the rising baptismal waters of the sea. He felt himself being lifted out of the ravine by a crane tied to a wrecking ball and placed on a raft tied to a ship headed to the equatorial waters under a waterfall of stars. They were not able to find his wooden leg before his journey over the mountain range and they called for scuba equipment and submarine to search under the frozen pond, and he raised his head as the tinsel of bereaved light fell over his eyes.

He fell asleep on New Year's Eve listening to the saxophonist who played jazz slapping heroin into the veins of his knuckles for a two dollar high. This was the Times Square falling one inch from the ground and rising back to the top of the world as the crowd square-danced with polka-dotted umbrellas and yellow scarves that illuminated the eyes of the vagrant musician who sought the gift of applause and redemption. He was known for his golden snap and melody on the bandstand. Fog cut the top of the trees threaded in blue light as the children drank hot chocolate and ate warm ginger cookies.

They sent photographs of Johnny Roach seated in his rented electric chair. One showed him taking out his false teeth provided by a local church, one showed him getting his last haircut, the one in front of the radio was taken at midnight as he listened to Lee Baby Simms on WPOP.

They sat with the devil and it was the devil's time. The choir, dressed in robes of light, lowered their heads to the man born with a New England Claw. They were told to write down their names and occupations and their next of kin. The velvet rope was pulled backstage and a curtain was lowered from the ceiling. Five minutes to show time left the devil on his bad knee. Bluebirds carefully wrapped in tinfoil were released from their cages into the theater. He spoke with his split tongue on a glass of Malbec as his red tail became caught in the blades of a cooling fan at his bedside. He uncurled his tail and it crackled like a whip. He whimpered into the shower to wash away the ash on his forehead. He splashed *4711 Echt Kolnisch Wasser Muelhens 3.0 oz EDC Eau de Cologne Original* over his tanned face, looked in the mirror and almost believed in the miracle inside his pale eyes. His eyelashes were burned during his fall out of the heavens and his descent into the iron skillet. Somebody had left the stove on in the underground lavatory as the city slept and the mustard gas seeped into the eyes of the damned and prosperous who awakened with a soul of the beast and clown lips painted with clay and brown faucet water. They punched the time clock and entered the ghost factory. They laid down the blueprint of the great world war and half world wars. They turned their heads to a chime outside the prison gate left hanging from the gallows one hundred years after the Civil War wounded were left writhing on hollow ground.

"The devil's third son was a sky pilot," they said.

He flew night missions over the city of glass. The bed frame inside the iron lung was made into an ejector seat at the exit window of the jet fighter. His one good thumb could release the lever if he wished and a yellow parachute blossomed into petals of light. It drifted for hours until radar off the coast tracked its descent into the Indian Ocean. One hundred sky pilots used their wings to soften the landing as it gently brushed against the buoys weighed down by small anchors tied to the ship.

Underwater cameras showed Johnny Roach raising a kaleidoscope to his window. He told them he was looking for one of those subterranean rainbows seen by the sailors drowned by a mermaid's hand. Had they seen his periscope set to the curvature of the earth or his fused pink spine that buckled in his rumble seat of desire, or was it the apparition of his body in a straitjacket seated in the electric chair on the day of his execution, caught between the living who climbed the heavenly rope or was it the petition of the dead found behind the painting, a family portrait, a cigarette thrown off the sidewalk curb, wine glass against the fireplace, the pool player's magic shot into the stratosphere of luck, a child's dream and fortune come to life, buttermilk on the front porch, the swing over the meadow, the young boy with nothing in his eyes who sat at his desk unmoved by his second grade classroom rushed out the door, what happened to Johnny's red-haired and freckled friend in his Buster Brown shoes, or his two buddies who walked in front of him on their way to Smith Elementary School as the car ran over them and into the field, had they, too, lived and loved enough to write what happened into their journals fifty-five years later, untarnished by memory, war, the harmony of the stars in a symphony of despair, the prisoners on a weekend pass and conjugal visits in purgatorio looking for a first kiss and last dance? The large brown eyes of the boy-soldier stared into the camera, and he lowered his head and nearly wept as if he had taken a wedding vow.

December 31, 2013

There was one half-eaten jar of freeze-dried Negro Peanut Butter left by the cripple ghost inside the pine cupboard in the small kitchen of the time machine. They served his last meal on a metal TV tray in front of his electric chair, the prison cafeteria served chunky Negro Peanut Butter and Fluffernutter to the inmates at their annual picnic with the police who profiled and lawyers who agreed.

It was New Year's Eve on death row. They opened the deserted bowling alley for the prisoners who were allowed on this one night to wear overalls and yellow pinstripes. Polka and rhythm and blues on 45s played through the wall speakers at each booth. Some of the prisoners danced with their wives and partners and children and some pranced with each other. They served bread, water, tea, biscuits, gravy, and grass-fed meats donated by the Wild Idea Buffalo Company in South Dakota and coffee roasted by Leaves and Pages Café in New Britain.

This was the territory of Wounded Knee, its small graveyard and Museum of the Dispossessed on top of a long sloped hill, tombstones tilted toward the horizon of the crippled ghosts, a temple of souls carried off in wooden carts by the retrievers of the living who had lifted the dead and thrown them into the rising river between two mountains, the way a man on death row might look into the scorched eyes of warriors riding wild horses into the high cliffs, the sound of a ragtime tom-tom jelly roll sleigh ride on a toboggan built for two lovers on a three-day pass of lavender grappa and Dutch Owl cigars, a tuxedo and spats, black dress and pearls, a chrysanthemum of kiss and tell, a bromide of flesh and circumstance, who is behind the reckless wheel of the town chariot, asleep inside the limousine of desire, half-alive on the highway between providence and despair, the two baptized infants in a cradle licking their serpent skin, the armies driven by the spoils of war and the hunger of gravity, collapsing at the walled gate into the failing arms of God, and some of those in attendance behind death's curtain asked if watching somebody put to death was like watching city chickens released at the midnight hour from the attic window of the brownfield and ghost factory roof first headed south until they were misdirected by the pardon on a rotary phone and were sent flying into rare snow and fog?

The *New York Daily News* under my father's arm, a black lunch pail, a Stanley thermos, the tumbler and quick silver moorings, a wooden ship in a bottle, time capsule filled with white muscadine grapes, honey blue, grape leaves, carpenter nails, air pump for the iron lung hot rod wheels, a set of Bible encyclopedias, missing back pages, the purgatory and hunger of gravity, weightlessness, how the brain, *the ghost in the machine*, knew everything and remembered nothing, built under a canopy of lace, chestnut, a wooden stump for a golden thumb, trill of the owl mouth, what tinsel of language uttered in darkness and captured in the backlit atmospheric heavens on the smoldering lexicon of God, the first spoken word, the appointment of beast and mother tongue curdled in the wild between the caverns of illuminated dust and sharp stone across the throat and bristle along the spine boiled in a kind of alchemy of laughter, the first kiss on the forehead, parted lips and parted company on the ocean of ice and pink tentacles floating between science and annihilation of species living and dead in a current under a covered bridge, the hapless town crier whipped the backside of his gray mare, death's carriage tumbled through the air, sardines and mustard, the weekly fifty-dollar U.S.

Savings Bond, boiled egg, apple, leftovers for ten thousand children, carried in whaling vessels, one continent to another, thrown overboard into the dismal waters of the heart, who sat in the throne of desire, raising their hand at the first sign of life underwater?

After the third shift, the factory horn blared, a signal to the fathers and mothers and children, awakened by the piercing shipwreck on a city sidewalk in front of the bushes, behind a cyclone fence, miniature corn in the front yard of the tenement, Park Street, the Blue Mirror Bar, the wool blanket for warmth, stick patch across father's chest, pruning back grapevines, the fertile swarm of blue bumblebees, eyes closed, hollow chest, bread rising, head lowered, last words and last breath, tumbleweed, twenty-one gun salute inside the iron lung, pillbox of false teeth, grapevines, a garden of winter collards, Mojave green turned to dust, radio signal from land to air over blue water.

"Can anybody know another's heart or widower's kiss?"

"Anybody out there?"

"What the hell's so funny?"

He held his hand over his heart as he lay still in his iron lung easily converted into a dog-legged tub by a pulling the light switch with his false teeth. It was built in the shape of a hammock and welded to the sides and strapped with thick rope used in ropes thrown over the pier to capture the dance of mermaids who cavorted the warm seas for a ship's captain. It floated below the blue coral stars and under the moon's wreckage and the retrievers of the dead sent out to recover the venom of sea snakes in search of the underwater miracle.

They sent a surprise box gift wrapped in aluminum foil and tiny red bow to celebrate his twentieth-century expedition on death row in a time machine set to explode on the anniversary of the moon landing and moon walk. During a lull in the sunlight as a rainbow appeared in his bathroom mirror, he sat up on his one elbow with the war wound bullet hole clean through the funny bone. He was able to pull the thread on the box and up jumped Jack, the beanstalk, that broke his eye socket. There was one-size-fits-all Velcro eye patch on the ventriloquist dummy that left Johnny Roach with a black eye inside the iron lung.

Ben Cocoa was first taken into the prison, on top of a mountain, former Shaker grounds, and when he looked out at the horizon, he swore he saw the circumference of the Earth and sky. There were large metal milk containers outside the main entrance filled with sand. I asked what they were and the guard said they shot bullets into the sand. . . I half believed him. I walked in and heard a large chorus of songs and chants and they said it was worship time. . . a "revival" inside a prison. Ben, the honorable executioner's guest, was allowed seating with the guards for lunch. He thought of the disappearing rainbow over the barbed fence. Suddenly, the siren went off and they wheeled a prisoner out on a stretcher. I was taken to the library. The small shelf of books were ragged and torn. It was a small group of men. I talked about my poems and books and read several. I sensed I reached out to them and they reached out to me. I gave them writing assignments. Ben left with his brown eyes lowered and heart unsettled.

Ben remembered the sound of the prison doors slamming shut like the jaws of Cajun gators. Those swamp stories. Legs and arms and heads found floating in debris. *Mercy.*

Ben was transferred to a small prison in Hastings, Nebraska, colorless, in a town with Hastings College. Midwestern ethos. Ben noticed a large castle door across and twelve paces away from the prison entrance. In Gothic lettering above the large doors: ASYLUM.

The *Omaha-Herald* reported the discovery of a burial ground behind the asylum. The state refused to release their names and ages.

This was not a regular dummy. It was set to speak only when a human felt alone and detached from its umbilical landing gear, and the rivets of memory needed a brief kiss and embrace with its small palms on his forehead. He found the battery inside the dummy doll and the green light inside its one eye was at five percent. It glowed red and yellow and green in the lap of his pajamas. He saw a candle inside the lighthouse, and he heard the voice of the seahorse above his head.

One wrong chess move inside the iron lung meant a gyroscope malfunction and a spittle of elixir out of the pink hourglass, broken vials and droplets of meningitis on his tongue, one lost year without a phone call on the rotary phone, a valentine, biting down on a plastic straw and his false teeth sent floating through the heating vent into thin air.

He was a partner to his own devices and allowed to choose one film, paraded as the last man executed on death row, for his last request seated in the electric chair, and he was also presented a vanilla-flavored breathing tube. It was Ingmar Bergman's *The Life of the Marionettes.* After his twenty-year reprieve and launch inside a time machine far above the war-torn cities and villages, he was shown a festival of films: *Sawdust and Tinsel, Under the Volcano, Wild Strawberries, Dr. Zhivago, El Postino, The Nude Howdy Doody, The Ghost of the World on the Plains, Mother's Last Dance,* and *The Night of the Living Blacks.*

He would have orange creamsicles at his last meal, redneck soup, pot liquor with dollops of sour cream, asparagus omelets, artisanal breads and cheeses, hummus, olives, pecan pie, summer sausage, salmon, and blackberries.

The prison doctor was given a court order to drill a small hole in his throat and place a voice box to complement the can-and-string walkie-talkie and upright Zenith radio with large tubes and dials.

If you cannot hear me, I mean no disrespect. I cannot speak well wearing a straitjacket inside the iron lung. My voice is low and disappearing. I have a voice box attached to an RCA Victor dog that sits on my nightstand. His eyes flash red and my violet verbs and mastodon nouns roll off his tongue. I was comfortable for years with this verbal agreement. I was on a list to retrieve a tongue transplant until the surgical team sent in from doctors on leave from the front lines decided it was best to place a small tongue revived and cut out of the mouth of a newly discovered and long-believed extinct luminescent frog into the Playdough mouth of the dummy doll that slept with him each night on a toy pillow sewn by the last surviving member of the Daughters of the Revolution. She used a needle carved out of a boar's leg and thread woven from the wings of the cicada that covered the salt fields.

Somebody played a violin in a meadow beside the Dismal River as the crowds gathered to view the first hanging of a man inside an iron lung. They raised the vessel off the ship and lowered it under the wild birch. The children rang the holy bells outside the local food shelter. The church folk sat in pews. One homeless man dropped his pants and urinated on the flag in protest of the execution. He was dragged by a wild horse into the factory furnace.

He turned the dial with the pencil between his teeth to the AM radio station. It was Muscle Shoals Studios in Alabama. They played Elizabeth Cotton's "Freight Train":

When I am dead and in my grave
No more good times here I crave
Place the stones at my head and feet
Tell them all that I've gone to sleep.

He held his daily journal, the aluminum ice tray, erector flaps cut into his numbed fingers. The first line, his last words: *12 Libretti for Two Daughters: The Ghost of the World on the Plains, Mother's Last Dance, Under the Volcano, Suddenly Last Summer, Wild Strawberries, The Life of the Marionettes, Ain't It Funny How Time Slips Away* (Joe Hinton's version).

He sat up in his easy chair on his back-porch, rocking into the feathers of gravity, Little League play of the century, tarred baseball on a collision course, moth balls inside a suitcase, family photographs, time's melody, cedar chest, frayed noose, attic of the birdcage, teacup science, chessboard, oil painting of the night school entrance sign, music box, drum beat, drum roll procession of star gazers under the gazebo. Who turned their back to the child with large brown eyes, blue blazer, tweed vest, white gloves, tinsel thrown over his shoulder by the helmsman, pulled the cart out of the mud and walked into fog and ruin?

They measured his thin body and broad shoulders to fit a shark-skin suit and left his narrow tie and money clip inside the soup bowl on the tray of his last meal. They examined his bucket of urine and burned the lapel miniature flag patch of his U.S. Army Corps jacket, torn off by the snow owl seen on the steeple of the prison chapel. It had flown into the attic window of the New Britain Mausoleum of American Art and was driven out by guards with broomsticks taken out of septic tanks behind the missile silo in the Great Plains after the dust had settled.

They cut the penny out of the one Sunday School loafer found in the tree at city hall. It was not clear if they had discovered the oldest human skull, a skeletal bird, the first human to raise his hand for blood and psalm after he painted the splayed beast. Had he witnessed the archangel mapping out the corridors of his soul as he fell out of the burning nest into the charred arms of his lover?

The waxed deck of his playing cards, cases of empty vodka bottles, cigarette cartons, peppermint twist fountain of youth at the five and dime penniless casino, citizens of God lined up for their last unlucky plug nickel and two-dollar bet placed on a goat-footed roadside roulette, knowing one drink in moderation would kill a one-eyed jackal, burn alive one alley cat in a barrel of trash and not make the one petrified monkey talk at the Goodwill auction, tied to a beggar's stick, riding shot-gun inside a knapsack on a hunchback joyride like the man who took out his false teeth and laughed in the back window of his pickup.

It was his wide-eyed insomnia strapped into the electric chair and rolled aboard a freight train headed to White Sands Beach that taught him to remain still in the iron lung.

On the morning of his execution photographers arrived with Polaroid Land Cameras and 35mm Plus X film attempting to capture the soul departing his illuminated body. He was dressed in burlap pants and top hat, opened umbrella, a puppet with pink eyes rested on his bad shoulder. The carnival monkey, a retired grinder, began to curse out of the voice box implanted into his chest behind its plaid vest.

Brotherman, goddamn, Brotherman, goddamn, Brotherman, god-damn.

The iron lung was lifted off the freight train into the wooden cart behind the Yellow Cab attached by a U-Haul ball bearing for his week-end pass into the Green Mountains, Breadloaf, Robert Frost, a change of seasons with stops at the Eddy Farm and Bishop's and Roger's orchards. He looked for a sign in the tops of trees and the night sky with his kaleidoscope like a helmsman drifting on the sea.

It was not the passage of time inside a rumble seat, it was how his memory danced in the unsettled air of recognition seated in the electric chair. There were clear signals observed at one end of the equator that he was the last man on death row, evident by the long thread of dust left behind by the crippled ghost bareback in a Western movie.

The children were born with small wings on the back of their necks, morning glory, heart-shaped whistle, charm on a doll's wrist, magnifying glass in a boy's hand held over a June bug, small as the beaded eye stitched into the wicked mouth of the red hen pillow, the spotlight above the Ferris wheel pulsing into the cumulus cloud into the heavens, monocle on the dresser, the lilac stars falling inside the hourglass.

The prison doctor noticed how the inmate's skin shed as he slept. The good country doctor checked the drainage of the "sleeping needle" they pushed into his neck vein to practice the deathwatch of old folks beyond their year and the deformed orphan. The doctor had seen the first case of eternal sleep on a young boy who nodded off in his biology class. He had been known to wet his bed after he listened to his mother scream, smelled her cigarette lips, heard her slapping the faces of his brothers and sisters, and the cursing doll under the Christmas tree, its pine needles breaking apart in March.

He watched a film of toy soldiers with rifles on the floor between two bunk beds, father with his handkerchief over his eyes, figure-eight highway on a pointillist landscape, drought on the human scale, landing and departure, love's certainty and restoration, blight and temporary gifts of rage.

He dreamed he had seen the discarded eyes of his late wife. He was given a pair of blue-tinted Polaroid sunglasses that polarized the sunlight through the sunroof above his rumble seat. They changed the color of the birch trees from white to a blue-green shade found under a line of weeping willows along the Dismal Swamp where the hunchbacked anthropologist and apologists of genocide uncovered piles of morel mushroom droppings left behind by prehistoric animals known to devour the stems and buds of lavender, lilac, and morning glory, using their prehensile dexterity to follow their herd into the shallow river until the great meteor fell out of the sky, turning the pastoral landscape and the sea into charred feathers that floated past the porthole inside the gas chamber unit attached to the iron lung, if electricity would not work, gas would be sent into his breathing tube, if gas would not work, the heat shield would be torn off by a nod of the warden's head, if heat would not work, they would try drowning in a waterfall of quicksand caused by detaching the spigot in the sink over the headboard, if drowning would not work, they would use electricity, and if electricity would not work, they would be surprised by his slow death and parade of alms left at the foot of his bed by the Helmsman of the Town Clock, and if he would not die in the manner of his request, they would bring out a firing squad of ten men wearing the black mask of Brown Zorro, a tall man with broad shoulders with a sword at his waist, who was taken by ship and left stranded on the unmapped and uninhabited island between two mountains, they would lift their long rifles and long knives, a well-mannered militia, taking short steps backward and forward, a choir to their left singing "Oh, Happy Day" to the beggars moved behind the prison gates, and if he would not die a glorious death determined by the prison doctor, under mysterious circumstances, prescribed his self-made equine elixir in a black bottle stamped with crossbones, it would be marked a homicide by the Pope of Letters, a man who received the Honorary Doctorate of Humane Letters, *Honoris Causa*, given by a small, private, Catholic university and the rare and distinctive Dominican sisters, who gathered their love of God and Christ into baskets of glory carried by the faithful believers of redemption and sacrifice, and they found the hour of his execution was the exact time they had crucified the Lord as he was lifted off the cross in his heavenly ascent cupped inside the charred hand of God, who laughed at the wicked and wept at the peasants who fell to their knees at the altar stone and lit candles and returned to the village and their armies sent their horses over the sea cliffs into flames, the children taken to a wishing well, pulled a rope and bucket, there was a flask once used by the alchemist who turned a semester of college into a worldwide wrestling enterprise, the gift by Satan's hand turned his luck into well-heeled fortune, his son joined the military police, he was hired at a prison for the criminally insane, known to wear long black boots and silver spurs, top hat and mask, he carried a bull whip, Taser, Mace, flashlight, Swiss army knife, and one expired jar of Negro Peanut Butter in his knapsack, stored inside his locker in case of a riot, his slow death brought a half-smile to a few faces behind the bullet-proof plexiglass viewing window, some bowed their heads, a shame known only to those who viewed such things from a balcony of desire, several collapsed under the weight of time and trampled the flowers under their feet into ash.

He was given re-runs of *Palladin, Sky King, Crusader Rabbit, Banana Man, Have Gun Will Travel,* and his favorite show *Death Valley Days.*

On his birthday, they attached his iron lung to the back of a twenty-mule team. He felt honored to be wheeled into the desert although a slight miscalculation of heat and refrigeration would be fatal. They found a baby sidewinder at the bottom of his portable toilet, a nest of scorpions inside his cuffed burlap pants.

The heat took what air he had left inside his breathing tube. His tongue swelled three times its size until the robotic arm at his bedside poured a potion of borax and cod liver oil into his mouth and nostrils. His eyes bulged. Fever. Cold sweat. The vial of swine flu vaccine saved his last sad ass day above the planet.

The warden sent out a call for war ships off the Macedonian coast. A reenactment of the Rockefeller Prison Riot went out of control. The prisoners seated and well-behaved under the live oaks became restless after opening their boxed lunches filled with sardines and mustard and soda crackers. Somebody tampered with the Kool-Aid and the guard-house monkey went wild inside his bamboo cage. It broke out and made a collect call through its voice box on the rotary telephone to the governor.

The riot police had muskets, ball bearings, silver bullets and canisters of nerve gas. They men were face down in mud and blood. Gunpowder lingered in the air. Their mattresses caught fire. Water hoses were cut. The alligators in the moat around the prison crawled into cells. Blueprints of underground tunnels connected to the outside world were stolen. Snipers were set up on the mountain range and picked off the unarmed men who gave signs of the cross. It was hunger, waste, high-water marks on the walls inside the cafeteria, a row boat and one paddle upstream, loud speakers and bull horns, classical music pumped into the asylum of beggars half-alive in their golden slumber, inside the prison, the reconstructed electric chair made out of hardwood and leather barber straps was removed and taken into the root cellar for safety, it was covered by a wool blanket of ghost stars, a replica of the Amazing Petrified Man smiled in the corner under a bare light bulb. Yesterday, in the prison chapel, a small group of former boxers had gathered for a Hopalong Cassidy sing-a-long.

Father Ben,

I was moving too fast between scenes, tripped on stairs offstage and twisted my ankle. I felt a few pops and went down. At the time, I was holding two pairs of bike handles (my own and a cast mate's). It could have been much worse.

My director and the crew got me ice/ibuprofen and put me in a cab right away to urgent care. (It was past 10 P.M. and they didn't want me going to ER cuz it would've taken too long.)

Got an X-ray and CT scan. No broken bones. But once I tried to put a little weight while the foot was in boot, I got so nauseous from the pain and lightheaded. Had to lay down for a bit.

There isn't swelling yet, just a bruise, but the dr. wants me to come back tomorrow morning. Then they'll send me on to get an MRI at another place. So I'm gonna do that early tomorrow morning.

Hurts bad, but my classmate Flordelino who's also in the show stayed in the cab with me the whole way home and walked me to my door. I have a prop cane from the theater and this boot. The urgent care ran out of crutches. Hopefully the place will have them tomorrow.

All of it is covered by worker's insurance. The director took cash out right away and gave it to Flordelino who then paid for my cab, etc. They will pay for everything if I need.

Haven't thought about what's gonna happen with the show because I'm supposed to be riding a stationary bike the whole time. But first things first. Gotta get this MRI. If it's a tear, I may need surgery. Hopefully it's not that bad and it will just heal slowly over time.

I'll let you know how MRI goes.

Love you,
Daughter Isadora

Purgatorio

(Tar Oil and Bluebird Feathers)

Merry Christmas, Daddy!

I love you with all of my heart. Thank you for your strength and patience, knowledge and selflessness. You're really the best there is. I'm constantly in awe of your beauty and charisma.

Your daughter,
Isadora

January 15, 1980

Dear Wendy,

My train rolled into New Orleans, on time, and I felt tired and dry, but I was full of your good apples and love. My bags (both of them) were waiting for me when I arrived. In the *New York Times* I found articles on Dance and New Orleans. In this letter I will tell you how much it means, to me, to be with you and how much it meant, for me, to share, with you, our families. At times I wondered if we could be together. I believe we can. Just as a wish unfolds before a lonely soul, you were there. Like a need reaches out to touch what it cannot see, you were there. And like a love nourishes itself forever on another's love we both were there. Every day I can hold you in my arms; every day I can talk, laugh, and sometimes cry with you. Every day I drew closer to the one person I love so much. Let's make a "bond" — a "commitment" to each other; it's not too late, and I need a one-arm massage, a woman who dances with the wind at her feet, a pair of hands to help me with my own.

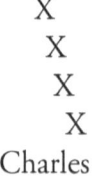

X

X

X

X

Charles

NEW YEAR'S EVE

IT IS A fearful thing to love what Death can touch.

There were clear signals you were not well fourteen
days and fourteen nights doubled over. The evening's
champagne was left unopened tied in blue ribbon like
death's bright palette. The horse-drawn carriage
arrived at midnight with pouches of a used and rare
blood type as the devil's fortune took the devil's turn
and catheters and picks left a territory of welts like
the discarded stars falling in your eyes. The hooded
driver passed the medicine bag to Dr. Bascom passed
down by his grandfather who bowed to the South
Dakota mountains wiped your forehead and took
your rapid pulse. This was not a part of the evening
news more than holy war and starvation of nations
only comfort to a husband with two daughters left on
the back porch with no crimes to unlearn who knelt
together like angels on the great plains. There were
clear signals you were not well with two weeks of
doubt until they scanned your organs as the fog lifted
over the Platte River a smoky black mushroom like a
newborn stillborn known only as a case number left
at the prom door. There was no wind in Nebraska on
New Year's Eve as the head nurse tapped your veins
for the morphine until your white count rose and your
platelets danced and your recovery made a good
country doctor flinch after a distant signal found the
artery of remembrance.

After the Rehearsal

We gathered your choreography of *Afro Psalms*
our wedding vow performance on marbled floors
at the Museum of Nebraska Art *MONA To Its Friends*.
You practiced for hours at Harmon Park's rock
garden raised by WPA flophouse workers free
room and board for the farmers and artists the
shapers of Central Nebraska's Stonehenge.
We gathered the African kalimba and rain stick
metaphors of black magic and voodoo blood
for our evening's curtain call in the corn palace
under a shower of circumstance and disease.
Forty-five minutes before the poetry reading
your dance and the art exhibit opening
we were seated in the small doctor's room half-
alive in thin aluminum chairs
among the scorched leaves in the hollow
and the bright wings of the angels noble
in their wild and hovering insignificance.
It was the doctor's first and correct call:
I am sorry to have to tell you you
have lymphoma.
There was nothing to be said.
We walked into the distant world
thirty minutes until our performance.
We would not tell our daughters tonight
and we gathered our poems and music
hollow instruments that moaned in our hands.
As we arrived and hurried into the museum

to a full house of literati and wise docents
the sandhill cranes and life studies seemed alive
with the avant-garde of the central Great Plains.
You were stronger than the hunger of gravity
and you had not doubled over for an hour
and the strong medicine they gave you made
you more of your second self.
I saw the throttle of pain in your eyes with
ten long minutes to show time.
Our daughters *Claire and Shelley* sat
in the front row with large eyes
small hands and their larger hearts
knowing something was wrong with you.
They had stared into the devil's wishing well
as you walked on stage they wished you well

In Memoriam

For Wendy Fort

TWICE THEY SAID you would not make it
and you awakened like a small bird in
its first dance outside its fallen nest.
Husband, two daughters, and friends
sat at your bedside at daybreak into
the evening until each minute fell out
of the heavens like a gold coin into the
lilac light that were your eyes. Your
chest rose and your breath fell and the
night nurse detected a slight murmur
in the parlors of your heart.
It's going to be all right mommy, *shhh, shhh*, Shelley whispered.
They held your hands for hours as Shelley sang into your eyes
that suddenly opened and you smiled and said to your
daughters: I love you, write it in your journal. They wrote it in
their journals in their bedrooms in your voice on your last day
on earth
before heaven you told Claire (16) and Shelley (12)
you would speak to them in their dreams. W*hat
am I going to do without you without the walks to
elementary school?
I did not want you to walk me.
It would be funny to my friends.*
What about our little dog Mojo in the park
who leaped like a deer in the tall weeds behind
the Windy Hills Elementary school?
It's going to be all right mommy, *shhh, shhh*,
Shelley whispered.

Claire screamed:
I don't want another Mom. She
won't see me graduate college
married or dance in the meadow
and soft shoe with Hines or Astaire.
She will be gone forever.
Claire comforted Shelley: You
will be fine.
You are beautiful
Wendy made you beautiful and there is
nothing to fear. Afterwards in the afterlife you
gave us the proper signals: Claire dreamed you
had left us and the morning clock stopped.
Weeks before your photograph that blew across
the room with closed windows and without the
Nebraska wind landed face up. Shelley wanted
to play the violin for you and they found it in
the dark locker halls. She played *Cripple Creek*
by memory though her music sheets were
in the case. Shelley's last song for you to hear
the symphony string filled the hospital halls
and lifted your spirit slightly from the hollow
ground to higher ground. After I heard your
last breath, Wendy, I awakened Shelley from
the fold-out bed and she touched your hollow
chest. She knew you were gone and asked:
Where did she go? Can you close her mouth?
The nurse closed your mouth. We walked
down the hallway and drove out of the
parking lot as Shelley wept in the backseat. I
suppose it was her young heart and age: *We
should have gotten a jar for her last breath*
something alive in a bottle to trick death?

The Antidote for Death

They found the antidote for death another's
wounded heart would never do. They were
no magic stones or treasure map only the
maimed animal's bottled blood stored in
bright vials in the root cellar until the
emergency or once latent disease called for
the melting of the wax seal for the ill poet's
wife or lost friend married to his own wife
with her own three children.
Your life would take another life. The planning
analyst who learned computers and sometimes
to hate them and bought one to write poems on
and to store them like jewels. *You said the poems*
became secondary to the machine crushed under the
weight of RAM and ROM and IBM.

You took a pen to three poems in twenty-four
odd and unblessed years. There were flashes and
interference intended to work on our kind of
work another degree in library and information
science more computers but you still had the
critical eye read and gave suggestions to a couple
of friends. You would return to writing for a
short time the good news and not so good news.
Your health was excellent in all respects except
for a bad heart and a small stroke and that heart
was beginning to fail. You were on a heart
transplant list had done better than they ever

expected. Your life would take another life. They
found the antidote for death another's wounded
heart would never do.

Wendy was a dancer, choreographer, and a poet's wife. We performed, despite Wendy being diagnosed with lymphoma at the Kearney Clinic, forty minutes before the opening of *Afro Psalms*. I am
writing this for those patrons, artists, and writers who attended the
Museum of Nebraska Art that evening, for what now seems a century
of evenings, to watch what would be Wendy's last dance performance.
Our two daughters, Claire and Shelley, sat in the front row.

Wendy had been weakened by her condition many weeks prior to
her performance. We rehearsed together in the Harmon Park Recreation Center; I read the poems, and Wendy danced like a noble angel. I
would share the stage with my artist-wife that evening, who performed
her brilliant choreography of *Afro Psalms*, and I was only able to read
my poems that evening because of the strength I had received from
her own isolated bravery and courage, the kinds of *higher places* we can
only imagine we are able to live.

During that long, faithful, and beautiful evening at the museum,
my heart broke apart in solitude and darkness. I witnessed my wife do
her best under the most unimaginable circumstances, with the audience, and what they did not know, with my daughters, and what they
were not told.

I also realized that evening, in another darker part of my heart, that
it would perhaps be the last time we would ever see my wife Wendy
and her spirit dance like a shadow larger than our just and miniature
world.

This story, Wendy's story, began under the elms that surrounded
Bushnell Park in Hartford, Connecticut, with the types of trees that
make us look toward heaven with its brief and eternal shower of hollow
stars and gold coins that fall to earth and into our hands. We met at the
outdoor jazz festival in Hartford a cool July evening as the saxophone,

cymbals, xylophone, and grand piano merged into a symphony of her dark hair, a perfect shadow that veiled her face and eyes. There was the carousel with polished snouts and painted hooves that seemed to circle the equator as the wild horses on their hind legs stampeded into wilderness and the ancient burial ground of slaves and forefathers.

Our twenty-one years of dance, poetry, and romance under the wreckage of the moon's grace was born in New Britain and Wethersfield, two towns two minutes and worlds away yet as much a part of the American dream and nightmare we called home. The brownfields of the factory town and the apple fields of the cove somehow merged inside the family pit where my father's hands churned molten steel into ball bearings and Wendy's father's hands stirred seed into blossoms.

There was New Britain and its three-story tenements and attic apartments, Hartford Avenue decades later named Martin Luther King Drive, a downtown with four theaters, the Strand, Embassy, Palace, and Falcon, a Central Park, and the old world five-and-dime stores, wrestling shows, in a time driven by the Thanksgiving football war between New Britain and Pulaski high schools. The black-and-white television turned into colors on the Ponderosa and left Amos 'n' Andy pale faced. The Vietnam War drew protests between the hard hats, long hairs, hardheads, and the black and white and blue collar working class poor who shoveled their own graves under willows after working their whole life in the city. It must have been the Beatles, Ali, and Motown between the bombs and Birmingham that turned us into poor little rebel angels in junior high cleats. Was it Wendy in the shadows at our first school dance as the teachers pulled us together, the tall with the short, black with the white, away from recreation dodge ball and the square-dance and into the rock 'n' roll Motown stiletto left on the afterschool schoolyard?

In the Hartford park we were under the spell of jazz and a bruised moon minutes away from our family and the New Britain polka and rhythm and blues and the Stanley Golf Course and the Shuttle Meadow Reservoir with its late-night romance on drives in Volkswagens still thinking about my baby and change my mind that never end.

We never understood how the first sight of love under the influence of the wind, rainbow, and music under the hollow stars would last twenty-one years and even when it ended the eternal dance of memory lives on in our daughter's smaller hearts.

It might have been the birds screaming for their brief lives under the Hartford Arch, the faces that appeared that day in the clouds in the photographs above the crowd, the howl in the tunnels below the city, the half-asleep chains inside the carousel, the beggar awakening with the crippled ghosts of Stowe, Stevens, and Twain in mid-conversation on the bank of the Connecticut River, the crumpled Stetson stolen from the Hartford Hat Shop floating under the covered bridge, how we picked it up, swash-buckled like thieves, and kissed.

There was a comfort in the broken city moon under the willow that brought us together, the dry ivy over the university walls, the morning tide of the Connecticut River, the beggar set afire by young thieves under the covered bridge, wild horses pulling urban chariots in the evening sky, the brownfields once factories where fathers toiled in the smoke and woe of forty years of unholy night shift wages, and the union brought sandwiches during a strike as they warmed their hands above the barrels of fire in snowfall. My father was a night shift factory worker, nine-to-five barber, and twenty-four-hour landlord in a three-story tenement with three attic dwellers in skyline apartments. Wendy's was a farmer's daughter. They worked hard until they died.

The city fathers held their genitals in the underground lavatory of the New Britain Central Park at sundown after the Memorial Day parade that I marched in for ten years. I wore a blue blazer, wide white navy pants, held a silver clarinet to the military march outside of the Burritt Music School. Our older citizens live in our old New Britain High School auditorium and classrooms. The Hartford Drive-In is a Sunday flea market. One no longer walks in comfortable shoes on a downtown street among the shops and restaurants that fed the black and white laborers, happily beat and bruised their wives and children and drank themselves into quiet deaths. They were given their wings by their misshapen belief in a wicked Manichean God and crippled ghost that roamed the factory railyard with red eyes and released the brakes of freight cars and swung its lantern with its brief candle of desire. The side of the black lunch box shows a rainbow above the smokestack.

I suppose this is another love story, one told a thousand times in a thousand ways, yet each time must be understood in its own way, how the feeble monocle is held and examines a specimen of the heart, the atlas of Eros, the way it drives us into passion and danger, and keeps us living as we do. I am not certain of this. I do know the ways in which we live do not always bring us the character some of us have been fortunate to have listened to as it was spoken in the great orations of King, John, and Robert Kennedy, yet we have been singed enough by a cynicism that has worn out the masters old and new. Love shadows hatred. Beauty terror. I wrote many awful yet important lines at a young age: *Nothing New Is Wanted Until the Sky Turns Black, Hatred Will Blow Itself Out.* Awful only because of its time. Important because without those lines I would not have been able to gather my signature title: *The Town Clock Burning.* There is a grace in self-knowledge, a humility scorned by our world that uncovers our phobias: spiders, Negroes, even family members. We are taught to hate others, even family members, at a young age, and rarely manage to become better people after nearly a lifetime of miseducation, but we are here to talk of the manner love brings us closer to the spiritual, how a few of us might manage to navigate the burning sails of the heart.

This memoir takes us on Wendy's journey through her light and darkness. She wanted excerpts from her journals in print. Letters written to and about her. I am here to keep her spirit and light with us as we journey into darkness. They say love conquers. It can never conquer unresolved grief. It can place a life, Wendy's life, and closer to our own, near her beautiful artistic shore. I take this page to write that I have met the first woman since Wendy's death and the first woman since meeting Wendy twenty-one years ago that I have felt as I wrote in my poem: *I met you the day I was born / and there was a certain comfort in this.* She is so much like Wendy. She listens. She is kind. She comforts.

She says she wears summer dresses. A summer dress in desert heat with beautiful eyes and a face like a blossom helped to a young man fall in love, want each word inked by the Love is brief, difficult to define, mis-used, and indefinable, and perhaps I am more certain about what love is not that I write this book unashamed of its contents, not knowing I would become a dancer's husband. *I do not love her / maybe I love her*, Neruda wrote in his book of poems, *Twenty Love Poems and a Song of Despair*. Perhaps we will become partners, imperfect pairs embracing under the heart's willow. I am not certain of this, only certain that she brings to me what I have longed for since my loss, and I am certain that my loss brings me closer to her in ways I do not yet fully comprehend. There are layers of stories in a single life left unstated and deflected by the manner of the writer's memory and imagination. For the rest of my life there will always be Wendy in others that I love, and I look forward to each moment where the living and the dead converge into one spirit, and her spirit can live on in others willing and able to do so without complaint.

We rolled a laundry cart several blocks down Esplanade into a sto-rybook building. In the evening Wendy and I entered the Maple Bar where customers could hear poetry readings, Roosevelt Sykes sing *I'll be a dirty double motherforya*, do their laundry, and join Everett Mad-dox who sat on his eternal barstool with endless rounds of bourbon until he nearly died a short year later a saint of the holy swamp mon-sters. This happened in forty-five minutes or less.

Wendy loved and cared for our two daughters. She helped me do the same. We never hit our children, slapped, or yelled at them like branded mules to the amazement of those who grew up *beaters and slappers*, the only way they knew to raise a child was to raise a fist. They simply believed they were superior, never wrong, and they lived in lagoons of denial, and there is no need to present their lies on this page. One sister's letter (and those who support it in the midst of Wendy's chemotherapy) is evidence enough that hate among immediate family members is the vilest human emotion. Those who teach their children the ways of hate leave no legacy of love on this page.

The Woman in the Petrified Forest

They say rain comes on Sunday the
first sign of love was thirst.

Had you looked into her wild and
mournful eyes a moment too long as
the warm winds shifted weightless
over the equator and migratory birds.
They say rain comes on Sunday.

Misguided by the harpooned moon bent
wings torn in their spiral flight turned
their wet shoulders downward into the
great nest and burial ground?

The last sign of love was sorrow the last
known remedy a canteen for the flared
heart and charred wing taken down by a
thin wire and low wind.

They say rain comes on Sunday the
last sign of love was thirst.

Were you the apparition of love a
soft shoe last dance embrace who left
the unadorned and immortal first
kiss under the reckless ship?

There was no harm in what you learned
with a noble savage asleep in your arms.
The pendulum moon over a barren acre love
in italics on the atlas of Eros.

They say rain comes on Sunday the
first sign of thirst was love.

The angel noble in love's carriage
with charred wing and top hat
swept over the village and swung its
mortal chimes over the two of us.

Had he pulled her necklace of fire
apart and taken each black pearl
between his teeth like a sword as
he rode the wild horse

a thousand miles to her chained door
and slept with the wounded beast on
its raw and charmed hooves in the
wilderness and nightfall?

They say rain comes on Sunday the
last sign of thirst was love.

What are two lovers to do? We take
care of our lives loyal to ourselves
and circumstance.
You would write these lines for us:

You and I would look beautiful together.
There is no doubt about that in my mind. Next
year will be pure hell
and two lives will make me crazy.

Maybe I will feel lucky. Do you ever
feel that you are standing on the edge
of a cliff?
Do you think I have sad eyes?

Do you ever feel that everything you have
ever known is about to fall apart? Today
after a short ride into this small town I will
see if you remember my voice.

I am going to town and get some food and
order some farm fresh eggs
I am such an old-fashioned person.
They say rain comes on Sunday.

The last sign of sorrow was love.

This is for the woman whose
first sight was fire and the
man and woman whose first
sight was love.

It was thirty years before she called
on marriage number two and five
children between two coasts after
missing the high school reunion.

A truck blind-sided her on I-95 and
totaled her car and awakened a
memory and need to call back from
her near death highway ride.

Half-awake and weary in
front of this bright screen and

this cup of black ass coffee
does no good and I miss you.

Were you the movie twin Audrey Hepburn
in a black dress and churchyard pearls on
the staircase who tossed her scarf off the
banister and into the wildfire?

The last sign of sorrow was love the
only sign of sorrow a kiss.

Letters

West Cork, Ireland
June 27, 2002
12:27 PM

Dear Charles,

It has been a long time, but we have been out of Ireland for over eight months, and only recently returned to our mail. We were deeply saddened to learn of Wendy's death, and consider it a great privilege to have known her, if only briefly. She was so brave, and looked so lovely, with her dancer's grace, although she had obviously grown frail. We also loved meeting your splendid daughters, and your account of Shelley's sorrow in the poem is extremely moving. Your opening image also moved us because here in West Cork small birds fall onto the grass outside our window. Please give our love to the children, and keep in touch. Thanks again for your hospitality in Kearney, where the lonely trains whistle through.

Did you go ahead with your plans for a book called *The Poet's Wife?* If so, we would love to see it. John's memoir appeared in England, to some praise, but has yet to make an appearance in America. Did you manage, in your travail, to send on the proofs to our editor at *The New Yorker?* Her name is Deborah Trainman. I presume you know of Alice Quinn, who could give lessons to a snail in slowness. Elizabeth's 3rd novel was published last Autumn, and she recently completed a fourth, so we are keeping ourselves fairly busy. Once again, our deepest condolences, and a warm kiss to you and your beautiful girls.

E and J
(Elizabeth Wassel and John Montague)

Dear Charles,

The first hint I had was your chapbook—for which I thank you—dedicated to Wendy. I e-mailed Hilda Raz who wrote me back with the terrible news of her death, and of the long struggle to save her that preceded it. I cannot help but think of Don Hall's wife Jane Kenyon, whose life followed very closely the same trajectory. I am so sorry—such a cruel end of young women of such talent. I remember meeting Wendy & think of how vivacious and attractive she was. I send you my deepest sympathy and warm regards.

Maxine Kumin
New Hampshire

Oct. 1, 2001

Dear Charles,

I never had the privilege of meeting your wife, but I have known you now for a few years, and I have met your two lovely daughters. When I heard of your wife's death, I wept. And on the long journey back to California, you were never out of my thoughts.

I have lost a son, and so I know something of grief. Don't be afraid to mourn and to mourn openly. You face a long, hard journey through the sorrow, but you will become strong enough to bear it.

And your wife will be with you. It is so odd—and so comforting—how those we love dearly stay with us. We talk to them and they respond in our hearts and imaginations.

I have you in my prayers. If you need someone to talk to, don't be shy about calling. You will need a few people who understand what you face. I was glad to see how much you are loved by your colleagues. Don't be afraid to reach out to them.

You have my deepest sympathy and are in my thoughts.

From my heart,
Dana Gioia
Santa Rosa, California

Dear Charles,

Thank you so much for sending me the relevant section from the Kearney Hub. And congratulations to you on the Wendy Fort Foundation. It is a brilliant idea for a memorial. After Jane's death, there were three separate, small Jane Kenyon memorial funds, one providing a scholarship for the MFA program at Bennington, another at the Michigan program, and a third supporting poetry awards in New Hampshire. Yours is so beautifully to the point.

You and I have been through such similar horrors. It's really good to know what you're doing. It isn't exactly as if one can really do anything about it!—but it is excellent to do something, at any rate!

Best wishes,
Don Hall
Wilmot, New Hampshire

Dear Charles, Claire, and Shelley,

We have thought, cried and talked about you all so many times since were received the shocking letter from Charles last January about Wendy's passing. I thought it was Wendy's end of the year card, picture, family information. Charles, your poems were almost too hard to read, and yet so compelling and direct that we had to reread and weep many times. We cannot imagine the pain of your loss, and wished and tried all this year to think of some way, something, some words that we could give you to ease your grief, let you know how deeply saddened we are. Thanks you so much for giving us the opportunity to contribute to the Foundation in Wendy's name.

Wendy was such a positive light. Our memories start with nursery school, Shelley and Claire about our kids' ages, parent helpers and then friends, violin lessons for Claire and family gatherings with Wendy's famous veggie spread. We knew we would not see you all very much again when you moved—but it seemed as though the adventure and opportunity for Charles was an incredible step, and from her letters and e-mails she sounded happy, that she had found a place for herself and your girls. We were proud of you all for being so brave to make such a radical move.

Wendy always showed such wisdom and at the same time a thirst for understanding of the strange, imponderable beauty and hardships of existence. Kate treasured seeing her weekly as Claire fiddled away. It is so wonderful to hear that Shelley took up the violin, and played for Wendy.

When you come to CT, we would love to see you, give you a meal, offer you a place to stay, anytime.

Please put us on the Foundation mailing list, keep us on your personal mailing list, accept our donation with love and memories of an incredible woman, wife and mother.

With much love,
Kate and Fred O'Brien

Dear Charles, Claire, and Shelley,

We are so saddened by the death of Wendy. Her last letters were extremely positive and full of hope. We had no idea her condition had worsened.

Of course, Wendy's letters never centered on herself. It was uncanny how her letters arrived on depressing days when I needed them most. They were vivid descriptions of her two greatest loves— her family and her dance. Her family was always foremost on her mind. Claire's growing up, Shelley's violin playing, Charles' poetry. She was so proud of all three of you.

The first time I ever laid eyes on Wendy, I thought she was the most naturally beautiful woman I had ever seen. It was my freshman year at UNCW, before I even knew Roy, and somehow I managed to get invited to an English department faculty party. Wendy was the first person I saw when I walked into the room, and she took my breath away. Naturally, I acted like the clumsy, seventeen-year-old idiot that I was, drank too much and babbled endlessly, so full of myself, my new-found freedom (and crap). Wendy listened intently, wisely, and never offered judgment or empty platitudes, even though I must have bored her to tears. Wendy had the ability to make other people feel special, when Wendy was the one who was truly special. I wanted to be like her so much. I wanted to BE Wendy Fort, to posses her quiet fire.

Throughout those first years, I had the pleasure of watching Wendy perform. One of the most beautiful dances I remember was an interpretation Wendy did which contrasted "City-Country." Her muscle tone, dancer's legs, and physical grace were amazing, but her spiritual grace made it even more awesome. One of Wendy's biggest talents was her ability to make the audience become a part of the dance. She made me, a flat-footed clam digger, feel as if I were up there on stage with her. For that, I always loved her.

After our girls were born, Wendy was always there for us when we needed her most. One of our scariest days was when Amber was a baby and we were living in that old house on Seventh Street. Amber was growing up rapidly, and we needed clothes for her but only managed to find a handful of changes to our names. Just as we were feeling our lowest and wondering what on earth we were going to do, Wendy appeared at the door with three large boxes of beautiful clothes for Amber, food, a baby carrier, etc! I can still see Wendy smiling as she came through the door with gorgeous baby Claire in her little cap and blue coat.

I always tried to model Wendy's gently mothering. She taught me so many things. (And Charles, you were the one who taught us the "football" hold for babies to ease an upset stomach!) It seems like a far away echo now, those play times with Claire and Amber and the creative dance classes Wendy taught for toddlers downtown. She was always so patient and loving with all of the children, teaching them to dance their own dance to the beat of African drums.

Wendy probably didn't even know how much she taught me or how much she touched my life through her own life. Over the years,

I have met so many empty people who are stagnant. But Wendy was always growing, always going forward, reaching for new truth and deeper meaning. I have always tried to pass the many things Wendy did for me and to other people. I will miss her so much, but I will never forget Wendy, and I know she will always be alive through the life she lived.

Thank you for the beautiful poems and for sharing those memories of Wendy. Please do keep in touch. If you are ever in the area, drop in and you'll always have a place to stay, food, etc. We would love to see all three of you. Please know that we are thinking of you and praying for you and love you more than you'll ever know.

Julie Buffaloe
Bowling Green, Ohio

A Poem for Wendy

(Love's Labour's Found)

There were no ferns in the meadow
Only children and beggars on the hill
With the lilac turning gray in evening tide
As we walked over the covered bridge.

We embraced cliffside overlooking the town
The trimmed vineyards and burning warehouse
Couples leaving pub doors and the backyard tree
Knotted into the human with ash over a nest of blue eggs.

Had I seen a lighthouse with its brief light
A torch thrown out of the heavens by a madman
Pegged the devil's fool by the ministers of the heart
Or a shadow moving across your sleeping face?

Shipwrecked under the hollow stars
The moon small under the northern clouds
Disgraced and smaller in the tidal pool
Nearly drowned in the moat of the last king.

There were no ferns in the meadow
Only children and beggars on the hill
And for years the missing treasures were your eyes
Until I found the antidote for love was love.

Ben Cocoa
May 22, 2000

LETTER TO WENDY FROM SISTER

Daughter's Letter to Her Father

Dear Dad,

September 2007

I want to write you this letter and tell you how much I truly care about you. I appreciate all you have done to help me get where I am now. I cannot believe I am here in New York. I am living my dream! Looking at the classes I may be taking is exciting. This year is off to a great start and I thank you for the advice you've given me so far and I look forward to getting more advice! We have spent four years together in the house getting to know one another better. You were there for most of all the football and basketball games I danced at and all of my performances on stage (both choir and theatre). I owe all of my talent to you and mommy. I wouldn't have as much love for the arts if it weren't for growing up with such loving parents as you. These past few months of summer have been a blast. I've enjoyed spending time with Claire and you at the Cafe and the YMCA. I am grateful to have spent time with you in a few new cities, Pittsburgh and Chicago. *Wicked* was the best gift ever! I do miss visiting Starbucks in the middle of the Great Plains, but we can do that when I get back over break. I am doing fine here. I love the campus . . . it's beautiful! People I have met are friendly and fun to learn new things with. What will make me more comfortable is to know that you are OK. If you ever need anything I am here for you. I love you with all my heart. We both know that life sometimes takes us in directions we least expect, but no matter where life takes me I know that I have you and I want you to feel the same about Claire and I. We are a family. Our relationship has grown so much and I know it can only get stronger in the future. Call me tomorrow. I want to talk to Little Eliot too. I love you soooo much! Tell Tinky hi give her some tuna juice. Give Mojo a spanking and hug . . . and after he's taken a bath spin him on a towel.

Love,
Shelley

November 2007

Hi, Daddy!

This little box was a gift from Mommy when I was in high school. I keep it with me during times of change. Inside is a necklace one of her dance students made after seeing *Afro Psalms*, and there is a tiny rose petal and a souvenir from our first trip from Connecticut to Nebraska. Keep it with you during your interviews!

Love,
Claire

P.S. I am on my way to the airport. Babies everywhere! I'm bored in Albany, but at least I got here. Taxi driver talked to himself, creepy old man on bus. Bad latte. Reading a book. Wow!

Reading Letters

Reading letters inside the iron lung was difficult enough, writing letters impossible. Before I wander off into a deep sleep on my long journey, I often speak into the monkey's voice box, hoping one day my recordings will be transcribed at the New Britain Public Library.

The iron lung started to fall into a black hole, and the Hawking Institute of Light and Gravity surmised it would be able to escape the event horizon during a lull in the Perseid meteor shower. Johnny Roach passed his time puffing on black licorice electric cigarettes and a long black pipe filled with Borkum Riff once smoked by John Gardner as he circled Dante's inferno on his motorcycle through the Green Mountains at Breadloaf. He sat on the long half-circle porch with Asimov during the long afternoons. He looked out and said:

"The loins of the mountains."

Asimov leaned his head and unruly hair into the sun with its long early 1970s sideburns like the ones he saw on his father and Fred Sanford. This was the blessing to the universe of the deranged and prosperous men who carried long knives into a battle royale between the haves and those had never seen the ocean, never left their hometown in Nebraska, never met a black man outside of prison or the asylum, never drove past 75 mph on I-80, never believed in the not believing of God and Satan wearing a kilt and driving a tractor between irrigated rows of soil left to drought and pig shit, they knew the aurora borealis, the shifting stars above the low center of their lives, a fountain of beauty under their feet on the hollow ground, aquifer of desire and the smell of money rising off the tarp and foul shower head, wash and dry cycle in the turbulence of fire clouds and the dust-to-dust in the vineyards and raindrops tapping the burnt-out drive-in, this is what was seen off the highway, driving east to the true Midwest, a family in a private prairie schooner with a wife, two daughters, a cat who ran into the wilderness following the blue eye of the moon's wreckage, headed south of the badlands, south of a wind that descended out of the inferno and out of the heavens and howled each night, the front yard hail storm and purple clouds turned black to orange into a tornado, lifting the roofs and pavement and bank notes blown into the sky as the animals were incinerated and school children prayed.

Whoever invented the bicycle built for two also invented a flying machine built for one prisoner. In Texas, they found the warden of the asylum had placed a video camera above the urinal inside the bathroom used by those who walked into the death chamber. The black eye of the camera rotated like a deranged cyclops after being run over by a jeep in a Hollywood movie trailer. The eye stared directly at the electric chair. It was first used by a young Edison in a dream, waiters brought trays of popsicles to the prisoners half-alive on a summer porch, the lilac they planted had grown and weaved into the barbed wire that surrounded the walls like tinsel under the moonlight in snowfall, he used the skin of peasants stretched and dried over tobacco leaves for the wings of the flying machine, although his bedwetting continued on the top bunk bed in his room as a child, he was no longer followed on Facebook nor praised as the sleepwalker inside his iron lung, he was known to suddenly become awake and healed, Parkinson's had left his body, pain had left his bones, and the pink flesh and threads inside his spinal cord and the wound at the back of his neck became whole, he danced and skipped along the pond in Bushnell Park, he tumbled and rolled like a child down the hill at Smith Elementary School, sky pilots lifting off at the Air Force base, a large red ball floating and rising into the air forever, his father's handkerchief once hanging from the clothesline above the grapevines, pushing the braided rope hand-over-hand out toward summer and the arc of human color, hoisted by the soldiers after night fighting and hand-to-hand combat with fist and bayonet, a white handkerchief in the left pocket of his sharkskin suit, raised outside of the flying machine, he surrendered to his life to the country that captured him as he ran AWOL into the wilderness, absent from his post, not intending to desert until he heard the voice of the archangel amputee, and saw him seated inside a row boat, fishing line cast into the baptismal waters, over his wool blanket and bad shoulder into the fog, there was a lighthouse, siren, blue coral, small fires, a compass in his vest pocket, one wing, caught in the hunger of gravity, pulled out of his back, fell out of the heavens, spin and fall, maple leaf, mid-air parasol, kiss, snowfall, corner kid, switchblade, high school sweater, typewriting class, stock options, ready for the homecoming queen and after-dance schoolyard rumble.

Johnny Roach fell in love at first sight. First among thousands at the Bushnell Jazz Festival under a blue sky, Dexter Gordon played in front of picnic tables set up for the wedding of the beggar's daughter, city folks danced around a maypole as they had for the spring equinox, first touched her hand as she closed her eyes and turned away, grounded, ignited, love's eternal twin, outside they took a broom to the snow on the cars, she drove and parked next to his car, embraced.

"May I kiss you?" he asked.

"Do you want to?" she asked.

Snow and dwarf stars. Snow owl. The velvet wolf. Their faces under the birch trees.

His peasant lawyers would ask for a stay until they gathered more evidence of his alleged crime against nature, war, and country. The prison doctor noticed a soylent blue tint in his brown eyes, on his wooden teeth and fingertips. His eyes turned colors like a whip. The Ministers of the Heart tossed rose petals on the floor of his jail cell, soiled mattress, the polka-dotted linoleum floor, and three floors to the basement into the nest of blue-yellow jackets. Was it Tom Thumb's luck spooled by the charred hand of God, gyroscope welded to the bumper of the flying machine, tied to the English saddle thrown over a fence at Lucy's Love Palace, he held a six pack, deck of cards, serpent's cane, jumping beans in his vest pocket, carved out of petrified wood, jumping beans inside his vest pocket, a thimble of his rare blood type drawn into a test tube before his execution.

They placed the soylent blue crystal ball in front of the electric chair. It was not what the future held for him, it was how the future held his past, and the present was a dance of embers inside the ghost in the machine. He set his Timex alarm to his feeding time and the compass to true north. He turned down the volume on the radio and then heard the telephone ring three times. There was no voicemail. The prison hourglass fell off his bedroom dresser, dust shoveled out of the hollow ground turned into a mist and filled his breathing tube inside the iron lung. He saw that on this night above the world there was love and it was rare.

"There are no black holes," he said.

The prison doctor and his staff concocted the elixir of death based on a recently unearthed cookbook under the Egyptian tomb of the African boy king Leo Africanus. There was beer and there was death. The elixir was to make the transition less painful yet workable. It was a handwritten hieroglyph green liquid mixed for hours with brewer's yeast, red clay, licorice, devil's claw, eye bright, absinthe, wormwood, lye, Drano, spearmint, and a secret sauce sautéed in pentobarbital smooth Negro Peanut Butter carried during the summer by horseback and the mayor's one-eyed mule in a charred sweet oak cask from the Blue Ridge Mountains of North Carolina and Tennessee to the prison gate. They poured it into the preacher's silver flask that he used with for his moonshine New Year's Eve midnight service. He was known in the backwoods of the brick steeple to take the flask from under his white robe and with one hand twist the cap and guzzle like a scalded hog thrown into the Dismal River.

A tiny droplet was found to be lethal for twenty-four hours, dispensed by a Walgreen's eye dropper or ground and stabilized into a single Bayer's orange baby aspirin. It did not work with cod liver only, something to do with the level of salt water and radiation in the bladders of captive dolphins and other marine life and the blue-faced chimpanzee who danced on its one leg at the county fair. The foreign press reported on protests for a meeting at the Hague for the release of Pussy Riot and the gay athlete imprisoned for wearing tights. At the zoo, they tested the potion on the gorilla, panther, baby hippo, tiger, llama, bluebird, chickadee, panda, canary, Minotaur, manikin, and the honey and African bees.

The long needle was inserted into his funny bone and threaded through the inside elbow, and in this case a bullet hole helped the prison doctor find the prisoner's corridor of flesh, illuminated by the Eveready flashlight between his yellow teeth, a searchlight into the man's eyes, anus, mouth, ears, penis, and nostrils, and the surgeon determined the gentleman was in perfect health to die in holy matrimony.

They lowered his iron lung head-first into a wishing well. It was tied to a wrecking ball and floated for three nights from the balcony of the Bushnell Theater in Hartford under the purple chandelier. The mop bucket was filled with pennies and blue coral and tied by a sailor's knot. Whenever he was moved in his iron lung, blood settled into his head and forced his eyes closed. Those who often made a wish vanished. Those who made one good wish spoke of the angel landing on their bad shoulder. Those who made two wishes at first were wrong. Those who made three wishes went from cuffed burlap pants to cashmere scarves after a thunderstorm filled the well. They found too late that the antidote for love was love and dumb luck a cousin to the fool.

The children fished for treasure using ball string and paper clip, and police were interested in a toenail claimed to a part of the unsolved murder of the can collector who rode side-saddle with extra large garbage bags on a twenty-foot bicycle he extended using chains and PVC pipe, and often had a large rooster riding in a basket on the handlebars. He was the retriever of aluminum cans on a bicycle built for his amputated left foot that took him weaving for a mile before he steadied himself and rolled into tight alleys, they say he did not see the speeding truck with no brakes flying down West Main Street and plowing into the wretched men and women who sat half out of their dimpled minds under their drunk parasols of grief, mouths open as the can man's warrior bird landed in the arms of the golden angel. There was a fountain where they cleansed their feet and sang "Amazing Grace," half-frozen donuts, lukewarm coffee, and free Bibles for the brokenhearted and forlorn citizens. The woman chain-smoked in her wheelchair. The young man lifted his long black coat of life over his neck and drank out of a long bottle of 151 rum. The church bell rang at South Congressional Church. The brass doors to the underground lavatories flew open, names of his high school friends on the war memorial broke off the wall. Who had claimed responsibility for the crime, threw stones through the church window, cut the climbing rope into the wishing well and what gentleman soldier on a weekend pass drove full speed and laughed like a champion as he rolled into a crowd of jolly good fellows in soiled burlap pants standing under the willow tree?

The iron lung was connected to the White House, a pardon from the electric chair might come after the lighting of the annual Christmas tree. The telephone operator held the call for three hours in case the retrievers of the dead sought refuge in the cathedral overnight.

There was no reprieve for the man cursing and shadow boxing a bare porch light on the cellar stairwell. He stopped, looked at the officer of the court, and pissed into a broken window, jumped into his jeep and ran over the chain a hundred times preventing the artists from using a driveway. He was a former taxi driver for the Yellow Moon Cab Company, with clients who once traveled the chitlin' circuit, broke the chains of gospel and barbed wire of rhythm and blues and made it to *Soul Train*. He was once a young jackal raised on gumbo and *The Weekly Reader*, a privileged and desperate fool who became a manager for a company of Mason jars filled with cleansed varieties of blueblood and given a job based on nepotism and the high school drinking club, no skills and artless.

"That's not art nor penmanship, they, and we, can't give that ruptured art away at the Goodwill, and the Salvation Army placed his canvas next to a White Negro Velvet Elvis above the men's room urinal upside down, he was the All-American, cursed, wretched, ageist, racist, and misogynist little boy blue. he was a child wearing a Travolta open shirt and gold chain. He was a child in a child's body, they read."

Using paste and chalk, he assisted in the gang rape of his best friend's girlfriend in sixth grade in his homeroom, and inside his overturned jeep he was given a ADBHAA (A Drunk Believing He's An Artist) at Dairy Queen, one day knowing too well that drunk and high and Lucky Strikes and art do not mix well without a gift or talent or vision.

Self-knowledge was once the highest form of intellect and confidence a fraud. The stop sign invented for us invited us to look both ways. How one appears to others when they open their door and walk into the world. The man in rags, the beggar in a top hat, a married man who knows he is gay and wears a muscle shirt to bed, the drifter who paused on the railroad track, looked up, and saw a whip-poor-will fall out of the sky.

He leaned over and turned on the left side of his thinning body without bedsores and looked out at the small planet Earth under the sunroof inside his diamond back iron lung. The periscope was able to record the fine lettering on the two-dollar bill on the mirror taped to the mirror inside Bob's Barber Shop. The backroom vitals of numbers sent on a black rotary telephone, a working class casino with nude magazines and Johnny Walker Red, Saturday morning was a family reunion for the city, a neighborhood church with children dropped off and placed into a chair above the chair, strapped into a straightjacket for the sound of shears inside their ears, arms flinging on a rodeo pony, high-pitched screams, a funny bone let me out of this chair before I throw a devil's fit, caught in a whirlwind of blades on the neck and hands on top of the forehead, holding down, capping the oil spill, the geyser of no return, after-school runaway-from-home kind of afternoon, children's haircuts 60 cents, adults $1.10, a shave with a straight razor like a pirate's sword. What brought the holy house down, Oak Street, Winter Street, Cherry Street, gone, and what determines what leaves, stays, what thrives like a congregation wading in the baptismal waters? Who holds the wrecking ball, a pendulum, the blade swaying above the heads of the world, globes of retreat and desire, a razor, leather strap, their golden snaps, witch hazel, lilac, candy store, firehouse,

Elk's Club, City Hall elevator grate, buildings falling, factory workers asleep, children rising, choir singing about the Old Rugged Cross, live chickens on Lafayette Street, Capitol Lunch special sauce hot dogs on a grill, feel the earth under your feet, rain on your lips, the workers on strike, shot dead at the factory gate on hollow ground? There was the Lord's Prayer on driftwood, hundreds of praying hands wearing white gloves on wallpaper above the mirrors, a sign with No PROFANITY! And No CREDIT!, Hartford Barber College, the sink with a small hose to rinse the heads of the laborers, three generals wearing starched white jackets, the black box that created shaving cream, a magical foam rising out of the depths of the underworld, small wooden folding chairs, red and yellow leather chairs with aluminum arms, three barber chairs that stood like redwoods with forged steel and red leather seats, white coats in the science lab of hair and heads and afros, 70s sideburns, white collars on pin-striped sheets, the holy garments of the barber-surgeons.

Ode to Our Public, Magnet, Private, and Segregated Schools Without Art and Music and Writing

He was the hairless artist in his thirties on the fifth floor, his *Playboy* and *Hustler* magazines under his pillow. She was the woman who danced without music or men. This is what high school taught our children who remain children on the down low. The quicksand imported from Georgia flowed into his breathing tube as he slept in the iron lung. A shipwreck on its side, it floated until lifted by a crane used tongs to lower him into the earth with dirt first. He taught his classes at university with the air tank attached to his vest and the hose pinned to the lapel behind a dried chrysanthemum they found inside his high school yearbook. The bulletin board photograph with a recognizable face thirty years before, a student who died in a car crash a week after graduation, ice sculpture, its center as brilliant as the second ring of Saturn, the opal eyes of his grandmother, a lantern in the caverns of the heart held high by the beggar's daughter, black strap molasses, the iron lung slid down the gangplank into the ocean like a psalm, her bouquet thrown into the undertow of the underworld, yellow-topped grasshoppers bounced off the screen door, the frost on the green stems of winter collards, Concord grapevines like barbed wire, bees swarm above his head, torchlight, lilac, root cellar, father's green factory pants and shirt, black boots, a candle at each table, linen, Roosevelt Junior High School, homeroom class lined against the wall for his first dance, shoe shine boy, snow shoveler, newspaper boy, school photographer for the Red and Gold, senior prom, White Sands Beach, driftwood fire, wine, dancing until the morning light, seahorses, sand dollars, first kiss in salt air, whistling "Scarborough Fair" on WPOP AM radio, a reunion of Love and Darwin in biology, caught between slavery, war, and redemption, was the apparition he observed God's charred hand his discovery of human as flowers trampled by the gods they created in their stooped image, furred hands reaching for the celestial globes of fruit, bluebird, webbed toes and curved spine, wingless, first steps into fire, wings, whiplash, split tongue, pink venom inside the hourglass, elixir between humans and beast, alchemy of the soul to brain, meteor shower, pulling the carriage wheel out of the mud, half-life of a ghost star, canteen, brass cash register, ivory keys, waterfall, mirage, bottle filled with pennies at the barber shop, clean-shaven, stepped off the footstool into the brownfield. The police officer on horseback drowned at Shuttle Meadow Reservoir trying to save a child with his lasso. Was this path a long walk into a blue coral Hell proper, her sad face inside a wishing well, the last dance and love at first sight in her uncoiled arms under a planet spun out of widower's silk?

He worked many childhood jobs: newspaper boy delivering 120 papers a day, snow removal with a shovel, snow blower, floor sweeper at father's barber shop, cross-country summer double sessions, indoor track, and outdoor track practice, gravel, long spikes, clarinet practice, tenor saxophone, first job at the Ace Cleaning Company.

"Job for life in the city," the man told us.

With a piece of white chalk inside the sores of his mouth, he had to write a hundred times on the blackboard:

His father worked at the Fafnir Bearings Company, factory man from 11 to 7 on the night shift making ball bearings forty years, a barber from 9 to 5 forty years, a landlord of the three-story tenement, and he rented the second, third, and attic apartments, holiday barbecues. Kept a garden and Concord grapes, Italian gentleman pruned the grapevines each fall…

Father loved his family.

"That's my son," he said.

Mr. Johnny Roach

I WAS BORN in working class New Britain, Connecticut. My father worked at the Fafnir Bearings Company, factory man from 11 to 7 on the night shift making ball bearings forty years, a barber from 9 to 5 forty years, a landlord of the three-story tenement, and he rented the second, third, and attic apartments, holiday barbecues. Kept a garden and Concord grapes, Italian gentleman pruned the grapevines each fall. I worked several child-hood jobs: newspaper boy delivering 120 papers a day, snow removal with a shovel and snow blower, floor sweeper at father's barber shop, cross-country summer double-sessions, indoor track, and outdoor track practice, lettered in all three, they called me a Jock-Poet and said I recited poems as I walked downtown, gravel tracks, long spikes, photographer, clarinet practice, tenor saxophone, first job at the Ace Cleaning Company. My career started in the Roosevelt Junior High gym when I fractured the side of my right foot playing dodge ball. It was the only day I missed school in twelve years. They placed a plaster cast below my knee to my foot. I caught the measles the next week. I broke the cast several times jumping in the wilderness.

As a lad, I tried to read every book in the world at the New Britain Pub-lic Library, and I won first prize in a photography contest at the YMCA. I worked as a photographer for the local newspaper The New Britain Herald. *I developed photographs on the old three-tray system, and I still have a few faded marks on my fingers when I didn't wear gloves and dipped them into the fixer. I used a plastic sheet on one roller and set the diamond shapes that transferred to another blue plastic on a roller that was sent to the newsroom production room. I listened to the police radio and jumped on my bicycle and photographed fires, protests, proms, and football games and the same day or next day "Photo by Fort" appeared on the front page.*

I wrote two short stories in second grade: "The Three Little Bears," my version, and a Halloween story titled "Booooooooooooooooooooooooooooo," with exactly twenty-seven o's. I graduated and won the undergraduate poetry prize, I actually won second prize but thought I should have won first. I received 5 bucks and bought 5 bottles of Boone's Farm wine I shared with other wounded freshmen. At Siena Heights College I was taught by poet John Woods who wore an ascot and drove a Triumph convertible with wire spokes on the wheels.

As an undergraduate, I attended the Cranbrook Writers' Conference held at the Cranbrook Art Academy in Bloomfield Hills, Michigan, three summers in a row. I also attended Breadloaf two summers before I graduated.

I left Michigan on a Greyhound with one dollar and found myself under a tree being taught by Mark Strand who had a red sweater around his neck and a tennis racket under his arms. At Breadloaf there was King Ciardi. There was John Gardner in his leather jacket smoking Borkum Riff in a long black pipe. I heard Robert Hayden read his poems and mocked by three other older black writers for not being black enough and I suppose not being political enough. I did not say anything although they completely misrepresented who he was as a writer and his powerful observations of a lynching and other subjects of his time and history. I should have said something. I did write a poem titled: "For Robert Hayden." It can be found in my first book. It mentions nothing about what happened as a young black man on top of the Green Mountains, but it does have everything to do with the event. Years later, after reading Marilyn Nelson's definitive essay "Owning the Masters," I created and moderated a panel at AWP inspired by Hayden and Nelson: "Afro-Formalist Poets: 'Owning the Masters.'" One good moment at Breadloaf was sitting on its long porch, as if I were inside a time machine with Isaac Asimov, his long 70s sideburns, running into the audience tearing cigarettes from the mouths of fools before he lectured without notes. I looked out at the Green Mountains, and I said to him: "The Loin of the Mountains," and he looked at me and nodded his head.

As an undergraduate I read The Stranger, Starship Troopers, *Kissinger. I took several courses in cultural anthropology, sociology, poly sci, theology of* peace, theology of social action, and liberation theology. I wrote also wrote poems instead of the required essays. That doppelganger to academe didn't last long. I was given five incompletes in my last semester. They locked me in a room with blue exam books as high as a cathedral ceiling. I passed and graduated with Honors in Creative Writing. It must have been the first such award, since they gave me textbooks: The Short Story and something about literary criticism. I still have them, and for the first time, as I write this, I understand why they did so.

As a fellow at MacDowell, I met Catherine Bateson, daughter of Margaret Mead, who was also in residence at the time. I only mention her roots because as an undergraduate I read a book called, A Rap on Race, taped discussions with Mead and Baldwin in London with controversial statements by Mead. I mentioned the book to Catherine, who months later, after leaving MacDowell, sent me the videotape of her mother and Baldwin. Blessings sometimes arrive in a shoe box.

Years later in graduate school I met Lillian Gish who to this day, to me, was a living ghost. I also performed in my first and last play. The director of the Hoo Doo Theater scripted the works of James Baldwin.

He was a visiting professor for as long as he wished at Bowling Green State University, and after he had flown in from Paris, he stood before the crowd and presented a masterful lecture.

I published a compiled interview with Mr. Baldwin, and I always call his short story, "Sonny's Blues," a poem.

I have won a few prizes and awards, and perhaps I might receive a few more. As Baldwin stated, "Write what you have to write." He knew too well of that premise in his support of William Styron in his battle with The Confessions of Nat Turner. I must note that I have been awarded tenure three times at three different universities, a record since recorded history or at least Aristotle. I mention it not for glory but a nod to insanity. I left each with my wife and two daughters as if on a Prairie Schooner drifting into the black hole of the dust bowl. It, no doubt, has taught my daughters that one can go where they need to go as Stafford knew. I loved/love teaching.

The fact that I was able to write and publish as much as I did was simply the voice of my father circling above my knotted head: Work, son.

My scholarship uses archival research on the creative process and what has been called Genetic Criticism. One example focuses on my poem "We Did Not Fear the Father." I gathered its entire text, first drafts to final draft, letters from the editors and publishers of The Georgia Review *and* The Best American Poetry. *I trace the entire poem from the original title, writing in long hand, correspondence with editors, suggestions on its form and content, final draft, and publication.*

This is one example in the title poem of my book: "We Did Not Fear the Father." It was completed in three years. The first year of drafts took the shape of a prose poem. The second year examined the form. There were shorter lines and stanzas in quatrains. I attempted to use the line "We did not fear the father" as the approximate line length of the entire work. The third year defined its metaphor, rhythm, and meter. I also used a longer line length: "We did not fear the father as the barber who stood," and I found the emphasis I had originally sought in the shorter form remained. I also sustained the poem's unity and its narrative elements by using the phrase as a refrain.

There are two key transitions in the poem. "We did not fear the father until he entered the tomb of noise. The ashes in the furnace are lifted by love and fear."

The son fears his father's weariness. We did not fear the father until he stooped in the dark and mortality even as his father lifts his sons and daughters like birds into the top bunk beds. The time clock was a pendulum inside his father's heart that kept him half alive.

The father had a wife, seven children, holiday barbecues, summer garden, and a small black and white fox terrier named Frisky. The father was a working man who toiled on the nightshift making ball bearings in New Britain, Connecticut (once called the Hardware City of the World) from 11:00 P.M. to 7:00 A.M. for forty years.

The father was a barber from 10:00 A.M. to 6:00 or 7:00 P.M., depending on the head count, for forty years. The father was a landlord in his three-

story tenement. He rented the second and third floor, and attic apartments. He was on call twenty-four hours a day. I wanted to capture the three jobs he held well as his fourth and fifth: he was our father and the scaremonger.

As a writer, I have been under the Anxiety of Influence, and as a lad, I have gone in and out of favor with a list of writers too long to name. It has taken me long years of reading, writing, and listening, at times, with a keen eye and heart, to know we do the best we can with such literary matters.

I have taught at the highest level of the university. My endowed chair presented me those rights and privileges we read, if we are so lucky in this deranged and prosperous world, on a college degree. I have received the Outstanding Scholarship and Research Faculty Award at the University of Nebraska at Kearney and the Faculty Scholar Award, Southern Connecticut State University. My work ("We Did Not Fear the Father" and "The Vagrant Hours," respectively) appears in The Best American Poetry 2003 and The Best American Poetry 2000. Carnegie Mellon University Press, under its Classic Contemporary Series, published my first book, The Town Clock Burning. My literary awards include: the 1996 The Writer's Voice Poetry Award (Judge: Grace Paley) for "On Being Invisible (For Ralph Ellison)"; the 1990 Poetry Society of America, Mary Davis Memorial Award, for my libretto Born on a River (The City of Wilmington, North Carolina), and the 1985 Randall Jarrell Poetry Prize for "The Writer at His Desk." I was the first editor and co-founder and first editor of The Xavier Review in New Orleans. Several of my poems have been translated into French and Spanish and published in France and Argentina. In 1996, I received a full residency at The McDowell Colony.

My undergraduate college now called Siena Heights University will present me with the Honorary Doctorate of Humane Letters, Honoris Causa, in May 2014. I am the founder of the Wendy Fort Foundation Theater of Fine Arts dedicated to my late wife a modern dancer and choreographer, and I am currently writing a novel: The Last Black Hippie in Connecticut.

He was the first man placed in solitary confinement inside the iron lung. The prison doctor and tailor were called in to record the exact measurements of his sharkskin suit. They were concerned about his height and the length of his sharecropper arms. Holes would be made at the end and sides of the iron lung to accommodate his feet and arms. The warden received letters of protest against making Johnny comfortable inside during his internment on death row. The court-appointed attorney wore a Madras bow tie and wingtips, to submit a writ of habeas corpus to allow for the holes. The court jester demanded justice and a key witness against Johnny recanted on the stand and said Johnny was at the wishing well far from the site of the crime. There was a stay of execution.

The holes were allowed.

Senators and House members gathered in the underground tombs below the city and listened to the church brethren plead for punishment that fit the crime against nature and humanity and a reversal of the holes was made before the justice of peace. The prison doctor was brought in by stagecoach to amputate Johnny's arms and feet. Both sides were pleased. There would be holes.

There would be holes in his feet and arms.

His torso floated in thin air on a breathing tube. They removed and converted a solar panel into a small wood stove underneath the iron lung. There was warmth, redemption, a star of brief wonder. They talked low of how his hands and feet suddenly caught fire and lowered the iron lung into lake water. The innocent felt safe. The criminal was made whole. Neighborhood watches were opened to the public. Free lanterns were distributed for the expected eternal blackout caused by nuclear winter and blotted sun, polar ice cap against a cruise ship, earthquake followed by a tsunami on the East Coast, poison cranberries, newborns without eyes, traffic light on the blink, minutemen vaporized by faith, the collapsed city, burning island, scorched surface of the earth, boiled alive, tarmac of flags, retrievers of the half-breathing spoils, flares across the night sky, salute to the brave and selfless armies of war and fame, survivors under the town clock burning, boarding a train headed for the shallow river, conductor for the waterproofed and flag-draped iron lung, tinsel of grief and amphibious grains of light. Punishment in the field became a crime in the city. Crime in the city became a punishment in the field.

Johnny Roach played solitaire and wore Google glasses with his lips on a breathing tube on his ride into Las Vegas inside a Prairie Schooner They made the chain gang carry shovels behind a twenty-mule team. The prisoner found the parachute wrapped around his iron lung three miles off course. It was to land next in Key West during the Hemingway look-alike contest. It was one of Johnny's last requests to grow a beard, participate, and win before his execution.

They found him among the palm trees wrapped inside a hammock. A Good Humor truck was sent to the scene, and they had to remove boxes of orange creamsicles to make room for the iron lung. They needed to lower his body temperature and emptied buckets of ice borrowed from the third-floor ice machine at Lucy's Love Palace. They had a parade for Johnny's homecoming and placed roller skates under the iron lung. School children were given the day off to pull Johnny down Main Street. The town folks and tourists were able to view the iron lung as he rested inside the backroom of a chapel illuminated by the holy ghost. They pushed flowers into the holes of the iron lung where his feet and arms had, at one time, gone limp.

He rested there for a week. The children were brought into town inside wooden carts. They ran into the vestibule and waited to hear the chimes of the Good Humor truck parked under a willow. They lowered their holy bells and blew out the white candles placed around the iron lung. One child claimed he saw Mother Mary on one stick of her twin blue popsicle. Two for a nickel. Although there was no verification, they wept at her feet. One child witnessed the noble angel land on the steeple, one saw Satan behind the wheel drag racing, wearing sunglasses, his gnarled tail wrapped around the radio antenna, listening to smooth jazz, a bottle of 40, wearing overalls, blue and brown disco platform shoes, jeans with a leather strip down the sides, top hat and magic wand he used to tap the head of each child after he had taken the guest elevator down to the basement where they had gathered in the baptismal water, the spigot was turned off inside the iron lung, the fresh air tank that pumped the elixir into the breathing tube malfunctioned in the heat and the blackbird in its cage let out a cry and fell to its side.

He read the story of Tom Thumb who was born in the back seat of a Cadillac convertible that drove over a cliff and overturned in the Mojave Desert and with his bare foot stuck under the gas pedal was the only survivor because of his short stature in the world. There was a rumor in *Reader's Digest* that Tom Thumb was kept inside the iron lung as a child. His parents thought of him as a doll asleep in the middle of a king bed with his burnt eyelash and viper tongue.

Tom's body was covered in straw and rolled under Johnny's thin mattress. Tom Thumb was buried with a 40-ounce bottle of Colt 45 malt liquor in his hand that had been broken by the wheel of a jumbo jet that had flown the iron lung from Switzerland. The pilot diverted the plane to Mississippi after he saw a halo in the cracked windshield and somehow glided the jet and landed in the last known cotton field in Dixie. Johnny tried to look away from the exit aisle where they had tied his rented iron lung to the aeroplane wings as a fireball and black smoke and trailed behind the tires and the landing gear snapped into feathers. Jeeps and soldiers with machine guns and ambulances with priests fell in line on both sides of the plane. The captain was able to pull the ejector button and was seen floating above a family barbecue pit with a wild hog being turned with the steering wheel of a 1955 Ford. His co-pilot was found upside down in quicksand, and his oxygen mask intact, accidentally filled with laughing gas in the machine shop, had left him convulsing on the shore of the muddy river, after the fire had burned his arms and legs to ash.

Tom Thumb was placed as a newborn into a small basket used for a crib at the local orphanage. They dressed him in a vest and sleeves of lace. Perhaps they gave him a top hat and wooden cane to suggest that despite his unnatural size he was beyond his years and commanded the respect of those who greeted him at the carnival of fools and freaks who observed such things as if what they saw attracted and repulsed their tongues against the cell bars and small window in the tent and the crowd turned their heads to the sky as Tom Thumb and Johnny Roach waved and the helicopter lifted off the makeshift air strip rooftop. Johnny Roach and Tom Thumb fell asleep half alive inside the iron lung nearly far enough away from a just and miniature world.

The helmsman, seated in the front of death's carriage, snapped his whip into colors on the back of the riderless horse.

"If you break a horse, you can break a man," he said.

They turned they heads as the broken wheel rolled down Main Street into the Tavern of Fools. One black man who talked loud and unclear drank Bombay gin out of his boot, spat, a woman in a long dress and pearls laughed alone in the corner booth, the ill-mannered young man, who knew little of himself and the world, wore a football helmet and a team jersey, and spoke of a wild caravan of nude women in his dreams as he placed his penis inside a mug of beer, and prepared to hunt for the strange beast sighted by a farmer under the harvest moon. Tonight Johnny was rolled to the middle of the dance floor under a chandelier of elves. They waltzed around the iron lung, in a quiet tribute and fear of the soldier who had won two purple hearts and a bronze star for the wounds to his head and spine and the valor he revealed placing a mask on the face and mouth of fellow soldier as the mustard gas changed the color of his brown eyes to milky white stars.

If you break a horse, you can break a man inside the iron lung, a runaway in a field, hog-tied to a post in the well of a ship, legs and arms fed to the sea, the body dipped in boiling oil, human heads staggered between rows of bluebird houses, genitals displayed in large jars, the poker player with his last silver dollar, charred remains of a child behind the bowling alley, fire spread across the rooftops, a seaquake once in a millennium, the altered coastline left a moraine from Maine to the Gulf Coast and a landscape of barbed wire, blue coral, smokestack, mortar shell, magnifying glass, uprooted graves pharmaceutical bottle, carpet, ball bearing, painting, newsreel, tires, wooden cart, baseball glove, church bell, gangplank, family Bible, chestnut, Vermentino, scarf, glue, manikin smoking a cigar, wingtip, ship in a bottle, music stand, stamp collection, butterfly, and the first edition of Webster's blue-backed speller.

The helmsman looked for a blacksmith to repair the broken wheel and nail one gold horseshoe to a pink hoof. The way he found salvation was how he removed the schoolboy loafers of the gentleman soldier on a weekend pass who wrote poems in one final act of war and gave a last kiss to the dying man in his arms.

Prison staff and the governor's office gave exclusive filming rights of the last execution to the *Daily Planet* newspaper. The lottery of ball and chain was created to allocate reservations for the world press. School children using toy metal detectors had recovered cannonballs from the Civil War under the monkey bars. Chains used on the ankles and wrists of former slaves were a perfect fit on Johnny inside the iron lung. The sunken ship off the Connecticut coastline provided the gray chains, anchor, lantern, gangplank, captain's wheel, and ship's log sent to the Supreme Court in the third act.

Although it would be televised live around the globe, those allowed to watch the execution behind the red velvet curtain, six feet in front of the electric chair, were given Polaroid Land cameras for sixty-second photographs to capture the instant of death and instant of knowing as if they sat inside a birthing room. There was a live feed sent to the space shuttle filled with Super Bowl videos and experiments on plants grown in the Garden of Eden.

Fifty thousand people gathered at Walnut Hill Park in front of a movie screen borrowed from Lowe's Drive-In and lowered from the roof of the music shell. Boxed lunches were prepared by the mayor's office filled with a bottle of Avery's birch beer soda, Capitol Lunch hot dogs, and kielbasa sandwiches. The Strand canceled a matinée of *The Sound of Music*. The electric chair would be taken to theaters of the world and introduced by Elizabeth Cotten singing "Freight Train." Elizabeth "Libba" Cotten (January 5, 1893 – June 29, 1987) was an American blues and folk musician, singer, and songwriter. Cotten

wrote "Freight Train" at 11 years old when she saw a train pass by on
the State University Railroad spur behind her house on Lloyd Street
in Carrboro, North Carolina. A self-taught left-handed guitarist, Cotten developed her own original style. Her approach involved using
a right-handed guitar (usually in standard tuning), not re-strung for
left-handed playing, essentially, holding a right-handed guitar upside
down. This position required her to play the bass lines with her fingers
and the melody with her thumb. Her signature alternating bass style
has become known as "Cotten picking."

They lowered and swung his iron lung into the freight train. Several other experiments were set up inside the machine. They sought
to discover the origins of life and language. The microbial beast swal-
lowing the bacterial foam, a beaker filled with Crispr, his bedside
kaleidoscope, the pot of hot grits over the gas flame, a photograph and
taped voice of a ghost, the splitting of the genome inside the human
heart into ten thousand psalms, a misfired volley by the hand of the
drunken sailor, a fleck of life born out of steam and mud inside rivulets
of desire, the third eye socket, tweed vest and pocket watch, twin drawings on Earth and Mars, the plants and animals, a species of rainbow
flora, the New England Claw under a stone fence, spelling bee, the first
word uttered by a human voice, *Becos*, alphabet of stars above the bassinet, tongue grown inside a dirt cellar, watercolors of the eye, wreckage
under the moon's grace, the baby grand and large red bow, helioscope,
the devil's tail caught in the ringer washing machine, what kind of life
first appeared in the smoke and woe tumbler of ash and sea meteor and
sky geyser, a five-inch waddle of flesh and thumb and finger able to
pinch a page of light and thin stone, and they spoke of birth and the
alignment of the moon, stars, and sun, nobody spoke a word as they
slept on hollow ground, mouths covered in thatch, the bloated calf in
the shallow river, a curse thrown down from the heavens into the lap
of the devil's throne, three wishes, fortune, a blessing made before the
vagrant hour of lost speech, sons and daughters marched into perpetual holy war under a chandelier of fire, half-globe and discarded maps,

one mile of ocean left to those who prayed, ten paces and a duel left to those who claimed a blood right, one mile of desert for those who claimed a kinship to water, three miles of fertile land for the keeper of the barnyard, a thousand miles of fence post for the retrievers of the buffalo, one mile of high cliffs for those who tamed the wild horses, a half-mile for the hooded birds trained on logs, one square acre of blue sky for the peacemakers who un-boarded the warships and staked their claim, one step into for the heaven sent eternal flame, the forlorn war-lords sent into quicksand, children who planted a mile of barbed wire left to the wakeful asylum who were also given the spoils of beauty, and there was nothing at the bottom of the rum barrel and nothing like one open hand reaching for gold coins spinning to earth.

What kind of life?

What kind of life? The life revealed in the letter of a man sentenced to death. It came down to choosing a sharkskin suit, double-breasted wool, or a prison-striped jump suit, rainbow green, topsoil of ocean tide, saltwater metallic undertow, two black pearl buttons, two-tone cordovans, spats, or wing tips, wristwatch, undershirt, no underwear for proper disposal of his urine and feces, tweed vest, a minuet of flesh and electric blood pulse in the open vein of his neck, photograph at the family picnic, dog whistle, rubber tube, wind storm, Weather Channel forecast of rain, blue fog settled over the city, anchor lifted out of the mud, wooden cart pulled under the town clock, silver dollar in a shoe box, typing his last words about seeing a dolphin of stars in a sweet dream, white flag, drowned body, heart-shaped scar on the cheek, left-over mustard and sardines, canteen, beauty and the beast, wedding plans inside the mausoleum of desire, kissed the hand of the ruby doll, lifted her body out of the bassinet and tossed her clothes into a laundry basket, rubbing alcohol over the joints of her arms, knees, open the wired jaw, prison shower closed, prepared for the possibility of a par-don on a rotary phone, prepared to be executed by the hanging judge and hangman's noose, silver bullet firing squad, long knives used to tear the ground thrown into the shadow behind a white sheet, burned alive inside a sleeping bag, tennis racket and boomerang in the trunk of the limousine, war monument flowers, solitaire, fishing pier, buoy, commandeered clipper ship, derailed freight and capsized boat, treading water, retrievers of the dead pause for a three-bank pool shot, stop talking and start chalking, barbed wire vineyard, carton of cigarettes, lunch tray, last request for a Victrola and 78s (Stravinsky, Hendrix, Beethoven, Miles, Beatles, Van Gogh, Stephen Hawking), repeating rifle, target on the chest, hollow point bullets, derby with a crossbow, false teeth, wire-rim glasses, he was awakened under moonlight and dressed in the prison chapel behind a two-way mirror, a bottle of *Echt Kolnisch Wasser No 4711 Original Eau de Cologne*, silver shoe horn, one dollar, money clip, Windsor knot, rock candy, a telephone rang twice, alarm clock startled Johnny, and he crossed his heart, read a psalm, tied his wingtips, and washed his face and hands in a bowl of rose water, looked out between the bars on his small window into the lilac garden. He twisted his jade wedding ring and placed it inside a Mason jar. He looked at the guard tower and saw a nest of starlings swerve into the tops of trees.

What kind of life? The healing and laying-on-of-hands inside the iron lung, a viper placed around his neck, a lariat of pearls, silver necklace on his daughter's neck, flesh pulled out of his broken spine, warm tentacles of the sea on his forehead, sea snake on his wrist, elixir, bitter, eye drop of venom, hot towel on his back, black widow, espresso cup, X, treasure map, amber alert for a buried iron lung last seen floating above the earth in stardust and satellite debris, astronaut urinal, stolen World Series hardball, stolen from the Governor's summer house on the Cape at low tide, small boats filled with black children from Hartford, Bridgeport, and New Haven, bearing a Bazooka Joe flag landed on private Connecticut shoreline, beached sea life and washed out eyes, the young boy dove into high water and swam to the pier, placed a map of his neighborhood into a bottle of Moxie soda pop and raised his to stake a claim on the open sea, captain of a reckless ship at sea, the young man held the rope and harpoon and struck the side of a gray whale half alive in nuclear run-off, bulging eye, snapped fin, caught inside barbed wire the underworld pool of time, nostrils that bled for months, hollowed shell of the sea turtle, otter bones, nest of blue eggs, hemp net of flora, blue coral, Chappie's brother-in-law to Loch Ness half-drowned face down and tossed into a geyser of oil and George Foreman Grill, here in the language of water was the alphabet of a salt throne, baby grand landed on the sea floor, notes of milky venom in absinthe spoons, *anchors away, anchors away, anchors away, we are starboard and charmed by the ghost stars that guide us to a faraway land with mermaids and sunken treasure and barrier islands kept from us for four hundred years after the hanging judge declared a reprieve for the retrievers of those lost at sea or thrown overboard in the hysteria of yellow fever, rickets, dysentery, did you see the blue mirage on the horizon between two mountains and forced the poison into the mouths of children after they waded into the undertow of the underworld?*

They found a smooth sea bottle inside a tin bucket buried in the family pit and placed it under the electric chair. Tom Thumb's black cape was pulled over his straitjacket. He broke the ivory walking stick over his knee, tossed a tourniquet of flowers over the bridge, swallowed a dime and threw a penny into the wishing well.

What becomes of love inside the iron lung? Spring arrives. Horse-shoes float. Croquet mallet. Unschooled fish. Butternut squash. Sunset Boulevard. *San Franciscan Nights.* Ben Cocoa laps rain water out of his hand. The people's truck threw boxes of popsicles under the maypole. Ribbon candy floated above the dulcimer. Goat-skin bottles of Spana-da. It was the year of the tumbleweed, finger though the bullet hole in the sculpture, rock 'n' roll and soul beyond the blues, a litter of chil-dren left inside a basket in the city hall elevator, rifles and reverie, bullet catchers in green fatigues, after a canteen of morphine and drip coffee, Johnny Roach was taken into custody for behavior unbecoming a sol-dier who threw his gun into quicksand, a peace offering after the night sky filled with tracers and bombs, shot in the head, shot through the helmet, shot through the elbow, left holes in the crippled ghost who rode shotgun in a caravan of de-boned sturgeon, it was a funny kind of

day with laughter in rain, a parasol caught in a clothesline in the tenement backyard, honeysuckle and barbed wire, white grapes, red and
yellow plum on a single branch, crabapple and rhubarb in the front
yard, chickens in cages, barrel, burning trash, something moved under
the ash, she had dropped newborn kittens into the flames, it was the
holiday neighborhood, The Blue Mirror Bar, Walt's Restaurant, The
Wedge, what is that sound, polka and rhythm and blues in the night
fog, blue bumblebees in a swarm above their heads, a Memorial Day
parade barbecue in honor of the fallen, *flowers to be trampled upon* by
the dispossessed gods who bathed in the fountain of youth poured into
dog-legged tubs with wine and honey and made love to peasants on
lamb's wool and sent out their warships, long hand of beauty, crowded
bus, subway, aeroplane, schoolyard, race track, gasoline, library, mall,
cruise ship, bowling alley, state fair, trigger finger, *Sky Pilot*, World
Series, Super Bowl, man-made earthquake, wedding ring, town clock,
equestrian jumps, cursive, ski jump, animal shelter, outdoor bluegrass
banjo, campus, post office, senior prom, graduation, cap and gown,
fiancé, sparkler, ice pond, Van Gogh, Uncle Ben's brown rice, Yellow
Cab to the diner in a blizzard, raspberry beret, rock candy, black licorice, square dance, twenty-mule team, blown into the hunger of gravity
and belly pool of time.

Johnny wrote a letter to his friend and lover:

Dear Wendy,

Before your leaving on Tuesday I wanted to tell you it was a good
day and night with you and there was no debutante ball in the world
that could hold a last dance candle for you . . . we started at Madison
Square Garden with you holding down your wide-brimmed hat in the
spring wind that warmed as the sun broke through the clouds . . . a
Yellow Cab brought us to the front of a sex shop and we walked to your
home to leave my Poet's Bag filled with Tarot and one good wish, there
was Olga (sp.) who seemed happy to see me entering your building and
life, the maid I think you said was simply surprised, I did not see many
men in your building, perhaps they were praying in their small rooms

for things they knew would not be answered . . . although it must have been their prayers that sent a psalm into the sewn mouths of your marionettes and a spirit that opened their eyes and raised their knobbed arms and legs in the dark, your angel boots with heels . . . the steep and broken steps into your building, the small café across from your corner, the way you removed your sweater over your head, we walked in all directions without direction, there was hyacinth, the *Strand Bookstore* where you saw time stir my memory, and we sat on a park bench listening to "Clair de Lune" . . . we stood and walked and shopped in your neighborhood of high-priced knee socks and entrepreneurs of the flawed heart, for our indoor picnic with good cheese and wine and the world watched over us, and as we crossed a street I played a jazz riff on your hand with my fingers, and if swooning made a claim on your heart, at that moment, l caught you as if you had fainted into my open arms on a train trestle, and one day I will look into your eyes and show you my way of *tying knots of breath around your body* . . . we sat across from one another, it seemed you were caressed under Madrid's copper light like a framed masterpiece, your beauty held by a shy beast, and you said something about handsome under the sailor's rope on the wall, and we sat at another cafe where the bartender knew your name and wanted to know more, a woman said she saw her own mother's eyes in yours and I was her father, we met a woman from France who wept twice, her roommate had hit her, although her tears may not have been real you offered her a part of your world, I sang a few verses of "In My Life" and you quickly joined me after a few lyrics: *There are places I remember / All my life though some have changed / Some forever not for better / Some have gone and some remain / All these places have their moments / With lovers and friends I still can recall / Some are dead and some are living / In my life I've loved them all,* and in your space with its fashionable cardboard coffee table stuffed with paper hearts like the puppets half-alive on strings, at the Mausoleum of American Art where you live, I read you three of my poems, we listened to jazz, we laughed and I nearly wept too with our stories of family and daughters and the way of the world, had black stonemasons built slave fences in Kentucky to keep themselves and livestock out on the border between heaven and hell? . . . you spoke of *The Book of Common Prayer*, and I knew the spirit in your heart was joy, with our first kiss you said my soft brown lips were made for playing any instrument perhaps a didgeridoo that soared with jazz notes and rhythm and blues of love and soul, and we kissed again and again and at one moment you must have called out Ben Cocoa, Ben Cocoa, a hundred times, and I felt as if there that there was some kind of happy god walking beside us and had brought us together in the chaos and magic of the world, I read a few of my poems to you: *I met you the day you were born / and there was a certain comfort in this . . . I gave you my breath / you gave me your own / When we met I was half in love with you.* We kissed. We parted. I threw you a kiss over the turnstile and you pursed your lips. Your face changed and I sensed a small sadness in our parting yet a larger joy in our meeting.

Ben Cocoa learned to shoot pool leaning over his father's arm at the card table and watching the one-armed player use his hat for a bridge at the Elk's Club. Three banks and a magic shot and "Stop Talkin' and Start Chalkin'" blared every five minutes. The crowd gathered around the pool table after Ben was challenged to four out of five games for a bottle of Wild Duck. The game would last for hours well into the morning before the milk truck delivered buttermilk to Mrs. John. There was low laughter and bad whiskey. It was a quarter to three and no sign of a thimble of honor in a game played on a hundred-year-old table made with lace hung on each corner where presidents once gathered after the war room. Tied three games, Ben needed a bathroom break, turned to the wall, shouted *Fuck me!* and pissed into his pork pie hat. The crowd went wild. They brought out cases of beer and Coca-Cola for the final game and handed out slot quarters for the juke-box and "Hello Stranger."

Somebody nailed a mallard to the wall next to a painting of the grand elk next to a lake and log cabin. The juke box played "Sunshine Superman." He walked into Guida's Dairy for a strawberry sundae with nuts and rode down Park Street hill and crashed as he turned left into the bushes. The sundae landed in a happy squirrel's nest, and Ben cried like a baby lamb pulled from his mother's teat for slaughter.

Johnny Roach took a bowling ball out of the trophy case and threw it down on the pool table like thunder and made a hole the size of the Sun. They called 911, and the man ran into the alley. The waitress almost caught him as he caught his foot in the sidewalk grill, but he left his work boot and ran barefoot into the snow.

Ben delivered Johnny a creamsicle behind bars. He was pardoned for reckless use of a bowling ball. The last game was never played. Ben and Johnny were sent to the front lines after signing papers at Selective Service Draft Board #1 at the Federal Building in Hartford.

It was a good day on Earth. It was a bad day in jail.

The Law of Land Warfare

They rolled the iron lung across the minefield and placed it on a freighter to New York City. It was lifted into a freight train and taken to New Britain, Connecticut's Central Park. Three gas lanterns were placed around his body, at his head, feet, and waist. The crowd stood for hours from the top of Broad Street to the front of city hall. The Band of Lepers played banjo and accordion. They were there to touch the metal frame and view his living quarters out of a periscope specially designed by the management of Stanley Tools and Connecticut Light & Power who found a solution daunting until they remembered how the Hubbell mirrors were based on a magnifying glass bought by a school kid who stole a Bazooka Joe bubblegum and used it in his science class the day Kennedy was shot with a silver bullet that floated into his neck and forehead like his bicycle streamer on July 4th as he burned the kaleidoscope wing of the monarch into black ash.

The mayor of New Britain declared all Section 8 housing moved and placed into one square mile on top of the mountain of waste he saw growing each year as a child growing with Johnny's father, Ben Cocoa, who drove the family into Boston and Fenway Park.

She re-named it Ugly Town in honor of the former Mayor and Chieftain Manafort who was said to be born with a pink spinal cord around his neck and saved by the high school nurse in the gym closet. The young UConn doctors examined the wrecking ball in his cuffed corduroy pants.

Ugly Town. Mines had to be placed at least 50 yards from public schools and libraries. The Chamber of Commerce called for the repeal of the law that required city workers to live in the Ugly Town they worked. Bomb shelters were opened from 5 p.m. to 8 a.m. for those caught in rush hour traffic and had to steer their cars back into the city of their birth.

In the first joint result from the world's two leading particle colliders, scientists have determined the mass of the iron lung to be the heaviest elementary particle, the top quark.

The measurement was made using the Large Hadron Collider (LHC) at CERN in Geneva, Switzerland, and the Tevatron at Fermilab in Batavia, Illinois. Four separate experiments found a joint value for the top quark of 173.34 (+/- 0.76) gigaelectron volts divided by the speed of light squared.

The recital was scheduled for a midnight service with candlelight, psalms, and hollow metal and wooden bells. Johnny Roach had stage fright since the second grade, and it continued as he lived inside the iron lung. He felt the warmth of candles pressed against the small vent next to his head as he stared at the miniature halos dancing across the ceiling like a chandelier thrown against the wall of heaven. The hollow bell was the sound of grief. It was at the center of what made us human and was stored outside the heart, something lost forever in the sea inside the hourglass and taken by the currents of ancient light into the charred hand of God who lifted us like birds into distant and newborn stars, one life worth living lost to the hunger of gravity. The metal bell was the sound of love. There was a wedding. Probity was written into courtly love. One was carried away by lust and betrayal and confidence. Probity was written into courtly love. *Ethos, Pathos, Logos, or something in the blood runs clean?* There was always the broken chalice, window, and back door, a ring discovered by a schoolboy picking wildflowers. The wooden bell was the sound of spirit. It was used to bless the darlings of the asylum. Naked and unashamed, they built a tunnel under their bedrooms with their bare hands and lanterns stolen from the church that led to the riverbank. They drifted without food in a canoe and came to rest under a covered bridge. One stood and pointed to the sky. Was it the shaking hand of the crippled ghost aligning the planets with the stars, dysentery of drawings turned into language, mirage of blue water, landscape of ten thousand freight trains, Atlas of Eros, black bird with emerald wing, on a step ladder raising the sun one kilometer to the east, dropping the furthest known source of light into the skillet of reason, a new life form waking inside a serpent's mouth?

"It was time to move the crowd," they said.

Four prison guards lowered a quilt over the iron lung like a veil. Johnny was fitted into a death mask a year before his execution, the last man put to death, the first and last man put to death inside the iron lung.

He saved a man's life. He took a man's life. A crew from Connecticut Light & Power was sent to towns surrounding the prison to raise the fallen power lines after the tornado left debris across half the state. Transformers exploded at the last execution, and there was no need for such a display of night clouds and rainbows against the moon. The missing were found three miles from the school bus floating under a fishing pier. There was something in the stars that half-blinked like the lilac light inside his failing wife's eyes. They placed a horseshoe upward on its vertical hoofs to catch the rainwater. It was time well spent in his search for luck and good fortune walking down the railroad tracks at the back of his father's factory. The sawdust they threw on the floor mixed with oil and his steel-toed boots almost glittered like Sunday School through the factory gate. He saved a man's life struck dumb by the automobile wheel of car driven by a woman who fainted in the spring rain. The traveling church brought donuts, hot coffee, and chocolate. The holy man held a microphone and spoke to the homeless about forming a choir of street angels and offered his blessings to those who stood before God and those without God. The search light illuminated the city chicken roosting on a smokestack. Two airplanes floated over the city.

Extinction

There were signs. Tiny green luminescent frogs that filled the rivers and lakes with stars disappeared. Johnny once captured them with his bare hands, small lanterns of grief, their eyes bulging and webbed feet in a Mason jar with screwdriver holes punched through the top, the tail of humans receded into darkness, its red tip like a blind man's cane, the rhinoceros, once a cabinet member in a mud bath, no longer rolled in the sun, its lacquered skin turned to dust, the zebra eye turned blue, starlings blown out of the smoke stack fell out of the sky into Easter baskets, one dog grew a yellow tongue out of its ass, a Kentucky bluebird was found on the windowsill of the Federal Reserve whistling "Dixie," in Connecticut, ten thousand Cyclops and orphaned newborns flown in from Europe were placed on ferry boats and discarded in Long Island vineyards, the sloth lost its hearing, a lion its mane, the giraffe became a pony, there was a Darwinian reversal of fortune in a mere year, man and woman reverted back to fruit and vegetables, those who once carried rocket launchers held long knives, those wearing clown sneakers and high heels awakened in loin cloth and barefoot, the tennis racket became a boomerang and in the alchemy of love and science a neutron bomb turned into a ball with chain, limbs fell off like wooden legs snapped into dust, armless and legless, the world suddenly calmed, those on a faraway island built a factory to manufacture one iron for each household, everybody was kept alive on a rotating schedule, portable used bottles of buttermilk and breathing tubes were attached to the bed frame to comfort those in sleeplessness, those on a Fiji island worked day and night for some years converting the army tanks of the world into iron lungs, land mines proved to be the last Darwinian notion of war and redemption, there were three land mines for each human, mammal, and sea creature, including the Manaphin, the inferno was the final sanctuary of the world. Johnny Roach was given a free subscription to *Esquire* before his execution.

She was no longer a nurse and became a soldier. The battalion of women was first created to acknowledge how one was taught to kill. It started in a pool hall with pinball machines. Green velvet on slate was a backyard breeze and barbecue with family and half the neighborhood children. One sat under the open garage child taste testers for Martin-Rosol and Mucke hot dogs and Avery soda. There was a red magic hot sauce with secret ingredients with a scent of wildflowers from sunrise to nightfall and the wild amber honey that rippled down the side of the second floor shed golden brown thick as the swarm of bees above our heads under the grapevines, four leaf-clovers, red and yellow plums, white grapes along the cyclone fence, cages filled with brooding homing pigeons and tumblers, ballet, tap, and apple orchard.

It was boot camp at the Fresh Air Center with a long rifle on a bad shoulder, live fire above her head in red clay mud, clay bird targets, tank driving school on I-95, parachute Avon Mountain, practice Morse code on a rehabilitated ham radio borrowed from the world headquarters in Newington, Connecticut, Girl Scout cookies, biology, frog pinned into wax, climbing tall buildings in a single-engine aeroplane lifting off the top of Walnut Hill Park into debris, wild rhubarb, ball bearings, binoculars, digging out of the snow with her army helmet, trumpeter, taps, folded American flag, widower's lap, how she turned her face to the Sun, iron gate staked into the one acre of heaven, what happened to the war medic trained in malaria shots, head wounds, soldier of misery, a green canvas canteen filled with holy water, ambulance driver smoking Lucky Strikes parked in the back of death row, copper penny on her tongue, the last young girl found guilty of murdering a six-year-old executed in the United States, churchyard mourners, salvation for the retrievers of the dead, peacemakers, taxi-drivers, unclaimed bag of clothes, last will and testament, family Bible, photograph, wingtips, belt buckle, shoe horn, money clip and a two-dollar bill, U.S. Savings Bond, covered wagon, Connecticut Yankee, bear trap, maple syrup, black strap molasses, salmon run, ferry boat, a bowlegged farmer on a bicycle built for two, Zenith radio tubes and electrodes attached to the electric chair pork pie hat, a man in dirt cellar setting perfect voltage to make a man's skin crisp, eyes boil, and, Ben Cocoa, the prison doctor, who worked as an army medic in Vietnam, stood behind the one-way mirror and listened for a moan, whimper, her last breath, and he stood up from his barber's chair, opened his black leather medical bag, and placed a stereoscope around his neck, crossed his heart and walked up to the woman, her head down and dressed in battle fatigues.

Do angels have human hearts? he thought.

The prison doctor placed his two fingers on her neck and a silver dollar on her breast and listened for a heartbeat. He tried to determine, using a mariner's compass, lowered from the ceiling into his left hand, the direction of her soul and its final resting place.

Honey Dripper Inside the Iron Lung

They placed the empty bottle of Vermentino inside the refrigerator above the porthole attached to the respirator coils and the breathing tube ventilator and used reverse osmosis to filter the ice and air. He listened to Robert Johnson sing the blues as he imagined making love in the red clay mud at boot camp. It was how her hazel eyes turned green as he kissed her and the lilac he sprinkled into her auburn hair, and he learned how water changed the color of her eyes too, although he never told her, wanting to keep one secret of her body left to his dreams, and he wished to marry her inside the iron lung. The community choir of retired factory workers would sing love songs. Children recruited from the ecumenical council of Connecticut imprisoned mayors and governors would hold candles against a Nor'easter. The underground tunnels flooded the city and uprooted trees and coffins. The National Guard was not sent into the city. Helicopters remained at their bases. The municipal airplane dropped flares into ballparks. They ran back into Yellow Cabs. There was no time for a wedding vow.

Johnny stared at the stars painted on the ceiling of the iron lung. He also looked for meteors in the periscope placed next to the smokestack on the outside of the chamber as he floated inside the iron lung at 35,000 feet above the earth. Johnny fell asleep at a quarter to three in the morning. His head was strapped to his pillow and he felt like he was wearing a concussion-proof NFL helmet provided by the Museum of Rollerball Studies at the MLA Convention, interviewees who also wore the helmets took small steps behind a parade of bagpipes on leave from Olympic curling, each was given a noisemaker for social security and checkered long johns for the long winter ahead, far below the stars he saw Earth, a crystal ball at the foot of his thin and soiled mattress began to turn colors, and he saw what he thought were faces of childhood friends and colleagues from the University of the Tar and Feather Brimstone Collectors who were also lifetime members of the Drunk and Depraved Administrator's Club closed to faculty weekdays and Saturday, he peered down through the holy stardust, there was lightning over a convenience store in downtown Detroit, the carcass of a horse tied to a backyard fence, a jukebox filled with Motown on the back of a pick-up headed due west, what he thought was a candle was a piece of candy left by his late wife inside the cup holder and picked up by his young daughter one day after her death as his daughter wept and he wept as if he was tumbling over some rainbow somewhere into a waterfall, a rubber tube around his waist, half-tethered to the stars and half to glory.

The scientist assigned to the prison's last functional iron lung placed Mason jars in the pine cupboards. There was a praying mantis with legs of a fetus, a rather large jar of hard-boiled prehistoric eggs of the flying octopus who lived half its life on land and half underwater near the New England coastal waters, split tongue of zebra, how gravity worked on the human body and mind, iced layers of memory inside a brain riddled with thought and consequence, a crystal ball above a dance floor with checkered tiles, illuminated squares, patent leather disco shoes, high-heeled boot-laced freak show on a Disney slide viewer, how the brain connected speech to gestures of the heart, a pink hourglass, rock slide buried the small town, followed by a dust storm, the sudden movement of a wooden doll's head became a marionette's change of address, how the wire connected to its jaw moved its eye socket made a spelling bee champion, the size of the flame inside a gas lantern, the amount of oxygen pumped into a breathing tube, the setting required for a coma, sleeping sickness, the gas mileage of a double-decker bus, iron lung on a bicycle rack tied to the front bumper, the amount of fresh air needed for those in a coma, the sleeping sickness that fell over half the world after the volcanic dust from the underworld seabed covered their roofs, lilac, and exhaust pipes, he observed the rattlers inside the buttermilk, and he felt like a ghost in a bath robe, and after brunch and jazz, a professor in a plaid cardigan and two-toned golf shoes, his open mouth full of butterflies and curses.

The warden approved of Ben Cocoa's last written request for his iron lung to be placed center stage at the Bushnell Theater and Hartford Stage Company one year before the date of his execution, a brass crystal lampshade with lace stage left, large dog-legged tub stage right, Victrola at the back of the iron lung, one bulb and string lowered to his head, one painting in a wooden frame, the shadow of a small pendulum swings back and forth slowly in a large picture window, chaise lounge, a vase of hyacinth next to audience members seated inside opened iron lungs bolted into the loges and walls far above the crowd, a young child brings Ben a music box, turns the key, places it inside the iron lung, and walks offstage into rain. They wept and tossed their blue roses, garter snakes, Tarot cards, hairpieces, lingerie, and clam diggers on the stage.

Ben Cocoa, Johnny's lawyer appointed by the Ministers of the Heart, defended him for thirty years on death row and had sought funds for a memorial service with full orchestra and choir. The reception was based on the early polling and public expectations of a guilty verdict given to an innocent bystander, a man who had pulled his fellow soldiers and town folks out of their dirt cellars into gardens brimming with fresh air, garlic, edible flowers, olives, sourdough bread, yellow goat cheese, and blueberry pie from Roger's Orchard.

East Haven: The Puritan Ethic and the Spirit of Christmas Past

He was given a plaque out of the dentist's office in the prison in a small room outside the commissary. Ben's gold tooth had fallen out of his mouth on the day of his execution after he took a large bite out of the Chunky Negro Peanut sandwich, a blue plate special on Passover and Good Fridays, they replaced his wooden teeth with fool's gold after a complaint from the Connecticut Civil Rights Commission came to his legal aid, after Weicker had passed the state income tax and the blue bloods traveled to the islands to hide their gold coins without tax or shame, the plaque read in small letters: This annual award is given to those who do not represent the less represented social classes: Spic and Spam Illegals and Niggers on a Weekend Pass can forget living without fear or being thrown into quicksand in East Haven or if their Mudhole is full, being driven to Jimmie's Smoke Shop in New Britain in a Yellow Cab. We forgive not our trespasses in the holy name, Amen. It was as if Ben Cocoa had never left Connecticut, pay-offs and bribes at the police stations, Manafort still destroyed tall historic buildings with a single blow of a gold-plated wrecking ball, the exit off the *Highway to Nowhere* still ended in New Britain, Tomasso Brothers canned tomatoes, Rowland was going back to prison, the mayors of Bridgeport, Hartford, and Waterbury ended up butt-fucking beggars on their bad knees brought into prison from Central Park in New Britain by the local police. It was determined the only plan would be to hire a flame-throwing Howdy Doody Kennedy to bring stability into a world of woe and enchantment.

Ben Cocoa wanted to be the first man to graduate from Harvard inside the iron lung. They transcribed lectures into violet verbs and mastodon nouns, and he was able to learn most of the languages of the known world. He had carried a red pocket dictionary and Mao, too. There was no pledge of allegiance to a flag waving and pointed to the landscape of Mars. Wild ghost stars creased the sky. There was a village of bluebirds and walking fish who grew large wings. The fish learned to climb into their houses and left small pearls inside tea cups. The wedding began at noon in Central Park, New Britain. The choir sang "Old Rugged Cross." Two people sat on fifty-year-old folding wooden chairs from his father's barbershop. The crowd that gathered ate twenty barrels of lobster donated by Yankees on the Seashore, a volunteer group of retiree gypsies who gave their life for their family, God, and country. Four men and four women were selected to lift and carry Ben to the top of Walnut Hill Park. The crowd looked out over the mountains for a sign of the second coming. They looked at the vandalized war monument and fading signature. The medicine man arrived in a death carriage and jumped to the back of the parade. He whistled, paused, and kissed their foreheads. There was no evidence of foul play only a pitchfork in the back of the pit bull on the back porch. No clues on who set the warehouse fires in the black and white city of thorns. Was it a blue moon, harvest moon, or blood moon that danced in their children's eyes?

They placed a circus-trained bear cub named Soviet Union on his mattress inside the iron lung. The prison doctor had studied the hibernation of the black grizzly before climate change altered its sleep patterns and they wandered into cities foraging for food in junkyards, Little League and badminton games, and backyard barbecues. Ben Cocoa loved Nestle's hot chocolate after a meteor shower and bed time. He was prone to hourly erections inside the iron lung, so they set his penis in plaster of Paris each day for his golden slumbers, a safety pin attached to his foreskin and fresh linen made him nod off into *the shining sea*. He winked at the photograph taped to his mirror and fell hard into matrimony. Ben was placed in a one-year study on weightlessness, isolation, and sleep deprivation. Weightlessness gave Ben a sense of power he no longer had in his brittle legs. He levitated and danced in thin air, and he was somehow able to breathe without a breathing tube on the back of his ear into his mouth, suspended animation on a high wire, landing face down into a down pillow, sleep deprivation, hot stove, mirage of space, time, stars turned brown turned blue turned white, yet it was isolation that led to his sustained hibernation, solitaire, one-way mirror, and he fell asleep in a few minutes holding a pink hourglass, and it was determined that he talked in his sleep and spoke in every known language, and he spoke fluently of every known bird, tree, and flower, and he spoke of cures for every disease and based on his waking notes with an extra fine pen in his mouth he was able to write on large moleskin sketchbooks that he had found comfort in the wild current of eternal sleep.

Ben dropped a twig of clove into a flask of black whiskey and lifted it to his blue lips to numb his broken crown. It was winter becoming winter again and VapoRub on his chest did not relieve his breathing and the wool blanket did not cover his toes. The lung was caught in the matinée of a sun spot and hurdled through time like a reckless ship at sea. Ben was always soft spoken even when he saw somebody in a jeep run into a barbed wire fence as if he would find salvation on the other side of the alley. The man lifted a boulder and dropped it at the back of a car as if the prehistoric opened the doors of hell that swarmed inside his bruised alcoholic mind. The man in the jeep kissed a spinster in dreadlocks who smoked weed twenty-four hours a day. She recoiled like a sea snake until her nose bled. The corridors smelled like spoiled chicken and funky broadway. The man in the jeep whispered bad sex jokes to his lover who also whispered bad sex jokes into his tin ears. The bad ass artist took a shit in the elevator for art's sake. He got his job knowing a drinking buddy. Job for life. Fast food olive oil and a hand job drinking a case of 40s in one afternoon on Valentine's Day.

He rose out of his chair as if he were the asshole of all time: "I drink like a hippopotamus and float like a hand-crushed can of beer in the Connecticut River."

Who the fuck do you think you are? Superman! You are always late! You don't participate! What have you ever done for the Art Co-Op! You are a motherfucker! You don't even change your underwear! You eat shit and scab pie!

The lover of theater and the man in the jeep almost made it into heaven as they stepped off the elevator.

The dentist was inclined to place electrodes, apply Murray's pomade, and Ray Charles sunglasses to Ben Cocoa's shaved scalp to monitor his pulse and determine how the lower regions of brain and matter converged into the featherweight of memory that connected tongue to spirit, how the past emerged somewhere in everyone's blood and the present disintegrated into the future, how the altered patterns found inside the beaker took the shape of the ghost in the machine and the kaleidoscope of her eyes brought Ben to his knees, the successful experiment of human nature, isolation, and particular physics, heli-copter pulley, a Good Humor iron lung on wheels, a makeshift hot-rod, particle board, bent axle, bicycle streamers, no brakes in zero grav-ity, steep hill, stop sign, green light, red light, flying over the sidewalk into Mrs. John's garden of rhubarb and tulips, rolled into the grass and sprinkler, the homegrown soapbox derby under a playground of factory bars, Ben and his backseat driver laughed and she cursed like a champion sailor, and we ran into the woods into the arms of the Green Lady wearing death's apparel blown off the clothesline, a wed-ding gown airlifted to a war zone, white candle, brass holder, chime, Mercurochrome, iodine, gas mask, blanket, handsaw, a blue fog lifted over the battlefield, dogs were sent into the trenches, most of the young soldiers were incinerated and those who were half alive stood in the baptismal waters.

The botched Oklahoma execution of Ben Cocoa has called our continued use of the death penalty in this country back into ques-tion. In many ways, the death penalty is an abhorrent attempt to sate an irrational cultural bloodlust, rooted in vengeance and barbarism and detached from data.

Ben Cocoa's execution was by all accounts a gruesome affair, as he gasped and writhed on the gurney, a vein collapsed and he suffered a heart attack. Ben grimaced and tensed his body several times over a three-minute period before the execution was shielded from the press. After being declared unconscious ten minutes into the process, Ben spoke at three separate moments. The first two were inaudible, however the third time he spoke, Ben said the word *man*.

There were always the sermons. How did eye-for-an-eye measure against thou-shall-not-kill? How is state-sanctioned killing somehow grandfathered out of that commandment? Then there's that issue of a constitutional prohibition against cruel and unusual punishment. How is something more cruel and final than death? And how do we deal with it when faced with a person convicted of administering cruel and unusual punishment?

Oklahoma botched the execution of a murderer convicted of administering cruel and unusual punishment. President Obama was asked about that execution, he did not categorically rule out capital punishment, but qualified that statement:

"[In] the application of the death penalty in this country, we have seen significant problems—racial bias, uneven application of the death penalty, you know, situations in which there were individuals on death row who later on were discovered to have been innocent because of exculpatory evidence. And all these, I think, do raise significant questions about how the death penalty is being applied. And this situation in Oklahoma I think just highlights some of the significant problems there."

Not only does the state play God here, but others will raise the issue of how expensive the whole process is. Appeals, due process, can double, triple, and more the costs of killing someone versus locking them up and throwing away the key.

We cannot deny we're a country raised on bloodlust. Capital punishment is the national DNA. We inherited our gruesome genes from

Britain well before we broke our bonds with that bloody empire that would execute someone for stealing a loaf of bread.

Our bloodlust puts us also into some dubious company. Only Bangladesh, China, Iran, Iraq, North Korea, and Saudi Arabia have killed more death penalty humans than us.

Some politicians have sought to reduce appeals and make executions more automatic, and therefore cheaper—removing that argument against the death penalty. However, it remains to be seen how the courts will view such haste.

Other proponents seek to institute even more checks and balances to ensure that no innocent person will ever be executed, but yet can anyone ever remove all doubt? And there's also the counter-argument that these provisions will make executions even more costly.

It's frightening that all these proponents use a rather macabre vantage to make their points. They are all spoken from atop the amassed graves of all those the state has executed. Is that, in itself, such a morally superior position?

But we must leave the sermon and return to the story.

It happened. Solitary confinement on death row. Ben Cocoa sat up in a folding director's chair and took a straight razor he stole from the commissary on Easter Day and hid inside the beautiful curls of his large afro and slice open his arm from the bottom of his wrist to the top of his elbow at the beginning of the machine gun bullet hole, a wound he acquired in WWII outside of Paris. The prison guard found him stretched on a soiled mattress flinching to Beethoven's Mass, C Major, Opus 86, and singing *Aleluia* to his stuffed parrot. They dragged him into the shower. He pulled out the razor. They stomped his hands with a claw hammer. The guard pulled a Taser gun out of his underwear, smiled, and aimed at Ben's groin. Electricity shot into his splayed penis. They tied a sailor's knot to his hands and ankles. Ben felt as if he were pulled by the Budweiser draft horses along the coastal waters and carried by the madrigal wings and dropped into the geysers at hell's border that reached the exhaust pipes of the iron lung providing some heat and well needed droplets of fresh water and air, he lifted his roped hand, branded by the warden's eight-year-old son, and pressed the sourdough bread against his lips like a wafer in the baptismal waters as they lowered Ben into a tub of dry ice.

It was Ben's Cocoa's birthday. He was allowed to draw straws with other death row inmates for a weekend pass to Ocean Beach in New London. Ben won. They chained his hands to the front of his waist and tied his ankles in frayed rodeo rope. Ben waded into the baptismal waters until the salt water turned his brown skin blue, a halo formed above his head. He turned to the lighthouse and stretched out his arms and dove into a high wave. The red and blue veins inside his translucent body pulsated as he fell into the undertow of the underworld. There was a table setting with holy candles, silverware, and a bell. The Captain placed his sword on his chair and stood for a toast to the prisoner shackled from his neck to his bare feet. They placed a ruby into the shirt pocket of each prisoner led to the edge of the gangplank before he was tossed into the great fires. Ben felt his pink spine come alive like a sea snake thrown out of a womb of a mermaid nestled inside the coral at the helm of a ship's wreckage. Ben awakened, dove, able to breathe underwater, touching black pearls and searching for unclaimed treasure drawn on a map of the world, and he looked over the landscape of the sea and started to pan for love and gold.

The man was born with a witless seed planted as he slept on a wooden birthing table and placed inside a canoe set adrift off in a Greenland storm and roped to the side of a large ship, anger born out of the devil's mural painted on the side of brick and mortar, pissed on by the drunk artist in Iowa overalls on a Saturday under the bright flag of the sun, colorless, blind, in a cloud of navy blue narcissism on a paint brush, pissed his beer into a bottle of 40, a boulder whiplash placed at the back and door of the tattooed motor car, how does one photograph a daemon invisible man? They discerned that *It appears, based on the timeline, this entire episode is based on subterfuge and ruse to counter one or two artists after being caught in a public rage, parking lot re-ordering, boulder redux, and mural recklessness.* He stood showing his gay side, face to face with the illustrated man in a face of bully dog limp dick boxing match and came back a second time for a third and final act, and he dressed like Elvis in *Jailhouse Rock* and Travolta in a disco dog competition with three legs, wide collar, open shirt, faker's gold necklace, golfer's jacket, marijuana sticks and a Lucky Strike up his ass, a kind of gentleman stool pigeon warrior, as a child had somebody placed the blue eyelashes of the devil on his chest, a second cousin gave the baby a golden shower into his bassinet as he dreamed of angels and prepared for war.

The Widower's Iris

BEN COCOA LOVED a woman and a woman loved him. There was lilac and peach, a glittering spring dress against black hair, violin under the husk of moon, brief kiss on low shoulder, butterfly on the stone fence, mist, clover field, lavender, the widower's iris, a crown of acrobats above the world in a dance, eclipse, maple leaves, without a net, high wire RPM, dish on a stick, the chandelier above the river, the rowers skim across a landscape of light, fog cuts the tops of trees, Vermentino sky, powder falls into buttercups, yellow turned into blue flags held by children rolling down Smith Elementary School hill that rose over the city, first night, second night, third night, lovers on a sailboat under the moon's wreckage, afternoon recital, dancers at the Black Box Theater at Brown, fourteen dancers in a rectangle of gravity, couples, one step forward, one step back, dancer of grief and circumstance, art for art's forsaken audience, what becomes of a dancer weeping as she danced, under a halo caught inside the hunger of gravity and poetry, applause, rite-of-passage, Ben sat down for the performance and held the widower's blue iris.

The woman was declared insane yet found criminally responsible for shooting her two children in the mouth. She once threw his school lunch box filled with a Ring Ding, and sardines and mustard, out of the homeroom window into the snow. Her partner and lover had tried to crack open a boulder with his one good hand, lift the chassis of a Mustang over the bridge into the shallow river, and with his pant legs rolled up in the river mud, he took a wood saw to cut the head off a blue mule goat at midnight. He was raised as a child to become a witch doctor and took her to the junior high school prom and homecoming game. They burned alms, skinned rats, ate brain and grits and walleye. As he turned the corner of redemption and salvation, her claws into his back, they sped down the country road on his motorcycle, she somehow jumped into the rumble seat, and he flew straight into the back of a Good Humor truck, he lost his left leg and right arm, her remains were collected and sent to the Peabody to study the patterns of his brain and the ghost in the machine. The head witch doctor was assigned to the prison after he discovered the healing properties for grief in a dream and revealed the hidden recipe to the bereaved.

What happened to the iron lung roasting on an open fire? Ben Cocoa's homeroom class decorated the iron lung with sleigh bells. It was set to be launched on the ski jump at the Vancouver Winter Olympics opening ceremony and canceled because of rainfall. They waited until spring. Ben was tethered to the wheel and lifted into the ski lift in Winnipeg, a small urn floating in the sea waves, thrown into the belly pool of time by the widower's cupped hands in a dance without music or men, birch, fog, lighthouse, wild horses, thimble of holy water, chalice, stained glass roses, carousel, tambourine, shackled broken hoof, birth canal, black pearl neckless, thin crescent moon on a pendulum, its blade swung high and swung low over the iron lung, one half of a human body left inside, the other half castaway inside a kayak on fire down the Connecticut River into the open sea and after the chimes held by the Minister of the Heart had awakened the retrievers of the dead, the international press and one university professor naked under his doctoral robe, awarded the Honorary Doctorate of Humane Letters, *Honoris Causa*, discovered in his eternal study of capital crimes that a clock that altered time altered punishment.

Pay Dirt

THEY SAY HER white robe appeared at each New Britain groundbreaking. Her bare feet floated in the background on the war monument to the last world war and present half-world wars. The names of hometown friends were carved into marble their bodies long turned to dust. The executioner lifted a brass shovel and pick axe and struck pay dirt. Two bank vaults full of two dollar bills were pulled out of the brownfield. The chariot race was scheduled for the 4th of July. Four prizes were awarded: a dozen gold ball bearings inside a music box, one complete set of antique wooden golf clubs including a Mashie Niblick, a baby grand piano, and an Honorary Doctorate of Humane Letters, *Honoris Causa*. It was the alchemy between pay dirt and redemption, derailment and goat-footed love, and what the dirt had covered the executioner's hands revealed.

Dante's Chariot

They stole the gold coins Ben had left inside a wool sock hidden under a sewer grate under the prison basketball hoop. A secret admirer, a woman afflicted with a beard at birth, sent Ben one gold coin each month for the last twenty-nine years, mint condition, a possible hedge against death row and the winter torch carried from the Wild Idea Badlands in a marathon protest against capital punishment to the unpaved streets of Ben's hometown in New Britain, Connecticut, against the parachute of the blues one found by accident in the field or city, where punishment in the fields became punishment in the city and punishment in the city became punishment in the field, bring the firing squad, rifles, helmets, a live grenade placed in the bed pan under the electric chair, the wrong extension cord, the hood placed over the prisoner's head, a trap door tarantula tap dance on the gallows of heaven, the human body falling at the speed of light into oblivion, thrown out of Dante's chariot, death's carriage brought to the prison door by the thin angel and white steed, men dressed in their military best, medals pinned to the chest, coiled gold braids over the shoulder, one bullet allowed in each chamber, one prayer for the deranged and prosperous gentlemen who wore black penny loafers and herringbone vests, pocket watches set to Saturn's rings and duck pin strikes at Laurel Lanes in Plainville, Connecticut, this was the way of the world, in its unremarkable movement under the stars, floated and the sky released its carpentry and left gold coins spinning to earth, one landed in the volcanic dust, one landed in Ben's hand as he walked on hollow ground, one landed straight up on its side at the prison gate, it happened at midnight, in the Bywater neighborhood in New Orleans, a few miles from Louisiana Avenue and St. Charles Avenue, a pelican mile from Audubon Park and the Maple Leaf Bar, the long bridge, narrow as Oswald's knife, Ruby's necktie, the alligator eyes under the moon's wreckage, the roped bridge over Texas Falls, the pink Cadillac in the homecoming parade on cobblestones laid downtown by a black man in Nebraska behind a mule, the black man who slept with a pitchfork under his bed, the armadillo struck by lightning and thrown into his dreams, who found out as a child that oxtail was a delicacy at birthday parties and thawing out frozen chitlins' and cleaning chitlins' was true North and homemade applause.

NEGRO PEANUT BUTTER

THE FAFNIR BALL Bearing Company was closed after the war and converted into the Negro Peanut Butter Factory after returning veterans were awarded loans and houses and employment for good behavior for good killing inside foxholes and aboard burning ships, player pianos were turned into Steinways, the baking soda divers into a wedding on the Brooklyn Bridge, the Fluffernutter was a conspiracy drawn inside the bunkers of the Confederacy, one good sandwich in a Lucky Strike lunch box was better than a stay of execution, and if human bones and teeth were changed into necklaces, rivers into highways, the Ogallala Aquifer into a sea of brains and pig shit, Pony Express into a Yellow Cab, meteors into nuclear clotheslines, platform shoes into penny loafers, wedding vow into death's carriage, Wounded Knee into White Clay Eaters, would a country allow Blacks, thrown into freight trains, lined up against the church wall, dropped into large jungle pots, stirred with kayak paddles, peanuts boiled with sea salt, chitterlings, raccoon tail, rattlers, and peacock, to be eaten by school children between two slices of wonder bread, Negro Peanut Butter, Spam and blackberry jam?

MATINÉE

THE MOVIE SET was designed for the reception in preparation for the midnight execution. The woman who starred in *The Woman of the Midnight Sail* and rejected after her audition for *Woman of the Dunes* arrived and was tied to a whipping post for a live performance. They announced each visitor at the bronze door: three Ministers of the Heart, Warden, the curator of the Mausoleum of American Art wore white silk gloves, abusive alcoholic vagrant uncle music teacher nicknamed Uncle Fuckhead by his talented students who wanted to learn the genius of jazz and as a young man called the men in Hartford porch niggers with glee and left his child and good wife who didn't believe in the arts including music far behind, the King of Pork Chops who leaned on one lamp post every night, the bald hip-hop without a college degree, who maligned spoken work in one language and Fool's English and kept a bucket of ice under his lawn chair, the crazy jane aunt who spoke in three tiny voices and used her fist on her little children who barely spilled lemonade at the Promenade Ball, and they taught their children to hate sitting in the easy chair, kept the family close knit and the darning needle piercing their hearts like the archangel holding a sword in one hand for the rabid wild boars and a staff in the other for the holy retrievers and relatives who sprinkled anti-Semitic and racist drivel over the world. Three minutes before the newsreel was to show the weekly body count the movie projector broke apart and the velvet curtain fell to the stage.

Sunday Stick

Grandpa Cocoa carried one golf club on Sunday disguised as a walking stick. He acted out bird-watching looking for the bluebird, yellow finch, crow's nest, owl eye, eagle claw, and he tossed a golf ball on the green and rolled a hole in one. He had *Civil Disobedience* in his long black coat and sat at the edge of the pier, stood and hit a long ball to the other side of the pond. Stanley Golf Course in New Britain. One hole for every citizen. One Mashie Niblick for each retired factory worker, broken glass inside a thermos of arsenic, schoolyard kaleidoscope, family photographs, unfurled light, ice chest, pitchfork, gold-plated serpent on their wrist, moon landing coronation of the working class, inveterate medals of honor, bugle, veterans, sundown, rainfall, six-gun salute, duel for pension, twelve paces to eternity, ribbon cutting ceremony, parade of broken bow and arrow, blackbird on a white birch, showdown, folded flag on her lap, letters, music box, cathedral of the dead, treatise of the living, consolation, red-brimmed hat, *leaning on the everlasting arms*, taps played and taps lingered in the lavender meadow.

DEATH ROW INTERLUDE

Dear Ben,

I found the song and lyrics to "The Death Row Interlude." Rerecorded, mixed, and mastered for the first time in 43 years during two weeks in May, 2014 at Northern Sky Music, Boulder, Colorado. Perhaps it can be used during your execution as the last song you hear on Earth.

mp3 of first studio mix is attached.

Johnny Roach

Dear Johnny,

I received your song last night. I have not yet listened. What in God's underworld had you find this piece from so long ago? I remember I wrote another piece for you. Of course, it is young stuff. I have a libretto that was commissioned and set to full orchestra and choir, but it has no special place in the one you performed.

I will listen tonight.

Thank you so much.

Do you recall the second song we worked on?

Sincerely,
Ben Cocoa

P.S. A few weeks ago I received an Honorary Doctorate of Human Letters, *Honoris Causa*.

Dear Ben,

You asked. Well, I'll try to keep the story short. Some time ago when "The Death Row Interlude" came up during one of our brief Facebook messages, I looked around for it, relatively certain I had an old lyric and chord sheet in exactly the files I thought they'd be in. But there was no trace. Over some months I went through every folder and file and box and book I had, gradually losing confidence in my original opinion that it would turn up. It never did. Two flooded basements and rebuilds later, plus one forest fire evacuation, and I had all the opportunities in time and space to unearth this relic. Except it never appeared.

Until about three weeks ago. My mother, in her 90s, had been on an eighteen-month decline toward what medical staff and caregivers told us several times over that period were her last few days. Margaret and I, with our son Graham, and my brothers with wives, and a niece and nephew gathered for Mother's Day in Prescott, Arizona, where mom was once again in her last days. Only this time the outcome was not medical opinion; it was more on her own terms. She decided to stay around long enough for all of us to gather once more, which was her wish, and then she passed two days later, which also was her wish, about two weeks ago.

Over the long term of my mom's last couple of years, it had become my job to organize and sort my mom's and our family's belongings, which was an enormous task, and could not have been done without the many hands that showed up to help. Just over two weeks ago, in a storage facility, waist deep in boxes and paintings, books and photos, I reached into one container and pulled out the album I recorded in Cleveland the summer of 1970. On it was, of course, "The Death Row Interlude." The thing is, it was damaged, warped and obviously unplayable. I felt taunted. Here was the song, but it couldn't be recovered from the old vinyl media. I put the record away with my things at the hotel anyway. Something would work out.

I looked into many ways to recover damaged and warped albums, and settled on the cave man approach. Find two smooth flat surfaces, place the album between them, and heat the sandwich in the oven for a little while and let the record flatten out. Two smooth unused floor tiles served the purpose and several oven attempts later I was able to get it just barely playable on the turntable, and from that pulled out the lyrics and the chords. The chords and lyrics, in my view anyway, were definitely worth the recovery effort. The recording, and the rest of the songs, on the other hand, were not. And I say not worthy in the most emphatic way, all caps, bold face, italics and exclamations points. This recording will never be heard. Years ago I had destroyed and disposed of my own copy of this album, and for good reason. No artist, no song-writer, no musician, no matter how accomplished or humble, would ever want that recording and those songs to be heard again. Except for "The Death Row Interlude."

Now to your question. Was there any other work of yours that we collaborated on, on that record? Maybe. There's one called "Wait Those Days" that may have been your lyrics, at least I have that impression. And another one called "Marilyn" which I think may have referred to someone you were connected with at Adrian for a time, and maybe you wrote lyrics about that. I don't know about either of those songs. The decades have done a job on those memories. If you recall either of them and having written the lyrics, and you would like them recovered, let me know and I'll give it the effort. But, frankly, if I were giving advice, I'd say don't go anywhere near them.

Well, I didn't keep this short, but the story is now told. The new mp3 recording and new rendering of "The Death Row Interlude" that I sent to you is just my way of attempting to do the work justice while in some way retaining the original sound and feel of it, and, parenthetically, retaining the word *groovy* in the lyrics. You may not like it, or you maybe you will. As with all works like this, that's out of my hands.

It's been a good ride getting to this point, and it took some amazing turns and unlikely twists to get here. Maybe there will be something in this that's worth it for you as well.

Johnny Roach

Attorney Cochrane,

I have made slight additions/changes:

I drove up to the Barista (drive through store) on Second Avenue. I looked out at Mr._____. I was prepared to order my coffee. He looked out through the drive-through window. He appeared wide-eyed and deranged. He proceeded to open the window, and he screamed and waved his hand and said: "Get out of here!" There were other employees inside the store. I said nothing to him. I did not order. I drove around the store . . . following the exit and south. Not knowing what was wrong; having no idea whatsoever what had compelled such awkward behavior from this public place of business, I drove back around. He left the building, and he proceeded to scream even louder with a rage I had not seen since watching TV as a child and observing the segregationists of the civil rights movement. His face was red. He was raging mad. He proceeded to say: "Get out of here! Get out of here now!" He said this over and over again while swinging his arms . . . he was like a rabid dog. I felt physically threatened by this rather large man. I did not leave my car. I was refused service. I was not served. I drove away. I should have called 911. I should have written to the Nebraska Human Rights Commission or whatever it is called. I should have called you, my lawyer, but I had recently lost my wife. After this incident, I developed and was diagnosed with high blood pressure. I have been on medication ever since.

I proceed with this in her honor, my daughters, all of his present and future customers, and for the city of Kearney.

Ben Cocoa

Dear Cochrane,

I am aware that there is a ten-day requirement to file a complaint on the Barista matter. It seems that that is such a short time, like a return on holiday merchandise, and it somehow trivializes an event that because of its very nature, might cause one to pause past those incidents, through "testers" or simple visits to this public facility, might provide further evidence and immediate legal action.

Best,
Ben Cocoa

December 3, 2005

To Whom It May Concern:

I brought the (enclosed) matter to the attention of Attorney Cochrane. I believe the deadline for filing a complaint has passed. I know I should have filed earlier, yet the very matter left me without the emotional and legal wherewithal to do.

Do I have any other options at this point in time?

Sincerely,

The Last Love Letter

Dear Ben,

You called me last night. I was half-asleep yet your voice stirred my senses. You spoke of reading my last will and testament and feeling love all around you. You read parts of my letter: A Prayer for Women, Race War, Prose Poem for the Poet's Daughter, and others. Were you falling in love with me?

You were falling in love with me. When I first wrote to you I said that although it takes time to know another's heart, there is, although rare, love at first sight.

It is almost midnight, and I had to write to you at this late yet hopeful hour. I await a phone call from the governor with my pardon. Apple created a special Death Row App connected by satellite to every prison where capital punishment is handed out for crimes against nature and nation. Your words you read to me last night on the telephone were unexpected yet not fully a surprise after our Saturday together. It was as if time for a brief yet eternal moment paused. I wept. Was it a blessing or a thin shadow that fell over us?

I just finished watching a movie and wanted to check my emails to see if you had left me something else or to ponder what had been written to linger a bit longer before going to sleep. It is very special our communication. My heart feels warm and tender in a happy way. I feel a little giddy like a teenager and yet full as a woman. You are doing something to me or maybe I should say I feel the best of me when I am with you and think of you. I am a bit scared that we are going too fast and that will ruin things or maybe that this is like a dream and I will wake up and feel foolish for playing at love. Are you not afraid? You seem more steady than me. Please be patient with me. I don't know much about dating or even about being with someone that makes me feel so alive both intellectually and creatively. I love your mind and heart. I also need to keep my feet on the earth. And as I said, many have told me "less is more." I get so excited like you. In some ways, I have a child's mind of wonder and excitement. I also know I can get caught up in the moment and lack the maturity of delaying gratification. But if what we have is real, I want it to last. I almost feel like I am in flight. So though I want to take you in, so much and so fast, I want to keep it real and not lose my balance. Let's take our time like drinking a fine wine. All of you with the songs, the poetry, your gentleness and loving ways need space to sit, to be still, and to take hold, slowly. A song tomorrow night would be great. I will listen to it over and over as I have with the others, treasure them and you, and dwell more in your head and heart through your poetry. Though I will want to respond to your song, I will wait to give you my heart in words if you can call me Monday night. It will be romantic to talk by the light of the moon after the sun has set. I feel much love. I am honored and happy to get to know such a beautiful soul like you. As the Hebrews say, you are a MENSCH!!

Sending you loving thoughts,
Wendy

To Mother Wendy,

Today, I'm eating pistachios and dates to remember you. I'm sitting by the water in the sun. I'm listening to "Magical Mr. Mistoffelees" and imagining you here dancing along by my side to the tape cassette recording of Cats. *I'm here in New York living the dream you encouraged me to chase. And though I'm not sure if my agent will send me out for an audition as a background dancer in this esteemed musical, I know that you're with me at every other audition I walk into. Every word I speak, every bit of dialogue I write, "every breath I take" (I'll be missing you—props to you #Daddy, sis and I love you), every move I make, every lover who has and ever will wrap me in their arms, all the heartache and moments of feeling lost, growing pains and #joy—you are with me. I have a part time job. I have friends who love me. I can wake up and drink a cup of #coffee. I have a beating heart that sometimes gets confused and makes out with strange men on the dance floor (it's okay, I don't go home with them and, fuck it, I'm still in my 20s). I wish you could see how strong my voice has become. How sometimes I feel like a #queen, and some days I feel like dirt. I'm confident now. More than ever. I'm getting closer to figuring out who I am, and how I identify. Black (hashtag #blackgirlmagic), mixed-race, whatever. I am yours and always will be. I usually post a picture of you on your birthday, but today, here's a picture of me. Cuz I am you and you are me. Love you, Mommy. Happy birthday!*

Daughter Isadora

They placed your father, Ben, into his iron lung on a wooden raft made out of railyard trestles, and roped it to the back of the ferry for a ride along the Connecticut River, past the school children who waved small flags of salvation, the town lined the shore, bands played Sousa at noon and practiced taps at midnight, and there was a certain comfort under light rain. This was the end of its journey, the last train out of San Francisco, runaway in the High Sierras, guarded by a posse of one-armed angels and a pit bull riding shotgun in a motorcycle rumble seat, they held a blue crystal ball for Ben Cocoa and observed the third eye of the enchanted beast at his bedside, he seemed to float above the lavender field, half asleep in the waters of the underworld.

What is this glass in my hand?

What is the recipe for golden slumber?

They appointed a board of scientists to find the ingredients. One cut out the eye of the walleye, one sought the bark of white birch, others brought the rattler of the Mojave green, goat hooves turned to dust, ghost star, lime dust, hair, goat hooves, blue coral, the alchemy of barbed wire and eternity, noose, trap door, they brought to the kitchen table, the language of death attached Morse code sent out to find death's carriage traveling on glass wheels into Machu Picchu, it was off course, a few miles from the equator, tethered by light to heaven's border, covered in tinsel thrown down by the devil's hand seated in the devil's throne, they walked for hours into the rain forest, they heard the choir, a headless bird white raven landed on Ben's shoulder.

What was this elixir they used to retrieve a life and take a life away in the mutilated days ahead?

Ben,

This is Wendy. Oh, my God. I ran all the way home to talk to you. It's 10 of 10. Ran all the way home to talk to you. I thought about you a lot today. And I'd like to date you exclusively if you are still interested and let you know that you're a wonderful man. I would like to get to know you, furthermore. I've been thinking about you today. Oh, God, I had a wonderful day. I did my art show with my women. I was thinking about you. Maybe you're sleeping. If you happen to be awake, call me. If not, I will talk to you tomorrow. I will check for your email. It will take me a while. Maybe in the morning.

Bye.

Wendy

LOVE LETTER FROM DEATH ROW

DEAR BEN,

I cannot wait to tell you that I love you
I love you through my heart
It is not of "new brain" or instinct
It is the spirit that rises from my chest
as I breathe a breath with you
And hold you in my heart darling,
charmer who hath won my heart and
walked the road of my soul . . . I love
this man
his politeness that speaks of love
His substance holds sway in my world I
feel small in his muscular arms and hope
he will hold me through the Night. I have
chills recalling verses articulated with
the sensitivity of this gentle Giant
I feel small in his arms insignificant
at times,
blocked by the light of his majesty
Shivering in the shade
Until he reaches out both arms and throws the clouds away
Splitting atoms, carving something of me out of the beauty of natural wood
An "uncarved block,"
He chiseled me into femininity made me feel like a
Woman of thin frame and wide hips
Held me in his arms when I would let
him I could truly love this man

I feel eternity in his eyes
I want to kiss his hands and let him know that he is the man.
The man that sits on a throne
King Solomon, a loving father who cannot bear
to have a child's life ripped in half. His eyes were
soft pools of love as he winced when I spoke of
my father's inability to love. I feel him in my
heart
freeing my caged soul that starves on shrinking pie
He is the promise of a better time when earth is
part of heaven "for earth is not sufficient
(but earth does not have to be) our only companion."

They raised the dead. First, they dismantled the antique wrought iron fence around the Fairview Cemetery, and threw the iron into pick-up trucks under a half moon, its pieces were sent to mansions around the world. The boneless thieves wore work gloves and escaped justice on earth and found themselves swimming in the inferno in the underworld. This was the first curse on the Hardware City of the World brought to its knees by fraud and circumstance, sirens, flames, floods knocked down smokestacks and spread embers that floated into the Shuttle Meadow Reservoir of the Damned and Prosperous. They raised the dead. Second, they paved a busway through a corridor of the dead. Death carriages on four wheels run over the gravestones, roses, wildflowers, and family photographs, left for their ancestors who had rested in peace after the taps were played and those seated in thin aluminum chairs stood in prayer and some of the sparrows that flew in a curved figure eight out of the church steeple guided by God's charred hand flew over the small gathering and dropped out of the sky like Apollo's arrow and sudden death into the windshield of a stalled bus in the middle ground of the dead and delirious ghosts.

My Dear Ben Cocoa, Sweetheart,

I'll send you a fb "friend request."

I do not believe in love at first sight. We have shared much with each other, but as we know love takes time. You do many wonderful things to me. In addition to being excited by you, being around you is helping me fall in love with myself in a big way. I know it sounds silly or maybe cocky, which it is not, but I must say maybe because you treasure me I feel special. Please know that I have much capacity to love and that you are the first man I have ever dated that could possibly be worthy of this great love. Historically, I have dated broken men and am now looking for someone who knows himself and feels full in himself. I cannot fulfill a need—make someone feel full and happy if he does not have a life that is full before meeting me. I want you to want me but not need me. Does that make sense? As my mother once told me, two halves do not make a whole. I am romantic but do not believe in bubble gum love or fairy tales.

Please tell me your nickname. I am curious and excited to share in that though I will call you whatever you prefer. I do not have a nickname though I like when you call me darling. When I think of you, I think sweetie and sweetheart though I am a bit shy to say it to you. I like terms of affection and love physical affection, so you need not worry about that! It will happen as we get to feel comfortable with each other.

Be good to yourself. You deserve it!!

Love,
Wendy
Provincetown

CNN Breaking News

THERE IS CLEAR evidence of the existence of the iron lung falling out of the sky 33.7 million years ago before capital punishment. The outline of the iron lung in the shape of a aluminum soda pop can was visible from infrared satellite photographs diverted from Direct TV into the homes of the bereaved. There was a mass extinction and the iron lung was all that remained inside the great crater called Popigai.

Popigai Crater.

Scientists claim it harbors industrial diamond deposits found on the rudder of an iron lung.

Popigai Crater is one of the ten biggest impact craters on Earth.

Impact winter could be the source of the Eocene extinction. Meteors colliding with the Earth can initiate a deadly global winter by saturating the Earth's atmosphere with microscopic particles that reflect the sun's heat back into outer space.

The Popigai meteor is the major culprit but three smaller Earth-meteor collisions around 35 and 36 million years ago are also suspected, such as the Chesapeake Bay crater offshore Virginia, Toms Canyon Crater offshore New Jersey and Mistastin Crater in Labrador, Canada. However, no other iron lung has been found at these craters.

These four craters have been ruled out because of their ages. Some dating attempts had determined that Popigai's impact happened 35.7 million years ago. Two million years' difference is too much of a time gap between a meteor collision and the mass disappearance of species. Another significant mass extinction killed the dinosaurs 65 million years ago coincides with another meteor clash 33,000 years ago, close enough chronologically to be a possible consequence.

No meteor can be directly blamed for the Eocene mass extinction, so many scientists have turned to climate change. They think that global cooling killed off many species.

There are some tell-tale markers of climate change. Scientists measure isotopes of oxygen, carbon and other elements in Eocene-age rocks and can estimate the Earth's temperature and greenhouse-gas levels. All of the evidence from the Eocene points that things started very warm and then became much colder and drier preceding the mass extinction. A distinctly sharp increase in temperature at the end of the Eocene indicates a brief but fairly extreme global cooling, which was followed by much warmer temperatures.

The timing of the Popigai Crater matches extremely well with that brief global cooling. The Popigai impact possibly created in very short time a global ice age, on a scale much larger than climate disasters after volcanic eruptions or the dinosaur-killing meteor impacts. The crash would have resulted in releasing massive amounts of sunlight-reflecting sulfur droplets into the atmosphere. And then they made a relatively quick recovery, geologically speaking, which ushered plants and animals on an evolutionary path to modern species.

Up to now, the Eocene was the last mass extinction in Earth's history. Snail species were decimated and toothed whales disappeared. The dramatic shift of European mammals, called the "Grand Coupure," a dramatic shift of the evolutionary progress of European mammals followed the Eocene-Oligocene transition.

The iron lung filled to the ceiling with a sulfur bubble bath now sold at Walgreen's as "Grand Coupure Body Wash" and sold at a discount at the death row commissary to wash and polish the body of those men and women executed by electric chair.

Fresh Air Camp

It was summer becoming summer again and the thermostat inside the iron lung malfunctioned and Ben started to dream of a Zebra lapping cool water. His shoebox Frigidaire often iced over and using the ice pick between his teeth to defrost took hours. They used ice blocks created by using dry ice and mercury for air conditioning and set single blocks into the porthole for ventilation at zero gravity. This was not fool-proof science. It was the shepherd with his goat-herd stepping on a narrow stone path of ruin into fog that cut the tops of trees that turned a rope bridge into a deep crevice into a single tight wire and thin air into mortal shapes. The air conditioning was a gift from the Death Row Welcome Wagon Society created by small town widows and large city patrons.

They considered using the iron lung for individual hide-aways during tornado and hurricane warnings, off the Atlantic coast they would be placed along the entire shoreline for sunbathers and hop-scotch kids, once inside the iron lung it becomes a floatable buoy, a resting place for the heart during turbulence, placed inside a mermaid net and dropped into the middle of the sea, a tidal wave lifted Ben's iron lung like a basket of Easter eggs and sent it to the highest peak, Ben learns during his one conjugal visit in twenty years that kissing was the ancient art, caught under its belly in the debris of coral and starfish arms clinging to round-stone, Ben awakened to the grand champion seahorse laughing inside his aquarium of desire and figs falling from the trees.

THE ARTIST AS MADMAN

THE ARTIST NICK-NAMED himself Howdy Doody with freckles on his cheeks painted by his art professor for extra credit. Mr. Doody signed his lease on time every year until he refused to do so for uncharted reasons after he threw a boomerang and broke the bathroom window of the police station. He was hog-tied and dragged down five floors of stairs and placed in jail for behavior beyond human consumption, a baby in a wet blanket left adrift on a fishing boat or was it a raft, a fishing pole line dragging for carp diem? The Vice-President of Safe and Happy Times at Community Central with her "Hit the Road Jack!" partner Arts Cafe among the black soot in the All-American city of the drunk, homeless, and proud, missionaries in second floor command center looking down at the bushwhackers pissing into four-leaf clovers, lovers of the poor, the dry ice man who melts in spoken word quicksand and hides in the far distant shadow of the real "Iceman" Jerry Butler with his ears covered by padded cell earphones on a city bus connected to a semiconductor no audience podcast, London School of Economics, no college degree, drinking buddy to a dim star who placed a boulder in a parking lot after a drunken Halloween scream out of control temper tantrum at a regularly scheduled meeting with a witness, who dunks his head inside a barrel of alcohol, a binge-drinking married misogynist, high-art low-intellect fart-joking couple who work nine to five, hired by a friend who enjoys a drunk partner, one who teaches children to act respectfully in the classroom and the ways of drama after living in a cuckoo clock nest of broken eggs and fried bacon and drunk vomit in the stairwell like the putrid rainbow cascade on the alley mural, a loveless skillet of desire without self-knowledge and ability to discern how computer-generated abstract art by the soft shoe shuffler was a critique of his own damned paintings completed by a drunk monkey painting abstracts seated on a music box, a monkey-grinder and his pet monkey holding a paint brush between his hairy toes for its Best of Show Public Mural Award, drinking as much as the drunks and homeless in Central Park, as loud and violent as the drunks and homeless in Central Park, *Leave It to Beaver* and artists to live how they believe they live and not how they live, the watercolorist who paints his wet dreams and fishing piers and high skirts in patent leather Easter best on a grim sidewalk, a manifesto philosopher with Disney World of color computer paintings on museum walls, a tattoo artist who pushes needles into Marilyn Monroe hips and lips, the President who dances a gifted hip-hop *American Bandstand* in riding boots and silver spurs, letters from her mother, the Afrocentric dreadlocked poster maker who smokes a wicked pack of Jimmy Dean weed with the ghost of Mr. Rastafarian for breakfast and unplugs a barrel of alcohol attached to the ice-maker, the large man who eats peanuts in his car and listens to Ayn Rand on cassette tapes and dances with the President like a diamond in wingtips at the New Year's Eve Ball, who is this dimpled artless fake art couple on a yellow-bellied dick ride inside a windowless jeep into Dante's *Inferno*, throwing wedding rice and roses into a sewer, happily ever after?

Howdy loved spam and beer and triple X-rated graffiti best of shows unfit for Basquiat and any southern gentleman. Howdy was confused by his open air jeep after the hurricane force wind blew a sunflower into the crack of his wooden ass. They tossed their empty beer cans out of their empty lives once a week, placed their empty canoes on the lake water, flicked a cigarette, vegan poetics, smoking tobacco, ganja, coughing, spitting into a frying pan, floating on the Dead Connecticut Sea with a large unhealthy ass, weary arms, swollen legs, and pink lungs. After one more last lazy swig of booze a flying fish landed in his mouth.

"His abstract painting is weeping," he said.

"I weep every time I look at it, even briefly," he said.

"I love bacon," the madman said.

"I love you like bacon," the madman said.

Mr. Doody, the first gay ventriloquist dummy doll, received his eviction notice for not paying full rent and annual increases for the flop-house penthouse with whips and chains, and baking soda that left burnt knot holes on his arms and legs and he was left alone having olive oil sex with a male rubber doll behind closed doors.

The madman writes letters to himself about noise and watering holes in the small knotted world of his imagination. The Henry and June artistasters of the former working-class neighborhood drank their booze as they stood in dark pools of urine ladled out of the dog-legged tubs where they lived spoiled by the wind chimes hung like tinsel on the hot, humid, and dreadful fire escape. He grew a humpback caused by long years of drinking acid rain in bottles in the green hills of the suburb, bent over like a young boxing champion left with a swollen brain at the Hospital of Central Connecticut. He used one hundred paint cans employing without irony a theory of computer-generated abstract painting to varnish and tap the restoration of the abandoned factories in New Britain, Connecticut, once called the Hardware City of the World, and he blamed the paint for turning his self-appointed masterpiece into the face of Dorian Gray. They dragged his drunken friends passed out on park benches and behind ivy bushes into emergency welcome wagons for the deranged as the prosperous mayor stared down from her second-floor office decorated in her 4th of July parade head-dress. He had created the first opium den found in the basement of a New England high school. He was released on his own recognizance without the self-portrait of his soul. He was given the curse of the ungodly blues as a gift that left his genitals mauled by a panther in his bedroom closet.

The Haunted Typewriter
Inside the Iron Lung

Ben Cocoa typed on his one-hundred-year-old Corona donated by the Salvation Army Band for writers on death row with infirmities. He used a doll-size absinthe spoon between his false teeth made of wood in honor of George Washington who wore them with those pulled out of the mouth of slaves as they received the holy ghost in the baptismal waters, the spoon was found inside a music box that played the Moonlight Sonata and Symphony No. 6 "Pathétique" in B minor, Op. 74, he was able to type one letter per minute, weightlessness gave him a strength that had left his body and spoiled his voice as his physical body gave up the ghost of his desires and he reached out to the falling stars as if they were small gifts to soothe the grief that embraced his chest and sleeplessness, too, was the offering he received in the long hours floating inside his iron lung in the delicious air and water that fed and nourished his skeletal body. I h e a r d a v o i c e a b o v e m y h e a d . W a s i t a p s a l m ? . . .

The Sugarfield

The young technician of the Department of Lungs placed a tiny seed under Ben's copper coiled mattress. It had caused him sleeplessness during the moonless nights, and he found watching a Sundance documentary on deadly spiders alive in small corners beyond his reach made the long winter months almost too unbearable in the vagrant hours. He had a recurring nightmare that his iron lung was lifted to the roof of a carriage pulled by a twenty-mule team under a sun that rained down on the iron lung and animals laughed and stomped the snakes under their hooves and Ben felt as if a curse had been placed around his neck by a drunk hanging judge until he awakened after the rope tethered to the harness snapped into feathers and the helmsman halted the processional after the last mule suddenly caught fire. Peasants in the sugarfield had their tongues cut out of their pink mouths for reading books and screaming: *Somebody ought to write a book about it. Somebody ought to write a book about it.*

Interview Inside the Iron Lung

I wish our meeting could have been longer. I wish my story for Sunday could have been longer. It really doesn't do you, who you are or why you are, justice. But let's hope for future stories. I'll look for the top 25 or whatever and send you the link. The hell with #16. I'd put you at least in the top ten. The prose poem I read in your diary, "Misty Blue," damn near wrecked me.

Johnny Roach
New Britain Herald

Love Letters to Ben Cocoa on Death Row Inside the Iron Lung

Ahh, Ben, I feel I'm starting to know you on a whole deeper level with this message . . . thank you, it feels wonderful!

Yes, I can understand the feeling of awkwardness & longing you describe after losing your wife. I felt so lonely & lost for a while on my own, even though I chose that path. It was so painful not sharing my daily life with a trusted companion, and painful having no one to express the intimate aspects of myself with, too.

It really jumped out for me when you mentioned looking at abandoned buildings for your project . . . along with the fact that you're making a film about the brownfields where you grew up. I've been looking at abandoned buildings & brownfields for years and envisioning urban gardens and animal pastures and community learning centers that encompass art & performance. My driving passion for well over a decade has been to help create a learning center that can become a template for urban community building and new forms of community sufficiency. People who live in these old neighborhoods so often don't have access to fresh produce or even to a decent grocery store, much less to artistic environments or activities. I find that my connection to the earth and art (literary and performing, especially) as well as to living creatures (dogs & horses are my deepest love) are absolute requirements for me to stay "sane" in this world, not to mention happy.

Neither of my folks went to college but both were highly self-educated. My dad was a correspondence-school trained mechanical engineer who got a couple patents through in the 1950s for the earliest versions of high-speed textile looms in factories, to help protect workers from losing fingers. He was a Dixieland jazz man. Some really good stories there. My relationship to him was complex, but he was a good father and a good man . . . driven & emotionally kind of vacant, but all the same he was deeply committed to his family. He died of what they used to call the wasting illness in the late 1970s when he was in his early 70s.

My mom was a secretary all her life, but she inhaled books and was part of the "Great Books" movement in the 1940s–60s. She had the entire Fall of the Roman Empire history series and had read it all. She could be a little pretentious at times . . . and she struggled with a lot of depression & anxiety all her life. After my dad died, she slowly began to own her life in a whole new way. She moved to Wisconsin then (my sister & I both lived there), survived a MAJOR depression, and got involved in AA there. (She first went into AA when I was 7.) She became a beloved "sage" in her neighborhood in Milwaukee, especially among women, and she really transformed herself as a mother & friend to my sister & I. She developed Parkinson's after she retired, which was excruciatingly painful to go through, but we were spared many long years of decline. She died ten years after my father, just before the millennium.

Perhaps I am wooing you. Death row correspondence. I thought after clicking send, I would have liked to have added each barefoot step on a sweet mossy path . . . Mmmmmmm.

He did. Get this: when he was about 19 or 20 he had his own band that he called The Lonesome Roadrunners. He played cornet and thought the trumpet was a far inferior instrument. God forbid anyone call his cornet a trumpet . . . they'd get a compressed dissertation on the difference.

In the 1930s, he walked the streets of Pittsburgh's south side, knocking on doors and offering to pay 50 cents or a dollar for jazz or big band records people didn't want. He slowly amassed well over 2,000 original recordings. By the late 1960s to 1970s, he caved in a bit and started buying *Readers Digest* collections of the old recordings, but till then, he took immense delight in going through his handwritten catalog and finding just the melody he wanted!

Clarinet is a beautiful instrument. Sax too. Ben, do you ever pick it up these days? Or do you play piano, like your daughters? I sort of always wanted to learn piano, but just wasn't that motivated as a young adult. My mother claimed she was "too tired to fight with me about lessons & practicing" when I was a kid, so I just took a few months of organ lessons as a teenager and taught myself a little guitar. But I love to sing.

I live in a rented 3-level townhouse that I love. It's very basic, very affordable, and my living room windows overlook a park. Private . . . but very nice neighbors. There's a community feel.

Yes, there is a guest room! My daughter's room . . . full of traces of her high school adventures. You would be welcome on your weekend pass although the chains on your ankles make conjugal romance difficult.

My death row cell phone number is 434-1599. I don't work this Saturday, so that's a good day for us to have a conversation. How does that work for you?

Your love.

P.S., my favorite Bergman film is *Fannie & Alexander*.

P.S.S., One of my "black dress" options is very much the peasant look.

P.S.S.S., I've worried about that older writer we both know, ever since talking with him that day . . . he seemed an alcoholic time bomb (my uncle was one, too, and died from it just last fall). I hope your stories aren't tragic . . . just interesting!

SKY PILOT I

THE YELLOW TAXI drones were sent by the Fox News Network and flown over the prison guard house on the night of Ben Cocoa's planned execution. There was a recording with commentary by Sarah Palin wearing a walrus. One drone lost its battery charge, caught fire, and burst into flames. It was designed as a identical twin replica of Huggy Bear inside his broken axle cab, his charred hands on the steering wheel as it flew into barbed wire. The black manikin doll with a Chatty Cathy ring for jive had a raggedy afro, long gold chains on his open chest shirt, long-brimmed hat with a wide cowboy stripe, platform shoes with a step ladder attached to the heels, he was he secret sharer of a forgiven state of cool, half-trickster, supple and divine, white and black hippie informants for the FBI COINTELPROL death row judge and jury hanging judges who planted land mines across half the world trying to stop civil rights and prevent peacemakers stopping the Vietnam war, there was a faint sound of the helicopter blades above in the fog above the tops of trees, there was one red eye blinking, a signal of unrest in the open sky, a ring, hand held sonar in the thunder cloud, Ferris wheel, *top of the morning, sir,* and the Black Panthers asleep on a waterbed never had a living chance.

The parachute was tethered to each end of the iron lung shaped like a root beer barrel from the candy store. Ben would be dropped from a dirigible over Times Square. They prepared the iron lung for a soft landing and then lifted down a blue fire escape by New York's finest and placed on a float. The first iron lung on Wall Street welded together with prehistoric amber rhinestones. Had they lined ten thousand lawn jockeys and burning lanterns along the parade route in honor of the world wars seen in a theology of epistemic injustice, alchemy, gallows physics, surveillance of body, apparition of time, negation of soul? Although he was still breathing and years away from his scheduled execution, they lifted one snapped ankle and began to wrap Ben's body in plaster of Paris, banana leaves, and lime dust. His head was left exposed and his mouth kept open by pinchers as he gasped the thinning air until the breathing tube was inserted into a small incision below his Adam's apple. Ben spoke in high-pitched and guttural noises, recited Shakespeare, and described a fishing pier where he had danced with his lover under the moon's wreckage. He lifted his head and heard a chime from a music box that had fallen just out of his reach.

The hanging judge called for several types of execution for certain death. Electrocution. Gas. Bow and Arrow. Wheel. Rope. Fire. Lethal Injection. Smoke. Explosion. Chains. Stone. Water . . .

OPTOGENIC USES IN THE IRON LUNG

BEN COCOA. SHY as second grade. He had signed a medical release form for his body to be dissected after his execution, vital organs removed and placed into Mason jars and barrels of single-blend black scotch. They flushed his pink lungs with fresh water out of the Shuttle Meadow Reservoir and examined his genetic code for signs of lasting love, how somewhere in everyone's blood there were clear signs connecting the brain to a mortal kiss and the soul to the emerald wing of the blackbird, and the particles of physics became the unseen particles inside the hourglass, what made them float and rise and bounce inside the cadaver's mouth and heart, its marbled tongue speaking the language of a last will and testament given by the scientist behind a curtain standing in front of a mirror designed to dissolve every source of light found in a single human eye, a curse or was any old penny a lucky penny?

"I see the earth men and their ruby dolls inside the periscope."

"Please send her letters to my iron lung."

"I can almost see her face in the widowed stars."

The Green Mountains

Ben Cocoa drove Little Eliot to the Green Mountains at Breadloaf. She performs the lead in *Troilus and Cressida* on the mountain top. He had not been to the Texas Falls in forty years, its plush cascade of water attempting to fill the low spots of the earth, the trestle of broken steps halfway into the underworld, the bridge over boulders, a brim of trees, gorge of blue and green tassels of rainbow flags blown into the air, Ciardi, perched in a fool's throne, filling his wine glass with the elixir of sin, Pack speaking of the wonder of the *Sonnetelle*, a science of poetics and the pastoral black caboose, and Asimov laughing at Ben looking out into the tops of trees and saying: *The loin of the mountain.*

The 1964 World's Fair

It WAS FIFTY years ago today and *Sergeant Pepper* had not begun to play. Ben's daughter Isadora performs in the World's Fair Plays at the Queen's Theater on the sacred grounds. Ben Cocoa was photographed in front of the Unisphere, one leg crossed, arm over the shoulder of one buddy, Ray Charles sunglasses, white plaid jacket, white Keds, a Roosevelt Junior High School field trip, New Britain Public Schools at their long-lost-best-witless-to-give-us-your-tired-and-poor-and-huddled-masses-yearning-to-be-free-at-last, highest unemployment and lowest income, parking garage with all-night bare bulbs lighting the universe, flags of the world above sky pilots bombs away flitter and shrapnel debris over the heads of sleeping children in a civil rights Vietnam fly over white crosses and a widow's thin aluminum chair, folded flag, taps played and outside the cemetery a transistor radio inside a bicycle basket and the schoolyard playground ribbon candy celebration merry-go-round singing it's a small world after all.

The Price of the Ticket in Space

I STEERED THE wooden circus wheels of my iron lung out of the New Haven Amtrak train station at approx. 1:00 A.M. in need of coffee and sleep. I had just returned by train from New York City after presenting a performance and book signing. I drove the speed limit past construction sites and continued on the exit toward the poorly lit Berlin Turnpike. I had not eaten much during the day and turned left into the MacDonald's parking lot for so-called nourishment. Yes. I should have taken the U-turn back on the Berlin Turnpike and into the parking lot. It was dark. The back seat of my car was full of books and the dog kennel basket. I was on my way into Newington to pick up my 16-year-old 8-pound toy fox terrier named Mojo from my mother's house. It was almost 2:00 A.M. My books and dog cage nearly came up to the inside roof of the back seat in the car. My pillow and head rest is always at the highest level to keep my rather large head straight and steady on the road ahead. I am a widower, and I raised my two daughters alone the past 13 years. I am semi-retired. I was a professor for nearly 40 years, and the last position I held was Distinguished Endowed Chair of English. A few weeks ago, I received an Honorary Doctorate of Humane Letters, *Honoris Causa*. I always wear my straightjacket and there are seat belts on my ankles, waist, and wrists. When I turned into the parking lot with the flashing lights behind me, I stopped, and as I always do when ordering something from a drive-through Starbucks, I released my seat belt, lifted my buttocks, and reached into the deep pocket for my wallet and identification to give to the officer. He said he thought I was not wearing a seat belt. How could the Officer of Iron Lungs see through my mile-high books and a dog cage, definitively, under the bare bulb light turning into a low-rent fast food parking lot, whether or not I was wearing a seat belt? I told him emphatically that I was wearing one. I would not drive, at night, inside an iron lung with a bumper made by the Department of War, without a seat belt on. If necessary, I am willing to take a lie detector on the Dr. Phil show.

Sincerely,
Ben Cocoa

P.S. The case was dismissed.

And if thy brother, a Hebrew man, or a Hebrew woman, be sold unto thee, and serve thee six years; then in the seventh year thou shalt let him go free from thee. And when thou sendest him out free from thee, thou shalt not let him go away empty: thou shalt furnish him liberally out of thy flock, and out of thy floor, and out of thy winepress: of that wherewith the LORD thy God hath blessed thee thou shalt give unto him. And thou shalt remember that thou wast a bondman in the land of Egypt, and the LORD thy God redeemed thee: therefore I command thee this thing today.
— Deuteronomy 15: 12–15

Besides the crime which consists in violating the law, and varying from the right rule of reason, whereby a man so far becomes degenerate, and declares himself to quit the principles of human nature, and to be a noxious creature, there is commonly injury done to some person or other, and some other man receives damage by his transgression: in which case he who hath received any damage, has, besides the right of punishment common to him with other men, a particular right to seek reparation.
— John Locke, "Second Treatise"

By our unpaid labor and suffering, we have earned the right to the soil, many times over and over, and now we are determined to have it.
— Anonymous, 1861

The Cement Mixer as Iron Lung

After a six-month flight and landfall in a Nebraska wheat field, they hoisted the iron lung into two halves of a cement mixer into a hammock of desire, its waterproof doors locked together like the prison gate at sundown, and the churning was heard from the solitary confinement of inmates who slept underground in the flooded underworld of their embrace and affliction, it turned twenty-four hours a day above a factory furnace, cooled by a running stream of saltwater poured over the vessel, and Ben started to sleep better inside a metal drum, the rise and fall of a raft thrown from a burning ship, the well done soldier-apprentice behind enemy lines lifted out of a trench and placed on the frontline, one hole through Ben's elbow were indentations on the outside of the iron lung. Ben was a bullet-catcher of crime, remembrance, and punishment tethered to the stars.

AVON LADY

THE IRON LUNG was hung inside a hammock at Central Park in New Britain, Connecticut. It was a hundred degrees, and the high humidity created droplets of condensation that fell into the mouth of Ms. Ruby who sat on the park bench without her banned grocery cart. She swung her cane against the sky.

"They may take my Wild Irish Rose, but I can still squeeze the grape," she screamed.

Ms. Ruby tried to pull down a knotted branch of the oak tree, holding the iron lung, with the handle of her walking stick. She cursed at Ben as he tried to sleep inside his tomb of noise. Her voice trembled and echoed off its walls like a church choir in a baptism of fire. The crowd gathered around the coffee and donuts. The man held a microphone and spoke of the devil at his side as he tried to awaken the gold angel that stared down at the world walking in despair. The angel opened her eyes for a few minutes and lowered her head as the wind stirred and the rain fell over the city.

"My mother was the first black Avon Lady in the city. I would have been one too, but they did not like me living outside the inside of a grocery cart. I started to drink and never stopped."

"I attended Weaver High School in Hartford. I wrote a book," she said.

Ms. Ruby whispered with a sadness one finds in a small child with large eyes into the speaker, next to the porthole, riveted to the port side of the iron lung, and told Ben she will drink until she dies.

Woe and Enchantment

Dear Friend,

It is evening. I stay awake late and always rise early.
They were far too young to know the days and months and years
ahead of them although they knew everything. I was only thinking of
their young grief. When Wendy first passed away (first?) I was completely obsessed with giving them a mother and a wife for myself. One
woman tried to take advantage of my position and fine house, another
was jealous of Wendy and those memorial boards my daughters created
. . . it was several years later I learned that all they needed was to see
me happy. I have not remarried although I might marry again. I have
been far too busy with my books and daughters for such a ritual. I have
not even partnered for any length of time yet it is time. I would like a
partner who might wish to know my creative process and writing life.
I would live with somebody if possible.

Your Friend, Ben

Dear Ben,

Thanks for your thoughts as you live inside your iron lung. It is
a journey. It seems right that your girls, especially now that they are
spreading their wings into their vocations and talents, should feel
now the wish for you to be happy. My older daughter long wanted
me not to remarry, but as her teen years advance, and perhaps as she
sees me talking often to and trying to help my widowed mom as
she gets older, what it means to have someone to walk along beside
you as you move on in life—seems meaningful to her in new ways.
My kids want to see me happy and they also want and need(ed?)
my attention, to know they were my priority, to see that in action.

What it means to love in the fall of life, vs the spring or summer, perhaps: knowing time isn't forever, able to live fully in the days in ways that for me, at least, weren't possibly in my youth (with its other tasks of living and learning). I have "inner resources," as my mom would say—I would rather be alone than with someone not right. My dream is of being understood and accepted, of being able just to be (even though of course love involves work over time, sometimes). My secret dream is of the kind of love described by Rilke in *Letters to a Young Poet*—"two solitudes that protect and cherish and salute one another." It's important to me to be a good teacher, to be kept honest by teaching, but so much less so than twenty years ago—now I want to develop my visions and ideas and questions as fully as I can, to live my spark of talent as fully as I can, to write things up and send them out into the world. Perhaps that is something like the wish you express. I would like a partner who understands this and who is a daily partner, a "I made coffee, do you want some" partner, a "you have flu, get back in bed" partner. The glorious and the mundane (sometimes not so clear where these are separated). I started out an essay writer and felt I couldn't/didn't want to teach nonfiction writing workshops like those I attended as an undergraduate—I have kept the flame alit, starting things, planning things. I have this in me too, not more important than the books I want to finish (Harriet Jacobs, deafness and child-rearing) but also important. To listen to my muse and know in my bones I haven't shirked, I've paid attention and respect and walked the walk. Today to New Hampshire to see a friend who works in Idaho and was there visiting relatives—took my friend's child who was a little overwhelmed by the number of smiling strangers and comforted, as I knew she would be, by *It's a Small, Small World* movie I had on my laptop for her to watch, to be taken away into. Lots of rain. Happy turn into Monday—sleep well, dream well.

Y. S. A.

Dear Ben,

Merrimack is about an hour north of Boston, next to Bedford. I don't lose my temper and am steady as can be. When is your birthday? Would love to chat about villanelles, graduate poetry classes, and (ah the saga) Life In The Academy.

Thanks for this. Lovely love letter—the details make it vivid and particular and save the awash with love overall mood and point from seeming like "love" of a familiar kind. I like the shift from detailed observed landscape and light to memories of girlhoods, from the timeless image of a butterfly to the timebound and evocative mention of *Seussical*. It seems right to open from that tunnel to the neighbors, the wider local world, makes the last line feel right and earned. Meriden is often our stopping point on longer drives to NY/ PA—we three might possibly come to a reading and signing, though that wouldn't be a conversation *à deux*. I also checked—Worcester is actually closer to both of us, halfway between us, a little more than an hour. I know two good Indian restaurants there, Bollywood Grill and Surya. Even though my kids are home with me now and their weeks of daycamp are done, they can stay together for the three-four hours that meeting you for a meal would involve, pretty much any time in August. So another option.

During the school year I get up at 4 to have time to work and be before the household day begins. Glad today to be back (I think) on a workable summer schedule, up at 6—need to finish the notes for my newest article, on the representation of deaf mutes, which I think matters because it is before the regime of sentimentalism came in—so dumb blacksmiths "count" as blacksmiths, as plebeians, workers skeptical about the middle class and Enlightenment dream of progress. It's made it through the first round at *Readings in American Literature*, a journal I generally love—fingers crossed. I have a chapter accepted to a volume called *Widening the Family*, on ways that changing perspectives on the family challenge what we think we know about the roles of children in American culture (my chapter is on life stories by several early 20th century American women in differing socioeconomic conditions), must be well into that before the school year begins as it is due in December. But the next thing I will face in my early morning work hours, after the notes are done today, is a revise-and-resubmit for an essay on the book called *Life and Times of Ida Wells-Barnett*, who was an indomitable investigative journalist, to *Women in Publishing*. I love discovery and have had to push myself to follow through and finish larger projects, like the Jacobs book. I just presented from it at a conference in Albany and am determined to complete it and move on to the project on deafness and childhood that seems to have arrived in my heart and spirit.

Your Secret Death Row Admirer

Dear Ben,

I read the news today how they launched your iron lung into space six months ago after you were given solitary confinement for prison misdeeds and frivolity of playing Motown at midnight in the unforgivable silence of the Tombs. You were the first to take flight in the movement of political prisoners to landscapes beyond Earth under a territory of the stars beyond our stellar blue oceans and ice floes that made the oceans rise and flood the great plains. They found a lost map blown out of a saddle bag on the Pony Express near Chimney Rock picked up by a surveyor of the heart.

Thank you for your words and these poems. "The Poet's Wife" —if I may say as a former wife, the title (and the phrase, "a husband with two daughters"—those girls are also her daughters, not only or even perhaps mainly yours in this drama?) makes her part of you in a way the rest of the poem does not, honoring her separateness, the life in her body alone, the death that came to her body alone. I love the way you make the Midwestern setting temporal as well as spatial; the most vivid and getting-through image of these is for me "knelt together like angels on the great plains," also the "newborn, stillborn" at the prom door. "Unequal to holy war"—I'm not sure I get the kind of contrast of personal, intimate vs global at work here, forgive me. It is so hard to grieve in poems in ways that honor the beloved and the work of grief itself in our lives, in life—that offer the self to get out of the way of the self. I like the passive agency in the last line, "a distant signal found the artery of remembrance"—the artery, blood, being remembered and itself remembering—makes her suffering both more vivid and more vast, even impersonal. Me myself, for what it is or isn't worth—I would like to be able to see her body specifically —that chin, that wrist, that changed way of sitting, that hair on the forehead. I will read more and write again later. So glad to have these poems and this correspondence.

Y. S. A.

Dear Ben,

Smiling as I make my coffee. Don't you think there are terrible solitudes and blessed solitudes? Suffering is certainly more terrible when it can't be shared. Yes, about Lawrence, though he's also the one who wrote, "All that matters is to be at one with you, the living God . . . Like a cat asleep on a chair, At peace, in peace, at home, at home in the house of the living . . . a deep calm in the heart . . .." So great to converse and be able to include these kinds of landmarks of my living. Wow, a Grace Paley connection! Which poem, which prize? Happy Monday . . .

A. B.

Dear Friend,

"Teach Us to Sit Still"
There is terror and absurdity wherever we walk. Yet to be with one and alone with or without a God . . . beauty and terror. Paley chose one of my poems for a national prize The Writers' Voice. It appears in my new and selected "On Being Invisible (For Ralph Ellison)" each us

to sit still as Pascal wrote and Eliot borrowed. Beauty or terror: this is what I do with my writing.

Your Prisoner Inside the Iron Lung Buried in the Dunes,

Ben

P.S. French Roast?

Dear Father Ben,

I Woke Up At 12 Midnight.

Thought I'd read some of your book, Dad. *We did not fear . . .* Marked out some pages for a new friend to read. Sometimes getting to know people, I just give them your book.

Then I read some of it. I guess I never read the Mrs Belladonna part. I skimmed it and saw some lines, made me sad. Couldn't read. I don't know how you did it. To write all that stuff, but I'm so proud of you for doing it. That takes a lot of courage.

Last year at the beginning of school, we had a workshop with our soon-to-be playwriting teacher. She had us go around and say one word that describes a parent. We went on to talk about how one word holds so much weight and meaning. She only asked a couple of ppl to say their word and the rest of the class made assumptions of what kind of person your parent is . . . I wanted to tell you that my word for you was *Brave*.

Among all the words I could think of, this one seemed the most close to who you are, who you have been for Little Eliot and I.

Thought you should know. I love you both so much and I'm thankful for you. More than I could ever say in words.

—Shelley

THE IRON LUNG OF THE DUNES

THEY FILMED THE execution for the World Wide Web in a move to resuscitate America Online. It was turned into a three-part miniseries after it took him three hours to die. They called his gasping snoring and his dying a heavenly light that lifted his body before dropping it into the eternal flames on a bed of hay and roses.

They hid the iron lung from poachers. Ben Cocoa, half-buried and half-alive, was prepared for the limitations of the human body. There would be fair amounts of electricity and a public utility gas chamber in a second iron lung built for the encore of executions planned for the holidays. Water torture inside his iron lung was determined useless based on false measurements of pain and the delirious effects of knowing how drowning was the third wave of a hand going down, down, down, a bag over the head, electrodes under armpits and clamped to male and female genitalia, flared nostrils, heating pad under a bed sore, counting black sheep set on fire, a blink and half-a-nod to anxiety, surveillance, the beating the truth out of lie, beating a lie out of a truth, beating the mouth until it pleads for mercy, carving into the flesh, pressing a smoldering X brand shaped like a crimson hand into Ben's temple until he fainted. They placed a mask over Ben's face and recorded his internal temperature and re-set his breathing tube. The sentry allowed the Ministers of the Heart to lower a man by frayed rope into the dune's sink hole used for solitary confinement, a wishing well.

A Dull Yellow Submarine

Ben was selected from one thousand prisoners on death row to board his iron lung inside a dull yellow submarine. The scientists were looking to the ocean as they had studied the moduli black harvest of the stars and brown dwarves they surmised mirrored the underworld of coral and luminous creatures that crawled the sea floor. How had they developed their high order of senses yet remained sightless and warm in the cold waters at depths beyond air and gravity, a cactus of starfish arms clinging to a round stone, the seaquake opened the underwater tomb releasing a porridge of venom into the freshwater reservoirs of time, and what became of the woman of the midnight sail, dressed in a white robe under the moon's wreckage, holding a telescope to the stars? They placed a necklace of urchins and sea charms on Ben's neck and crowned him king of the sea cliffs and a survivor of the coastal waters that rose out of the ocean inside the iron lung as the blindfolded manikin fell to earth.

Beehive Blues Inside the Iron Lung

They replaced his straitjacket with a bug-proof Easter coat. They sized his increasingly small head with a Model A Mann Lake CL(!!) Stingless Binding Square Folding Veil with Zipper. There was Ben Cocoa at rest wearing a bee coat and patent leather penny loafers with untouched 1943 copper pennies in his eyes and shoes. The nest of African honey bees was cryogenically frozen and placed in his meatless freezer with blue ice cubes used for his favorite ice tea with lemonhead drops. The bees would be released in case of a gravitational shift of the stars. Ben would pull the emergency cord above his head like a pendulum inside the iron lung that opened the moon roof into a diamond shaped window to the galaxy. Ben operated his appliances with the tip of his swollen tongue. He used the beggar's knife he placed in his apron during holiday dinners between his frost-bitten toes to cut through wires connected to his breathing tube and freed his descent from the fault lines between light and darkness, a small bellows under his one good arm resuscitated him during layovers between this burning planet and that hollow dying star. If the bellows failed, he would need a single bite from a single bee to draw blood into his forehead and breath into his parched lungs, he inhaled what he expected to be his last breath from a long filter attached to a bubblegum Marlboro cigarette, a video played in the medicine cabinet mirror, a bluebird flew out of a smokestack, the police found a wedding gown on the fire escape, it took two hours and fifteen lethal injections to kill the last prisoner on death row, and Ben sought comfort in how he lived and nestled the hourglass filled with bee venom between his teeth like a World War II spy in a flophouse movie.

Ebola Inside the Iron Lung

HE RECEIVED A birthday gift from the Crippled Daughters of the Confederacy of Dunces who left flowers at the prison gate in honor of the rapidly executed. It was wrapped in fuchsia onion skin with a small red bow. He placed his bandaged thumb into a hole on the side of the box. He pulled out a long string attached to a video electric eye. He kissed the box as if he were kissing the hand of royalty at a world boxing match. He lifted his personal Ebola necklace, sold at the Family Dollar for old-school green stamps, and placed it around his neck, it was like a chain of pomegranate seeds and ivory porcupine teeth that glowed in the crawl space of the underworld in the half-light of prayer and evolution, a necklace, a charm bracelet with tiny carved wheelchairs, white dove, Yellow Cab, a bar of soap, noose, rotary telephone, headphones, Quaker Oats, scalpel, fishing hook, diploma, head hog cheese, hourglass, ruby slipper, it was a gift placed on the thin wrist of the newly dead and sold to the living at a discount, the emergency squad rolled a gurney into the root cellar under a bare bulb and placed a death mask attached to a half-empty oxygen tank dug out of a trench with canisters of nerve gas with golden shovels, they inserted a long reed straw into the mouth of the death mask and placed two calls, one to the Minister of the Heart and one to the Retriever of the Dead, a young child played a xylophone until Ben's blood ran clear inside his breathing tube.

Finding the Brains of Isaac Asimov and Isaac Hayes Inside a Glass Jar Under a Dog-Legged Tub at Breadloaf

Ben's body was kept half alive in suspended animation under dry ice, a one-minute black-and-white newsreel showed how his planned electrocution caused a major blackout in most cities in the world, the power grids had been struck dumb by solar flares and cosmic karma left over from the old-age hippies who marched and sang and made love in sweet mud after the iron lung rose out of quicksand transported from the Amazon River and Himalayan churchyard, there was evidence of a supernatural event, the holy cross on a steeple caught fire in broad daylight, a cloud of starlings above a war monument flew into the sewer behind the Dismal River, a manikin at the local toy store opened its eyes, the cashier wiped a speck of blood under its left eye, moon flares changed the color of the night sky to oxblood, the prison staff turned the iron lung on the devil's rotisserie each hour, Ben had found a certain comfort in this, face up, face down, his body tossed above a Rolodex of feathers and ash.

Ben hung his Ebola necklace on the mobile above his soiled mattress inside the iron lung, Earth's porcelain gift, it might have been in the stars, the alignment of Mars and Nebraska, Pluto and Connecticut's last black hippie, a page torn out of the yellow pages in 1969, found in a wallet under the grate outside the Blue Mirror Bar, Jude's last name and phone number, a week after the Senior Prom and the ride to White Sands Beach Gary and Debbie, how a life was changed by another life, how lives were changed by other lives, how the world was changed by a single life, how the universe was changed by a single act of war, how the taking of one life led to the taking of another life, a string theory of the first living organism, upright on two legs, sprinting into despair and oblivion.

The Witless Seed

Ben read about a well-disposed truth, how the brain was created by the charred hand of a god that trampled humans like flowers, a convergence of prayer and spoiled meat, part-time soldier and witness to depravity and the witless seed somewhere in everyone's blood, planted by a hoe and grown in the baptismal waters, not a curse on the world we inhabit, a curse on the body we inhabit, the soul we desire, and the voice above our heads, the burning sail, volcanic ash, stone and timber dragged for a century, a city built inside the corridors of the sea flowers, Neptune's hoppin' john, and those who breathed in deep waters breathed on land and those who breathed on land found pestilence in deep water and those who breathed in deep waters found love on land, what had one become on death row between three meals and one hour of light a day, a wheelchair used by the wounded without eyes, arms and legs, refugees, burnt hair, broken jaws, led by the Crippled Ghost in a white dress holding a staff, floating above the trenches, stooped over the flames, and started to dig into the sand for the human treasure, a witless seed buried by the retrievers of the dead on a covered bridge inside a clearing in the wilderness, and she stepped lightly on the inferno's tilted landscape, looking for Earth's wounded and Earth's gift, left to those who survived on land and walked into embers that bloomed in the fog, finding the dead and raising the dead.

THE *PIETÀ*'S SHADOW
IN THE DEATH CHAMBER

BEN COCOA HELD the Virgin Mary's soft hand as he sat in the electric chair. The warden had placed a black veil over his eyes and cape over his shoulders, death's apparel, a blue halo formed above his head, the vagrant hours filled his cell, a painting of the *Pietà*, his fiction in front of a mirror, turned colors, the honor guard of executions raised their hands, white gloves and took slow steps under rain and saluted the iron lung as one guard in a top hat stepped forward and opened a music box. He took out the Town Crier's skeleton key, presented to him after he emerged speaking in languages thought to be lost to war and natural disasters, after living for years inside a cave under the waterfall. He turned the key once and listened to Ben's voice at the end of his breathing tube breaking into a psalm, he turned the key twice and a bell rang on the ventilator, and he turned the key three times, opened the window, and observed how Ben had lived in his last hours, a painting of the *Pietà*'s and her curved spine and cloven feet, the Town Crier hung a curtain over the porthole, yet it would not stop the angelic light, would not stop the throttle of pain that shook Ben's body, would not stop the embers shooting out of his clenched teeth and shut eyes, and it would not stop the birds screaming for their lives and the vagrant hours and blue halo of fire above his head.

Wrecking Ball

One almost expected invisible arrows to drizzle out of the sky, propelled by war and desire, ten thousand poison-tipped blow darts, dipped in a misery stew of celibate wild boar, Mojave green, pot liquor, brown rice, and albino haggis. Nobody saw what was coming tonight, the apparition at the screen door, a stair of the third floor, a blue ghost at the window a few miles down from Lucy's Love Palace, the cement mixer parked in front of city hall, opened like a morning glory, and they lifted the iron lung into the water, it was built to float in turbulent waters and survive harsh winters, insulated by the feathers of the white raven and crushed human bone, the prison had orders to move the iron lung into a lavender field as a final resting place until a meteor shower under the harvest moon placed the county jail on high alert, they placed Ben on a death watch and the exact time of his execution was determined by the boat's sundial. Before his fifteen lethal injections of tainted breast milk for bountiful punishment, Ben was given the elixir out of the king's chalice. He looked at a photograph of her lilac eyes and a thin arrow pierced his chest. The doctors pushed the mop pail under his cot, tightened his straitjacket, long needles in his arms, neck, thigh, penis, his body swelled into a large circus balloon tethered to the stars, he would die under his cot, drowned in the dismal waters, he was revived, half-alive on his mattress, he would die under the trestle he was revived in the high cliffs, he died.

BLUEBLOOD

IT WAS ALL about the sandwich. The turmoil started at Capitol Lunch known worldwide for its famous secret sauce, workers from the factory and city hall, famous because it was secret or secret because it was famous? The recipe was kept underground in a safe deposit box at the Burritt Mutual Savings Bank and lost during its demolition followed by the loss of five local movie theaters. Those citizens of neighborhood news and history claimed the sauce was stolen from the buried vault of a slave who taught himself to read under penalty of death and who served it on the plantation with his own original mixture of tea, witch hazel, and devil's claw. The family died off after thirty years of hiccups and pus, but this is not their story, this is the story of the anvil used by the king's horseman who turned bad luck into a horseshoe and dust into holy water.

The retrievers of the dead had pulled their wooden cart bearing the iron lung to the front door three days before New Year's Eve. The three ex-convicts who turned into beggars for God ordered thirty-six Mucke and Martin Rosol hot dogs for the public viewing stand built out of pine and tar and feathers for the execution. The trap door was devised using medieval standards of woe, enchantment, and courtly love. What was read as redemption in scripture was a curse, the crystal ball's landscape of misfortune, a hanging noose, a bluebird pulled into a chimney, one snap of the golden thumb.

Sky Pilot II

THEY BUILT A solid-state record player with a gyroscopic needle next to Ben's head inside the iron lung. When he was a freshman he played "Who'll Stop the Rain" for 72 hours straight dressed in a Ghandi robe, sandals, and rose-colored wire rim glasses. His roommates declared war, broke the door, and threw the record and phonograph out of second floor window. Ben, who tried to stop the rain, too, was pleased they had done so and passed a bottle of Boone's Farm apple wine to the "Break Out the Jams, Motherfuckers!" crowd on the college green.

Ben also requested an 8-track machine with videos of the March on Washington, Freedom Riders, Chicago 7, Black Panthers and Leonard Bernstein, and the 1968 Democratic Convention. Hoover's FBI had planned to manufacture segregated iron lungs with WHITE ONLY signs forged in Pittsburgh steel and Stanley rivets. It took a flea-bitten beggar who found Hoover's papers in a trash can in the alley nicknamed Transvestite Spies Need Work Will Travel for Love, Food, and Sex.

Inside the iron lung, Ben played his songs whenever he wished for as long as he wished. He listened to *James Brown at the Apollo, 1962*, Herman's Hermits, T. S. Eliot reciting *The Wasteland*, "San Franciscan Nights," "Sky Pilot," *Jimi Hendrix and the Band of Gypsys*, Motown, and *Sergeant Pepper's Lonely Hearts Club Band*, and he found love under summer rain on a white beach, on a greyhound bus headed to New York City into the Midwest, hitch-hiking to a wedding in Cleveland, picked up by the state police and taken on a ride through Ohio into Kent State, stuck under a thunderstorm and a bridge, his thumb catching a milk truck headed into Ann Arbor on Memorial Day, half in love with a printmaker, nobody home, nobody half alive in the city, outdoor concerts on Sunday, levitating above the arboretum, listening to Sam and Dave, and Blood, Sweat, and Tears, and Joan Baez. Ben was half-way home until he received #105 in the lottery of petrified wood and a draft notice to be present in downtown Detroit at 8:00 A.M. and as he rode the bus he looked up at the sky and named the constellations and forgot the name of the cheerleader he never kissed.

Murder and Suicide
Inside the Iron Lung

THE IRON LUNG was recalled not for a malfunction in its steering wheel taken from a 57 Chevy at the Willow Street Junkyard, but to turn the hourglass. It seemed to Ben that unknown physics had set *the ghost in the machine* off course and the pig lard and pot liquor caused a spark and altered its gears. Ben had caught a small portion of a sun flare in his magnifying glass he had kept since Smith Elementary School and burned the middle of its center, and they prepared a crew to repair the hourglass. It would take a year-long journey into the outer regions of the soul captured in the falling light and nettle of rainbow and broadcast on twenty-four hour news cycles around the globe, what enemy carved the spoils of war, yet it was not the kaleidoscope of colors he observed in the nappy afro stars nor the soul in its descent into the heart's inferno, it was the nature of the crime and how the crystal ball on the mantle filled night with falling embers of sleep that left God's pastel fingerprint on the cellar window, had he looked for something rare under his throne, stared into the captain's periscope and dipped his arm into the undertow of the underworld, sketched the terror in the battlefield and raised a hand for blood, hunger, thirst, alchemy of the cross, birthright, *knife*, blueblood, *crippled ghost*, birthstone, *roped bridge*, keen immortal worship, stepped lightly into a killing field, walked to the mountaintop, gathered wood in the Green Mountains, and what startled Ben awake made him weep on his bed of grief or was it God's charred fingers that moved across his cheekbone, tinsel falling over his deep-set eyes under the widowed light that arched his spine, half awake and weeping profusely in the weary arms held by the undefined air under the earth's smoldering stars under the weightless embrace of solitude a brief kiss on the low shoulder, what he thought was in his life on the pier of remembrance and landscape of tilled and water-colored fields, trench warfare, barbed wire, mustard gas, the last man who night crawled until he saw a halo of fire rise over the equator.

Ben stooped over the stone fence and drank out of the peasant's gourd pulled out of a wishing well. He entered the iron lung unjustly convicted on death row and left the iron lung a harvester of the stars and holy ruin.

Sweet Cigar, My Darling

So. The young man was shot seven times in the back and the back of the head. The crowd gathered on the town green under the town clock. It was late summer. There was a bronze leaf on the hanging tree at the shore, a needle boat and rowers on the lake, a man in a long black coat left a parasol at the churchyard door, a harpist played "Für Elise" in the lilac garden, the sky darkened and the choir of children with webbed feet ran into the root cellar. The violinist took shelter under the grape-vines. Lightning traveled across the telephone wire and clothes line and through the picture window into a large mirror above the fireplace.

Ben examined the small faces that appeared in a photograph at the back of the wedding album, clipped ears, beveled eyes, and pursed mouths *purgatorio.* Were these the faces of woe and enchantment collected and captured in the mortal light, half-alive saying: *I am here, this is how we breathe, there is light and there is no light, there is hunger and there is no hunger, there is love and there is no love, there is life and there is no life, there is laughter and there is no laughter, there is fire and there is no fire, there is air and there is no air, there are voices and there are no voices, there is war and there is no war.*

It was how the light was altered after the first light. It was the spool of darkness after the first darkness. It was the birth after the first stillborn. It was a lullaby after the birth before they captured the holy city. It was love after the first love. It was war after the first war.

Ben fell asleep in the iron lung after reading psalms. He met his first and only wife at the Bushnell Jazz Festival under a blue sky, drive-in movie, night train to New Orleans, wed under a cathedral of moon and chalice of stars.

My last request before my execution was a sweet cigar, my darling.

Dear Beguiled University:

I am grateful to receive this high honor from Beguiled University based, in part, on the writer's life that started for me as a freshman and English major. The writing started here has taken me to many universities, but Siena is the one university that defines my life, heart, and the larger world. My wife passed away thirteen years ago. My two daughters, Little Eliot and Isadora, are not seated here today. They attend graduate schools on the East and West coasts, but they are all in two of my two poems I offer to you:

Prose Poem for Little Eliot

January 7, 1985, 3:23 A.M.

Winter brings my wife a child and your birth arrives with the morning tide like wings alive in a jar. The sunflower seeds and thorns bloom in your hands, Claire, and we walk in the mist and draw circles in the sand. I read your palms like a map and there are small islands and mountain roads rising in your summer eyes. Is my daughter the dancer, actress, artist, gifted in language or song? I search the form and proper length to write one impossible verse to place into your hand. The unspoken metaphor falls like a meteor into this simple throne of time I've built for you and your birth arrives with the morning tide like wings alive in a jar.

For Two Daughters

for Little Eliot and Isadora,

There is no history in their eyes as they tap
the lilac drum and birch, roll out the silver
necklace into a straight line over the stone
and open wound.

The light brown yet darker daughter
sits on the father's back porch and
reads a poem to the brown yet
whiter one under his arms.

There is no history in their eyes only
the ancestral trick light pulling the cart
out of the mud and war with mules,
peasants, and slaves.

There are one thousand metaphors, a
father's fortune in their eyes: hollow
star, broken wheel, caboose, wild
horse, wings over a blue pond.

Their father's pen replaces the hollow star
with a broken wheel and drops a whistle
on the train as wild horses graze and stare
at the wings above the blue pond.

There is no history in their eyes
only two daughters in the backyard
hidden under the cellar door. This
is their evening of metaphor.

Thank you.

Voice Box

THERE WAS NO good way to begin. Ben lost his voice inside the iron lung. He was no longer able to record his thoughts on the cassette tape needed after the reel-to-reel broke apart and snapped into feathers, into the alphabet of mastodon nouns and mortal verbs, his voice pulled from his past, defined in the present, and partitioned into the future. The reel-to-reel was tethered to a black rotary phone and Ben felt like Clark Kent posed as a detective in a film noir trying to hide behind a dumpster in the alley behind the Belvedere Restaurant, beggars foraging the kielbasa, sauerkraut, black ants roasted under a child's magnifying glass, a song traveling through space, eternal keyboard of God, a surgical hole in the esophageal throttle of time, a voice box attached to Ben's neck brace and breathing tube, the experiment without gravity and the force-fed mallard, he recited "Loveliest of Trees" in a pirate's voice, a bottom dweller in the aquatic stratosphere of speech, the voice box was a gift placed inside a cedar chest, it had been pulled out of the chest of the ventriloquist dummy doll found in the basement of the New Britain Mausoleum of American Art, on loan from the Institute of Higher Living in Hartford, once used to study the effects of syphilis on black citizens and LSD on soldiers in one final act of war, and what happened to the human voice before and after execution, the harmony, archangel, melody, red violin, bellow, tenor saxophone, screech owl, the Backyard Poetry Theater in New Orleans, Bywater, steamboat, breech, high-water, whiplash, Mardi Gras, Don Pardo, "Iko, Iko," James Brown on the second floor, Junior Walker and the All-Stars on the first, Café du Monde, *café au lait*, chicory, the Holy Bells of Jackson Square, Napoleon's bare feet, Jax Beer, up to the knees in mud and jazz and blues and a twenty-four hour gospel trolley to the inferno.

They pumped sphagnum, peat moss, and quicksand over the electric chair to weigh down the particular physics of dying without a voice and to preserve his hollow bones. They left a bottle of vintage Loch Du at the foot of Ben's bed to provoke laughter in the sentry outside the chamber's viewing stand. One man was known to throw himself against the one-way mirror, a woman clawed at the glass for her lover and falsely accused murderer, one guard on a weekend pass volunteered to videotape and Spotify the exact moment of the body left the soul, the bare bulb on a frayed string above his head smoldered and exploded into angelic light and they stood before the man who would not die, a monument to those prepared to kill and those who had killed and those followed the crime and recorded the punishment in the field, they placed a veil over the dying man's eyes as if he were a king in a king's throne, it was the last song inside the voice box, a taxi cab carousel ride for a lower species and high order of the human need to kill what had killed.

Venom

THERE WAS A global search for a small amount of lethal elixir able to kill in three seconds, before he would open his blind eye, before he would raise his hand in surrender, before he would make one wish for salvation, before he would claim insanity for planting mines under the segregated swimming pool, before he walked into the War Bound recruitment center for the deranged and prosperous young men sent off to the front lines, before sleep had good reason, before he opened his mouth and recited a curse learned in the backroom of voodoo and despair, before he would break the leather straps on his ankle, wrist, and neck and throw a brick through the stained glass, before he was able to raise a potable snake-skin drinking gourd to the lightning.

They used a fresh and fatal dose of the sea serpent mixed into the secret recipe from Satan's holiday feast injected into Ben's mandible at the first Good Housekeeping laboratory built by scoundrels in Hell proper where the prison guard fed the homeless holy grits and tar babies out of ladles. It was a hell of a night to find yourself alive and well in hell. They lined up outside the local church built by slaves. School children carried water from the wishing well. They released the farm animals and captured North Carolina wild horses that first had to be broken and used to drag the iron lung over fallen timber and snow. They called the alchemist on the prison phone to mix the potion into a mortal green and rainbow divine. The elixir was administered by three beggars as they stepped out of the hardware city of the world's tent city behind the five-and-dime enterprises. The crowd danced in the street and fell asleep on the sidewalk outside the beer garden after the hoses used to suckle alcohol until brain dead were tampered and they fell sick after eating stolen sea bass and bratwurst dipped in a bad batch of sauerkraut accidentally mixed with rat poison. They used one eyedropper placed in a brown paper bag. They removed Ben's Zorro mask. One second, drop in the right eye, one long breath, drop in the left eye, two seconds, one half-a-breath, three seconds, death.

IF YOU CAN BREAK A HORSE,
YOU CAN BREAK A MAN

HE AWAKENED FROM his golden slumber with spiders in his mouth.

The headline news emerged on his iPad on loan from the Stephen Hawking Foundation. The letters moved across the small screen like the Wall Street alphabet of coins. The Poet's Wife Murdered in Bowling Green Ohio Found in a Doglegged Tub in the Rail Yard. The professor had completed his book of poems titled *Hard Candy*. His wife had grown back her hair that was set on fire by a curse at a faculty reception.

The periscope in the iron lung was replaced by a miniature model of the Ariane 5 ECA in orbit 100 million miles above the earth. The infrared setting allowed for sightings in the corridors of the heart and the lower regions of despair. He telescope was able to pick up the sounds of animals and voices. He saw one man remove a horseshoe from the Arabian stallion with its high tail carriage and whispered: *If you can break a horse, you can break a man.*

Ben had requested the sailor's telescope after reading the back of a Sergeant Rock comic book and the ads for a pocket camera and *Grit* newspaper, America's Greatest Family Newspaper. Ben pulled his shade over the iron lung's sky roof. Placed a veil over his sunken eyes. Ben was able to observe and read the Dead Sea scrolls, execution by firing squad, noose, gas chamber, electric chair, lanterns on the coastal waters, ghostly figures running into a cave, the Amazon washing volcanic ash into surrounding villages, he was able to record the manikins of pestilence on showroom floors, Robin Williams played with toy soldiers wearing granny dresses on a chessboard of smoke, woe, and laughter, the hardscrabble boardroom war room board game for those who believed they were kings walking barefooted over hot coals, fighter jets, the angels used parachutes, minefields airlifted by helicopters and dropped on schools and roads and farmland, oil fires, flares above large cities and small towns, and he watched a man wearing a black robe over his head, red eyes, and pants shoved into his boots, and he pulled out a knife and beheaded the man and placed the man's head with its eyes asleep between his shoulder blades under his neck where yesterday his wings had began to grow.

The mother and father lifted sons and daughters out of the bath and kiddie pool into the low ocean tide, cupped their bellies and swung them like lanterns into the tainted sea. Lifeguards handed out ladles for the swimmers with parasols holding mop buckets filled with radioactive salt water and lemonade on the beachfront property, custodians of rainbow currents, oil surfactants, and plutonium time-released beads of light floating inside bloated jellyfish, thin nuclear plant rises on the horizon, boat launch, hula hoops, orange creamsicles, seaweed, 5 cents a Dixie cup of mouthwash, *teach a man to fish and eat a fish*, a thimble of uranium (thorium), minor actinides, neptunium, americium, and curium, Yucca Mountain Repository for the Witless Seed, and was not what happened to our ancestors on the highly selective farms worked by the peasants boarded in the cheap motels on the Berlin Turnpike, it was not what happened last year or years ago after the weddings and tossed salad, it was what happened to our children after the first 100,000 years of eternal residue, after the great tomb doors borrowed from the 1901 savings and loan bank vault built for the next world war and Tommy Gun, opened at the front stairwell to deep geologic storage containers, those who entered collapsed a few feet away, coughed, shed their skin, and died, after the missiles sent the prehistoric by-products of a Thanksgiving fireplace into space toward the sun, the rocket man who wore yellow living gloves released the cargo door that released a billion tons of nuclear spittle each earthly minute, collected during the global dust bowl caused by volcanic eruption and earthquake and a child's tilted swing set, it was hoped the immortal sun would dissipate the nano-nuclear fog or at least by sending it to other planets and galaxies beyond our own, give those blessed in the fountain of youth and in their later years afflicted with a maimed body powdered, dressed, and mummified like a holiday manikin a chance to wash their hair in cascading moonlight, was it the work of the unpaid long-distance swimmer, born without eyes, who dove into the underworld lake to unrecorded depths and retrieved the holy bells attached to the waist of a ruby doll placed in a showcase window after the karmic-tainted water she swallowed was one example of the unexpected deranged and prosperous life well-lived and gone?

Get Plenty to Eat

Get plenty to eat the day before your execution, the prison doctor told Ben Cocoa.

Ben Cocoa's father was born and raised in Eufaula, Alabama. Ben's mother was born and raised in Efaula, Oklahoma, and I leave that story for another morning. Ben had heard the story from his great grandfather over Thanksgiving dinner.

A (white) mob from Eufaula once went looking after Preston Fort. In town, a white man slapped him but Preston Fort went to work on him with his pocket-knife and almost cut him to death.

That (white) mob stopped by Mr. Clark's store, about a dozen carloads of them. The KKK gang told Mr. Clark that they were going after that nigger Preston Fort. Mr. Clark told them they better get plenty to eat because if they went messin' with the those Forts, some of them were not going to come back.

But that (white) gang had gone back to Eufaula. That (white) mob decided to go back to Eufaula. Those Forts were scattered all around in the woods with their rifles and shotguns waiting for them.

Bish Fort could strike a match with his rifle and when they would go bird hunting he would take his rifle and kill more birds than the ones with shotguns.

http://www.amazon.com/Witness-Injustice-Jr-David-Frost/
dp/1604738863

The Black Widow in a Red Dress

They sat in pews carved by the hand of the Crippled Ghost and threw roses over the burial ground wearing black robes and white gloves that panned for light in their grief under the hollow stars, it was the red dress worn by a widow, scripture read by a holy man, bluebirds swayed in the tumbling sky,

"The earth received his body and the heavens his soul," he preached.

They said Ben had shot the man through one eye. The defense claimed it was a ruse to bring up a petty crime inside a candy store. Teachers who read Ben's short stories in second grade wished for his life to be saved. Ben had missed only one day of school in twelve years the day he fractured his foot coming down on his right foot from the sky playing dodge ball in the Roosevelt Junior High School gym at recreation on Wednesday. The prosecution claimed it was the witless seed in Ben's blood and the specks of stardust among the delicate wings of DNA found under his fingernails. There was a single pubic strand of black hair dyed blonde. It would take a miracle to shoot a man through his eye and top of his head without leaving a trace of evidence, and there were signs of a struggle inside the iris garden behind the gas station outside the Petrified Forest.

They were held in a trance until they heard the preacher proclaim:

You want to be a nigger and call your woman a whore.

They pushed a long thin needle through his eye and into his brain and they showed the procedure on the weekly death row newsreel. The Negro Dr. Frankenstein wore his oxblood boots and threw Ben's wedding ring into a glass jar in the root cellar. There was a school desk and broken clock. He lit a long white candle and placed it under a painting of a night train on a bridge in Belgium. The choir walked out the back door and rang a bell with each of their steps, paused at Ben's webbed feet, and rang the bell one last time.

Ben's Letter to the Pardon Board

What if there were less of things in New Britain: fewer gopher holes snapping the ankles of wild horses, numbers to count, engines to start, dentists with yellow teeth, skyscrapers, weddings, beachfront property, Main Streets, park with music shell, eighty-five-year-old restaurant, pool hall, cigarette, bubble gum cigar, spousal abuse, football, basketball, baseball games, hockey fight, coin collector, cheese, banker, volcanic ash, smoked kielbasa, Starbucks, public library, pre-school, one prized Macaque monkey in a beauty salon, blue suede shoes, ethnic strife, yellow, coal, anthropological dig under a brownfield, magician, drunk, pothead, addiction to coffee, East Haven, rock 'n' roll, soul, polka, false teeth, town clock, wheel chair, lilac, full moon, sourdough bread, black licorice, dancing in the streets, shoe without laces, floating armadas, small dog, blind ventriloquist, harmonica, violin lessons, pigeon, city chicken, wildfire, a bonds bailsman on every corner, deer tracks in snow, time clock, smokestack, barbershop poles, Cadillac, birch tree, honeysuckle, pit bull rolling in a dirt cellar with arrow in neck, fog, church bell, track and field, prison cell, library, burning car tire, backed up sewage, underground lavatory, wingless bird, sad-faced manikin, jazz in schools, report card deficiency, fractured foot, measles, plaster cast, two-headed child, mustard, land mine, Halloween candy, human, grape, White Sands Beach, boomerang, pillow fight, religion, infantry, iron lung, washboard, angel, baptism, winter collard, money, poetry, museum, tornado, earthquake, UFO above city hall, plasma, Picasso, yo-yo string theory, Radio Free Poetry, Hendrix, Miles, Beatles, Motown, Stravinsky, Beethoven, Van Gogh, Stephen Hawking, blast furnace, music box, skeleton key, factory, homeless, poverty, bail, bond, dark chocolate, reservoir, Mausoleum of American Art, men who beat women, police officers who beat minorities walking through Central Park in New Britain.

The Life of the Marionettes

Two BOXES ARRIVED at Ben's porthole. The first was a pair of newlywed marionettes with strings attached for the death row talent show. The gentleman with a thin goatee was dressed in a pink jester's coat, white pants, red lipstick, and black magician shoes. The gentlewoman had red hair, white dress, lace, pink lips, ivory pendant, pearl necklace, tan ribbon at her waist, and white bridal shoes. They hung from the heating pipes on the ceiling of the iron lung like a mobile above a bassinet. High eyebrows were poised in laughter and miniature hands held a teacup above a doily, their mouths sewn together in black thread.

Whose charred hands bounced them above Ben's head in a dance under the moon's wreckage, two knobbed heads bowed in mortal shame, two dolls nearly alive in their pastel cheeks, and lifted them out of a rain storm, voiceless except for whimpers in the smoke and medicine cabinet mirror, arms raised, elbows bent, one low shoulder, knees bent, long eyelashes, eyes opened, thumbs out, lucky penny in the back pocket, they had floated down from the sky, two unfurled angels released from the backstage cedar chest, placed on a music box turntable, *Blues Sonata*, the last dance unearthly twins who boarded a clipper ship headed to their honeymoon past the equator of despair toward the new world of spring and fall, lilac, autumn torch, lantern raised on the underworld roped bridge, bomb shelter, clean water, jelly beans, children fold paper clowns under their school desks, ten-week survival after warm winds dissipated, handmade silhouette of a crystal ball on the fireplace, valentine taped to the bedpost, a call-to-arms, chandelier, two-way mirror, blue nest of flowers, wicked vicar, witness to the playground thief and rumble, take a bow and offer a plate to lost languages and courtly love, choir of the dispossessed, carousel ride into the oblivion of desire, two night swimmers in red life jackets across the lake, a curtsy to the crowd, pull and jerk, marriage of the ruby dolls in the root cellar, brief kiss on knotted wood, prison escape over the moat and barbed tinsel in the life of the runaway marionettes?

LAUGHTER IN THE IRON LUNG I

THE SECOND BOX was filled with dormant African bees that came alive under weightlessness. Ben opened a manual inside the box published by the Connecticut Hysterical Society under the Good Housekeeping motto. It described five methods often used for the execution of prisoners in the United States. They transmitted episodes into the iron lung on a 24-hour video loop of Dick Gregory, George Carlin, Bill Cosby, Jackie Gleason, *Sanford and Son*, Richard Pryor, Dave Chappelle, and Lenny Bruce.

LETHAL INJECTION

First adopted in 1977 in Oklahoma . . . inmates are strapped to a gurney while needles are inserted into the veins and the drugs are pumped in. This method is often seen as the most humane of the five because the inmates are supposed to be sedated before they die. Inmates, though, have been known to writhe and talk during poorly carried out injections . . . all states used a three-drug protocol that included a sedative, a paralytic and then the final, fatal drug to stop the heart. Because of drug shortages and legal challenges that claimed the paralytic drug could mask an inmate's suffering, states are now experimenting with several different protocols . . . some states are adopting a one-drug method that is essentially a massive overdose of a sedative. Other states are keeping a multi-drug protocol but experimenting with different drugs.

ELECTROCUTION

New York developed electrocution as an alternative to hanging—which was often a gruesome public spectacle—and executed the first inmate by electric chair in 1890 . . . prisoners are strapped into a chair with electrodes placed on their heads and legs. Saline-soaked sponges are placed between the skin and the electrodes to aid conductivity . . . the voltage, the number of jolts and the length of time they are administered vary from state to state. Executioners usually give more than one jolt of electricity, to make sure the inmate is dead. Executioners can't give one long, continuous jolt because the person's body could start to burn. Instead, they let the body cool down for a few seconds between jolts.

It is unknown whether the person being electrocuted is rendered unconscious by the shock or is merely paralyzed and unable to yell out . . . electrocution usually kills by sending the inmate into cardiac arrest, but it could also cause brain death first. "Or it could be both brain death and heart death."

After Tennessee executed Daryl Holton by electric chair in 2007, a method he chose, state medical examiner Dr. Bruce Levy said Holton died when the electricity stopped his heart. Holton also had burns where the electrodes contacted the skin. And Levy said inmates sometimes suffer broken bones when their muscles clench violently during the shock, but that did not happen with Holton.

GAS CHAMBER

Nevada developed the gas chamber in the 1920s as an attempt at a humane method of execution . . . it had "horrific problems" from the start. The original idea was to pump the gas into an inmate's cell while he was sleeping, but there was no way to keep the gas contained, so they built a chamber instead . . . inmates are strapped into a chair and the chamber is filled with cyanide gas, which kills by asphyxiation. The inmates are fully awake and conscious as they suffocate.

FIRING SQUAD

This method has been used as recently as 2010 in Utah at the request of a condemned man there . . . the prisoner is strapped to a chair, as in electrocution and the gas chamber. A cloth target is placed over prisoner's the heart. Several shooters are given real bullets but one or more are given blanks. Assuming the shooters hit their target, the heart ruptures and the prisoner dies quickly from blood loss.

HANGING

Before 1890, hanging was the principal method of execution across the country. The prisoner stands over a trap door while a noose is placed around the person's neck, and then the trap door is opened and the prisoner falls . . . by design, the fall breaks the prisoner's neck and kills him or her . . . but that has often not been the case. In some cases, prisoners have been decapitated from the fall. In other cases, they have strangled over the course of several minutes.

Reefer Madness Inside the Iron Lung

Ben never got high. He was a child begging the world for a good sleep inside the iron lung. His insomnia began one afternoon after he fell out of a hammock held by two posts used for the prison clothesline, and he was knocked into a coma after his large forehead hit a marbled crystal ball thrown out of the warden's window during his temporary gift of rage.

Several prisoners were known to awaken decades later as weightless skeletons inside a cryogenic eggshell. There was no known cure for sleeping sickness and the Kind of Alaska that caused Pinter to weep without consolation.

The prison doctor lifted the tincture and squeezed droplets of Mercurochrome rose, lavender, jasmine, hemlock stew, and vaporized THC used with VapoRub to stir the senses.

The three executioners were given one hollow point bullet and one blank cartridge, one hourglass filled with a secret and deadly concoction and one hourglass to revive a human pulse. Razor blades were placed under their tongues to cut the throat of the convicted in case the other methods failed. One out-of-date method was based on the RCA Victor phonograph, a well-behaved dog sitting next to the electric chair, ears perched, listening to a harpist. The Queen's Victrola was carried and used as a living room prop to calm those behind the death watch one-way mirror until it was discovered that playing the 78s calmed the dying and afflicted and its half-inch four-pointed needles were similar to those inserted into the neck, elbows, and plump veins of the accused and convicted members of society.

The prison chaplain, who wore a Pharrell hat with a pirate feather to confession often sat outside in the corridor, was known to burn frankincense on the evening of executions, reading psalms, singing

"We Shall Overcome," Pete Seeger, Woody Guthrie, and a former cellist in his high school band, he found music a plum nearly comfort to those on death row who carried the pitchfork blues on their backs and a Bible in their hands. The clock was set to chime at a quarter to three in the morning. The wild boar that escaped on Thanksgiving from the prison cafeteria was found half alive in the barbed wire, the prison guard fell asleep with one eye open and a bow and arrow across his shoulder. It was night and the time for lies.

Electrocution in the Iron Lung

THE SCIENTISTS AT Good Housekeeping received federal funds in 1967 to supply each prison with a solar powered electric chair. It was designed to be lowered and hibernate under snow during the winter and raised during a spring thaw. Some of the portable battery packs were tied around the necks of animals known to dig holes into hollow ground for good sleep. They found the groundhog useful and one toy fox terrier named Mojo relentless in his former male self in search of bone. Sunlight altered the sleep patterns of prisoners on death row and experiments in isolated confinement only heightened their sense of displacement. The lack of sunlight created a lack of air in the lower regions of their brains.

They tightened shock collars around the necks of prisoners on death row and practiced the amount needed for the afternoon nap or to induce nightmares inside a cell the size of a shoe box used by Happy Jack the Black Kiwi King at Grand Central Station who was renowned for his waxless shine. Happy snapped his nappy rag on the penny loafers worn by prisoners before their execution after one prisoner died during a hunger strike protesting the sole use of World War II black boots.

The prison doctor was known to check a pulse using his middle finger or bad thumb broken by a street hustler who noticed him carrying a medicine bag and demanded a test for strep throat, aspirin, and catfish bladders disguised as cod liver oil.

It was night and the lilac wild. The hand-cranked stars seemed to tremble in the hands of the crippled ghost who looked out at the sky from a small window in the root cellar under the electric chair. He sat at the school desk, throwing ice into a bucket, turning the handle, creating a current. He shouted for the executioner to attach a live wire from a lamp post and connected to the governor's red rotary phone to the temple of the man seated on his throne of embers and broken glass. Ben pissed into the bucket of snow. There was snow, hooves, footsteps, dogs sent to capture the escapee. It would take more than ruin to find the proper amount of voltage required to kill before smoke seeped out between the teeth.

GAS CHAMBER INSIDE THE IRON LUNG

THERE WAS A gas leak left undetected under the chair on death row. Several prisoners who ate in the cafeteria and who had not been reassigned to solitary confinement for unruly behavior had placed notes in the warden's suggestion box about a lingering scent that reminded them of pot liquor.

The odor awakened Ben from a deep sleep inside the iron lung. He was able to maneuver a toothbrush into his mouth and drag it across the bars of his cell like vibes over a hot stove. He knew there was something raw and malicious in the air. The week before they had been served sardines and mustard in tin cans until a jolly good fellow decided to cut open his neighbor's carotid while he lifted his spoon of calf liver broth to his lips. They flew Robert Redford from the Eugene O'Neill Theater to the prison by helicopter to quell the disturbance and landed in the center of the basketball court followed by Fox News and the Dallas Cowboy Cheerleaders.

The company men of war and fame who invented and used nerve gas in Ferguson, Missouri, had not planned on one man, crowned in laurel, and seated in death's throne inside a circle of rose petals, to rise out of his chair, freed out his stirrups by a minor earthquake that cracked the cement floor where he had bowed and prayed to the crippled ghost, and burst a pipe in the stone wall of the root cellar that spewed gas under every bunk bed in the prison block.

The prisoners, including one pregnant woman, were placed on thin futons borrowed from the Museum of the Summer of Love, and blankets still covered in Woodstock mud, once used by two teenagers, who kissed and rolled in the barnyard of rock 'n' roll, and listened to "The Times They Are A-Changin'" on a transistor radio, sung by The Last Back Hippie in Connecticut, who was noted in the 1969 New

Britain High School year book, to be destined for university, nearly drafted by the U.S. Congress, barefoot on a college campus, long white robe, wearing rose-colored Gandhi glasses and sandals in the middle of a large lecture room listening to Biology 101, the world, its wars, singing "We're on the Eve of Destruction," a cartoon of body counts and the sound of stained glass windows breaking a treble of the undeserved heart.

Firing Squad in Front of the Iron Lung

They blindfolded Ben Cocoa during the daylight hours inside the iron lung so he would find comfort as he faced the firing squad wearing his Sergeant Pepper jacket and brown Zorro mask. The leader of the firing squad, selected by a straw vote and a snap of the golden thumb, brought a flask of black whiskey, green canteen, compass, and a sundial for the exact setting for Ben's sundown execution. The public event, well advertised on prison social media coined *The Facebook of Death*, was scheduled at the World Famous Hanging Tree somewhere in everyone's blood in Mississippi.

They carried swords at their sides and they also had rifles on their shoulders, if one was still alive after the firing squad, they would place a newly minted copper penny in each of the eyes, a leather strap tightened across the forehead of the prisoner also prevented the neck from falling to one side before the shooting, which allowed for the body to sway, rise, and fall like a marionette.

It was at the junior high school dance. Boys on one side. Girls on one side. Girls in square dance skirts. Boys with cleats on their shoes. The teacher pulled Ben together with a girl who stood as tall as a skyscraper. It was rock 'n' roll and Ben thought: *She was just seventeen and the way she looked was way beyond compare.*

It was winter becoming winter again. The wind carried the leaves into the electrical wires above the defunct gas chamber and snapped them into dust. Those who stayed home on their porches on the evening of the execution heard thunder in the snowfall and saw lightning in the hills above the Waterbury Holy Land cross. There were no survivors on the Glastonbury-Wethersfield Ferry. The church bells rang and the black lamp posts on the town clock green dimmed and left small clouds of nearly smokeless powder.

Although the five men selected from the Navy Seals stood under a thunder cloud with lightning above their top hats, they lifted their Mannlicher Carcano C2766 rifles made for executions per order of the U.S. Congress after taking two-dollar bets on which bullet would be determined by the Ferguson, Missouri, medical examiner, the exact whereabouts and immediate cause of death. Was it the one charmed silver bullet in the chest, one magic bullet in the forehead, or a 6.5 millimeter bull's eye into Ben's thick glasses?

Ben walked like he didn't ride the bus, side-to-side like a pigeon, a city chicken on its way to roost in the backseat. He drank Ovaltine out of his green Stanley thermos on his ten-minute break on the factory floor, downtime, waiting to punch out on his ball bearing landscape, a parking lot circled by barbed wire, working overtime, a short walk into the storefront, pinball machine, percolated coffee, good to the last living drop.

Ben learned to shoot pool with his one good eye, steel-toed boots, and baby powder inside his black aluminum lunch box that made his wrist click into place, slot quarter per game, side-rail maze, bank shot, gyroscopic vision, anti-gravity eight ball into outer space and back to earth, fast track, breaking his pool stick across the back of his wife's neck.

If you find a crippled ghost in your house, what do you do? You watch over it, the small floating head, its pursed doll's mouth, pointed ears, almond eyes. You lift yourself up with your elbows and drink out of your goblet of holy light. You live your life.

This is autumn becoming autumn again, a kind of misunderstood blue, call, no answer, a valentine of leaves, coronation of grief and desire, *roses are red*, violets falling into a wishing well.

Ben throws his letters and old family photographs into a stream, not to discard, an offering, speaking to her at night her arms become wings, pitchfork blue, yellow plum. There was a bicycle stolen on a holiday and left in the alley of the corner filling station, chandelier blue at the Lithuanian Hall, Mojave snakeskin, pigeon's opal eye turned sideways, Concord grapevine, wooden gold club, marble hole, storage house, Victrola, back porch, steel rail set in concrete, clothesline, winter garden, Ben's old man stepping behind a tiller of light.

What kind of blue does one feel inside the iron lung pulled by a ball and chain down a retractable conveyor belt on a carousel of prisoners made to fill a trough of water for the peasant kings? Ben was almost comfortable dressed in fireproof fatigues inside a cocoon of silk and tar rolled down a gangplank into the landscape of the sea. They filled the gas chamber with nerve gas and shoveled coal until the embers floated down from a white birch.

A bird from some strange blue planet landed on Ben's bad shoulder, and he wept in the kind of way one might for a man under a bare bulb dressed in torn elbow patches on a professorial tweed jacket after his featherweight and lifeless body is lifted out of the electric chair.

Ben saw a woman wading in a blue pond, blue horse, front legs bent, hind legs stamping dirt into the air, reaching the haunt of the cliff, falling backward into rock, going under, drowned by the miniature men and their ruby dolls.

What was found under the volcano thrived in the baptismal waters, a life study, self-portrait, inside the oblong mirror, factory gate, elixir spouting from the inferno, mule's tooth, land mine, shipwreck, ivory skeleton key, Minotaur's pink hoof?

It was said that those who slept better than the retrievers of the dead, returned home to a bowl of grits, spoon of buttermilk, rosewater, hot bath, and ash tossed at the foot of their beds from the urn of former death row inmates, executed not by long knives, birthright.

The Hangman's Noose
Found Inside a Pyramid

Ben was sent to Egypt inside his iron lung and pulled by rope into the netherworld tombs found half-way between Hartford and purgatory.

The body of the executed was wrapped in tar and feathers once used by the Mississippi Citizen's Council for those exhibiting civil disobedience at water fountains, bus stations, and toy lunch counters. The body was first prepared using layers of sweet Vidalia-Georgia-on-my-mind onionskins, Crisco, and they discovered a set of stairs inside the pyramid that led to the lowest level of hell and another set of stairs that led to higher ground for those who might enter the chamber of the Ministers of the Heart.

Ben read the morning newspaper with his anti-gravity French press coffee, the article expounded on the first man who raised his hand for blood, who taught his child to respect his elders by taking a straight razor and cutting slow ragged lines into his son's scalp, his welts were leeches half asleep over his torso.

They welded a bassinet next to Ben's spring mattress inside the iron lung, a mobile of animal crackers rotating, rising and falling above the golden slumber, rosewater, luminous black wings of the noble angel, above his head in the electric chair to keep a prisoner mesmerized at ease, keep his knees from breaking out of the leather barber chair straps, used to slap and sharpen the blade's hollow ground, and after his last cigarette, he realized he was taught to curse the infirm, gay, female, religious, and ethnic diversity.

The green flies around his eyes snapped him awake, and he was blindfolded and told to take three deep breaths. They lifted his charred feet into a bucket of lard. He was told to open his one good right eye, and threaded a needle through the eyelid attached to the gas chamber vent used to open the jaw of the marionette. The curtain to the viewing room was opened six hours after the beginning of the execution and they applauded the man's untimely demise, with a standing ovation, those who raised their hands and punched a child's teeth out into a bedpan used by the prisoners for thirst and to conduct electricity after they kicked them for the very idea.

The physicist wrote: *The disaster and warning would arrive at the same time.*

Ben often turned his head and looked over his shoulder into the trees for a sign. He had learned how the fault lines of the past, in its glory of time poured into a fountain somehow combined with the present into a readable imprint of the future.

There was rain. The woman walked and held a parasol of rags. Ben was under her spell, blindfolded, stepping lightly. He fell backwards into a net of roped stars.

The prisoner on death row was half-awake and dying, the mannequin kissed and recoiled, the mime paused in the middle of a tightrope over a gorge, his cleft-foot the devil's Florsheim, letting go, masquerade ball on the ocean, debutante waltz, Mojave rattler in a glass cage, hammock and whiplash, stage fright and wishing well, one drop of venom in the buttermilk, thirst, boxing gloves and brass-knuckle keyboard, champion of the netherworld, who skinned the blue mule and placed it on the outdoor barbecue and the cafeteria's Thanksgiving menu. The prison chaplain read the blessing for those on death row and flung holy water against the side of the iron lung and threw down the witless seed on the hollow ground of the prison cemetery next to the great oak that grew into the iron gate with branches in a web of barbed wire and grace and a pocketknife valentine with the names of twins who in their life sentences were separated and placed in solitary confinement for hiding love poems inside the soles of their shoes. They were once allowed to throw confetti inside their cells on birthdays until the cell was set afire by a toaster used for frozen raisin and cinnamon bagels donated by the Salvation Army of Wives who danced and shook their bells and skirts in the snow on God's death watch with a velvet wolf.

Taps were not played and flags were not folded for the executed. The homework over the holidays given to schoolchildren was to find a first prize death mask made out of silhouettes from the death row inmates using magic markers and number one pencils in a palette of death's colors and portraits of their demise and disguise.

Autumn Leaves Inside the Iron Lung

THE PRISON MEDICAL staff ordered small piñata bags filled with maple leaves, hung above Ben's head, and released by voice commands with a password on loan from Anonymous. Ben was awakened each morning by the taped recordings of crickets and a video of the blossoming morning glory in slow motion. The atmosphere inside the iron lung, its gravity and weightlessness, added years to his prison sentence. One year was the equivalent of ten thousand days inside a time capsule riveted with heat shields and retractable soapbox baby stroller wheels with the hardest known wood used for axles, and its *NASCAR for Negroes* designed steering wheel provided the proper grip for Ben's mechanical marionette hands attached to insulated rubber gloves saved for the electric chair for a test of the remains of his black, numb, and blue fingernails, Ben took control of the ship's wheel, a helmsman floating in the sea among ghost stars and he touched the well-preserved follicles inside the meteorite he found half-buried in the prison garden, the meteorite turned to dust after he blew from his breathing tube he thought was connected to laughing gas, it was the belly-up jaw-breaking kind of laughter he experienced in college as he read a story he imagined on a paper bag and the entire room nearly burst into flames in a down-home out-of-this-world chuckle falling on your knees buckets of magic brownies and tubs of Columbian gold smoked to a fine herbal essence of barbecued lobotomy sign-off the world turned into one comedy lost in the archeological dig that uncovered lost tablets of jokes written by the holy jester hired by a spoiled boy king who rubbed his knees together trying not to piss on his top bunk bed and they stood against the wall each holding a bong of water and weed and at this moment with its legs crossed at the top of the Ann Arbor Arboretum, Ben levitated for the first and last time in his life and he looked down at the landscape and cornfields and saw her entering her downtown artist loft on Memorial Day and the early morning and for the first love of his life, a print-maker who wore her braids short and he believed he had once kissed her red lips for hours and it was like the burning of leaves.

What became of the last known recordings in Ben Cocoa's personal 8 track play list (songs and albums): *In My Life, Sergeant Pepper's Lonely Heart Club Band, Time Slips Away, Dancing in the Dark, As Tears Go By, Master Jack, Magic Man, Cat Named Dog, Handsome Johnny, Freedom (Motherless Child), Johnny Too Bad, The Harder They Come, Fish Cheer/I-Feel-Like-I'm-Fixing-to-Die-Rag, Darlin' Be Home Soon, I Had a Dream, I'm So Lonesome I Could Cry, Cowgirl in the Sand, What's Wrong, Invocation, She's Gone, If I Were a Carpenter, Reason to Believe, Simple Song of Freedom, Dhun in Kaharwa Tai, Momma Momma, Coming Into Los Angeles, Amazing Grace, Oh Happy Day, I Shall Be Released, Joe Hill, Sweet Sir Galahad, Swing Low Sweet Chariot, We Shall Overcome, Jam, Evil Ways, Fried Neckbones, Rock Me Baby, Going Up the Country, Let's Work Together, On the Road Again, St. Stephen, Dark Star, Turn on Your Lovelight, Dreams of Milk and Honey, Southbound Train, Born on the Bayou, Green River, Bad Moon Rising, Proud Mary, I Put a Spell on You, You Can Make It If You Try, Everyday People, Dance to the Music, I Want to Take You Higher, Stand!, Summertime, Piece of My Heart, Ball and Chain, As Good As You've Been to This World, I Can't Explain, Pinball Wizard, We're Not Going to Make It, See Me Feel Me, Summertime Blues, My Generation, Volunteers, Somebody to Love, White Rabbit, Ten Years After, Tommy, Band of Gypsys, With a Little Help From My Friends, Summer Dresses, I'm Going Home, Ain't No More Cane, The Weight, Foxy Lady, Fire, Voodoo Child/Stepping Stone, Star Spangled Banner, Purple Haze, Hey Joe.*

Declined Invitations: The Beatles (hard to come together), Jeff Beck, Iron Butterfly, Joni Mitchell, Lighthouse, Ethan Brown.

Canceled Acts: Led Zeppelin, Bob Dylan, The Byrds, Tommy James & the Shondells, Jethro Tull, The Moody Blues, Spirit, Mind Garage.

The warden had placed Ben's vintage collection of singles and LPs under Mister Electric Chair one at a time during a year of executions.

They had planned to use eggs taken out of Sherwood Anderson's Easter basket, but the family disapproved of such folly in the face of high unemployment and perpetual wars observed by citizens of distant planets putting their lingerie on a clothesline.

The wicked were known to dance naked in the wilderness or on stage with a half a million strong, and given his last request, watching *Woodstock* from the porthole of the iron lung was the best thing that ever happened to last black hippie from Connecticut besides making love in the mud.

Bread and Water at Yucca Mountain

It was night and the time for lies. The iron lung was tethered to a yellow submarine borrowed from the Maritime Museum of Mermaids, Ben slept well as they skimmed above the underground lakes and when they dove into the dark waters that collapsed into starfish arms clinging to round and supple stone, he found the opal dancing eyes of sea creatures looking into his porthole, their bodies were like rubber inflatable water bottles filled with faucet water over his mother's sink and placed with Vick's VapoRub on Ben's young chest, their coral fins disappeared into the coral landscape, and as the water level fell, the iron lung sun roof retracted using its Polaroid electric eye, and Ben found that it was in total darkness where signs of life were visible, the way one follows intuition in a corridor, root cellar, fog over the stone fence, covered bridge, the military prison convoy, machine gun turret aimed at the peaceful demonstrators against the war, *Hell no we won't go!*, behind the lights ahead of them and so on, a long line of drivers and retrievers of the dead in army jeeps and ambulances arriving to pull the young out of trenches and into body bags, taken to the mouth of Yucca Mountain, taken down in coal bins, at rest on hollow ground, dressed in green fatigues, zipped into polyurethane body bags, oxblood or wingtip instead of black infantry boots, canteens on their belts, lips sewn together by silk thread from Vietnam, bow tie, buttoned collar, New Britain High School sweater, class ring, GED, fast food award, bicycle streamers, country music, *Love it or Leave It, Change It or Lose It,* it was how the sea moved the flora in slow motion, sea snakes floating as if they were tethered to the ghost stars in reverie, how the taps sounded at his brother's gravesite, the soft sound of bombs from a distance, church bell, chandelier, telephone operator, funny papers, the unknown soldier, last-second three-point shot, *Dancer in the Dark, The*

Machinist, Boxing Helena, Dr. Zhivago, Ben ate popcorn with brewer's yeast and a witless seed became stuck inside the bellow of his coal burning stove and he realized that living in the iron lung was living underwater and by breathing underwater he was learning to live and breathe on land.

There were moments of splendor living inside the iron lung. Ben's Timex alarm clock had a lime green tint that glowed in the dark, he pulled the shade on the porthole window and a jack-in-the-box flew out of the box with a feather collar, he reached for the cupboard and lifted the dummy doll off its pillow stuffed with rubber olives, he took off its shirt and pulled the string attached to its hollow spine, its eyes and mouth opened, flashed its human teeth, and started to speak one word in every language in the world, programmed by Homeland Security by order of the courts, this was a four-letter word with only one meaning, scrawled on Egyptian walls by children left in the dunes, who climbed down the stairs into the underworld cellar with bags hung low from the ceiling by guards holding spears and gourds on their waist filled with water harvested from desert aquifers, some of the citizens fell into a state of grace after hearing the voice of the crippled ghost and walked for hours in the garden of the sacred wood, the hands and feet of those on death row were dipped in bronze, a Dairy Queen surprise, known for its rapid conductivity in a mop bucket to the fontenelle, their flesh burned well and their hair quickly turned to ash under their pork pie hats, the dog collars worn by the prisoners had brass rivets, Ray Charles sunglasses were optional, the last man walked behind the warden and chaplain, a leash held by the executioner wearing a black robe, bow tie, and loafers with pennies from a porcelain piglet above the commissary closed on blue Connecticut Sundays, they rotated the prison staff to avoid PTSD that flared with love at first sight and the holy bells struck numb on Good Humor trucks at Walnut Hill Park, there were signs of autumn and signs of good fortune: the Ferris wheel in the underworld was jump started by the two men caught in the Dr. Petit murders, although they were sent back to a landscape that they had first thought was heaven and soon realized they had been set on fire with recycled Goodyear tires around their necks. There was a long line at the Lake Compounce wooden roller coaster, and they waited in the rain for their turn to take a short ride inside the chariot. The bodies of the executed were placed on the caboose of the carousel train that led to the iron lungs lined up at the equator that led to a funhouse of gravity.

The Tangled Wood

THE ALCOHOLIC NAMED Buster Brown lived in a shoe box on the second floor never to be seen or heard from again, another heard voices and threatened himself and others and never sought help from anybody, king of the seven-card draw, dulled mustard tattoo on his wrist, another alcoholic in prison for being a child who beat his woman over the head with a bucket of worms and carved his name on her chest, one in-law bum who lived in the suburb, found upside down in his tub, nine bottles of vodka at his swollen feet, never got it out of his heart, something in his childhood, something tangled and gnarled, a living kiss in blood and desire, he wrapped his arms around himself like a straitjacket, a two-bit drunk in a carnival of thorns, another fed her daughter into a bloated feral child larger than life, feeding Crisco at the trough, appetite will as appetite does for those addicted to the crushed beer can, teeth on a whistle of despair, the twelve pack for dinner, a twenty-four pack weekend pass into oblivion, permanent damage to the ghost in the machine, smokers who do not know and may never know, black hole in their lung, smoke inside a brand new house, a broom against a rug stirred dust and the living ghost, five thousand dollar tournament and I can own the world, the runaway one-armed bandit losing his mind, another speaking in tongues at a graduation dinner, howling and dancing alone was not a crime only insanity, measured by a fall off a cliff, a tempest of the heart, never had a full-time job for any length of time, not enough saved for one bicycle tire, not enough time for a family, children, not enough time for a life of one's own, eat a hundred church dinners in a year and one ended up with pan-fried bacon, chitterlings, and tar and feathers growing out of their spine, a beautiful mother living the last years of her life inside a wretched house, black mold, bugs, vermin, another living alone in a wishing well gone dry without a daughter and son, nothing gained in the apple orchard or barbershop, a few pennies in the piggy bank. Was this the life they led in their imagined wars inside houses of shame and bigotry that fell to the ground in a sudden wind and the backyard fence dragged from the sea by the Great White Father and the Great Brown Father and what was that hanging from the tree?

Laughter in the Iron Lung II

Laughter was not allowed inside the prison. There was a microphone planted under Ben's memory foam pillow that allowed the scientist to monitor the sleep patterns and nasal laughter during periods of REM and the effects of gravity on Ben's sinus and snoring. Disturbances of sleep in the animal world were known to be called by slight axis shifts in floating planets, underwater earthquakes, and solar flares. Digital radio and TV signals collapsed into the hunger of gravity. There was reason to believe the splinters in the windshield of the iron lung were made as the iron lung passed through the magic dust of the red planet that made Ben fall asleep for seasons at a time like a small animal under a crawlspace lifted by the charred hand of God. Ben was given a Rolodex once used to record redlining by Connecticut banks to remove tons of dirt each day and bury pipes and change the course of sewage and the river that ran like a waterfall under Hartford. The water filled the corridors of tunnels that ran patients underground from the Institute of Living to the Bushnell Park carousel for moonlight rides and after the offices cleared and the citizens were well fed by waiters and fell into good sleep.

Ben had read about the New Britain Skull and Bones, a group of limp doctors, sterilized architects, and manikin mayors and governors, who displayed their wings of courage by stealing public funds for gold plated dog-legged tubs, cruises to China, limousine drives to the casino, and the occasional gift of Styrofoam cups of powdered hot chocolate and watered-down coffee, set up on a table in a ruse of dice, a playpen at Central Park in New Britain, a pigpen for those human among us who needed more than the gift of ruin and the curse set upon the world written in a voodoo villanelle written by a grandmother in a root cellar: *You will hear something coming behind you.*

Ben turned to his bedside Timex set to November's end. He held the holiday saber that hung from the ceiling. He watched a video of the prison riot. The submarine cleared of mustard gas and decommissioned after shell shock and was restored for missions of peace but never made it out of the sweet water on the New England coastline.

OEDIPUS, TEXAS

AFTER A COMPASS malfunction, a shadow fell over the sundial and sent the iron lung over Oedipus, Texas, a ghost town used by gamblers, rustlers, and used by a hanging judge for the most comfortable electric chair in the country. They spread the legs of the prison artist incarcerated for running over a young boy. The boulder he placed on the back of his jeep rolled over the boy's head. It was a clear case of negligence of the highest order. He was placed on death row despite a letter from his grandmother written to the judge on a Valentine's card with a scar-shaped heart.

My nephew would not stop drinking. He started on Halloween. The Lords and the Earls pummeled him and threw him into the underground lavatory at Central Park in New Britain. He awakened with his head inside the urinal with a photograph of the mayor bearing a stogie from Jimmy's Smoke Shop. He ran for his life in the snow.

This was Oedipus, Texas, on any Sunday. The fathers would take their sons armadillo hunting. They would follow their small paws to the riverside and wait to cut off their tails with long carving knives. They were paid for their armor used to create midget football helmets to prevent NFL-type concussions on soft baby skulls. They would find road kill too and disembowel their natty flesh and howl together at the crescent moon. The son caught what had fled from the wilderness, charming, feral. The father looked into his son's flat brown eyes.

"What you killed was never alive," he said.

"Look for movement in the hollow," he said.

"They stir under the crawlspace in the early morning," he said.

"*They hide in the fog, too. You can wait on the bridge and aim for the back of their necks,*" he said.

"*They will fly and flip into the air like pinwheels,*" he said.

Out of the Foxhole
and Into Death Row

Ben wrote one half of his letter in a foxhole and the rest on death row:

I first looked into your wild and mournful eyes. You kissed my lips. I had read about the warm winds shifting over the equator and migratory bird misguided in flight by the harpooned moon. Their bent wings were torn in their spiral flight, their shoulders downward into the great nest and burial ground. His top hat floated above the steeple and its mortal chimes. You and I would look beautiful together, and maybe I felt lucky. Do you ever feel that you are standing on the edge of a cliff? Do you think I have sad eyes? Do you ever feel that everything you have ever known is about to fall apart? I am going to town on my next weekend pass and get some farm fresh eggs. I found the last sign of my sorrow was your love.

The autumn leaves from the tops of distant trees fell over the soldiers as they spread handfuls of lime dust over the bodies of the fallen. Each leaf had a face and each face had a name. The ghosts stood over their own bodies, separated by the force of mortars and the sleeping sickness of nerve gas as tanks rolled over them in a quiet plunge of wheel, flesh, and soil, the tiller of the great war, relentless, and the unsteady town clock, a coil of light covering the holy bell, Ben drank fetid water out of his green canteen taken out of a wishing well, covered himself in a stick-patch blanket of wool looking for good sleep and acquaintance, he heard the muffled sounds of the fallen, young men in their requiem of light, shadow, and redemption, a psalm was read by the Minister of the Heart. Was it a curse that had taken them into shallow waters and baptismal fire, the angel noble on a wild horse, the archer bearing invisible arrows, the crippled ghost of their country, their hands turning into great serpents where earth is not sufficient and earth is their only companion, what led them to war led to ruin, the tall ships broke apart between two mountains and the men swam to shore and fled into the fire with the animals, they had prepared their keen metallic wings for war in a masquerade of the living and dead who were buried without their shoes in a field of lavender?

Saggin' Pants Inside the Iron Lung

There were times Ben had to pull up his corduroy pants. He used the sharp end of a clothes hanger between the gap in his lower yellowed teeth. Prison dentistry had taken X-rays of his jaw and perfect bite. Ben was fitted into the original Emmett Kelly clown mask to disguise his drooped left side, pirate eye, bruised lips and root beer mouth. The calendar pinned to the ceiling was dated 1967 b.c., a typo caused by a slight earthquake in the Blue Ridge Mountains after the tape machine was placed under the altar stone during a chorus of holy snakes consecrated by a young boy with rickets, bitten in the eye by a pink viper skinned at birth and placed into a Mason jar with nail holes used to nail the front door shut during a windstorm.

"Glory is what glory commands," they sang.

"We walk in the shadow of death," he preached.

"We are the temple," they sang.

"We drink the blood and heal the curse," he preached.

Who was the man in a clown mask barefoot and face up in a gutter? He claimed his family name was Cocoa and he was a descendant of the makers of O'Doul's and Nestle's Quick Drying Cement.

They shuttered the windows of city hall and burned the holy books, race records, archival musings and architectural sites, priceless paintings and manuscripts, buried and forbidden languages, and the town clock was left burning, its smoke seen from Walnut Hill Park among the beggars who pulled weeds out of the rose garden and rolled bicycle tires into Shuttle Meadow Reservoir with branches snapped by the ice storm after lightning killed three handicapped golfers at Stanley Quarter Park almost re-named The Wethersfield #2 Rumsfield-Sammy

Davis, Jr. Golf Tournament until the New Britain Chamber of Commerce protested with picket signs and marched nude from Batterson to Willow Brook Park, picking up passengers from neighborhoods, summer homes, crack houses, filling stations, and a free holiday dental clinic.

Iron Lung as Lifeboat

There was a war. The mother was pulled into the lifeboat with her baby wrapped in a black shawl. She wanted to drown with her child. They tried to resuscitate the baby. They waited until its mother fell asleep. She awakened with her hands and arms still holding her child although she was only holding the light of its body. The movie studio needed to re-create the ocean, supply ship, German submarine, and a lifeboat filled with Steinbeck characters, a black man who worked in a kitchen on the water, a wealthy woman who used her wedding ring tied to a frayed string to catch a fish. They had planned to suckle on its skin to draw out water. They had tried to pan for water as if they were panning for gold on land during a brief rain and held the cloth and captured only droplets for their parched tongues. It was the whiskey they had given to the man with the amputated leg. They used his empty shoe to beat the German who had hid his compass and flask until he let go and drowned. The newspaper ad proclaimed: *Reducto, Slayer of Fat.* The hero of a war was often paraded through a town square, a bouquet of flowers, followed by children with toy drums who ran alongside the hero and into the lavender field. The town crier played peasant songs on his piccolo.

One soldier, not knowing the war's end, walked out of the mountains and pushed a canoe into the lake, it was nightfall, moonless, light rain. He stood and saluted. He raised his rifle and shot a hole into the iron lung and through the pink hourglass. Ben thought for a brief moment the prison firing squad had identified his whereabouts guided by a compass and the dwarf stars. It was one soldier's misfired firepiece, dereliction of duty, folding the widow's flag, six-gun salute, a barefoot, half-burned, whiplashed, feathered man fleeing a mob into hollow ground, chased by hellhounds and kept alive by rainwater and a small fire he saw burning inside the abandoned mineshaft as he sped down on four wheels welded to the iron lung by U.S. Steel using the leftover armor of Panzer tanks.

Winter snapped the vineyard into dust and the harvest was gone. The church bell rang and a woman lowered her veil. They roped Ben's iron lung to the back of the lifeboat to save one man and almost saved the world.

The Iron Lung Libretto

BEN WROTE A death row libretto for the ghosts who walked into the chamber. He set it to a pipe organ and choir titled: *Requiem for the Twenty-First Century*, a retired daredevil who swung above the crowd without a net and held a rope between his teeth, played rock 'n' roll organ in the 1960s, lived and loved with hippies in the hills, rolled and inhaled joints as large as Cuban cigars, took a submarine to Key West, competed in the annual Hemingway Look-Alike Contest wearing a large afro and red sunglasses, hitch-hiked to a wedding in Cleveland, picked up by another wedding party, the bride and groom in the front seat of a VW Bug that caught fire after a joint thrown out the window blew back and landed between Ben's thighs, weed, smoke blowing out of their nostrils like shooting stars, Ben late for the wedding rehearsal, perfect pitch, out of key, rolling down the interstate, pipe organ blues, the bride and groom on their knees, one, one more, one more toke.

The bride threw her Earth Shoe through the stained glass window and the groom stood naked at the altar stone, the reception party ended up at Big Boy's, free hamburgers and fries, tumbleweed connection, night of the living blacks, apple pie, candles in the meadow, Alice's Restaurant, lottery of ball and chain, Vietnam, flowers in your hair, Breck, honeymoon at Monterey, Otis Redding, Altamont, Woodstock, 2014.

What happened at Woodstock?

They say somebody drowned in quicksand.

They were going home.

They made love in the mud.
Half a million strong stood in the rain.
Angels rode shotgun in the sky.

Requiem for the Twenty-First Century

Ben Cocoa looked into the nest of blue starlings under the town clock on a precipice between order and desire, the metamorphosis of departure and grace in everyone's blood, the witless seed, attic lantern, music box, spooled thread, disfigured mirror. He watched the vagrant hours like gold coins spinning to earth.

He decided to discover some unknown falling star from the port-hole of the iron lung that would be named Ben Cocoas Africanus. Ben remembered Mr. Wizard and the comfort he found inside a test tube, microbes embedded inside petrified rock.

The prison doctor placed a stethoscope on the man's hollow chest as he sat in the electric chair and examined him for a sign of life or a sign of death? Had he discovered a long dying or proof of living?

His hand suddenly caught fire, they said. The prison chaplain put out the flames with holy water, and the doctor placed gray silk gloves on his knotted wrists.

"There is nothing sadder than a young drunk," he said.

The manic-depressive, narcissist, alcoholic, on death row, dispossessed from a blue crystal ball, unable to steer the ghost in the machine, misaligned heart, the holy tableau, tarot cards under a thin mattress, Ouija board in the tombs, the voodoo doll villanelle thrown into the fireplace, white candles in the root cellar, haunted typewriter, old tires, one room schoolhouse, human skin lampshade, what story had he read about the woman who cut out the back of a chair and sat inside to listen to the guests, and felt their bodies of those who sat in her lap, and she found a certain comfort in this. They spoke of fine arts, politics, and magic carpets, there were smoke rings of Borkum Riff, and 4711 Original Eau de Cologne, clove, beedi, hookah ghost, frankincense, and the tap of a right foot, and she felt their hips and dangling legs, and she fell asleep embraced by a halo of humans, arched spines and tail-bones as she listened to the grammar the ruling class inside her throne of desire and felt their long arms and puff adder hearts.

New Year's Eve Inside the Iron Lung

(December 31, 2013)

Ben Cocoa wrote a letter to the Board of Pardons. He had been reluctant to address the procedural concerns on the use of supportive letters written in his behalf. One letter was from his Baptist minister. He had attended Sunday school and church service from 9:30 A.M. to 1:30 P.M. for eighteen years, and Rev. Starling, whose golden arms swung like a chariot as he proclaimed God's fortune and the devil lurking in the blues of a mumbling train, one letter from a Harvard law professor who kept one of Ben's assignments on the Mideast conflict completed over forty years ago inside a manila folder, and Ben gathered quotes from Tolstoy, Gandhi, and King, and he prepared his own poems to recite to the angry twelve men who would determine if Ben would be freed, executed by firing squad, drowned in a dog-leg tub, seated on a throne of lilac and electrocuted, thrown down a temple of stairs into the underworld, sent out on a burning canoe over Niagara Falls, arms and legs pulled apart by Budweiser horses during a small-town Memorial Day parade, tar from the superhighway and feathers from a city chicken used as squab at the annual National Arts Club picnic, a thread from Billy Budd's peacoat woven into the noose found inside the hanging judge's hope chest made out of cedar and balsam, one silver bullet forged out of a sniper's rifle fired at Dealey Plaza, hot coals stuffed into the mouth, placed into the charred sweet oak whiskey barrel with head, arms, and legs protruding like ornaments on the aluminum Christmas tree, thrown from the caboose of the runaway Orient Express moved to the High Sierras in one final act of war, left naked in the Petrified Forest, night, smoke signals, Mojave green snake thrown at his feet, a monkey left at the guard tower, without its eyes, laughed in the rumble seat, they threw a blanket over its head and beat the stuffed monkey into silence with a duck pin, it was a full harvest moon and the time for lies, redemption, mercy, pardon, peony and exile, half-forgiven by a panel of scarecrows dressed in full military dress, who raised their rifles in the corn field and shot toward the back of Ben's head and the scarecrows opened their eyes.

Where is the basketball money we raised?

In honor of the Champy Lake Monster Art Show?

No. It was for the revival of art in a working class city.

The Mural of Greatest Art on Earth

Whose money?

Our damned money!

Is it inside a bank vault, penny jar, or dirty sock?

The money was stolen by a crazed half-artist exhibitionist who wants her own shit done immediately while ignoring the worth in others, he said.

Our newly elected and dutiful treasurer wanted me to send a note to the co-op making us aware that she was aware that we need to shut the front door tightly during the freezing weather, he said.

We might wish to avoid the bullshit stampede of a passive aggressive non-intellectual sloth, he said.

We are in rat's alley. It was a stew of rubbers, beer piss, cigarettes, and blunt cigars smoked by the near homeless in the artist lofts built above the underground tunnels where the lungs of children filled with TB in the lavatories of the inferno that ran under Walnut Hill and Central Park.

There is a rat on a telephone speaking in a lost dialect of lemon rind and blackened cheese, a two-foot city rat who ate backyard city chickens in wire cages, a rat wearing gym socks and hip-hop scalawag headphones, a rat who loved *American Bandstand*, and danced at the high school prom in a plaid jacket, thick gold chains, open chest, a rat who was alcoholic with a money clip tied to its tail and the memory of a child left drifting inside a canoe on Batterson Park, who swam underwater too long and rose to the surface thinking it was half-human with eyelashes, a rat who believed in war and the mortal fling of the arrow, deprived of heart and desire, and the cops found him singing the blues and calling out the names of the city fathers who sent a wrecking ball into the walls of the ghost factories.

THE NEGRO PEANUT BUTTER COMPANY

THE NASA ELITE supplied the iron lung cupboards with a year's supply of small jars of Negro Peanut Butter. The jars were processed and sealed in large steaming vats inside warehouses built at the seaport. Those who arrived by land, air, and sea were brought there by yellow taxis and one rehabilitated submarine found listing off the Ivory Coast. Ben Cocoa enjoyed his Negro Peanut Butter and grape jelly sandwich and often loosened his neck brace and seat belts on his ankles and waist. They had sent a basket of Wonder Bread with its edges cut with perfect corners. Those who arrived in the daylight were blindfolded and led to a gangplank and given their last rites as they fell backwards into a vat stirred by fans, boiled peanuts, human flesh, bones crushed by a wrecking ball, sourdough, kielbasa, light spam, and espresso beans passed through the intestines of a blue monkey found while doing the back stroke on the Amazon River. The last ingredient was a state secret created by Homeland Security for the sake of the nation, designed by fugitive war criminals in the executive suite during lunch meetings, this peanut butter was made to be eaten with nigger baby candy sold in candy stores across the nation mere feet from every elementary school, black licorice carved and pressed into a black baby inside a small box inside a small hand inside a small mouth, wafer, revelation, Ben imagined a blue halo above his head, the sky turned peanut butter blue, they found a jar in the town clock burning, one behind the mayor's desk, saltines, sardines, a silver bullet found inside a jar of Negro Peanut Butter won a two-week vacation at the warehouse of their choice, a two-story limousine, silver knife, gourmet K Jelly, two flash-frozen Omaha Negro Lamb Chops, fresh ground peanuts, a make-up kit filled with vials of powdered Nigger Lips, and the entire 8-track Home Shopping Network volumes 1-12 Christmas Blue Plate Special with

Negro Liver and Grilled Onions based on the old plantation method of search, desist, destroy, and cracked jars were found next to the Confederate canteens half-a-world and half-a-war away, a twenty-mule team delivered the peanut sauce to remote locations directed by satellites through wind, fog, dust storms, and when the rainbow shined and the Nigger Lips opened there was joy.

Sergeant Pepper's Lonely Hearts Club Band and the Iron Lung

Ben read that *we are ultimately alone* among the borrowed stars that he saw dance above his head. The iron lung floated into the darkness, a wayward dirigible caught in the hunger of gravity, the blossomed wing of the wingless bird, the evolutionary marriage of the witless seed, stone, water, stepped into a winter garden, barn leaning into the sun, car axle in the doorway, RV on concrete stilts, frost burning the stems of winter collards, Mojave green snake nesting inside a boot, desert pool, ghost tiller, a mirage of love, canteen of desire, the elliptical moon asleep in white birch, stone fence, chimney rock, embedded tracks of the prairie schooner, dinosaur teeth, the one-eyed and wild mastodon, beehive above a waterfall, a bluebird flew into the fog above the Dismal River, choreography of the sun-dial, longing inside the iron capsule, feather pillow, rainbow fish below the ice, the unsteady compass, wing-tips inside the iron lung, conductor's wand, sun flare, naked like blown glass, sleeplessness, lavender, articles of the sea dog, anchor thrown off the tall burning ship, knotted noose, the hanging captain swore on a Bible, raised his hand, the nest and gangplank were set on fire, release of the wounded mermaid, pulled gold coins out of the thief's eyes, headed to shore inside hush boats, the flag was lowered, a declaration written, war declared over, eye patch removed, white flags raised to no particular physics, a distant radio signal tethered to the stars picked up the sounds of a faint and dying heart, the cooling fan started working, heat shield, they lowered his bunk bed by remote control where he had slept, rotated, and found himself raised to the ceiling and face down, the heat shield and weightlessness returned to the cabin, protest music played, a rumble seat had been welded to the side of the iron lung and a breathing tube connected to his helmet, he thought he was inside a flea motel, movie theater, matinée, tag sale, soda pop, Memorial Day parade, military march, church bell, and Ben Cocoa awakened from his sleeping sickness aboard the iron lung for three years after he felt a brief kiss on his low shoulder and she disappeared and he turned the large dial on the short wave radio and heard that Earth's soil was saved from drought and love was rare and there was a certain comfort in this.

The Cartographer's Wheel

The Cartographer's Wheel was connected to the iron lung's oxygen system that supplied purified air pulsating out of the spokes of meteors released into goblets of crystal that dissolved into beauty connected to Ben's breathing tube, *connectomes* that sizzled in quicksand, birth under a rock slab, the indefinable light, how the wheel turned inside the pink hourglass, Ben's voice box:

"I sleep in the vagrant hours," he said.

Connectionism, how a voice is heard by another in the language of water under stone and the splitting seed, there was a yellow chicken at his bedroom window, the wind chime outside the attic window, a distant radio signal on Ben's transistor radio discovered outside Rapid City, South Dakota, AM radio transmitted to a hollow star, Ben left his black iron skillet on the stove too long,

"I awake out of winter's slumber," he said.

It was early afternoon and too soon for laughter, the kind of *ha ha hell* heard in the birthday screen porch, sixteen candles, Polaroid, mothers who broke their high heels on a sewer grate, fathers who swam naked to shore, a breathalyzer attached to Ben's breathing tube and a VW Bug steering wheel lowered by a wink of his left eye, he enjoyed the bumper car weightlessness, the dirt track feel of gravity and air whistling through the vents, the hum of monarch, screech owl, and aerial hiss of the radiator at his feet, what divinity waged war against war, gave voice to a spindle of crackling light, a wireless unknown contraction, found salvation between black and black, the wedding dress at railroad salvage in New Haven, toys placed inside the iron lung, aluminum Christmas tree tethered to its bumper, red light, green light, blue light, snowfall outside Ben's window, snowfall inside the iron lung, the story of the Hartford Circus Fire, the Great Flood, the earthquake that split the Yankee earth, a white candle burning in the attic, *epigenome*, floating upside down straightjacketed inside his convertible iron lung.

My Body Is on Fire Inside the Iron Lung

THE WARDEN KISSED Kafka's ghost and placed a black glad doo-rag over Ben's head, the guard kicked a spittoon thimble of tobacco cud as he walked and chewed snuff on a death row night shift, the platoon of duck hunters sent to retrieve the iron lung as it parachuted into the Burning Man Festival, the iron lung lifted by crane and placed on a freight train of scorpions, coal, and sidewinders that entered the vents and were captured on dry ice, Ben was allowed to wear the same straightjacket, coiled like a viper and seated on the electric chair, it was the hiss and curse of the underworld, somewhere in everyone's blood, surrounded by goat hooves and a horse shoe thrown upside down in heaven and thrown right side down in heaven, was it luck or the how the rain fell over the city and they rolled Ben in his wheelchair over the Corinthian bridge and they watched the devil rise from his pewter throne and place a brief kiss and spell on the pink mouth of the woman of the midnight sail, a sonata played in the back room, a barber chair, refrigerator, rotary phone, numbers, nudie magazines, Jesus, Martin Luther King, and Kennedy, a dog whistle for the golden retriever tied to the bag lady's shopping cart, three men who resembled those seen on the grassy knoll stood and charmed the world with drunkenness and frivolity, one leaned into the shoulder of the other and leaned into the shoulder of the other that collapsed and folded his wings on the sidewalk, Ben had met the *Iwo Jima* of the homeless, deranged, and depraved who ate gay onion rings wrapped in bacon, a number of former veterans, one without memory of language and charred tongue, one with his nails ripped out of each finger, one without shoes, one wearing the mayor's Playtex living girdle tied to the belt of his carpenter pants, the daily insignificant drawing of tap water, church coffee, transistor radio, *bringing in the sheaves*, wires attached to the spinal cord made for eternal sleep before the siren called for the executioner to pull death's curtain and serve sourdough bread and holy water inside the hourglass.

They placed his bare feet into a mop bucket to conduct the brunt of electricity into his toes that would echo and spiral out of his dry mouth and pallid eyes, and the Minister of the Heart was called into the chamber to lay his hands upon Ben as he danced and bobbed in the electric chair, seized by the charred hand of God, and the minister stood over Ben, and he swore he heard laughter under Ben's hood, and he swung out his hands as if the holy ghost had embraced him and he turned his head to the blue halo that formed out of the tainted light above Ben's head, a séance of voices under Ben's hood, the tarot of the underworld for a moment caught him by surprise, a temporary gift of rage and remembrance, last request, buttermilk, clown mask, funny papers, one French lesson on a 45 record, metal cleats on Beatle boots, plastic clarinet reed, and they played a recording from his diary: *I was in one of only two plays I have ever performed in at what was called The Protean Theater in downtown Hartford. The theater was big as a closet. It was a Brecht play . . . some combination of* The Way the Earth Moves/ The Life of Galileo. *It was a protest play against the bombing of Hiroshima. We wore tights and held large silver swords in the park. We met at the Bushnell Park Jazz Festival. 8,000 people. The saxophonist Dexter Gordon was playing. He appears in the film* Round Midnight. *I had my 35mm camera and took photographs and saw Wendy through the lens. We went to dinner. I left three days later for my first tenure track job in New Orleans at Xavier University. Wendy visited me one week later in New Orleans, and she moved down and we lived together for two years . . .* Ben had his voice recorded on a reel-to-reel tape and installed under the iron lung's steering wheel, easily accessed by a deformed foot, hand, or straightjacketed arms, although the tape was disarmed by distant signals from SETI and picked up the complete seasons of *American Bandstand* and Dick Clark in tears after performances by Chuck Berry and Chubby Checker: *It was the devil's music, it would make your teeth fall out and your hair turn blue . . .* Ben understood the bass line, lived by the bass, and wished to be executed by the bass, and they wired the electric bass to a double bass, and they attached his electric baseball cap to the full spectrum of sound that would make the color of his eyes change into a prism, into orbs of the mortal black and blue and wailing lavender prehistoric light often inhaled by a last breath.

The Proprietor Who Ran the Family Theater Showing *The Sound of Music* Hung Himself (Or Was He Noosed and Hooded?) From the Balcony Chandelier in the Strand Theater

He sat in the loge seat, stage left, and after a splice of the reel, he lowered the screen and pulled the rope that lifted the red curtain, and he pointed the film projector at the center of the white sky, a storm cloud descended from the ceiling and covered the seats with a fine powder thrown from the pocket of the ventriloquist seated in the balcony with his dummy on his lap, who after turning its eyes away from the star and screen, took his lower jaw and wooden teeth and bit the hand of his master. The ventriloquist was surprised and tossed the dummy off the balcony into the crowd, who carried his broken body into the basement to repair its mouth and weary arms and legs. It was the ghost of the Strand Theater, the demolition of historic movie houses in a city that became known as Ugly Town, demolition without a world war, a war against a city of factories and workers and families, a ghost of the hardware city of the world, the city buried each year under a million tons of concrete until its town clock collapsed, and the city's last smoke stack, rising out of the earth next to the railyard, a fistful of embers spread over the tenements, strip malls, bail bondsmen, court house, a million-dollar store All-American city, industrial arts, trade show of toasters bought and sold in America, it was the ghost of the city who hung himself in the balcony, although the Keystone Cops removed evidence that would have called for a Henry Lee investigation, under suspicious circumstances and wild speculation that his body was lifted to a chair by ushers in fake uniforms, a monkey grinder arrived at the grand opening of *The Sound of Music*, polka and rhythm and blues, the red-capped monkey clapped its cymbals on cue, somebody had kicked the chair out from under the gentleman who watched movies as a lad and was mesmerized by silent films and newsreels, and at the Saturday matinées, wearing his penny loafers, bow tie, and red vest, greeted the movie-goers with a salute and the tip of his cane. He found his life in the movies seated in front of the screen under the borrowed light, and after the film broke apart inside the projector room it filled with candlelight, he found a certain comfort in the kind applause he received after they had placed the thick rope around his neck.

HE WALKED LIKE HE DIDN'T TAKE THE BUS

THEY STARTED USING red carpeting leading to the electric chair for Ben Cocoa who for years walked like he didn't take the bus. He lived inside the iron lung for years during the appeal after receiving the death penalty, falsely accused of hunting bluebirds with a hand net. Instead, he placed the net over the head of NYPD's finest and was chased into Times Square where the young cop placed a chokehold on a suspect who sold loosies in front of the Dollar Store, the one-armed police officer locked his arm wrestling under the man's neck until his eyes closed, and the officer heard a lullaby from the ice cream truck, and he swore in his deposition that a blue halo had formed over the thief's head as it slammed against the sidewalk, as a thimble of wintergreen fell out of his mouth. Were these the vagrant hours, grandfather clock, flop house theater of the manikin angels, cathedral of ghost stars, the woman who danced without music or men, arctic ship, self-portrait inside a locked room, smoke, jade, peat, charred sweet oak cask, a wee dram of black whiskey?

The demolition team, during Ben's sleeping sickness, mistakenly placed him into a cement mixer instead of his reserved iron lung, and Ben was spun into a daffodil of thorns, until the warden received a signal from his red telephone used to retrieve the governor's call, a last minute pardon at 11:59. They removed Ben from the cement mixer, lifted him above their heads and marched behind the riderless horse who fell like a psalm on Sorrow Road. It was not how the execution was planned. There would be the archer with a bronze arrow and one hand-carved bullet on the breakfast plate, the guard lowered the rope that dropped the velvet curtain in front of twelve thrones behind the one-way mirror, a three-minute slide show, ten thousand years of taking a life for a life in the wonderful world of color, a bluebird landed on Ben's shoulder and his eyes opened. It was not sleep, it was beauty that brought Ben back from the human curse, and he looked out of his porthole and down at his broken feet, half-asleep and lifted his eye patch, a meteor crossed above the tall ship and sea cliff, and he felt his weightless body almost pummeled into consciousness and redemption.

Ben thought they had boarded, rolled, and lifted him on a bus with a round trip after a photo shoot at the *Hartford Courant* after the *Herald* closed its door after a centuries of local news about the city rulers, rustlers, and buckaroos of New Britain. He found they had thrown out the one-door lavatory and cut out the row of back seats to make a bedroom for the iron lung. It was a one-way ticket toward some distant planet outside known galaxies and dwarf star factories that dispensed the demons and earthly pleasures for travelers caught in the hunger of gravity and weightlessness on a city bus headed to the mall. The bus driver wore a black hat, red scarf, and his large hands turned the ship's wheel into a storm of coral embers on the corner of Park and Stanley. He took a turn on four wheels straight into the side of the Blue Mirror Bar, ten thousand quartets of glass floated into the air, each a story with the disfigured face of a peasant who swallowed the black soot, and the suntanned city fathers, horse thieves riding a bareback race for foxhounds at Shuttle Meadow Reservoir and Stanley Gold Course.

Ben's last wish and testament before his execution was agreed upon by the Minister of the Heart and Pardoner of Sins, two gentleman who carried themselves with ivory cane and teapot civility. They requisitioned the tool and die welders to attach Mashie Niblick wooden golf clubs to the both sides of the iron lung so Ben was able to lift himself into the electric chair with ease, into death's carriage, dressed in a three-quarter-length black cashmere coat, penny loafers, filled with two lucky copper pennies, mint condition, a blue-plate special made to conduct the proper amount of lethal voltage pumped into his pink vein and broken spine.

The door of the iron lung was camouflaged with palm leaves and barbed wire, the medical doctor, who lost his stethoscope to a sudden gust in the American Cup, was brought in to find a pulse for the newly executed, if it was determined there was no pulse, a call was made on a red rotary telephone to attempt resuscitation, if a pulse was found, it took a steady hand and middle finger to avoid a wrong number on a bus ride carousel into a factory gate furnace, a Morse code, collect call, sent out to heaven directly to the warden was received as a busy signal. The phone booth, left standing under the highway to nowhere by city proclamation, used by appointment only for meetings with Satan's merry workers, last seen bobbing in the Connecticut River, caught fire.

Ben fell in love with Frankenstein at the movie theater when he was nine years old, something about those brass rivets bolted with a Stanley drill into the side of his neck and the assemblage of inflatable body parts he found placed inside the iron lung, something called a city that built ghost factories, men on stilts who lifted bricks to men on roof tops who built smokestacks made of red clay and penny bugs, a requiem of the twenty-first century in a time capsule, something about how steel melts inside a furnace, the alchemy of desire, the palace, not for beauty, a road built out of a wooden cart, the bronzed man who walked behind the palomino, laying the cobble down, a stone house with a stone fence, chiseled into round stone, something in the hand flew away into the scalding air, this was the science of woe and enchantment, rain, embers floating into birch trees, town clock, stagecoach, chained at the waist, falling backward into the lake, meteor above the crescent moon, a palette of ghost colors, a quarter mile to the covered bridge, Ministers of the Heart, wild horses, the blue tarantula placed on Ben's bad shoulder to awaken, heal, as he sat in the electric throne, resuscitation followed by execution, hanging, firing squad, roped, boiled in oil, was it how they tightened his barbed wire necklace before his last meal and testament, found the proper fit and width of his wingtip shoes, his tuxedo, suspenders, bow tie, how his collarbone snapped into dust as he swung above the crowd, how he became half a man, a transfusion of eyebright for the third eye and devil's claw for his re-attached hand, until they realized how his fingers reaching out to the sky was a sign of comfort, the nerves under his hand were soldered and connected to the back of his head that nodded like a marionette on a wind chime, it was time for him to fall asleep and dream about what he had seen as he awakened, something about her eyes, the rare air of circumstance and collapsed landscape, a scarecrow, bluebird, the rowing out of fire?

CAROUSEL

IT WAS SATURDAY. Rain turned to ice. The Yellow Cab was delayed, blocked by a caboose stalled in front of the entrance to the ball bearing factory. The Willow Street Junk Yard provided scrap metal transformed into pellets of steel used inside the engines of fighter jets and helicopters, a playground for the neighborhood park below the swing sets, monkey bars, and slides, lowered into the rainbow oil puddled at their feet, iron, steel, dogged-legged tub, the copper teeth inside the crane's mouth, silver spoon, precious blue metal, emerald headlight glass, front door knobs, chicken wire, cellar door to a root cellar, sinks, toilets, Victorian, sewing machine foot pedal, Victrola, lampshade, false teeth, pick-up truck bumper, and under the ice and mud, a model, an electric chair carved out of hardwood, leather straps intact, a steel plate inside the helmet, blue visors to protect the eyes, placed on each seat inside the viewing stand, green pairs of Polaroid sunglasses for inmates to protect them from the ultraviolet aura caused by the increased voltage charging the battery in a black box placed under the electric chair to monitor the impulse of the warden and executioner and the pulse of the inmate, it counted each breath and measured how long it took to inhale the gas, the speed and trajectory of silver bullets used by the firing squad, the weight of the ball and chain on the ankle, how the inmate exhaled what he had taken deeply into his lungs, the minutes allowed to enter the chamber, a grammatical and spell check of the last words, the amount of effort and drag used to pull the lever on the one-armed bandit pre-set with the exact temperature on the sun's surface and set the amount of voltage dispersed through a silver barbed wire into threads of copper connected to the bedpan under the chair, as if the jerky movements of his arms and legs were normal circumstances with the electrified barbed wire, skull cap with a freshman beanie, and what they saw in his eyes before the veil of tinsel was placed over his face.

His father was a hardworking amputee who played a mean piano with his left hand. He swung a mean strap, but not the kind that's slung on a barbershop chariot. His one arm did double duty, so he had a forearm the size of a '48 DeSoto's front fender. We didn't "spit into the wind," and we didn't "mess around" with—him.

Marcel Marceau Inside the Iron Lung

The hammer-thrower turned his waist, curtsied, and flung his ball and chain like a meteor into the Sun.

It was how Ben buttoned the collar of his coat against the sea wind. He had walked under the moon's wreckage after the lantern he held for a century snapped his wrist into dust. It was his love that started as a whisper, ice folding over ice, blue coral, waterfall, chandelier of fire, a temporary gift of rage, newsreel, velvet rope, curtain of light, the couple seated in the balcony loge kissed, black dress, pearls, red shoes, boutonnière.

The Pullman porters lifted the iron lung into the bunk bed. It had been carried through the Amazon River on a houseboat, tied to a canoe, left anchored in the mountains, placed on a rubber-tubed raft, lifted on the backs of marines in basic training until Ben's passport was declared fake, void of birthplace and circumstance, Ben's fingertips dipped in hot tar, up to his neck in ash, hog-tied to a freight train, air brake, elephant horn, bread basket, goat cheese, French bread, olives, Vermentino, saxophone, white birch, ginger ale, *pop ate the weasel, jack.*

What happened to Ben happened to the world. He took notes on the yellow lined 8½ × 14 legal pad provided by the New Britain Public Library Perennial Flower Club, a silver vase of daffodils and dandelions were placed in a corner of the gas chamber near the candlelight and used to prevent accidental leaks, the songbirds Heckle and Jeckle had messages tied to their claws, the alarm was pulled, the fire engines arrived, and hoses with sensors attached sought out the mustard gas, canaries flew out of the prison chimney like a psalm, the blackbirds with yellow eyes were screaming for their lives, the holy bell, chimes at the end of the clothesline above the grapevines, the cab hit the curb and tore a phone booth off the sidewalk, a small man who had sat on Ben's lap had placed a collect call to the liquor store.

Ben shared his canteen with his prison mate, his secret-sharer, the one he saw in the oval mirror attached to the bars of his cell, and he looked out of his porthole, at the stars above his knotted head, and he noticed what floated in the air settled into dust, the blue-winged grasshopper tumbled out of a summer screen, flew upward and burrowed into a cloud.

Ben Cocoa was first sentenced to hard labor in a labor camp disguised as a hideaway for the daughters of the Confederacy who cleansed their sins with moonshine under the pecan trees, spreading their legs to the general who surrendered his country on a white horse and spent the rest of his life in search of gold treasure thrown into the Cape River. Ben's sentence was overturned by a declaration written by Amnesty International, the gentleman's agreement was for a re-trial held on Gullah Island. Ben was sentenced, not for desertion, it was for not raising his rifle above the trench line against enemy fire and tanks blessed in barbed wire, and he was dragged out of the tunnel of light reading his poems, Tolstoy, Gandhi, and Martin Luther King, Jr. Ben had covered his naked body in mud and lime dust to ward off night crawlers, bluebirds, and the waste of the living and dead soldiers in their bright cuffs and corsages, it was a time of war and beauty, a brief kiss on her low shoulder, smoke rising in village, the riderless carriage, barber shop pole, wingless bird, gold coins spinning to earth, midnight chime, browned water, undertow under the battalion, bed pan, penny in the eye, summertime, bloated calf.

Ben, the first prehistoric man who walked on two legs one hundred thirty-five million years ago, headed to a requiem for the twenty-first century. He became a refugee who crawled under the town clock burning, caught in the belly pool of time, there was no redemption, eternity one mile away, he placed his rifle on his chest, a conscientious objector, working class factory worker on the night shift, U.S. Savings Bonds inside his green Stanley thermos, sardines and mustard, stirring his white fires of beauty inside a barrel outside the factory gate, union, on strike, smokestack, time clock, the leaflets dropped from the dirigible read: War Is Over, Surrender Your Heart and Disable Your Weapons, he tried to rise out of the chair, he coughed into the gas mask, the leather straps were tightened on his ankles, waist, and wrists, and they whispered to Ben that executions were part of the armistice in a world of lilac wild and marionettes, and they offered him a last fair deal, and he ran for his life in the snow.

So.

They pulled Red Tarbox out of his bunk bed at the *Salvation Army* next door to New Britain High School. They pinned a badge to Red's thermal and deemed him the Executioner of Ben Cocoa inside the iron lung and Johnny Roach seated in the electric chair.

Tarbox was the name in large red letters on the mailbox for upstairs at the Diamond Bar. Red Tarbox tried to pawn his mother's wedding ring at Polumbo's Jewelry Store on East Street. The bookies in the back room eating wedding cake gave Red a working-man's beatdown. The henchmen broke his toes and stole his shoes. Tarbox limped around the corner to St. Thomas Aquinas and tore down a boarded window and climbed inside for redemption.

The newspapers deemed New Britain the City of Blight after a former Mayor T. BlowFly claimed that City Hall was filled with thugs and inmates. T. BlowFly, father of the present Mayor, Ms. Butter-worth-Barnum-BlowFly, tried to reverse himself against the very social media where he posted and boasted his racist ethos. Tarbox was thrown out of elementary school for tipping a cow off John Downey Drive. It rolled down and was run over by a Guida's Dairy truck headed to a meadow. He was the person of interest for the Night of Fires that lasted several weeks and burned down an abandoned building long set for demolition and Urban (Negro) Removal. Tarbox often walked into Glabow's Bakery and was given leftover pierogis and latke pancakes. One evening in the back room he pulled out a knife and murdered six employees who were preparing blue-plate specials for Eastertide.

BEN COCOA, PROFESSOR OF BLACKSMITHING

Himes focused so sharply on his release from prison that he'd almost forgotten he was black.

Himes, as both an artist and a man, forces us to rethink the degree to which black people live in reaction to oppression yet may also elect to be implicit in it.

"Black Americans are the most neurotic, complicated, schizophrenic, unanalyzed, anthropologically advanced specimen of mankind in the history of the world."

—Chester Himes, *If He Hollers Let Him Go*
from *Chester B. Himes: A Biography*, by Lawrence P. Jackson

THE FIRE SPREAD like fog over the prison
left swollen bellies 372 dead in the city
and the tilled crops of corn and tobacco.

The underground tunnel that connected
heaven's linoleum killing floor moan
to the congregation of the bereaved

autopsy of the soul called to the yard
to identify charred bones and collect
false teeth, census record, wedding license,

birth date, blackened corpse, and water fountain,
bodies, pacifier, bronzed baby shoe,
for the warden-stiff happy birthday cake.

He brought his senior class to a brothel
for comfort in the blues and moonshine-flask
showed them what he learned behind metal bars

find a baton in the ass of a man
a black man denied hospital treatment
and assigned bare-two-hand latrine duty.

Appendix 2

HE WAS NICKNAMED Johnny Roach. Before he was executed, he spent fif-ty-three years lying flat on his back inside a 7-foot-long iron lung that breathed for him on death row waiting for the electric chair and rumble seat in the time machine. His lungs, along with the rest of his body, were paralyzed by a police bullet inside the Lithuanian Hall. His confinement to the massive respirator hasn't stopped him from graduating from high school, attending college and writing a book. He says he is always in pain. The doctor says he has beaten all odds.

"The iron lung produces a positive and negative pressure on his lungs that make the lungs expand and contract, like bellows."

"He can speak when he is breathing out," Harrison said.

"I didn't think he would last through puberty because his lung capacity was so limited," he said.

From Wikipedia:

In 1670, English scientist John Mayow came up with the idea of external negative pressure ventilation. Mayow built a model consisting of bellows and a bladder to pull in and expel air. The first negative pressure ventilator was described by Scottish physi-cian John Dalziel in 1832. Successful use of similar devices was described a few years later. Early prototypes included a hand-oper-ated bellows-driven "Spirophore" designed by Dr. Woillez of Paris (1876), and an airtight wooden box designed specifically for the treatment of polio by Dr. Stueart of South Africa (1918). Stueart's box was sealed at the waist and shoulders with clay and powered by a motor-driven bellows. The first of these devices to be widely used however was developed by Drinker and Shaw in 1928. The iron lung, often referred to in the early days as the "Drinker respi-

rator," was invented by Phillip Drinker (1894–1972) and Louis Agassiz Shaw, Jr., professors of industrial hygiene at the Harvard School of Public Health. The machine was powered by an electric motor with air pumps from two vacuum cleaners. The air pumps changed the pressure inside a rectangular, airtight metal box, pulling air in and out of the lungs.

Iron lungs were first used to sustain life in 1928. Positive-pressure airway ventilators largely replaced them in the late 1950s, and only about 75 to 100 are still in use in today, said Cheryl Needham, product manager for home ventilators at Respironics, a Pittsburgh company that makes and maintains respiratory equipment. In some cases they are not used all the time.

About 200 iron lungs exist that can be re-circulated among people who need them, but production of iron lungs ended decades before the time machine.

An angled mirror rigged above him in his prison cell allows him to make eye contact with the guards and prisoners. He has mastered "sip and blow switches" that allow him to control a television set. A voice-activated computer allows him to write. He is writing his autobiography to show those on death row they should never give up.

"It's amazing what you can accomplish if you see someone do the same thing," he said in a halting, high-pitched voice.

The person using the iron lung is placed into the central chamber, a cylindrical steel drum. A door allowing the head and neck to remain free is then closed, forming a sealed, air-tight compartment enclosing the rest of the person's body. Pumps that control airflow periodically decrease and increase the air pressure within the chamber, and particularly, on the chest. When the pressure is below that within the lungs, the lungs expand and atmospheric pressure pushes air from outside the chamber in via the person's nose and airways to keep the lungs filled; when the pressure goes above that within the lungs, the reverse occurs, and air is expelled. In this manner, *the iron lung mimics the physiological action of breathing: by periodically altering intrathoracic pressure, it causes air to flow in and out of the lungs. The iron lung is a form of non-invasive therapy.*

One iron lung from the 1950s is in the Gütersloh Town Museum. In Germany, nowadays less than a dozen of these breathing machines are available to the public.

The first clinical use of the Drinker respirator on a human was on October 12, 1928 at the Children's Hospital in Boston. The subject was an eight-year-old girl who was nearly dead as a result of respiratory failure due to poliomyelitis (often called polio or infantile paralysis). Her dramatic recovery, within less than a minute of being placed in the chamber, helped popularize the new device. Boston manufacturer Warren E. Collins began production of the iron lung that year. Although it was initially developed for the treatment of victims of coal gas poisoning, it was most famously used in the mid-twentieth century for the treatment of respiratory failure caused by poliomyelitis.

Danish physiologist August Krogh, upon returning to Copenhagen in 1931 from a visit to New York where he saw the Drinker machine in use, constructed the first Danish respirator designed for clinical purposes. Krogh's device differed from Drinker's in that its motor was powered by water from the city pipelines. Krogh also made an infant respirator version. In 1931, John Haven Emerson (February 5, 1906 – February 4, 1997) introduced an improved and less expensive iron lung. The Emerson iron lung had a bed that could slide in and out of the cylinder as needed, and the tank had portal windows which allowed attendants to reach in and adjust limbs, sheets, or hot packs. Drinker and Harvard University sued Emerson, claiming he had infringed on patent rights. Emerson defended himself by making the case that such lifesaving devices should be freely available to all. Emerson also demonstrated that every aspect of Drinker's patents had been published or used by others at earlier times. Since an invention must be novel to be patentable, prior publication/use of the invention meant it was not novel and therefore unpatented. Emerson won the case, and Drinker's patents were declared invalid. The United Kingdom's first iron lung was designed in 1933 by Robert Henderson, an Aberdeen doctor. Henderson had seen a demonstration of the Drinker respirator in the early 1930s, and built a device of his own upon his return to Scotland. Four weeks after its construction, the Henderson respirator was used to save the life of a 10-year-old boy from New Deer, Aberdeenshire, who was suffering from poliomyelitis. Despite this success, Henderson was reprimanded for secretly using hospital facilities to build the machine.

"Unclear Future for Executions After Inmate's Slow Death"
By Andrew Welsh-Huggings & Kantele Franko
01/18/14 03:25 AM EST (AP News)

https://apnews.com/general-news-4b13bd4f012f427f9b-c05a675d552d7f

"Family, Experts: Ohio Execution SNAFU Points to Flaws in Lethal Injection"
By Tom Watkins, updated 5:53 PM EST, Fri January 17, 2014 (CNN)

Son of executed Ohio man breaks silence after botched execution. "This one was different," says witness to execution McGuire was convicted in 1994 for the rape and murder of 22-year-old Joy Stewart. Killer's family say they will file suit next week to stop any such executions in the future. Lawyer questions whether they have the standing to do so.

https://www.cnn.com/2014/01/17/justice/ohio-execution/index.html

Johnny's Last Testament on This Planet

Mr. Boland, Hawker Media,

When I first responded to you, I didn't think that it would cause people to reach out to me and voice their opinions. I've never been on the Internet in my life and I'm not fully aware of the social circles on the Internet, so it was a surprise to receive reactions so quickly.

I learned that some of the responses on your website were positive and some negative. I can only appreciate the conversation. Osho once said that one person considered him like an angel and another person considered him like a devil, he didn't attempt to refute neither perspective because he said that man does not judge based on the truth of who you are, but on the truth of who they are.

Your words struck a chord with me. You said that my perspective is different and therefore my words have a sort of value. Yet, you're talking to a young man that's been judged unworthy to breathe the same air you breathe. That's like a hobo on the street walking up to you and you ask him for spare change.

Without any questions, you've given me a blank canvas. I'll only address what's on my heart. Next month, the state has resolved to kill me like some kind of rabid dog, so indirectly, I guess my intention is to use this as some type of platform because this could be my final statement on Earth.

I think empathy *is one of the most powerful words in this world that is expressed in all cultures. This is my underlining theme. I do not own a dictionary, so I can't give you the Oxford or Webster definition of the word, but in my own words, empathy means "putting the shoe on the other foot."*

Empathy. A rich man would look at a poor man, not with sympathy, feeling sorrow for the unfortunate poverty, but also not with contempt, feeling disdain for the man's poverish state, but with empathy, which means the rich man would put himself in the poor man's shoes, feel what the poor man is feeling, and understand what it is to be the poor man.

Empathy breeds proper judgment. Sympathy breeds sorrow. Contempt breeds arrogance. Neither are proper judgments because they're based on emotions. That's why two people can look at the same situation and have totally different views. We all feel differently about a lot of things. Empathy gives you an inside view. It doesn't say "If that was me . . .," empathy says, "That is me."

What that does is it takes the emotions out of situations and forces us to be honest with ourselves. Honesty has no hidden agenda. Thoreau proposed that "one honest man" could morally regenerate an entire society.

Chuck Colson, former advisor to the President once said that they were passing laws to be tough on crime, but they didn't even know who the laws were affecting. It wasn't until the Watergate scandal and Colson himself going to prison that he learned who the laws were affecting. Colson ended up forming the largest prison ministry in America. He also foresaw in his book The God of Spiders & Stones *that America was forming a new society within its prisons. Basically, that prison would become a nation inside this nation. He predicted that over a million people would be locked up by the year 2000. The book was written in the 1980s. Now, its 2014 and almost two million people are locked up. It's not that crime is the issue. Crime still goes on daily. It's that the politics surrounding crime have changed and it has become a numbers game. Dollars & Cents. You have people like Michael Jordan who invest millions of dollars in the prison system. Any shrewed businessman would if you have no empathy for people locked up and you just want to make some money.*

I don't agree with the death penalty. It's a very Southern practice from that old lynching mentality. Almost all executions take place in the South with a few exceptions here and there. I was raised in California. Coming from the West Coast to the South was like going back in time. I didn't even think real cowboys existed. This state is a very "country" state, aside a few major cities. There are still small towns that a black person would not be welcomed. California is more of a melting pot. I grew up in the Bay Area where its very diverse.

The death penalty needs to be abolished. Life without parole is still a death sentence. The only difference is time. To say you need to kill a person in a shorter amount of time is just seeking revenge on that person.

If the death penalty must exist, I think it should only be for cases where more than one person is killed like these rampant shootings that have taken place around the country the last few years. Also, in a situation of terrorism.

If you're not giving the death penalty for murder, then the government is already saying that the taking of one's life is not worth the death penalty. Capital murder is if you take someone's life and commit another felony at the same time. That's the law in this state. That makes a person eligible for the death penalty. The problem is, you're not getting the death penalty for murder, you're actually getting it for the other felony. That doesn't make common sense. You can kill a man but you will not get the death penalty . . . if you kill a man and take money out his wallet, now you can get the death penalty.

I'm on death row and yet I didn't commit the act of murder. I was convicted under the law of parties. When people read about the case, they assume I killed the victim, but the facts are undisputed that I did not kill the victim. The one who killed him pled guilty to capital murder for a life sentence. He admitted to the murder and has never denied it. Under the that law of parties, they say it doesn't matter whether I killed the victim or not, I'm criminally responsible for someone else's conduct. But I was the only one given the death penalty.

The law of parties is a very controversial law. Most Democrats stand against it. It allows the state to execute someone who did not commit the actual act of murder. There are around 50 guys on death row in the state who didn't kill anybody, but were convicted as a party.

The lethal injection has become a real controversial issue here of late because states are using drugs that they're not authorized to use to execute people. The lethal injection is an old Nazi practice deriving from the Jewish Holocaust. To use that method to kill people today, when it's unconstitutional to use it on dogs, is saying something very cruel and inhumane. Peo-

ple don't care because they think they're killing horrible people. No empathy. Just contempt.

I understand that it's not popular to talk about race issues these days, but I speak on the subject of race because I hold a burden in my heart for all the young blacks who are locked up or who see the street life as the only means to make something of themselves. When I walked into prison at 19 years old, I said to myself, "Damn, I have never seen so many black dudes in my life." I mean, it looked like I went to Africa. I couldn't believe it. The lyrics of 2Pac echoed in my head, "The penitentiary is packed / and its filled with blacks."

It's really an epidemic, the number of blacks locked up in this country. That's why I look, not only at my own situation, but why all of us young blacks are in prison. I've come to see, it's largely due to an identity crisis. We don't know our history. We don't know how to really identify with white people. We are really of a different culture, but by being slaves, we lost ourselves.

When you have a black man named John Williams and a white man named John Williams, the black man got his name from the white man. Within that lies a loss of identity. There are blacks in this country that don't even consider themselves African. Well, what are we? When did we stop being African? If you ask a young black person if they're African, they will say, "No, I'm American." They've lost their roots. They think slavery is their roots. Again, its a strong identity crisis.

You take the identity crisis, mix it with capitalism, where money comes before empathy, and you'll have a lot of young blacks trying to get money by any means because they're trying to get out of poverty or stay out of poverty. Now, money is what they try to find an identity in. They feel like if they get rich, legal or illegal, they've become somebody. Which in America is partly true because superficially we hail the rich and despise the poor. We give Jay-Z more credit than we do Al Sharpton. What has Jay-Z done besides get rich? Yet we see dollar signs and somehow give more respect to the man with the money.

A French woman who moved to America asked me one day, "Why don't black kids want to learn?" Her husband was a high school teacher. She said the white and Asian kids excel in school, but the black and Hispanic kids don't. I said that all kids want to learn, it's just a matter of what you're trying to teach them. Cutting a frog open is not helping a black kid in the ghetto who has to listen to police sirens all night and worry about getting shot. Those kids need life lessons. They need direction. When you have black kids learning more about the Boston Tea Party than the Black Panther Party, I guarantee you won't keep their attention. But it was the Black Panther Party that got them free lunch.

People point their fingers at young blacks, call them thugs and say they need to pull up their pants. That's fine, but you're not feeding them any knowledge. You're not giving them a vision. All you're saying is be a square like me. They're not going to listen to you because you have guys like Jay-Z and Rick Ross who are millionaires and sag their pants. Changing the way they dress isn't changing the way they think. As the Bible says, "Where there's no vision the people perish." Young blacks need to learn their identity so they can have more respect for the blacks that suffered for their liberties than they have for someone talking about selling drugs over a rap beat who really isn't selling drugs.

They have to be exposed to something new. Their minds have to be challenged, not dulled.

They know the history of the Crips & Bloods, but they can't tell you who Garvey or Robeson is. They can quote Drake & Lil Wayne but they can't tell you what Jesse Jackson or Al Sharpton has done. Across the nation, they gravitate to Crips & Bloods. I tell those I know the same thing, not to put blue & red before black. They were black first. It's senseless, but they are trying to find a purpose to live for and if a gang gives them a sense of purpose that's what they will gravitate to. They aren't being taught to live and die for something greater. They're not being challenged to do better.

Black history shouldn't be a month, it should be a course, an elective taught year around. I guarantee black kids would take that course if it was avail-

able to them. How many black kids would change their outlook if they knew that they were only considered 3/5's of a human being according to the U.S. Constitution? That black people were considered part animal in this country. They don't know that. When you learn that, you carry yourself with a different level of dignity for all we've overcome.

Before Martin Luther King was killed he drafted a bill called "The Bill for the Disadvantaged." It was for blacks and poor whites. King understood that in order to have a successful life, you have to decrease the odds of failure. You have to change the playing field. I'm not saying there's no personal responsibility for success, that goes without saying, but there's also a corporate responsibility.

As the saying goes, when you see someone who has failed, you see someone who was failed.

Neither am I saying that advantages are always circumstantial. Sometimes its knowledge or opportunity that gives an advantage. A lot of times it is the circumstances. Flowers grow in gardens, not in hard places. Using myself as an example, I was 15 when my first love got shot 9 times in Oakland. Do you think I'm going to care about book reports when my girlfriend was shot in the face? I understand Barack Obama saying there is no excuse for blacks or anyone else because generations past had it harder than us. That's true. However, success is based on probabilities and the odds. Everyone is not on a level playing field. For some, the odds are really stacked against them. I'm not saying they can't be overcome, but it's not likely.

I'm not trying to play the race card, I'm looking at the roots of why so many young blacks are locked up. The odds are stacked against us, we suffer from an identity crisis, and we're being targeted more, instead of taught better. Ask any young black person their views on the Police, I assure you their response will not be positive. Yet if you have something against the Police, who represent the government, you cannot sit on a trial jury. A young black woman was struck from the jury in my case because she said she sees the Police as "intimidators." She never had a good experience with the Police like most young blacks, but even though she's just being true to her experience, she's not worthy to take part as a juror in a trial.

White people really don't understand how extreme it is to be judged by others outside your race. In the book Trial & Error: The Texas Death Penalty *Lisa Maxwell paints this picture to get the point across and if any white person reading this is honest with themselves, they will clearly understand the point. I cannot quote it word for word, but this was the gist of it . . .*

> *Imagine you're a young white guy facing capital murder charges where you can receive the death penalty . . . the victim in the case is a black man . . . when you go to trial and step into the courtroom . . . the judge is a black man . . . the two State prosecutors seeking the death penalty on you . . . are also black men . . . you couldn't afford an attorney, so the Judge appointed you two defense lawyers who are also black men . . . you look in the jury box . . . there's 8 more black people and 4 Hispanics . . . the only white person in the courtroom is you . . . How would you feel facing the death penalty? Do you believe you'll receive justice?*

As outside of the box as that scene is, those were the exact circumstances of my trial. I was the only black person in the courtroom.

Again, I'm not playing the race card, but empathy is putting the shoe on the other foot.

The last thing on my heart is about religion and the death penalty. There are several well-known preachers across the South that teach their congregations that the death penalty is right by God and backed by the Bible. The death penalty is a governmental issue not a spiritual issue. Southern preachers who advocate the death penalty are condoning evil. They need to learn the legalities of capital punishment. The State may have the power to put people to death, but don't preach to the public that it's God's will. It's the State's will.

If God wanted me to die for anything, I would be dead already. I talk to God every day. He's not telling me I'm some kind of menace that He can't wait to see executed. God is blessing me daily. God is showing me His favor & grace on my life. Like Paul said, I was the chief of sinners, but God had mercy on me because He knew I was ignorant. The blood of Abel cried vengeance, the blood of Jesus cried mercy.

There are preachers like John Hagee in San Antonio who have influence over thousands of people, who not only attend his church, but also watch his TV program, and hear him condoning the death penalty. Hagee doesn't see his Southern mentality condones the death penalty, not the Scriptures. There is absolutely nothing in the Bible that condones the way this state executes people today.

Southern preachers use Scriptures like God telling Noah, "Whoever shed's man's blood, by man his blood shall be shed." "That's murder. Under our law, you cannot receive the death penalty for murder. There is no such thing as capital murder in the Bible, where murder must be in the course of another felony. Yet, they preach capital punishment is God's will. Even if you're guilty of capital murder, it doesn't mean you'll receive the death penalty. People get the death penalty when a jury has judged them to be a 'continuing threat to society.'" "That means they are deemed so bad that they have no hope of redemption or change in their behavior. That is the only reason a person gets the death penalty. They are supposed to be the absolute worse of the worse, so terrible that they cannot live in prison with other murderers."

That in itself is contrary to the whole Christian faith that believes no one is beyond redemption if they repent for their sins and put their faith in Jesus Christ. For a Christian to advocate the death penalty is a complete contradiction.

As easy as it is for a preacher to stand up in the pulpit with a Bible and tell thousands of people the death penalty is right, I challenge any preacher, John Hagee or any others to come visit me and tell me that God wants me to die. Martin Luther King said, "Capital punishment shows that America is a merciless nation that will not forgive."

Again, Mr. Boland, this is only my perspective. I'm just the hobo on the street giving away my pennies. A doctor can't look at a person and see cancer, they have to look beyond the surface. When you look at the Justice system, the Death Penalty, or anything else, it takes one to go beyond the surface. Proper diagnosis is half the cure.

I'm a father. My daughter was six weeks old when I got locked up and now she's 15 in high school. Despite the circumstances, I've tried to be the best father in the world. But I knew that her course in life is largely determined by what I teach her. It's the same with any young person, their course is determined by what we are teaching them. In the words of Aristotle, "All improvement in society begins with the education of the young."

Sincerely,
Johnny Roach

P.S. Forgive me for being long-winded, but I was speaking from the heart. Thanks for the opportunity.

Ben Cocoa, Brother of Johnny Roach's Victim, Shares His Story

Previously, a post from Hamilton Boland on Hawker shared a statement from a death row inmate named Johnny Roach. The letter from Johnny is touted as the last statement Johnny may make on Earth. Tuffpo has it as a must read. Johnny is on Death Row for his involvement in a stabbing murder committed during a robbery in November of 1998. I'm about to comment on Johnny's statement without having read it. In fact, more than likely I will never read it. I imagine it is not much more than the statement he made in court to my family. My name is Ben Cocoa, and it is our brother, son, grandchild and cousin, the forever 33-year-old, who was killed by Johnny and his two accomplices.

The facts of the case are readily available on the Internet, but allow me to plainly restate them here. My brother was killed on November 29 1998. It was roughly seven to ten days before this date when, unbeknown to him, my brother received his death sentence. Johnny, according to his testimony, needed money so that he could move out of his parents house and into an apartment with the mother of his child, his girlfriend. Johnny decided to rob my brother.

Johnny was an aspiring rapper who had been recording music at my brother's self-owned recording studio. (An important note here is that Johnny was not a business partner of my brother's as has been claimed elsewhere.) This was a self-made independently owned recording studio, by the way. My brother had leased an old apartment complex office, and with his own hands, and the help of our father, fashioned it into a affordable space for struggling local musicians. He offered low rates for artists who, much like himself, could not afford more spacious digs. My brother had no apartment of his own; he would crash on a couch at our parents house or, more often, sleep on a makeshift bed on the floor in the studio. He eschewed nicer living quarters so that he could pour his available money into the studio.

Johnny Roach knew well that he could not rob my brother's studio equipment without being fingered to the police by him later. So it was, seven to ten days prior, Johnny made the decision to end my brother's life. He enlisted the help of two others. That night (and this is all from on-the-record courtroom testimony and statements he gave police in his confession) the three men made the recording appointment. They were there for roughly two hours working, recording, my brother sitting at the control console. Johnny admits to then grabbing him by his hair, yanking his head back and pulling the kitchen knife he brought with him across his throat, slicing it open. My brother jumped up and grabbed at his own throat from which blood was flowing. He began to fight for his life.

At this point Johnny called to one of his accomplices who rushed into the room with another knife. His accomplice then stabbed my brother 25 times. My brother collapsed, already dead or dying—we will never know. The final stab wound was at the back of his neck; the knife plunged in and was left there.

He was then covered with a sheet and the three men proceeded to tear out as much equipment as they could and load it all into the van they drove there. As they were loading they were spotted by an off-duty sheriff who called out to them. They took off running, and were eventually caught. The evidence was overwhelming; DNA, fingerprints, confessions. This is and was an open and shut case, as they say in all the cheesy TV murder investigation shows. One defendant was offered the choice of a trial by jury, which could end in a death sentence, or he could avoid the death penalty by admitting his guilt. He chose to admit his guilt. Johnny, given the same choice, apparently decided to take his chance with a jury trial.

During the trial, testimony from the Medical Examiner revealed that it was not technically Johnny's injury to my brother that caused death, but the subsequent 25 stab wounds. Johnny's defense team seized upon this as a defense tactic against a murder charge, and Johnny joined that opinion. Never mind that Johnny delivered the first attack. At one point while he was on the stand testifying, he asked to speak to us—my brother's family members. He looked us square in the eye and exclaimed "I didn't kill your son. He was one of the nicest guys I ever met, but I did not kill him." Johnny's reasoning was that since the ME cited the 25 stab wounds as the cause of death and not the throat slit committed by Johnny, he was technically not guilty of murder. You can make of that what you will, but it seems any reasonable person would hold Johnny as culpable in the murder as the other defendant who finished him off. So the long and short is this final statement is based in a fantasy that Johnny has convinced himself of. All evidence to the contrary, it seems he denies he is a murderer and therefore he feels he should not be executed for the crime.

And now to the Death Penalty issue. I must stress that I speak only for myself here and for no other family member. Our extended family is much like the rest of the United States. We are a large American family. There are Liberals and there are Conservatives in our midst. There are pro-death penalty and anti-death penalty folks in our tree as well. I am one of those opposed to the death penalty. As far as I can remember I have been in opposition to it. My brother was not opposed to the implementation of the death penalty. We used to debate the topic often. Sometimes vigorously.

During the trial the prosecutors in the case decided to use me on the witness stand in an effort to give my brother a voice. He was one year older than me. We had been roommates the whole time we lived with our parents. I was the best man at his wedding. I hesitate to say I was happy to testify, since it remains the hardest thing I have ever done in my life. But I willingly agreed to testify on his behalf. At the trial, the first thing the prosecution wanted to do was to introduce my brother to the jury through my words, so I was the first witness called.

After I was sworn in and sat in the chair, the prosecutor handed me a picture of my brother. It was a postmortem picture. It was a close up of his face from the neck up. His eyes still open. The gash from Johnny's knife visible. I let out a gasp and when the prosecutor asked me what the picture was of I told him, "It's my brother." Through tearful testimony, I tried my best to bring my brother back to life in that courtroom. When I got off the stand I reached for my father's embrace and sobbed as I had never before and have not since.

As I wrote earlier, this was an open-and-shut case and the jury did not take long to return a guilty verdict. All that was left was the punishment. During the punishment phase the prosecutor outlines the State's case for the death penalty and, of course, the defense argues for the sparing of the defendant's life. I'm sure if you asked, under the Freedom of Information Act, you would be able to wade through the trial documents; the prosecutor's case was convincing for a death penalty verdict from the jury. Johnny Roach did not grow up on the wrong side of the tracks, he came from a family wherein his father, a career military man, and his mother were still happily married. Johnny was not defended by a court appointed lawyer; his defense was comprised of a well paid for and well known private practice firm. Johnny had a history of arrests and in fact was out on bail when he participated in the murder of my brother. He had, weeks before, assaulted an off-duty police officer who had stumbled upon Johnny attempting to break into a house.

During the trial somehow, apparently, the defense team got the idea that some of our family might be opposed to the death penalty and called my father to the stand. Nothing my father said could help their defense. When they called me to the stand the defense attorney asked me what my thoughts on the death penalty were. I knew what he was doing. He was hoping I would confess my opposition to the death penalty, thus maybe sparing Johnny Roach's life. And I could not assist him in good conscience. I've thought often in the years since if I did the right thing. If, when push came to shove, I suppressed my own true thoughts in an effort to avenge my brother's murder. This is what happened. The defense asked me what my opinion of the death penalty was. And I said, "I don't think it's relevant what my opinion is." And I paused. And I don't know where it came from, but I then said, "But I can tell you what my brother thought of the death penalty." And the defense attorney asked me, "What was his opinion?" And I said, "He always told me that if there was no question of the guilt of a murder defendant, that the death penalty was a just punishment." I'll never know for sure, but it's a pretty good bet my brother's words uttered through me sealed Johnny's fate.

After everything, I'm still opposed to the death penalty. I have no intention of witnessing Johnny's execution but I have no intention of fighting to stop it either. Does this make me a hypocrite? Maybe, but that's for me to live with. I harbor no illusions that Johnny's ceasing to exist will ameliorate the pain I feel daily from the loss of my brother. The truth is I rarely think of Johnny or the other defendants. I think of him more. Those thoughts are more important to me than anything else. Certainly more important than any last statement from Johnny Roach. Though I purposefully skipped reading Johnny's statement, I did read through the comments. I have to say to my fellow death penalty opponent friends: Keep up your fight. It is an honorable one. But do not use this man, Johnny Roach, as your spokesperson, as your example of why the death penalty should be abolished. The death penalty should be abolished because it is wrong to kill another human being. Not because a Medical Examiner said your knife wound did not cause immediate death. Johnny Roach is not worthy of your good and kind hearts. He has never accepted culpability or expressed remorse. He is responsible for viciously ending the life of "the nicest man he ever met." Responsible for ending the life of the nicest man my family ever met.

ABSINTHE

BEN COCOA WOULD ask for New Britain Martin and Rosol kielbasa and sauerkraut, and Ben also demanded twelve Capitol Lunch
hot dogs with its special sauce sent to the jurors, judge, and viewers
behind the two-way mirror in front of the electric chair. He wrote in his
appeal letter that he wanted a blue crystal ball filled with absinthe, so
he might read his misfortune in the green lilac wild. His last heavenly
drink, distilled wormwood, fennel, anise, green fairy dust, sugar cube,
absinthe spoon, thujone, spirit in a bottle set up at The Old Absinthe
Bar on Bourbon Street, and the bed pan placed under Ben Cocoa's
electric chair, his yellow urine would make Prague's holy bells echo
and sway throughout the village, the stagecoach stopped at the trough,
horses knelt as if in prayer and on their hind legs raised their hooves
under the moon's delirium, laughter bellowed out of their stalls, a place
where straw ignites in the corridor, hands reaching into a dumpster,
falling into the light green kaleidoscope of the mad chef who dropped
a plate of liver and onions on the mayor's lap, who stood up like a general, a paté of silver dollars fell out of his pants, and he took his glass
of absinthe and sang a song, something like a gospel and his ancestor's
blue mule that was set afire one the riverside, its teeth were pulled, its
pink spine buckled and arched like a praying mantis, trench warfare,
canteen, kerosene lantern in the fog, tied down in straightjacket, high
collar, barbed wire, grenade dropped into a tank, gas chamber, and the
warden sent his staff sergeant to Walmart and Costco for a six-foot
extension cord with a copper plug ground at the executioner's request,
that would handle the necessary voltage required for the electric chair,
and jumper cables in case of a blackout under the moon's wreckage,
and if all else failed a thick lynch rope, frayed yet usable, and the choir,
angels wearing patent leather penny loafers, sang a dirge behind the

electric chair, removed their shoes, and the conductor found two new pennies for the last meal and last rites, the green fog in the water, the sugar cube burning, sweet chariot drops fell into the absinthe, crystal ball, and bed pan, and the drank a toast to the first execution on New Year's Eve.

UGLY TOWN

BEN COCOA WAS born and raised in Ugly Town, a sub-division of Wilmington, North Carolina, a short walk from Whitey's Restaurant and the Cape Fear River. History recalls how the governor was found running nude in Airlie Gardens, how the Confederate Army threw the smoldering bodies of black businessmen, wives, and children into the Cape Fear River.

Blue starlings filled the sky as they buried gold coins under the boarded houses of Ugly Town.

This Is Their Story
This Is Their Song

This is their story and this is their song.
Buddhist priest sat and set himself on fire and his heart
would not incinerate.
They wept and sang to study war no more.

The deformed children are straightjacketed
until small pox buries them in boxes.
Lay down my sword and shield
for a story on the end of the world.

The sky pilot dropped leaflets that ignite
and float in surrender and blossom.
How high can you fly?
People wept at body bags on TV.

Music followed them into the trenches. Young men cut
down and trampled like flowers.
We shall not be moved
uprooted and sent to the inferno.

His arms moulted and his spine buckled
until it snapped into flames like a psalm.
Napalmed girl.
The angels on horseback looked down on them.

Holy men pray to raise bloated children from their winter
sleep. What has spring revealed?
Bullet in the skull.
We ask why our children have gone mad.
Look what we have left them.